P9-CSV-929

Emma Miller lives quietly in her old farmhouse in rural Delaware. Fortunate enough to be born into a family of strong faith, she grew up on a dairy farm surrounded by loving parents, siblings, grandparents, aunts, uncles and cousins. Emma was educated in local schools and once taught in an Amish schoolhouse. When she's not caring for her large family, reading and writing are her favorite pastimes.

Jan Drexler enjoys living in the Black Hills of South Dakota with her husband of more than thirty years and their four adult children. Intrigued by history and stories from an early age, she loves delving into the world of "what if?" with her characters. If she isn't at her computer giving life to imaginary people, she's probably hiking in the Hills or the Badlands, enjoying the spectacular scenery.

EMMA MILLER

Redeeming Grace

&

JAN DREXLER

The Prodigal Son Returns

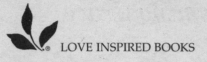

LOVE INSPIRED BOOKS

Recycling programs for this product may not exist in your area.

ISBN-13: 978-0-373-20974-3

Redeeming Grace and The Prodigal Son Returns

Copyright © 2017 by Harlequin Books S.A.

The publisher acknowledges the copyright holders of the individual works as follows:

Redeeming Grace
Copyright © 2012 by Emma Miller

The Prodigal Son Returns
Copyright © 2013 by Jan Drexler

www.Harlequin.com

Printed in U.S.A.

CONTENTS

REDEEMING GRACE

Emma Miller

But by the Grace of God, I am what I am.
—*1 Corinthians* 15:10

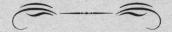

Chapter One

Kent County, Delaware…October

The storm beat against the windows of the house and rattled the glass panes. Since the early hours of morning, the nor'easter had hovered over the state, bringing high gusts of wind that ripped loose shingles on the outbuildings, sent leaves and branches whirling from the big shade trees and dumped torrents of rain over the Yoder farm. It was almost 10:00 p.m., nearly an hour past Hannah's usual bedtime, but she'd lingered in the kitchen, reading from her Bible and listening to Aunt Jezzy sing old German hymns while she knitted by lamplight.

Neither Irwin, Hannah's foster son, nor her two youngest daughters, Susanna and Rebecca, had retired for the night. The young people seemed content to remain in the kitchen, warm and snug, sipping hot cocoa, eating buttered popcorn and playing Dutch Blitz.

Today had been a visiting Sunday, rather than a day of worship, and so it had been a relaxing day. Usually, on visiting Sundays, Hannah's household would have

company over or share the midday meal with one of
her married daughters or friends. But the nor'easter
had kept everyone home. Simply getting to the barn
and chicken house to care for the livestock and poultry
had been a struggle.

Footsteps in the hall signaled Johanna's return to the
kitchen. Hannah's oldest daughter had taken her two
children up to bed earlier and stayed with them, reading aloud and hearing their evening prayers, until they
dropped off to sleep. Katie, two, had adjusted easily to
the move to her grandmother's house, but Jonah, now
five, was still difficult to get in bed, and once there, he
was prone to nightmares. Since Johanna and the children had returned to live with Hannah, almost a year
and a half ago, the boy often woke the entire house in
the middle of the night screaming, and nothing would
satisfy him but his mother's arms around him.

"Did you get them down all right?" Hannah asked as
Johanna appeared. Hannah thought her daughter looked
tired tonight. The strain of her husband's illness and sui-
cide and the need to return to her mother's home had
been hard on her; now she was learning the struggles
of being a single mother. Even with the support of her
family and friends, it was a difficult time in Johanna's
life. Hannah knew that Johanna worried about her son,
and prayed that God would ease Johanna's mind.

"Katie was fine, but there's a loose shutter on the
bedroom window, and Jonah was afraid that a monster
was trying to get in."

Hannah glanced at Irwin suspiciously. Even though
he was almost fifteen, he still behaved young for his
age, probably as a result of his parents' death and his

being shuffled around. "Have you been telling him stories about trolls again?"

Irwin's face reddened and he feigned innocence. "Trolls? Me?"

"Under the corncrib," Susanna supplied, looking up from her cards. She nodded firmly. "*Ya.* You said there was trolls with scabby knees, fleas in their ears and buck teeth."

"Did not," Irwin protested. "Moles. I might have said there was moles under the corncrib."

"*Were* moles," Hannah corrected.

Johanna frowned. "Find someone your own age to tease."

"But I didn't," Irwin insisted, hunching his shoulders. "Must have been one of Samuel's twins who told Jonah that."

"We'll discuss it tomorrow. With Jonah," Hannah said, marking her place in *John* with a red ribbon. She closed the big Bible. "Past time you were in bed, anyway. You'll have to leave early to get to school in time to start a fire in the woodstove. After all this rain, the schoolhouse will be damp."

"Maybe the storm will get worse," Irwin suggested. "Maybe there will be so much rain the school will wash away."

"I doubt that," Johanna said. "It's built on high ground, with a brick foundation."

Reluctantly, Irwin stood up, unfolding his long, gangly legs. He'd grown so much in the past three months that the trousers Hannah had sewn for him in June were already high waters, short even for an Amish teenager. She'd have to see about new clothes for him. Irwin was shooting up faster than a jimson weed.

She'd never regretted taking him in after his parents died in that terrible fire, but an Amish teacher's salary went only so far. Like everyone else, she had to watch her pennies, especially now that Johanna and the children had come back home to live. Not that Johanna was a burden; she contributed as much as she could. She had her sheep, her turkeys and her quilting, as well as the sale of honey from her beehives.

Johanna picked up the empty popcorn bowl and Irwin's mug. "I think I'll turn in now, Mam. I have to finish that quilt for that English lady tomorrow."

"You think you can?" Aunt Jezzy asked. "If it's still raining, Jonah will be stuck inside again all day, and—"

"I know," Johanna agreed. "He has so much energy, he'll be a handful."

"I can take him with me to Anna's," Rebecca offered. "He can play with Mae. The two of them are less trouble when they're together."

"Would you?" Johanna said. "That would be so much help. Katie follows Susanna around like a little shadow, and if you take Jonah for the day, I know I can finish those last few squares and press the quilt in no time. The lady's coming for it Tuesday afternoon."

Irwin went to the kitchen door. "Come on, Jeremiah," he called to his terrier. "Last chance to go out tonight. You, too, Flora." The sheepdog rose off her bed near the pantry and slowly padded after Jeremiah.

Abruptly, a blast of wind caught the screen door and nearly yanked it from Irwin's grasp. He grabbed it with both hands, stepped out onto the porch and then immediately retreated back into the kitchen, tracking rain on the clean floor. Irwin's mouth gaped and he pointed. "There's somethin'…somebody…Hannah! Come quick!"

Jeremiah's hackles went up, and both dogs began to bark from the doorway.

"What's wrong with you, boy?" Johanna said. "Don't leave the door open. You're believing your own tall tales. Who would be out there on a night like this?"

Hannah tightened her head scarf and hurried to the door as Susanna, now on her feet, let out a gasp and ducked behind Rebecca.

"I don't see—" Hannah began, and then she stopped short. "There *is* someone." She stepped through the open doorway onto the porch.

Standing out on the porch steps was a woman. Hannah sheltered her eyes from the driving rain and raised her voice to be heard above the storm. "Can I help you?" she called, shivering. She couldn't see any vehicles in the yard, but it was so dark that she couldn't be sure there wasn't one.

"Who is it, Mam?" Johanna came out on the porch behind her.

"An English woman," Hannah said. She motioned to the stranger. "Don't stand there. Come in."

Johanna put a restraining hand on her arm. "Do you think it's safe?" she asked in German. Then, in English, she said, "Are you alone?"

The girl shook her head. "I…I have my son with me." She turned her head and looked behind her.

Standing on the lower step was one very small, very wet child. Instantly, Hannah's caution receded, and all she could think of was getting the two of them out of the rain, dried off and warmed up. "Come in this moment, both of you," she said. She stood aside, grasping the door, and motioned the English people into the house. Seconds later, they were all standing in the middle of the kitchen, dripping streams of water off their clothing and faces. The young woman was carrying an old guitar case and a stained duffel bag.

For a long moment, there was silence as the Amish and the English strangers stared at each other amid the still-barking dogs. "Hush," Hannah ordered. Flora immediately obeyed, but Jeremiah circled behind Irwin and kept yipping. Hannah clapped her hands. "I said, *be still.*"

This time, the terrier gave a whine and retreated under the table where he continued to utter small growls. And then Susanna broke the awkwardness by grabbing a big towel off the clothesline over the woodstove and wrapping it around the small boy.

"He's wet," Susanna said. "And cold. His teeth are chattering."

"*Ya,* I'm afraid he is cold," Hannah agreed. "Please," she said to the young woman. "You're drenched. Get out of that sweater."

The stranger, her face as pale as skim milk, set down her things and stripped off a torn gray sweater. In the lamplight, Hannah could see that she wasn't as young as she had first thought. Mid-to-late twenties probably. Her cheeks were hollow and dark shadows smudged the area beneath her tired blue eyes. She was small and thin, the crown of her head barely coming to Johanna's shoulder. But her face in no way prepared them for the very odd way she was dressed.

The woman wore a navy blue polyester skirt that came down to the tops of her muddy sneakers, a white, long-sleeve blouse, a flowered blue-and-red apron and a man's white handkerchief tied like a head scarf over her thin red braids. The buttons had been cut off her shirt, and the garment was pinned together with what appeared to be safety pins, fastened on the inside.

No wonder Irwin and Hannah's girls were gaping at the Englisher. For an instant, Hannah wondered if this was some sort of joke, but *ne,* she decided, this poor woman wasn't trying to poke fun at the Amish. Maybe she was what the English called a *hippie.* Whatever she was, Hannah felt sorry for her. The expression in her eyes was both frightened and confused, but more than that, she appeared to expect Hannah to be angry with her—perhaps even throw the two of them back out into the storm.

"I'm Hannah Yoder," she said in her best school-teacher voice. "Did your car break down?"

The Englisher shook her head and lifted the child into her arms. "I...I hitched a ride with a milk truck driver. But he let me off at the corner. We walked from there."

"Where were you going?" Johanna asked. "The two of you rode in a milk truck? With someone you didn't know?"

The Englisher nodded. "You can pretty much tell if somebody is scary or not by looking at their eyes."

Johanna met Hannah's questioning gaze. It was clear to Hannah that for once, even wise, sensible Johanna was dumbstruck.

"I'm Hannah," she repeated. "And these are my daughters Johanna—" she indicated each one in turn "—Susanna and Rebecca. This is Irwin." She turned back toward the rocker by the window. "And Aunt Jezzy."

The stranger nodded. "I'm Grace…and this is my boy, Dakota."

"Da-kota?" Susanna wrinkled her nose. "That's a funny name."

The young woman shrugged, holding tightly to the child's hand. "I thought it was pretty. He was a pretty baby. I wanted him to have a pretty name."

She had an unfamiliar accent, not one Hannah was familiar with. She spoke English well enough. Hannah didn't think the stranger was born in another country, just another part of America, maybe Kansas or farther west.

"Oh, you must be as cold as the child," Hannah said. "Rebecca, fetch a blanket for our guest."

Grace held out a hand to the warmth of the woodstove. Hannah noticed that her nails were bitten to the quick and none too clean.

"Are you *Plain?*" Hannah asked in an attempt to solve the mystery of the unusual clothes.

The woman blinked in confusion.

"You're not Amish," Hannah said.

"Maybe she's Mennonite," Aunt Jezzy suggested. "She might be one of those Ohio Old Order Mennonites or Shakers. Are you a Shaker?"

"I'm sorry…about the apron." Grace brushed at it. "It was the only one I could find. I looked in Goodwill and Salvation Army. You don't find many aprons and the only other one I saw had something…something not nice written on it."

Hannah struggled to hide her amusement. The apron was awful. It had seen better days and was as soaked as the rest of her clothes, but the red roosters and the watermelons printed on it were definitely not like any Mennonite clothing Hannah had ever seen.

"Would you like some clothes for your little boy?" Johanna offered. "We could dry his trousers and shirt over the stove."

Grace pressed her lips together and nodded. "That's nice of you."

"And something hot to drink for you?" Johanna suggested. "Tea or coffee?"

"Coffee, please, if you don't mind," Grace answered. "I like it with sugar and milk, if you have milk."

"We have milk." Susanna smiled broadly.

"Maybe Dakota would like some hot milk or cocoa," Hannah said, noticing the way the boy was staring at a plate of oatmeal cookies on the counter. "He's welcome to have a cookie with it, if you don't mind."

"He'd like that," Grace stammered, shifting him from one slender hip to the other. "The cocoa and a cookie. We missed dinner...being on the road and all."

Hannah thought to herself that Grace had missed more than *one* dinner. The girl was practically a bag of bones. "Let us find you both some dry things," Hannah offered. "I've got a big pot of chicken vegetable soup on the back of the stove. That might help both of you warm up." She smiled. "But I'm afraid you're stuck here until morning. We don't have a phone, and it's too nasty a night to hitch the horses to the buggy. In the morning, we'll help you continue on your way."

"You'd do that? For me?" Grace asked. She sniffed and wiped her nose with the back of her hand. Her eyes were welling up with tears. "You don't know me. That's so good of you. I didn't think... People told me the Amish didn't like outsiders."

"Ya," Hannah agreed. "People say a lot about us. Most of it's not true." Then she looked at the stranger more closely. What was there about this skinny girl that looked vaguely familiar? Something… Something… "What did you say your last name was?" she asked.

Grace shook her head. "I didn't."

Hannah had the oddest feeling that she knew what the stranger was going to say before she said it.

"It's Yoder." The young woman looked up at her with familiar blue eyes. "Same as you. I'm Grace Yoder."

Chapter Two

"I'm Grace Yoder," Grace repeated, gazing around the room expectantly. "And I've come a long way…from Nebraska." Standing here in this fairytale kitchen, her clothes dripping on the beautiful wood floor, all these strangers staring at her, Grace was so nervous that she could hardly get the words out. "We went to Pennsylvania where he grew up, but people said he moved here. I hope this is the right house. We're looking for Jonas Yoder." She paused for a long moment. "Please tell him his daughter and grandson are here to see him."

"Was in der welt?" the older woman in the rocking chair, Aunt Jezebel, exclaimed. *"Lecherich!"*

"Ne," the oldest sister said to Grace. Her expression hardened. "You've made a mistake. Jonas Yoder isn't your father. He's ours."

The younger girl, Rebecca, looked at her mother. She was holding a blanket she'd just fetched. "Tell her, Mam! Tell her that she's wrong! It's a different Jonas Yoder she's looking for. She can't be…" She took the hand of her younger sister, the one who looked as if she had Down syndrome, and squeezed it tightly.

"Absatz," Hannah said. "Stop it, all of you." She moved closer to Grace and touched her chin with two fingertips, tilting her face up to the light. She looked into her eyes, and when she spoke again, her voice was kind. "What is your mother's name?"

"Trudie," Grace answered. "Trudie Schrock. She was Trudie from Belleville, Pennsylvania, and she was born one of you— Amish."

"Trudie Schrock?" the older woman said loudly from her chair. "I know that name. Trudie's aunt was a friend of Lavina. Trudie was the third daughter in the family, tenth or eleventh child. The Schrocks had a lot of children."

"And her name was Trudie? You're sure of it, Aunt Jezzy?" Johanna—the one with the attitude—asked.

"Ya. For sure, Johanna. That Trudie's the only one who didn't join the church. It hurt her family *haremlich*...terrible bad. Her father was a preacher, which made things worse. But there was never any talk of the girl being in the *family way.* Trudie left home and they never heard from her again. Must be some other Jonas this girl's looking for."

Grace didn't know what to say, but she knew she'd come to the right house.

Hannah shook her head. *"Ne,* Aunt Jezzy. Jonas told me, before we married that...he and Trudie Schrock... that I wasn't his first serious girlfriend."

"But not..." Johanna twisted her fingers in the hem of her apron looking from her mother to Grace and back to her mother again. "Dat would never... To make a baby with a girl not his wife. He couldn't have..."

"Hush," Hannah said. "Don't be a child." She waved toward the table. "Come and sit, Grace. Was your mother certain? That Jonas…" She sighed, was quiet for a moment, and then went on. "I should have seen it the moment you walked into my kitchen. You have my Jonas's red hair…his blue eyes. And you have the look of your sisters."

Grace swallowed, feeling a little dizzy. This was even harder than she thought it would be. She felt as if she was going to cry and she had no idea why. Her gaze moved from person to person. "I have sisters?"

Hannah nodded. "I'm Jonas's wife, and that makes my daughters—our daughters—your sisters." She waved toward the stunned girls. "These three are your sisters, and there are four more. Ruth, Anna, Miriam and Leah. Leah is in Brazil with her husband, but the other girls live close by."

Grace's knees felt weak. Her stomach felt as if a powerful hand was tightening around it, but at the same time, the feeling of relief was so intense that she thought she might lift off the floor and float to the ceiling. This good woman, this Hannah believed her! They didn't think she was a con artist. Giddy and light-headed, she took the chair that Hannah offered. "Could you tell him I'm here?" she asked again in a breathless voice. "My father?"

"Did your mother send you to find him?" Hannah asked, a little bit like the way the police asked questions. Grace had never been questioned by the police, but her Joe had. Many times.

Grace shook her head. "She died when I was eleven. She never told me anything about her past. A friend of hers, Marg, told me what little bit I know. She and my mother danced…*worked* together in Reno. Trudie and me moved around a lot, but she and Marg shared a trailer once when I was little."

"Your mother?" Hannah asked. "You called her Trudie?" Lines of disapproval crinkled at the corners of her brown eyes.

Grace nodded. "Trudie was nineteen when I was born, but she looked younger. She never wanted me to call her Mom. She said we were girlfriends, more like sisters. I think it was so guys—*other people*—wouldn't guess her real age. She was pretty, not like me. She had the most beautiful blond hair and a good figure."

"Verhuddelt." The older woman muttered as she retrieved the ball of yarn that had fallen out of her lap and rolled across the floor. "Such a mother."

"No," Grace protested. "She took good care of me. I never went hungry or anything." *Well, not really hungry,* she thought. Memories of sour milk and stale pizza washed over her, and she banished them to the dark corners in her mind. Trudie had always done her best, and she hadn't run out on her like some other moms. Grace had heard lots of horror stories from the kids she'd met in the Nevada foster homes where the state had stashed her after her mother died. Raising a child alone was hard—Grace had learned that lesson well enough. She wasn't going to let anybody bad-mouth Trudie.

"She did the best she could," Grace said. "She was smart, too, even if she didn't have much education. She could speak German," she added. "When she was mad, she always used to..." She trailed off, remembering that the angry shouts had probably not been nice words.

"I'm sorry that your mother passed." Hannah sat down and reached out to Dakota. "Here, let me hold him. Rebecca, could you get that cocoa? And hand that blanket to Grace."

The sister named Susanna offered a big cookie. Dakota shyly accepted it, but bit off a big bite.

"Remember your manners," Grace chided, accepting the blanket and wrapping it around her shoulders. She was so cold, she was shivering. "Don't gobble like a turkey. You'll choke."

Susanna giggled. "Like a turkey," she repeated.

Dakota nestled down in Hannah's lap, almost as if he knew her. His eyelids were heavy. Grace was surprised he'd been able to stay awake so late.

Hannah ran her fingers through Dakota's thick dark hair. "How old is he?"

"Three. He was three in January."

"His father?"

"Dead."

"He's little for three," Aunt Jezzy observed.

"But he's strong. He was always a good baby, and he's hardly ever sick. His father wasn't a big man." Grace looked into Hannah's eyes and tried to keep from trembling. "Could you tell Jonas I'm here? Please. I've come a long way to find him."

"How did you get all the way from Nebraska to Pennsylvania? Do you have a car?" Hannah asked.

Grace sighed. Her father's wife was stalling, but she didn't want to be rude. After all, Hannah had let her into the house and hadn't kicked her out when Grace told her who she was. "We had a car, but the transmission went out on the Pennsylvania Turnpike. It wasn't worth fixing, so we left it." She looked down at the floor. No use in telling them that the insurance had run out two weeks ago and that she had barely enough money for food and gas to get them to Belleville, let alone repair a 1996 Plymouth with a leaking radiator and 191,000 miles on it.

"So you went on to Belleville and then came here looking for Jonas?" Hannah looked thoughtful.

"I'm not asking for money. I don't want anything from him or from any of you. I just want to meet him." Grace chewed on her lower lip. "Since Trudie died, I haven't had any family." She hung her head. "Not really." She looked up again. "So, I thought that if I found my father…maybe…" Her throat tightened and she could feel a prickling sensation behind her eyelids. Grace took a deep breath. She didn't need to tell her father's wife the whole story. She'd save it for him. She looked right at Hannah. "I need to talk to my father. *Please,*" she added firmly.

Hannah clasped a hand over her mouth and made a small sound of distress. "Oh, child." She closed her eyes for a second and hugged Dakota. "Oh, my poor Grace. It pains me to tell you that your father…Jonas…he died four years ago of a heart attack."

Grace stared at her in disbelief. Thank goodness she was sitting down; her legs felt a little weak. Dead? After she'd come so far to find him? How was that possible? *Bad things come in threes, and if you don't expect much out of life, you won't be disappointed.* Her mother always said that. But the awful words Hannah had just spoken were almost more than she could bear.

Her father was dead, too?

Dear God, Grace thought, *how could You let this happen? First my mother, then Joe and now my father.* Now she was glad they hadn't eaten since her breakfast of Tastykakes. If she had anything in her stomach, it would be coming up.

"I'm so sorry," Hannah said. "It must be a terrible shock to you. We've all had time to get used to Jonas's passing. We miss him terribly. He was a good man, your father, the best husband in the world."

"Not so good as we thought, that nephew of mine," Aunt Jezzy observed, more to herself than the others. "Not if he fathered a child and didn't take responsibility for her."

"Hush, now, Aunt Jezzy," Hannah softly chided. "We shouldn't judge him. Jonas was a good man, but he was human, as we all are." She kept her gaze fixed on Dakota's sweet face. "He told me that he and Trudie Schrock had made a mistake, and that he'd repented of what he'd done. She left, suddenly, without telling him. No one knew where she went. She just left a note, telling her father that she didn't want to be *Plain* anymore. Jonas never knew about you," she told Grace, lifting her gaze. "You have my word on it."

Grace nodded, trying to get her bearings again. Trying hard not to cry. What was she going to do now? Her whole plan had been based on getting to her father. She was going to come to him, tell him the mistakes she'd made and beg him to let her into his life. She was going to promise to make only good choices from now on, to find a good man who wouldn't lie to her and deceive her. She was going to tell him she wanted to become—

"So." Hannah smiled at her with tears in her eyes. "What do we do now, you and me? Where do we start, Grace Yoder?"

Grace felt shaky, her mind racing. What *did* she want the Yoders to do with her? What was her plan B? Joe always said you had to have a plan B. "Maybe I could have that cup of coffee?"

Hannah chuckled. "You have your father's good sense, Grace. Of course you shall have your coffee, and the soup I promised. Then we'll all take ourselves off to bed. You'll stay here tonight, and I won't hear any arguments. I'll put you and Dakota in the guest bedroom."

"You'll just let me stay?" Grace asked, truly surprised by Hannah's kindness. Especially after the news Grace had just dumped in her lap about her husband. "You don't know me. I could be a thief or an ax murderer."

Hannah smiled at her. "I doubt that, not if you're Jonas's girl. A straighter, more God-fearing man never lived. He might have stumbled once, but he never faltered. I'm sure you're as trustworthy as any of your sisters."

Susanna giggled. "A sister."

"Thank you," Grace managed. "Thank you all." She looked at the women and the boy, all looking at her.

Exactly what she was going to do now?

Grace hadn't thought she'd be able to sleep a wink, but she'd drifted off to the sound of rain falling against the windowpanes and the soft hum of Dakota's breathing. And when she'd opened her eyes, it was full morning, the rain had stopped and the sun was shining.

My father is dead, she thought. She'd come all this way, only to find out that he was as lost to her as Trudie. She felt numb. What was plan B? Where did she go now? What did she do?

"I'm hungry," Dakota said, interrupting her thoughts.

"Can I have more cookies?" He popped his thumb in his mouth.

"No cookies this morning," she said.

No one had said a thing about Dakota's dark skin the night before, but she'd be ready for their questions. When Hannah and her sisters asked, and Grace was sure they would, she'd tell the truth—that Dakota's father had been Native American. Marg had said that the Amish were backward, old-fashioned and set in their ways. Grace hoped that didn't include judging people by the color of their skin, because if they couldn't accept Dakota, then she wanted no part of them.

But they hadn't *seemed* to care.

Grace looked down at Dakota's little face as her mind raced. Plan B. She had to have a plan B. But maybe... maybe plan B should be the same as plan A. Or close. Why couldn't it be? Hannah had been so nice to her. So welcoming.

"Cookies aren't for breakfast," she told her son as she got out of bed and put her arms out to him. "But I'm sure Miss Hannah will be able to find something for you in her kitchen."

Just thinking of that kitchen made a lump rise in Grace's throat. It was exactly the kind of kitchen she'd expected to find in her father's house, only better. It was big and warm and homey, all the things that the kitchens she'd known in her life weren't. And the Amish she'd met last night, even suspicious Aunt Jezzy and tough Johanna, were right for Hannah's kitchen.

What would it have been like to grow up here? she wondered. *To belong to a world as safe as this one? To be part of a family who could welcome total strangers*

into their home and feed them and give them a place to
sleep without asking for anything in return?

It all seemed too much. She'd just do what she'd always done when things got scary or uncertain. She'd do
what was most important first and worry about the rest
later. And now, finding something to feed her hungry
child was what mattered. Plan B could wait.

She tidied the two of them up in the bathroom, took
Dakota by the hand and, heart in her throat, led him
back to the spacious kitchen.

Grace could smell coffee, bacon and other delicious
odors coming from the kitchen as she walked down the
hall. "Now, you be a good boy," she whispered to Dakota as she led him by the hand. Nervously, she slicked
his cowlick back and tried to pat it down. "Show all
these nice people just how sweet you are."

Hannah, two of the sisters that she'd met the night before and Aunt Jezzy were gathered at the kitchen table.

"Miriam's taking my place at the school this morning," Hannah explained. "You'll meet her, Ruth and
Anna later. And this…" She waved toward a thirtyish
brown-haired man in a blue chambray shirt and jeans
sitting at the head of the table. "This is our friend John
Hartman. John, this is Grace."

Grace nodded. He didn't look Amish to her. His hair
was cropped short, almost in a military cut, and he had
no beard. Definitely not a cowboy type; he was nice-
looking in an old-fashioned, country way.

John rose to his feet, nodded and smiled at her.
"Pleased to meet you, Grace."

"He's having breakfast," Susanna explained as John
sat down again. "He eats breakfast here a lot. He likes

our breakfast." She picked up Dakota and sat him next to her on an old wooden booster seat in a chair.

"I stopped by to check on one of Johanna's ewes that got caught in a fence and Susanna caught me and… forced me to the table."

Grace wanted to ask if he was a farmer; it sounded as if he knew something about animals. She liked animals, especially dogs, and she'd always felt more at ease around them than people. The best job she'd ever had was working at a kennel where she cleaned cages and took care of dogs boarded there while their families were on vacation. Trying not to say the wrong thing in front of her new family, though, she decided that the less she said to a strange man, the better.

Susanna laughed. "You're silly, John. You said you were sooo hungry and Mam's biscuits smelled sooo good."

"I did and they do," he agreed.

"He wanted to get married with Miriam," Susanna happily explained, offering Dakota a cup of milk. "But she got married with Charley."

John's face flushed, but he shrugged, and looked right at Grace. "What can I say?" He grinned. "Always a bridesmaid, never a bride."

The others were laughing, so Grace forced a polite smile. John seemed like a stand-up guy, a real gentleman. As she accepted the cup of coffee Hannah handed her, Grace couldn't help wondering why her half sister had turned John down. If a man as good-looking as John, who had a job he could work when it rained, asked her, she'd marry him in a second.

Chapter Three

John finished off two slices of scrapple, two biscuits and a mound of scrambled eggs, but as much as he normally enjoyed Hannah's cooking, he may as well have been eating his uncle's frozen-in-a-box sausage bagels. He couldn't take his eyes off the attractive, almost-model-thin redhead, wearing the strangest *Plain* clothing he'd ever seen on a woman.

Her name was Grace. A pretty name for a pretty girl. He knew he would have remembered her if he'd ever seen her before. She was obviously related to the Yoders; she looked like Hannah's girls. From the attention she was giving the boy, she was probably his mother or at least his aunt. He didn't look like the Yoders, though. And the two of them sure didn't look Amish. So why had they spent the night here?

John was Mennonite, and among his people, staying in the homes of total strangers who shared the same faith was commonplace. Mennonites could travel all over the world and always be certain of a warm welcome from friendly hosts, whether it was for a weekend or a month. But the Amish were a people apart and rarely mingled socially with outsiders, who they called *Englishers*.

"'Come out from among them and be separate.'" 2 *Corinthian* 6:14. It was a verse that John had heard quoted many times since he'd come to join his uncle's and grandfather's veterinary practice. Because he specialized in large farm animals, many of his clients were Old Order Amish. Mennonites and Amish shared many of the same principles, and because he'd come close to marrying a Yoder daughter, he'd gotten to know the Amish in a way that few *Englishers* did.

Who was this mystery woman with such a haunting look of vulnerability? And what was so important about Grace's visit that Hannah—who *never* missed school— had taken the day off from teaching? John couldn't wait to get one of the Yoders alone and find out.

He lingered as long as he could at the table, having more coffee, eating when he wasn't really hungry and trying his best to engage Grace in conversation. But either she didn't answer or gave only one-word responses to his questions, intriguing him even further.

Eventually, he ran out of excuses to sit at Hannah's table and glanced at his watch. "I hate to leave such good company," he said, "but I have an appointment out at Rob Miller's farm." Repeating his thanks and wishing the others a good day, he gave Grace one last smile, and left the kitchen.

Hannah followed him out onto the porch, carefully closing the door behind her. "Well, what do you think?" she asked, drying her clean hands on her apron. "Of our visitor?"

He wondered whether to play it safe and be polite or to be himself. Himself won. "Um…she's nice. Pretty."

He met her gaze. "But, Hannah, I'm confused. Grace isn't Amish, is she?"

"*Ne,* John, that she isn't."

"A friend of the family from out of town?"

"None of us had ever laid eyes on her until last night. She came to us out of the storm, soaked to the skin and near to exhaustion. She'd been hitchhiking."

"Pretty dangerous for a young woman," he observed, not sure where the conversation was going.

John could tell that Hannah was pondering something, and that she wanted to talk, yet the Amish tradition of intense privacy remained strong. John waited. Either she would share her concerns or she wouldn't. No amount of nudging would budge her if she wanted to be secretive.

But then Hannah blurted right out, "Grace is my late husband's daughter."

"Jonas's daughter?" John stared at her in disbelief. He'd never heard that Jonas had been married before. "Jonas was married—"

"Jonas and Grace's mother never married. She ran away from the church. Jonas never knew she was in the family way."

John couldn't have been more shocked if a steer had been sitting at Hannah's table this morning. For a moment he didn't know what to say. Jonas Yoder had been one of the most genuinely kind and decent men he had ever known. It just didn't seem to fit that Jonas would... "You're certain this isn't a scam of some kind?" He couldn't imagine that the young woman he'd met inside could do anything dishonest, but Uncle Albert had often told him that he was naive when it came to seeing who or what people truly were. "She's not trying to get anything from you? Money or something?"

"She's asked for nothing. She came here looking for Jonas and I had to tell her he'd passed."

Poor Grace, he thought. *How terrible for her. But how terrible for Hannah, too. Not just to hear this news, to learn the awful truth about her beloved husband, but to have to tell his child that he was dead.*

"I…believe the girl is who she says she is," Hannah admitted, going on slowly. "Jonas told me…confided to me his affection for her mother, Trudie. Jonas was under the impression they were courting, then Trudie left the church and her family and disappeared. Jonas never knew anything about a baby. I would suspect her family didn't, either."

"It's possible, I suppose." John glanced out into the farmyard, feeling so badly for Hannah. Not wanting her to feel uncomfortable. This kind of thing was a delicate matter. Unwed young Amish women occasionally got pregnant, but it didn't happen often. And when it did, there was repentance, then a quick wedding and the matter was settled. "She has the same color hair as your girls."

"And Jonas's blue eyes."

John glanced toward the kitchen door, picturing again the guarded expression in the young woman's gaze. "I thought there was something familiar about her. She favors Johanna, not as tall, and she's a lot thinner, but…"

"Too thin by my way of thinking, but Miriam was always slender, too."

John nodded. It hadn't been easy, coming to accept losing Miriam. But after two years, he could see her or hear her name without feeling as though a horse had kicked him in the gut. And he could see that she'd made the right decision. She wouldn't have been happy leaving the Amish, so as much as he hated to admit it, Charley was right for her.

"How do you feel about Grace coming here?" he asked. "It must be a shock to you."

"*Ya,* a shock. It…is. My Jonas was as capable of making a mistake as any of us. As much as I loved and respected him…" She shrugged. "A bishop, my Jonas was, but I knew him to be a man first. His girls think him perfect." She chuckled. "And the longer he's dead, the more perfect he becomes."

John grinned. "That happens a lot, and not just in your family. My mother and father didn't always see eye to eye, but once he died, Mom promoted him to sainthood."

Hannah laced her fingers together. "Whatever Jonas's faults, he repented of them and asked God's forgiveness every day. When he passed, he left me the means to care for his children and myself and nothing but good memories." She walked down the steps and into the sunshine.

John followed her, giving her a moment before he spoke again. "You are the most remarkable person, Hannah Yoder. Most women would have been furious or so hurt, so bitter that they couldn't have considered inviting the girl into their home."

"*Ne.*" She shook her head and slowly slid down to sit on the top step of the porch. "I am not remarkable, only numb, like after you hit your thumb with a hammer. Before the pain starts."

"But you didn't take it out on Grace. That's what matters. You had compassion for a stranger."

"Why should I blame her? None of this is Grace's fault. She's innocent. I need to remember that. My girls will look to me to see how to treat her, as will the community."

"I'm just saying, as your friend, that you have a right to be upset." He folded his arms over his chest. "Her coming here changes your family. Forever."

"And her," Hannah said. "I don't believe she has had an easy life. Her mother died when she was a child."

"So she's left without a mother or a father?" *No wonder she had the look of a lost puppy,* he thought. But then, he corrected himself. *Not a puppy, but a feral kitten, wanting so badly to be loved, but ready to scratch to defend itself.* "So now that she's here, what are you going to do with her?"

Hannah frowned ever so gently. "Honestly, John, I have no idea."

Later, after John left and the breakfast dishes were cleared away and Rebecca and Jonah had left for the other sister's house, Grace watched as Johanna settled at the kitchen table with a pile of quilting pieces. Her daughter sat beside her, playing with her own squares of cloth. Just as the night before, Johanna seemed stiff and reserved. Grace couldn't blame her. It wasn't every day a stranger showed up claiming to be a long-lost sister. Katie, however, was all dimples and giggling personality in her Amish dress, apron and white cap.

"How old are you?" Grace asked the child.

"Drei!" Katie held up three fingers.

"My goodness, you're a big girl for three," Grace

said. She and Dakota were the same age, but Katie was nearly a head taller and much sturdier. Shyly, her son hid behind her skirt and peered out at Katie. "Come out and meet Katie," she said, taking his hand. She squatted down so that she was closer in size to the two of them. "Katie, this is Dakota."

He stared at her, and Grace ruffled his hair. No matter how much she slicked it down, his coarse Indian hair insisted on sticking up like the straw in a scarecrow. No wonder Joe had grown his long and braided it. "Say hello," she urged her son.

"'Lo," he managed. Grace could tell that he wanted to play with Katie. Since she'd had to pull him out of day care back in Nebraska, Dakota had missed his friends.

Katie put a finger in her mouth and stared back.

"She doesn't speak English very well yet," Hannah said, walking into the kitchen. "But she understands it. Most children learn when they start school, but Jonas always insisted that we use both English and Pennsylvania Dutch at home, so the girls wouldn't feel uncomfortable among the Englishers." She looked at Johanna. "I know you need to get to your quilt, but if you, Grace and Susanna could hang out the wash, I can get that turkey in the oven." She glanced at Grace. "I hope you don't mind. We all pitch in to do the housework."

"Sure," Grace said. "I'll be glad to help. Tell me what to do."

"I'm just glad we've got sun and a good breeze," Hannah said. "We're expecting company this afternoon, and I've washed all the sheets. If it had kept raining, they would have been a mess to get dry."

"Right," Grace mused. "No electric dryer." Then she considered what Hannah had just said and started to get nervous. About her new plan: plan B. "You're getting company? I guess I picked a bad time to show up here."

"Ne," Hannah said. "It's a big house. Friends of ours, the Roman Bylers, have relatives moving here from Indiana. Sadie and Ebben King bought the little farm down the road from us. They'll be part of our church. Two of their sons and a daughter, all married, live here in Kent County, so they decided it was time to move east. They'll be staying with us until the repairs are done and they get a new roof on."

Grace wanted to ask why the Kings were staying with the Yoders instead of their own relatives, but she thought it better to keep her questions to herself. She didn't want to be rude.

"They have one boy left at home," Hannah continued. "David. He's their youngest. He's like our Susanna. Special."

It took Grace a second to realize what Hannah meant. The son must have Down syndrome like Susanna. She nodded in understanding.

"Get those wet sheets, Johanna?" Hannah asked.

Minutes later, Dakota and Katie were happily playing together under Hannah's watchful eye in the kitchen, while Grace, Susanna and Johanna hung laundry on the clothesline in the backyard.

As Grace hung a wet sheet on the line running between two poles, she took in her surroundings. It seemed almost too good to be true to Grace. The white house, the wide green lawn with carefully tended flower beds, and not a car or TV antenna in sight. The only sounds she heard were the breeze rustling through the tree branches, the creak of the windmill blades and the joyous song of a mockingbird.

Johanna, her mouth full of clothespins, was intent on attaching a row of dresses—blue, lavender and green dresses—while Susanna and Grace hung items from an overflowing basket of towels and sheets. Grace eyed the dresses and aprons wistfully. Today she'd put on a clean blouse from her bag, but she didn't have another long skirt or apron so she'd had to put the same ones on again. Susanna and Johanna both wore modest Amish dresses in different shades of blue with white aprons and stiff white caps. Grace felt foolish with her men's handkerchief tied over her hair, but no one had mentioned it, so maybe it wasn't as bad as she thought.

Susanna hummed as she worked, but her older sister was clearly out of sorts. After a while, Grace took a deep breath and peered over the clothesline at Johanna. "I don't blame you," she said in a low voice.

Silence.

"I can see how it would be upsetting," Grace went on. "Me coming here."

Johanna reached down for a boy's pair of blue trousers. "If you must know, I'm not sure I believe you. I don't want to see my mother hurt."

Grace felt her cheeks burning. She'd expected her stepmother to be the one who would try to deny her, not a sister. Not that Grace had even expected a sister. She'd never allowed herself to think any further than finding her father and hoping he'd claim her. Oh, there had been a family in the background in her daydreams, sort of a shadowy idea of younger brothers, but never in a million years had she considered that she'd find seven sisters.

And Johanna had been a surprise. She and Johanna looked so much alike, almost like twins, although Grace was shorter and skinnier. It was weird to Grace, seeing a stranger who looked so much like the face she saw in the mirror every time she brushed her teeth. And their light auburn hair, a shade you didn't often see, was exactly the same color that Marg had said that Grace's father's had been.

"Trudie's man was a ginger-haired, blue-eyed Amish hottie," Marg had told her.

Grace was so sorry she'd never get the chance to meet Jonas. It wasn't fair. But when had life ever been fair to her?

"Think what you want about me," Grace said stubbornly to Johanna. "I'm here, and I'm just as much Jonas's daughter as you are."

"Maybe," Johanna said. "That remains to be seen."

"What are you arguing about?" Susanna demanded, pulling the clothesline down so she could see them over a row of towels. "Don't be mean, Johanna."

"I'm not being mean."

"Are, too." Susanna planted her chubby hand on one hip and stuck out her chin. "Mam said be nice to Grace. She's our sister."

"She might be our sister, but she might not, Susanna Banana. She might be a stranger just *pretending* to be our sister."

Susanna shook her head. "I like her, and I like Dakota."

"But what if she's trying to trick us, just saying she's our sister?" Johanna argued.

"Doesn't matter," Susanna said firmly. "Maybe God wanted her to come here. She needs us." Her head bobbed. "*Ya,* and maybe we need her. It doesn't matter if she's a real sister. She can be one, if we want her to, can't she?"

Grace turned toward Susanna as tears gathered in her eyes. "Thank you," she managed, before dashing across the grass and back into the house. She wanted to go into her room, to fling herself on the bed, shut the door and try to reason this all out. She didn't trust herself to talk to Hannah or anyone else until she'd regained her composure.

"What's wrong?" Hannah asked as Grace came in the back door.

Grace rubbed at her eyes and sniffed. "Nothing. Must be allergic to something."

"Ya," Hannah agreed. "Must be."

"This is hard," Grace admitted, folding her arms over her chest and looking down at the floor. "I didn't think it would be this hard."

"It is going to be hard for all of us. Maybe Johanna most of all." She glanced at the two children who were busily sorting wooden animals in a toy ark in the center of the floor. "Come with me." She motioned, and Grace followed her into what appeared to be a big pantry off the kitchen. "So the children won't hear," she said quietly. "Don't be too quick to judge Johanna. She has a good heart, but she's had a hard time these last few years. She is a widow, too. Did you know?"

Grace shook her head. "No." So Johanna had lost her man, too? It was creepy how much alike they were. "I'm sorry to hear it."

"He was sick...in his mind," Hannah explained. "Wilmer took his own life. Johanna couldn't manage their farm on her own, so she came home to live with us. For a long time, things were not good with her and Wilmer, and she finds it hard to trust people."

Grace nodded. "I can understand that."

"The two of you have common ground," Hannah said. "You both have small children that you love. It's a place to start, *ne?*"

"Maybe." Grace sighed. "But why can't she be like Susanna and just accept me for who I am?"

Hannah smiled. "We should all be like our Susanna. She is one of God's special people. She was born with a heart overflowing with joy."

"You believe me, don't you? That I'm Jonas's daughter?"

The older woman hesitated only a second. "*Ya,* I do."

"Then…" She peered into Hannah's eyes, thinking about plan B. This was it. This was her opportunity to speak up. "Can we stay—at least for a little while? I won't be a burden, I promise. I'll get a job and pay room and board, and I'll pitch in like everyone else." She glanced at her feet, then raised her head, her eyes wet with tears. "But I need to be here."

"You can stay as long as you like."

Grace looked into Hannah's eyes. "I didn't tell you the whole truth last night. About coming here."

The older woman's face didn't change.

"I did come here to find my father. To meet him. But also…" She thought of Dakota and the life she'd led, the life she didn't want for her son. That was what gave her the strength to spit it out. "I came to Seven Poplars to tell my father that I want to be Amish. Like him."

Hannah looked away. "Oh my, Grace." She sighed.

"It's not impossible, is it?" Grace went on. "Especially because my father—and technically Trudie—were Amish?"

Hannah turned back to her and smiled wryly. "It's not so easy. Sometimes Englishers say they want to be like us, but the world calls to them, too loudly."

"I've seen the world," Grace insisted. "It's too loud."

Again Hannah smiled. And this time she patted Grace's arm. "Best you stay awhile and see if this is the life for you before you make big decisions like that. But whatever you choose, you and Dakota will still be family."

"But I've *already* thought about this for a long time." Grace tried not to sound whiny like Dakota sometimes did. Now that she had plan B straight in her head, she wanted to put it into place. "Being Amish feels right."

"First, you live with us and see how you like it. See if it *still* feels right to you once you've walked in our shoes. In time, if you still think this is the life you would choose, we'll talk to the bishop and see what he says. But first, you must learn *gelassenheit,* the ability to submit your will to that of the elders, the church and the community."

"I will! I'll do anything you say, if only you won't turn us away."

Hanna studied Grace closely. "Can you turn your back on the world? Can you give up your automobiles, your television programs, your telephones and live a *Plain* life?"

"I can. I promise you that that's what I want."

Hannah took her hands. "Then we will try, together. And may the Lord help and guide us every step of the way."

Chapter Four

"Wake up, *Schweschder,*" Susanna called, pushing open Grace's bedroom door. "Wait till you see! Mam sent you new clothes. And Plain clothes for Dakota, too."

Grace stifled a groan. Surely it couldn't be time to get up yet. It wasn't even light out. How was Susanna always so happy this early in the morning? Still, Susanna had called her *sister,* and the word glowed warm in Grace's heart. At least *someone* thought she belonged here.

Susanna placed a kerosene lamp carefully on the dresser, and a circle of soft yellow light spread across the room. "Mam says it's time to get up."

"I'm coming," Grace promised. Getting up before dawn was hard. She'd never been a morning person and rarely came fully awake until her second cup of coffee. Groaning, she pushed back the heavy quilt. She was no quitter. She'd do whatever she had to do to prove to Hannah that she was worthy of becoming one of them.

The room was cool and the feather ticks and quilt that covered the bed toasty. Dakota was snuggled beside her,

black hair all spiky and one arm wrapped tightly around
his stuffed bunny. Intense love for her son washed over
Grace. Dakota was what mattered most in the world
to her. His welfare was more important than anything
else. The past three days hadn't been easy, but the worst
had to be behind her if Hannah had sent them Amish
clothing. If they dressed like the rest of the family, it
had to be easier for them to fit into the household and
the community.

Dakota sighed and burrowed deeper under the covers. She'd tucked him into the trundle bed as she had
for the past three nights since Irwin had carried it down
from the attic. She knew he should be sleeping in his
own bed, but every morning, when she awoke, Dakota
was in her bed. Back in Nebraska, he'd slept alone, but
since she'd uprooted his life, he didn't want to be apart
from her, especially at night. And who could blame
him? Seven Poplars was a world apart from a trailer
park on the wrong side of the tracks. If she was confused, how much more must Dakota be?

"Mam is making blueberry pancakes," Susanna supplied cheerfully. "And today the Kings come. To stay
with us." She bounced from one foot to another in excitement. "Do you want me to take Dakota to the potty
and brush his teeth?"

"Would you?" Grace leaned down and whispered in
her son's ear. "Wake up, sleepyhead."

Dakota sat up, yawned and rubbed his eyes. A lop-
sided grin spread over his face when he caught sight of
Susanna. Sometimes, Grace found Susanna's speech
a little hard to understand, but Dakota seemed to have
no trouble at all. He'd taken to Susanna, as Joe would
have said, "Like a cowboy to hot biscuits."

Thoughts of Joe were bittersweet, and Grace pushed his image away. So many mistakes…but then there was Dakota, her precious son.

Susanna held out her chubby arms, and Dakota scrambled out of the bed and bounced into her embrace. "I'll help him get dressed, too." Dakota waved over Susanna's shoulder as she scooped up a small shirt and a pair of blue overalls and went happily off with her.

Grace's pulse quickened as she looked at the neatly folded stack of clothing. Her hands trembled as she reached for the white head covering on top, but when she picked it up, she couldn't help but be a little disappointed. It wasn't a proper *Kapp,* not like the ones Hannah and her daughters wore. It was white cotton, starched and hand-stitched, but more like a Mennonite head covering than Amish. She'd seen Mennonites in the Midwest; they sort of dressed like everyone else, just more modestly.

The long-sleeved calico dress was robin's egg blue with a pattern of tiny white flowers that fell a good three inches below her knees. It wasn't new, but it fit as if it had been made for her. And once she tied the starched white apron over the dress and added the dark stockings and sensible navy blue sneakers, Grace had to admit that it was a great improvement over the outfit she had arrived in. But it definitely wasn't Amish.

"Small steps," she murmured under her breath. "I should be grateful that Hannah didn't toss me out in the rain." Instantly, she felt guilty for her lack of patience. She dropped to her knees beside the bed and offered a fervent prayer of apology and thanks. "I'm still fumbling in the dark, Lord," she whispered. "I came here looking for a father, and instead You showed me the possibility of a whole family. Help me to do what's right for Dakota and me."

Grace knew that she had much to atone for and much to learn. But surely, a merciful God wouldn't give her a glimpse of heaven, only to snatch it all away.

"Grace?"

Grace rose hastily and turned to see Hannah standing in the open doorway.

"I'm sorry," Hannah said. "I didn't mean to disturb your prayers."

Grace felt her cheeks grow warm. How long had Hannah been standing there? Had she heard her prayer? Unconsciously, Grace put a hand to her cap, checking to see if it was securely pinned in place. "You didn't… I mean, I was done. I…" She hesitated. "I thought… These clothes aren't…"

"They're Plain," Hannah said. "Not Amish, but not English, either. Halfway, as you are, Grace. Actually, the dress is a gift from your sister Leah's Aunt Joyce, by marriage. She's Mennonite. Leah married into the family."

"Anna told me that Leah and her husband, Daniel, were missionaries in Brazil. I didn't think that was allowed…."

Hannah's features softened. "Our way, the Old Order Amish way, must be chosen freely by each person. I can't deny that I was surprised that Leah chose another path to God, the Mennonite path, but I accept it as part of His plan."

"Oh." Grace couldn't imagine that her sister would want to leave Seven Poplars for Brazil. And to be Amish and give it up…

"Leah's husband, Daniel, has an aunt nearby. Joyce

and I have become friends. When I saw her at Byler's and mentioned you, she said that a niece had outgrown some dresses that might fit you. Joyce dropped them off yesterday, but they were a little long."

"I always have to hem stuff," Grace said. "I'm short."

"Your father wasn't a tall man." Hannah folded her arms. "I hope you like the cap and apron. Rebecca sewed them for you."

"I do." Grace took a deep breath. "And I appreciate the clothing. But I don't want to be a burden. I'll get a job just as soon as I can and contribute money to the household." She thought as she spoke aloud. "There must be hotels in Dover. I've worked in housekeeping a lot and most places have a big turnover. I'm not sure what I'd do for transportation. Is there a bus—"

"Ne." Hannah shook her head. "Not permitted."

Grace looked at her. "You mean I…we aren't allowed to use public transportation? Is there a rule against—"

Hannah's eyes widened. "You cannot work in a hotel. Housekeeping for English is sometimes allowed in private homes, but the bishop must approve it. He would never allow a woman to work in such a place."

"Being a maid is respectable," Grace argued. "We hardly see the guests at all. I wouldn't be alone. Two girls work together to clean the rooms."

"Too worldly. At Spence's Auction you could work, or at Byler's. Even Fifer's Orchard. But not as a hotel maid. We keep apart from the world."

Grace stared at the hardwood floor. "I'm not sure what I can do, then."

Hannah sighed. "I'm sorry, Grace. If times were better, Eli and Roman could use you in the office at the

chair shop. But this winter there's barely enough work
for the men."

"I know the economy is bad," Grace said in an attempt to remain positive. "But I've worked since I was
fourteen. That's why I thought housekeeping—"

"*Ne*. Maybe Johanna would let you help with her
quilting. She sells her quilts in English shops."

Grace grimaced. "I can't sew. I'm all thumbs when
it comes to replacing a button."

"Maybe her bees. She has nine beehives and col-
lects honey for—"

"I'm allergic to bees." Grace's shoulders slumped.
"The last time I was stung, I ended up in the emergency
room. I didn't have insurance, and it took me two years
to pay off the bill."

"Then we'll have to keep you away from the beehives. We don't have insurance, either." Hannah met
Grace's gaze. "We Amish put our trust in God, and if
the worst happens, we help each other to pay the ex-
pense." She smiled. "Have faith, Grace. He brought
you to us, and He won't abandon you now. We'll put
our heads together and find a job for you." Her eyes
twinkled. "One that Bishop Atlee and even my sister-
in-law Martha will approve of."

From the way Hannah's nose wrinkled when she
mentioned Martha, Grace had a feeling that Martha
might be harder to please than the bishop. "I don't believe I've met her yet, have I?" Since she and Dakota
had come to the Yoder farm, there'd been a steady
stream of visitors, but she didn't remember anyone
named Martha.

"*Ne,* you haven't. Martha, Reuben and their daughter,
Dorcas, have gone to Lancaster to a Coblentz wedding.

Reuben is a Coblentz." Hannah brushed the wrinkles out of her starched apron. "Now we should eat our breakfast before it gets cold. It will be a busy day, and I don't want to be late for school."

"If you would tell me what you need done before you leave, I can—"

"Johanna knows. And I should be home before the Kings arrive. We don't expect them until supper time. It all depends on what time their driver picked them up this morning. They spent last night with relatives in Ohio and still have a long drive today."

"It's good of you to have them stay with you."

"Roman's house is small, and they have children. Ebben is a second cousin of your father. They could have stayed with their daughter and her husband, but they live over by Black Bottom. Better Ebben be here to see to finishing their house. You'll like Sadie, a sensible woman with a good heart. Full of fun. Always the jokes, Sadie."

Pondering how different Amish life was than what she'd expected, Grace followed Hannah out of the bedroom. She'd thought her father's people would be stern and solemn, sort of like modern-day Pilgrims. Instead, she'd found gentle ways and easy laughter, making her realize just how much she'd missed out on by not being raised as one of them. *If I had,* she thought, *everything would be so different. And I wouldn't have so much to ask forgiveness for....*

When they reached the kitchen, Grace saw Rebecca, Susanna, Irwin, Aunt Jezzy and the children already seated while Johanna carried a steaming platter of pancakes to the table. Susanna was pouring milk for the little ones as Rebecca slid sausage onto Jonah's plate.

No one seemed to mind that Katie already had a mouthful of applesauce before silent prayer.

Dakota looked up at Grace and grinned. She stopped short and stared at him. Dakota's handmade blue shirt and overalls were identical to the ones worn by Johanna's Jonah. Grace had been meaning to trim his hair. It grew so fast that it always needed cutting. But now, she saw that the style was just right. Black hair or not, Dakota looked exactly like any other little Amish boy. Fresh hope welled up inside her as she blinked back tears of happiness. She would make a life for them here. She had to. They could never go back to living as they had before.

"Coffee?" Johanna asked as Grace slid into an empty chair.

"Yes, please, but I can get—"

"I'm up. Mam?"

Hannah nodded, and Johanna returned with the pot.

The odor of fresh coffee assaulted Grace's senses. She knew from every other cup she'd enjoyed in Hannah's kitchen that the brew would be just the way she liked it—hot, and strong enough to dissolve a spoon, as her mother would have said. Johanna took her seat, and Grace bowed her head along with everyone at the table, including the children.

A moment or two later, everyone was digging into breakfast, more interested in the delicious meal than talking. It gave Grace time to compose herself and smile at Johanna. "I'll be glad to help you get ready for your guests," she murmured shyly.

"Willing hands are always welcome. Anna, Ruth and Miriam are coming over once they finish morning chores at home. Between us, we can roast a turkey, prepare enough food for company and get the house shining."

"And me," Susanna reminded. "I can help."

"You're always a good helper," Johanna said. "And you'll do us a big favor if you can keep Jonah, Katie, Dakota and Anna's Mae out of trouble while we're busy."

Susanna giggled. "We'll make oatmeal *kichlin*. With raisin faces."

"Cookies!" Jonah chimed in. "I like cookies."

"Me, too," Dakota echoed. Katie clapped her hands. As Johanna had said, Katie was just learning English, but it was clear she understood everything being said at the table.

Grace was just accepting the platter of pancakes from Johanna when Irwin's terrier began to bark. Surprised, Grace turned to look toward the door. Surely her sisters wouldn't be here this early in the morning.

Hannah rose, motioning to the others to remain at the table. When a knock came, everyone stopped talking. Hannah removed her scarf and quickly put on her *Kapp*.

"I hope nothing is wrong," Aunt Jezzy said. "The sun isn't up yet."

Hannah opened the door and laughed. "John, you are an early bird. Come in. We're just sitting down to breakfast."

Rebecca cut her eyes at Johanna and stifled a giggle.

"John!" Susanna cried. "It's John."

Everyone was looking at him, but John didn't seem to mind. He stamped his feet and rubbed his hands together. "It's cold out there. You don't have a cup of coffee to spare for a frozen friend, do you?"

"Of course." Hannah chuckled. "Take off your coat and come to the table. We have plenty."

"I was hoping you'd say that," John answered with a grin. "I've been up all night with one of Clarence Miller's cows."

"Bad off?" Johanna asked.

"Delivered safely of twin heifers," John pronounced. "Although it was a near thing. The first one was breech. If Clarence hadn't come for me, I'm afraid they would have lost all three."

"Thanks be to God," Aunt Jezzy said.

John tucked his gloves into his coat pockets and hung his coat on a hook near the door. "I didn't come empty-handed," he said to Hannah. "Clarence just butchered two days ago. He insisted on giving me a ham and a pork loin. I left them in the cold box on the porch. You're welcome to them, and I know you can use them with company coming."

"Grace." Johanna nudged her. "Could you set a plate for John and pour him some coffee?"

Grace nodded. "Sure." John smiled and winked at her as she got up, and she felt herself blushing. What was it about him that made her feel as if she had two left feet? She'd always been more at ease around men than women. But John Hartman was different. When he looked at her, her wits scattered like fall leaves in a windstorm.

"Don't put yourself out for me," he said. "I know where Hannah keeps the cups."

"No," Grace insisted. "You sit. You're company." Thinking about John was distracting, but it made her feel good that Johanna had asked for help. It made Grace feel warm inside to welcome someone into the house.

For a few minutes she could almost convince herself that she had always been one of them.

"Look at you," he said, making a show of staring at her. "Dress and apron, prayer cap."

Grace's throat clenched. Was he making fun of her? "Hannah gave them to me," she said. It came out a whisper.

John saw that his teasing had upset her. "I think you look fine," he said with another warm smile. "More than fine. I think you look…"

"Plain?" Hannah said, coming to his rescue.

"I was going to say pretty," he answered. "*And* Plain. Nice. The blue brings out the blue in your eyes."

Now everyone was staring at her. Woodenly, she walked to the stove and reached for the coffeepot.

"Watch it!" John warned, lunging across the room and throwing out a hand to block her arm. "You need a hot mitt. You don't want to burn yourself."

Grace yanked her arm back almost as fast as she would have if she had been burned. For a second, their gazes met, and she saw the real concern in John's eyes. Then she took a step back. "Sorry," she managed. "I didn't think."

"Ne," Susanna said. "You don't want to get a burn. Becca did. Becca burned herself on the stove. She got the blister. Mam had to put medicine on it."

John found a hot mitt and handed it to Grace.

"Thank you," she said. "That was dumb of me."

"Not dumb," he answered in a deep, rich voice. "We all make silly mistakes." He opened a cupboard door, removed a mug and held it out to her. She forced her hands not to tremble as she filled the cup nearly to the brim. "Thank you, Grace Yoder," he said.

Rebecca giggled.

"Come back to the table, you two, before breakfast turns to ice," Hannah called. "You say both calves were heifers, John?"

He gave Grace a warm grin before turning back to the table. "Pretty calves, both of them. Big. A little tired, but they were both on their feet and nursing when I left the barn. Clarence is lucky. They'll make a fine addition to his dairy herd if he decides not to sell them."

"Late in the year for calves," Irwin said between mouthfuls of pancake.

"Or early." John took a chair. "Clarence didn't intend for her to calve in November. He said Reuben's bull broke down the fence between their farms and got into his pasture."

Grace was grateful that the conversation had turned to animals and away from her. She'd heard lots of talk about livestock around the rodeo, and she'd grown used to it. It was clear that John was dedicated to his work. He didn't seem the least put out that he'd had to miss a night's sleep in one of his client's barns. Even on such a cold night.

"I saw your lights as I was on the way home," he was saying. "I hoped that if I threw myself on your mercy, you'd feed me. Yesterday morning, Uncle Albert insisted on making oatmeal from scratch. It was awful, as thick and gummy as paste. He thought it was wonderful, and there was no way I could get away from the table without eating a bowl the size of my head."

Susanna giggled. "The size of my head," she echoed.

"I can't imagine what it would be this morning for breakfast," John continued, glancing across the table at

Grace and smiling with his eyes. "I was just hoping it wouldn't be more oatmeal."

"Ya," Irwin agreed. "Probably so."

"That or his French toast," John replied. "And he always burns that. Says charcoal is good for the digestion." Everyone, including Grace and John and the children, laughed at that.

"It must be hard for the three of you," Hannah said. "Three men with no woman to cook for you."

"It's a heavy burden, I can tell you." John grinned again. "I'd do the cooking, but the truth is, mine is worse than Uncle Albert's."

As the meal continued, Grace tried to convince herself that John was just a friend who had stopped by unexpectedly, that she had no reason to think he was paying special attention to her. She tried to eat, but even the coffee seemed to have no taste at all. She forced herself to concentrate on finishing the single pancake she'd put on her plate before John had arrived.

"Another reason for stopping by, besides starvation," John went on. "The young man who cleans our kennels hasn't come in to work for three days. He didn't even call to let us know he had quit. We're desperate for help. I was wondering if Irwin might like to come by after school for a few hours and maybe half a day on Saturdays? What do you think, Irwin?"

"Me?" He looked up. "I don't know, John. Are they big dogs?"

"You like dogs," John said. "Look how good you are with Jeremiah. You'd be cleaning cages, doing some grooming, helping with—"

"Don't know." Irwin stared at his plate and pushed a piece of pancake into a pool of syrup. "I've got chores…

and homework. Saturdays I'm pretty busy here on the farm."

"Nine dollars an hour to start," John said. "And I could arrange for you to have a ride to the clinic. You wouldn't have to—"

"I could do it," Grace interrupted.

Everyone looked at her.

She took a deep breath. "I used to work in a big kennel. I'm good with dogs. And…and I need a job."

John looked surprised. "It's hard work, Grace. Dirty work."

She looked him straight in the eyes. "I'm not afraid of hard work. And I know dogs. I like them and they like me." She glanced at Hannah. Unable to read her face, she looked back at John. "If you'll give me a chance, I promise you won't regret it."

Chapter Five

"I'd have to talk to Uncle Albert," John said. "But...I don't think he cares who is hired, just so he and Sue aren't doing the cleaning. She's our new vet. Dr. Susan Noble. Just joined the practice in the spring. She's the one who helped us get our small-animal business running."

A lump the size of her coffee cup knotted in Grace's throat, but this was too good an opportunity to miss. This was a job she could do. *Please, God,* she prayed silently. *Help me convince them that I'm the right person. If it's Your will,* she added hastily.

She knew all too well that she'd often prayed for things that hadn't come true—from praying that Joe would recover from his terrible accident, all the way to praying that her old Plymouth would make it to her destination. God didn't always answer prayers, but she believed that He had His own good reasons. And it didn't keep her from praying.

"I...I'd do a good job. I know I would," Grace heard herself say.

John glanced at Hannah. "Is that something that your bishop would approve of?"

"Cleaning the cages? Is that what you need?" Hannah turned to Irwin. "You're sure it isn't something you'd like to consider?"

Irwin scooped up a forkful of pancake and jammed it in his mouth. "Got homework," he muttered. "Don't like strange dogs."

"*Ya,* we all know how dedicated you are to your education," Hannah said without the hint of a smile. Rebecca twittered and Johanna hid her amusement behind her coffee cup.

Susanna had no qualms about speaking her mind. "*Ne,*" she said. "Irwin hates school. He doesn't do his homework unless Mam makes him."

Irwin washed the last of his breakfast down with milk, mumbled an excuse and fled, grabbing his coat and hat as he went out the door. Jeremiah scrambled after him, hot on his master's heels.

Hannah chuckled. "I think we can safely say that Irwin doesn't want the job, John. Maybe you *should* consider Grace's offer. I see no reason, because she'd be working for you and your grandfather and Albert, that Bishop Atlee should disapprove. Charley's sister Mary still cleans house for you, doesn't she?"

"Yes," John replied.

"You'll give me a chance?" Grace asked eagerly. "I have kennel experience. My foster mother bred all kinds of dogs and sold the puppies. I cleaned cages, fed and groomed dogs, delivered puppies and did basic medical care for five years."

"How many dogs did she have?" John asked.

Grace shrugged. "It depended. Sometimes more than

a hundred." She met his gaze. "I suppose it was a puppy mill, but Mrs. Klinger took good care of her dogs. She had a vet that came out to the house regularly. She fed her dogs well, and their cages were always clean and dry." *I should know,* she thought. *I spent enough hours on my hands and knees scrubbing them.*

"Five years." Hannah was watching Grace. Making her self-conscious. "How old were you?"

Grace lowered her gaze to her cup of coffee, then looked up again. "Twelve when I went to live with Mrs. Klinger."

There were three other foster mothers and a group home before Mrs. Klinger, in the year after her mother died. After that, Sunny Acres Kennel didn't seem so bad. Grace had had to work hard seven days a week, but as long as she kept up with her chores, behaved herself in church and didn't fight with the other foster kids, Mrs. Klinger was nice enough to her.

At least she'd gotten to stay in the same school longer than she ever had before. It wasn't like when she lived with Trudie. With her mother, she missed a lot of school. Once, when Grace was eight, she'd gotten off the school bus to find their trailer empty and all their stuff gone. She'd sat on the step crying until long after dark before her mother came back for her.

"It sounds as if you have the experience we need," John said.

Maybe more experience than I care to share or you'd want to hear about, Grace thought as she clasped her hands together under the table where no one would see. Her stomach clenched. She didn't like deceiving good people, but if they knew her for what she really was, they'd show her and Dakota the door.

John nodded. "Let me see what Uncle Albert thinks while Hannah checks with Bishop Atlee."

It was all Grace could do to not let out a sigh of relief that no one had asked why she'd ended her stint at Sunny Acres at age sixteen. What would they think of her if they knew she'd run away from the foster home? She'd had her reasons, good reasons, but quitting high school and living on her own hadn't been easy. Many a night she'd slept in someone's barn or went to sleep hungry. She'd never stolen anything and she'd never begged. Somehow, with God's help, she'd survived. And she'd never quit going to church wherever and whenever she could. Somehow, sitting in the back of a church, no matter which denomination, had helped to fill the emptiness inside her.

John looked at his watch. "Yikes. I have a surgery this morning. I'd best get back to the clinic." He rose from his chair, taking one last swig of coffee. "Thanks for breakfast. Again."

"And thank you for the ham and the pork loin," Hannah said with a smile. "You're welcome to come to dinner when we cook it."

"I just might take you up on that." He turned his attention to Grace again. "I promise to have an answer for you by Monday. If you're certain you want the job."

Grace nodded. "Definitely. So long as Hannah… and the bishop approve." She hoped that working in the same place as John Hartman wouldn't be a mistake. He had a way of making her pulse race and her thoughts scatter every time he smiled at her. It was a pity he wasn't Amish. If he had been…

Grace glanced down at her plate and tried to keep from chuckling aloud. If John had been Plain, she'd have made no bones about setting her *Kapp* for him. Because the surest way to make certain her future was secure in this community was to find an Amish husband and tie the knot. If she married into the church and had a home of her own, then no one could ever say she and Dakota didn't belong.

All the way back to the clinic, John thought of Grace and wondered if hiring her would be the right thing to do. He liked her, and that was the problem. If she didn't work out and he had to let her go, it would be awkward, to say the least. But if she did a good job, it would be a relief to know that the cleaning was done properly by someone experienced and reliable.

He wished he knew more about Grace. When Miriam had turned him down for Charley Byler, he'd been badly hurt, so much so that it had been over a year before he'd gone on a single date. Since then, he'd gone out with three different women, two members of his church. He'd enjoyed their company, but none had intrigued him the way Grace Yoder did. There was an air of mystery about her, and he had a feeling that she was someone special.

He chuckled out loud. It had never occurred to him that he might find another potential mate in Hannah's kitchen.

Then he grew serious. What was wrong with him, thinking such things? After he struck out with Miriam, he'd vowed to never become involved with an Amish girl again. And while Grace wasn't Amish yet, it was clear that it was her intention to join the community.

How crazy would it be to risk the same disappointment? Ultimately, Miriam had chosen the Amish Char-

ley over John, a Mennonite. When John had asked
Miriam to marry him, he'd offered to convert to her
faith if he could continue his veterinary practice. Considering everything, he now felt that would have been
a huge mistake and he would have come to regret it.
Thank goodness Miriam had realized that, even if he
hadn't, at the time.

He'd been born and raised in the Mennonite Church,
but he hadn't taken his religion seriously after he'd
left his mother's home for college. Like a lot of young
adults, he'd been tempted by the world. He was proud
to say that he'd never drank alcohol or used illegal sub-
stances, but he hadn't always made the best choices.
He'd definitely spent too many Sunday mornings sleeping late instead of going to hear God's word.

But after Miriam had married Charley, John had realized how empty his life had become. He'd accepted
Uncle Albert's invitation to attend a worship service at
Green Spring Mennonite, and he'd only missed Sunday
services when veterinary emergencies prevented him
from going. He'd started with the regular worship service and then found himself involved in volunteering.
He'd put himself through college working as a carpen-
ter, so repairing homes for seniors or helping to build a
community hall was rewarding. He'd even participated
in a church-sponsored trip to the Ozarks to construct a
refuge for abused women.

Returning to his faith hadn't been dramatic or sudden. It had happened slowly, but the strength he gained
from knowing that his life was moving in the right direction was vital to his well-being. He'd found peace
and purpose. And now, he'd reached a point in his life
where he wanted a wife and kids, if God blessed him so.

John hoped he'd make a good husband and a good dad. He'd always liked kids, and he wanted a chance to be the kind of father he'd never had. It had been important for his own father to provide financial support, but it had come at the cost of spending time with his only son. John had always believed that his father loved him, but he'd never been able to bridge the emotional gap between them.

Being a good veterinarian took long hours, but John intended that—if he did have kids—he'd make time to take them fishing, to read bedtime stories and to help with Little League, 4H and, most importantly, to worship with them. He promised himself that he'd remember to show affection and tell his children that he loved them, even if he had to insist on rules they didn't understand.

John hadn't come to those conclusions by himself. What wisdom he had concerning the relationship between a father and his children he'd learned from Uncle Albert, the rock who'd always been there to listen to and guide him.

John knew himself well enough to realize that he was sometimes too quick to form opinions. He'd known Grace Yoder only a few days, and he should have had the sense to be cautious. Yet, he couldn't deny how he felt. The truth was, being in the same room with her made his pulse quicken and his spirits rise. It was too soon to tell if she was as attracted to him as he was to her.

For all he knew, she might have a boyfriend or even be engaged. But he didn't think so. Because she carried the Yoder last name, in spite of having a son, he guessed she was single. If only she didn't have her heart set on becoming Amish... When he married, it would for a lifetime, and he didn't want something as important as faith to strain the bonds of his and his wife's union.

He chuckled to himself as he pulled into the clinic parking lot and parked beside his uncle Albert's pickup. He hadn't even asked Grace to go to a movie with him, and already he was picturing her as his wife. He decided to talk to Uncle Albert tonight at supper about hiring her as the new kennel attendant. Grace needed a job, and the practice needed a dependable employee. It would be foolish not to hire her just because he was attracted to her.

If Grace worked at the practice and he saw her every day, it wouldn't take long before he'd find out if there was more to his attraction than her pretty face and cute figure. Instinct told him that Grace was as lonely as he was. From what he could gather, she'd had a difficult life, but didn't feel sorry for herself or want sympathy. It was obvious that she was independent and possessed a keen mind, and she seemed to be an excellent mother. What he had to discover was whether she had a loving heart and a strong belief in God to go with those sparkling eyes.

"Hannah's sure that she's telling the truth?" Uncle Albert said as he removed a family-size aluminum container of lasagna from the oven.

"Are you certain that's been in long enough?" John's grandfather asked. "Last time it was still frozen in the middle."

"I set the timer," Uncle Albert said. "John, would you get those paper plates off the counter? And a roll of paper towels. I forgot napkins again."

"Nothing wrong with paper towels," Gramps insisted. "Works just as well." He poured cranberry juice into three tall glasses. "And get the cheese, will you, John? Parmesan, not the slices of Swiss."

John chuckled. "And I was thinking Swiss." The few meals the three of them could share were always haphazard. And Gramps had a running joke about the cheese, even though John had been six and visiting for the weekend when he'd removed sliced Swiss from the refrigerator to go with canned spaghetti and meatballs Uncle Albert had heated.

Gramps laughed, folded his newspaper and added it to the stack of magazines and journals that took up a large section of the dining room table. John passed forks around and took his seat. Uncle Albert offered a brief grace before returning to his questioning. "This young woman you're talking about hiring... What did you say her name was?"

"Grace," John answered. "Grace Yoder. And I'm sure she's who she says she is. She's one of Jonas's girls, all right. She looks a lot like her sisters—petite, like Miriam."

"And as pretty?" Gramps teased.

John grinned. "Every bit as pretty. But that's not why I think we should hire her. I like her and—"

Gramps groaned. "Here we go again. What's with you and those Yoder girls? Two years ago you were head over heels over Miriam Yoder. And now—"

"Hannah's a fine-looking woman," Uncle Albert remarked as he scooped out lasagna onto the paper plates. "It's no wonder she has attractive girls."

John hesitated, finding his uncle's comment interesting. If he didn't know better, he'd think Uncle Albert had a thing for Hannah Yoder. "What I was trying to say about Grace Yoder is that she has five years' experience working in a kennel," John said, trying to bring the conversation back around. "We're desperate for help, and Melody is willing to swing by the Yoder farm and pick her up on her way to work."

"It's fine by me." Uncle Albert shrugged. "So long as Hannah won't be upset if the girl doesn't work out. Has the bishop given his say so? You know the Amish, John. They have their ways, and they're set in them."

"Aren't we all?" Gramps asked, and they all chuckled.

"So it's settled." John cut a piece of rubbery lasagna noodle with his fork, trying not to imagine what the Yoders were having for supper tonight. Not supermarket lasagna, that was for certain. "I can offer Grace the position?"

"Of course you can hire her," Uncle Albert said. "We're making you a full partner on the first of the year, aren't we? We trust you, John. If you believe in the young woman, that's good enough for me."

Six o'clock came and went, then seven, too, without word from the King family. Johanna removed the turkey from the oven, wiped her hands on her apron and glanced at Hannah. "Maybe we should go ahead and eat, Mam. The children are hungry."

"I'm hungry, too," Susanna declared from the doorway.

Grace sat down in the rocking chair and pulled Dakota into her lap. It had been a busy day, what with the cleaning and preparing a large dinner for their expected guests. No, she corrected herself, *supper*. The noon meal was what her Amish family referred to as dinner. She'd have to get used to that. "Maybe we could feed the children," she suggested hesitantly. "It won't be long before it will be time to put them to bed."

"No bedtime." Dakota wrinkled his face. "I'm not sleepy."

"A good idea," Hannah declared. "Susanna, if you wouldn't mind eating with the little ones and keeping an eye on them, we can set the small table up here in the corner."

"I can eat with them," Irwin said, abandoning the adult status he usually assumed. "I'm starved."

"Fair enough." Hannah returned to the stove. "If you think you can get those long legs of yours under the table."

"Ya," Susanna agreed with a wide smile. "The little table with the benches."

"Grace," Hannah called. "Would you help Irwin carry the table and benches in from the pantry?"

The next half hour was occupied with the children's meal. The warm kitchen glowed with the soft light of kerosene lamps and the soft voices of Hannah, Rebecca and Aunt Jezzy. Outside, November blackness had settled around the farmhouse, but Grace felt snug and happy. She was content to sit and watch as her son ate and chattered with his cousins. Already, Dakota was using a few Pennsylvania Dutch words. *He fits in,* she thought. *As if he'd always lived here in this safe and loving haven.*

When the children had finished, Grace helped clear away the dishes and silverware before bathing Dakota and leading him, protesting, to bed. She tucked him with his stuffed rabbit, helped him say his prayers and kissed him good-night.

"I like this," he said sleepily. "Can we stay here to-morrow with Jonah and Katie?"

"Yes," she promised. "And the day after that."

"All the time?" Dakota asked. "Can we stay forever and ever?"

"I hope so," she answered. She didn't want to leave Seven Poplars any more than her son did. She knew they couldn't expect to take advantage of Hannah's hospitality forever. Sooner or later, Grace would have to find a permanent home for them.

But first, a job.

"Sing," Dakota urged.

"Hush, little baby,

"Don't say a word," she sang softly as she stroked his head.

"Mama's going to buy you a mockingbird.

"And if that mockingbird don't sing..."

Dakota's rhythmic breathing told her that he had dropped off. Taking the lamp, she walked quietly out of the room and closed the door behind her. Her thoughts were still on the possibility of the kennel job at John's veterinary practice. The position seemed heaven-sent, but if she got it, she would have to be careful. She would see John Hartman every day. Regardless of how much she liked him, she'd have to guard herself against him. She'd have to regard him as her boss, nothing more.

Her future and Dakota's lay with some as-yet-unknown Amish man. She would seek out a decent man of the Old Order faith, allow him to court her and marry him. She knew that before the wedding, she'd have to confess her sins, ask forgiveness and be accepted into the church. That would lift a huge burden off her shoulders. It would give her the first real peace she'd felt in a long time. It would be a new life, heartfelt and honest, one in which she could spend the coming years serving God and her community. It was the only way, and John Hartman had no part in it.

Chapter Six

When Grace returned to the kitchen, she found Hannah standing at the back door peering into the darkness. "Have the Kings arrived?" Grace asked.

"No." Hannah closed the door. "It's starting to sleet."

"Early for such bad weather," Aunt Jezzy said.

"Not for Nebraska." Grace stood beside Hannah and looked out. "By now, they're having snow."

"I kept thinking they'd arrive in time for supper," Hannah murmured. She turned to the others. "But there's no reason for us to wait any longer. It could be that they were delayed on the road, maybe spending the night with friends again."

Grace started to ask why they wouldn't call if they were delayed and then remembered that Hannah had no telephone. When she'd asked about it, Anna had told her that there was a phone at the chair shop for emergencies, but once Eli and Roman locked up for the night, a ringing phone would go unanswered. It was against the *Ordnung* to have a landline telephone in a home, and cell phones were looked upon with disapproval by the elders.

"How is Anna?" Hannah asked, changing the subject, perhaps to ease her own concern about the lateness of her guests. She walked to the stove where the prepared meal waited.

To Grace's delight, Anna and her youngest stepdaughter, Mae, had spent the afternoon at the Yoder farm. Next to Susanna, whom she adored, Grace thought she liked Anna best of the sisters she'd met. Anna seemed as open to welcoming her into the family as Susanna. Ruth, the oldest, was pleasant but a little formal, and Grace had spent so little time with Miriam that she didn't really have an impression of her yet. Thankfully, all of them, including wary Johanna, were kind to Dakota.

"Gut...gut." Aunt Jezzy began to talk about how happy Anna had looked and how pink her cheeks had been. "She and Samuel are right for each other," the woman said as she removed her knitting needles from her worn canvas bag and began to work on her project. The wool was white and soft as a kitten's fur. Grace hadn't been able to guess what she was knitting, and she hadn't wanted to appear nosy by asking too many questions, although a hundred buzzed in her head.

"I'm glad," Hannah said as she began to slice the turkey. "Becca, could you mash those potatoes?"

"I'll do it," Grace offered. It was obvious that her cooking skills were hardly better than Susanna's, but she could mash potatoes with the best of them, especially because there were mounds of newly made butter and fresh milk to stir in. They'd boiled a giant kettle of potatoes and kept them warm on the back of the stove.

"Ya," Hannah agreed, but suggested that Grace first dip out just enough for the six of them. "We'll leave the

others unmashed, and one of you can make potato salad tomorrow. You can drain them and put the pot in the cold box on the porch for the night."

Rebecca dished up one bowl of green beans and another of creamed corn while Susanna carried applesauce, bread and butter to the table. Again Grace marveled at how smoothly the work went with so many hands to help. It was almost like a dance, with everyone knowing their places and what to do—everyone but her. There were smiles, jokes and laughter bouncing around the cozy kitchen. It might be sleeting and nasty outside, but here, in Hannah's house, was a sanctuary from the world.

"How's the blanket coming?" Johanna asked their aunt as they all gathered around the table.

"It goes quickly." Aunt Jezzy smiled. "It should, as many as I've made of this pattern."

"She's over the morning sickness?" Hannah asked. "I know it troubled her some." She glanced at Grace. "God willing, our Anna will be blessed with a baby in late April or May."

"May Ruth and Eli soon find the same happiness," Aunt Jezzy said, pushing her knitting bag onto a counter. "She's almost as excited about this coming baby as Anna is. She's already sewn a half dozen gowns and undershirts for the little one."

"Ruth was married two years ago," Johanna explained. "She wants little ones badly, but so far nothing. Neither she nor Miriam have gotten pregnant yet. It must be hard for Ruth and Miriam because Leah and Anna were married after them. Leah already has a baby and now Anna has one on the way."

"It took your father and me a while," Hannah said,

"but after Ruth, there was no trouble. I have no doubt that you girls will fill this house with grandchildren. All in God's time."

Susanna giggled and put a finger to her lips. "Don't tell Anna's got a baby in her belly," she whispered to Grace.

"A secret?" Grace glanced at Hannah, unsure what to say. Anna and Samuel already had five children, from his first marriage. Anna was younger than she was, and Grace couldn't imagine being the mother of six.

She supposed that she would have to become accustomed to the idea if she wanted to marry again. Most Amish families were large ones, and it would be good for Dakota to have brothers and sisters. She loved children, but considering how difficult it was to be a good mother to one little boy, six young children seemed overwhelming. *So much to learn,* she thought.

Johanna glanced at her with a pleasant expression. "What Susanna means is that we don't talk about it to people outside the family."

But they didn't hide it from me, Grace thought. *Is Johanna starting to like me?* More than anything, she wanted to break through to Johanna. She had the feeling that once Johanna accepted her, the other sisters and the rest of the community would follow.

"And say nothing to the men," Rebecca put in. "Especially not to Samuel. They all know, of course. Men gossip worse than women." She twittered. "But we all pretend not to know about Anna's blessing."

"In this house, between us, we talk, but say nothing to Anna unless she does first," Johanna advised with a serious look. "Some people worry that it's bad luck to say too much about a baby before it arrives."

"But each one is welcome." Hannah motioned for silence for grace. "And each child a blessing to the parents, the family and the church."

They had finished the delicious meal and were clearing away the last of the dishes when Grace heard a horn and the sound of a vehicle pulling into the yard. "Is that the Kings?" she asked.

Rebecca went to the window. "*Ne,* it's a truck. The Kings hired a van."

Johanna opened the door and went out onto the porch. "It's John Hartman," she called. Rebecca grabbed two coats off the rack and hurried after her older sister.

Susanna was halfway across the kitchen when Hannah waved her back. "*Ne,* it's cold out there." She shook her head. "You stay inside. I don't want you catching a chill. We'll find out soon enough…"

"It *is* the Kings, Mam," Rebecca shouted back. "They've come with John."

Grace couldn't help but feel a rush of excitement. Why was John here again? She knew it was too soon for him to tell her if he could hire her or not, but the thought of seeing him made her a little breathless. *It's just the promise of a job,* she told herself. *If I'm lucky, he'll be my boss. Nothing more.* Her life was finally falling into place, and no hunky guy with an easy smile and a twinkle in his eye was going to prevent her from doing what was best for her and Dakota.

Not two minutes later, John, along with an unfamiliar Amish man and woman, and a young man, were stamping onto the porch. Sleet covered the woman's cape and bonnet and the men's hats and coats. All of them were smiling and talking at once as introductions flew and coats were hung up and coffee poured for the guests, all but the son, the one Grace had heard Aunt Jezzy mention as David.

Grace tried not to stare at him, not because he was odd in appearance or because he obviously had been born with the same challenges as Susanna. It wasn't his short stature, bowed legs or chubby body that held her attention. What was so unusual was that when David pulled off his snowy black hat, he was wearing a fast-food chain's cardboard crown under it. Beneath the crown curled an unwieldy thatch of yellow-blond hair. David had sparkling blue eyes, bright as cornflowers, a dough ball of a freckled nose, a wide mouth and round, rosy cheeks. He reminded her of a carved wooden boy she'd once seen on a Swiss cuckoo clock in a department store window.

David gave Grace a sweet smile and then turned his full attention to Susanna. His smile became a wide grin and he stared unabashedly at Susanna, who had become pink-cheeked and giggly. "Hi!" he said in a husky voice. "I'm King David."

Susanna beamed. "I'm Susanna Yoder."

"Hi, Su-san-na." He bounced from one high-topped shoe to the other. "Hi."

"Hi."

"I'm King David," he repeated.

"You look like me," Susanna said. "Mam, he looks like me." And then to David she said, "Will you be my friend?"

"*Ya.*"

"David, remember your manners," his mother said softly. Sadie King was a stocky little woman with eyes that Grace decided had once been the exact color of her son's. Love and kindness radiated from them as she spoke. "Your name is David King."

David nodded vigorously. "King David."

His mother chuckled. "Pay no heed to our David. It's his way. He loves that paper hat."

"However did you end up in John's truck?" Hannah asked.

"Van broke down." Ebben King wrapped his hands around a warm mug of coffee. "On Route 13. South of Wilmington. Bear?"

"The van had to be towed to a garage," Sadie explained. "We couldn't think of a way to let you know."

"Our van driver wanted to stay in a motel across from the garage," Ebben added, "but we didn't care to do that. David likes his routine." He trailed off with a shrug. Ebben was tall and slim with graying hair and beard and round wire glasses.

"The tow truck driver, Jay, goes to our church," John explained. "He would have brought the Kings himself, but he was on duty all night. Lots of need for tow trucks in this weather. He knew that I had a lot of Amish clients, and he thought I might be willing to give the Kings a ride to their destination."

"Is *gut,*" Ebben said. "So kind of you to go out of your way on such a night."

John's dark eyes twinkled. "Glad to help out. I would have spent the evening ordering supplies, anyway. By the time I get home, Uncle Albert will have it done."

"Once again you prove what a good friend you are," Jezzy said. "Come now, sit down and eat. You must all be starved."

"Not me," John said. "I'll just—"

Hannah gave him a look. "John Hartman, you can

eat a little. So much the girls cooked, and the turkey is still warm."

John, through a willingness to be amiable or because he was really hungry, allowed himself to be ushered to the table along with the Kings. And this time, once Grace had helped to serve up the food family-style, she found herself sitting beside John. Not that she could eat another bite after the earlier meal, but it wouldn't have been polite not to join the others at the long table.

The Yoders and Kings obviously had news of friends and family to share, but they spoke in English out of kindness to her and John and made an effort to include them both in the general conversation. Susanna was unusually quiet, but whenever Grace glanced her way, she saw her youngest sister staring at David. And if he looked at her, she hid her face in her hands and giggled.

"I think Susanna's made a new friend," John said quietly to Grace.

She nodded. "I think so, too."

John laid down his fork and leaned closer. "I talked to my grandfather and my uncle. If you get the okay from your bishop, we'd like you to start at the clinic as soon as possible."

"Really?" She looked up at him. "That's wonderful!" In her excitement, she must have spoken louder than she intended because Aunt Jezzy looked at her in surprise. "Sorry," Grace said, lowering her gaze. "John says that I can have the job. If it's all right," she added.

"I'm sure Bishop Atlee will agree," Hannah said. "He'll be here Saturday for apple pressing. I'll ask him first thing." She smiled. "You remind me, Grace, if I forget. It will be a busy day, a lot of neighbors coming."

"Am I still welcome to bring our apples down?" John

asked. "Uncle Albert is still talking about the fun he had last year. I think we've got about ten baskets in the cold storage. Granny Smiths and Arkansas Black."

"Of course." Hannah passed the potatoes to Ebben for a second helping. "And bring your empty gallon jugs. Our cidering gets bigger every year. Last November we had more than a hundred here." She glanced at Sadie. "If the weather is good, we'll have the men set up the tables outside and eat in the yard."

"It will have to get a lot warmer than this." Ebben looked toward the back door. "Have you seen the sleet coming down outside?"

Aunt Jezzy laughed. "You aren't used to Delaware yet. The saying is, *if you don't like the weather, wait an hour. It will change.* It's always a surprise to me, I can tell you, me coming from Ohio."

"Easier winters here than in Indiana." Ebben returned his attention to his plate. "According to my sons."

"They'll be here with their families Saturday," Hannah said. "And your daughter. They all promised to come early and stay late."

"I can't wait to see them," Sadie replied. "We don't have any means to visit anyone until Ebben can buy a new buggy and a driving horse. We had to sell our buggy when we held the farm auction. And the livestock. Too expensive to ship them east."

"It must have been hard to part with your animals," Hannah said.

"Ya," Ebben agreed. "It was, but this place is much smaller than our old farm. I'm not a young man anymore."

"If you're looking for a dependable driving horse, you should talk to my brother-in-law Charley," Johanna suggested. "He deals in livestock, and I know he has at least two suitable horses for sale."

"And a cow," Sadie put in. "I make my own butter and our David likes his milk." She smiled at David. "Are you certain you can eat more turkey?" Her son nodded and kept chewing.

"So you'll be here Saturday?" Grace asked John.

"Try and keep me away. I'd come for the apple pies if nothing else."

"I've never been to a cidering," Grace confessed. "I'm sure Dakota will like it."

"I know he will," John agreed. The others continued to talk about cows and horses, but his attention remained on her. "More children to play with than he can count. How is he doing? Is he settling in?"

"Yes, he is. It's kind of you to ask. And kind of you to offer me the job," she added, "considering that you're taking my word on it that I've had experience."

"I'm sure you'll do fine," John said, helping himself to a serving of chowchow and more coleslaw. He grinned and dabbed at the corner of his mouth with a snowy-white cloth napkin. "It's hard to find good help, and if we suit each other, you'll be doing our practice a big favor."

But will I be doing myself a favor? Grace wondered. John was a nice guy, a sweet guy, from all appearances. He'd done or said nothing that would cause her to believe his interest in her was anything but professional. But that didn't keep the oxygen from draining out of the room when he walked into it, and it didn't help a bit that when she dreamed of an Amish husband later that night, he was wearing John's face behind a neatly trimmed brown beard.

* * *

As Aunt Jezzy had promised, the weather did change. By Saturday, the temperature had risen to the sixties and the sun had dried up the soggy yard and fields. By eight o'clock in the morning, a stream of buggies was rolling up Hannah's lane. Grace had never seen so many Amish gathered in one place at one time.

"More than last year," Anna said as she supervised a pair of blond-haired boys unloading endless pies and baskets of delicious-smelling baked goods from her family buggy. "Careful with that bowl of maca-roni salad, Rudy," she called to one of them. "We don't want it spilled on the ground for the chickens." She waved. "Naomi!"

A tall girl, about ten or eleven, wearing glasses, helped two younger girls out of the buggy. "*Ya,* Mam. I'll watch they don't get under the horses' hooves."

"Take them into the house, *Schippli.* The big girls are minding the children this morning. You find your friends and have a good time."

"What did you call her?" Grace asked. "I thought her name was Naomi."

Anna chuckled merrily. "She is my *lamb,* my sweet Naomi. Always she helps without me asking. The twins…" She shook her head and laughed again. "Full of themselves, Peter and Rudy, but good boys. Not a lazy bone in their bodies. See how they help *Gross-mama* down from the buggy. They'll make fine men. *Grossmama,* come. Meet our Grace." Anna leaned close and whispered. "Don't let her upset you. She has a sharp tongue, but she'll make your son gingerbread cookies and spoil him endlessly."

"Grace!" Hannah called from the back porch. "We need you."

"Pleased to meet you," Grace said to the elderly woman, then dashed off gratefully to help in the kitchen. From what she could gather from Rebecca, and remarks Miriam had made to Ruth, their grandmother had been a difficult person *before* old age had begun to cloud her reason. Grace hoped for a good relationship with her, but she was afraid that *Grossmama's* reaction to her son's illegitimate daughter would be less than positive. Grace didn't know if she was ready to confront the matriarch today.

Because so many in the community would be gathered at the Yoder farm for the cider making, she hoped she'd meet some of the eligible Amish bachelors. Aunt Jezzy had hinted as much, explaining that there were nine church districts in the area, and Rebecca or Grace might meet someone they liked. Grace wished she was dressed like her sister in a neat blue dress and white apron and *Kapp,* but she felt pretty in the green calico dress that Hannah had hemmed just in time for Saturday's celebration. If she didn't look exactly Amish, Grace thought that she looked properly Plain, and she'd taken care to get her smaller cap pinned on so tightly there'd be no chance of it coming loose during the busy day.

She hoped that it wasn't the wrong thing to do, actively searching for a husband, but if she didn't make an effort, how could she expect someone to court her? *Court her.* A shiver of excitement made her chuckle. It sounded so old-fashioned, so wholesome. She and Joe hadn't had much of a courtship. He'd stopped and picked her up along a lonely road where she'd been hitchhiking. It had been an unconventional relationship from the first night she'd laid eyes on Joe, and it never got much better. But that was all in the past. God willing, things would be different here in Seven Poplars, and she'd get a chance to live her life in a better way.

"Grace!" Rebecca poked her head around the door. "Hurry! It's Bishop Atlee. He's in the front room and he wants to see you."

Grace opened the door a little wider. "Did your mother ask him?"

Rebecca grimaced and threw her hands up to signify that she had no idea. "But he wants to talk to you. And he looks—"

"As though he's going to agree?" Grace suggested with more optimism than she felt. Her heart plunged. If she hadn't been prepared to face her grandmother, she was twice as unready to meet the bishop.

"Serious," Rebecca finished. And then as Grace hurried through the kitchen, crowded with busy women, her sister called after her, "Good luck."

Chapter Seven

Grace clasped her hands together to keep them from trembling as she stepped through the wide doorway into the Yoders' parlor. She'd never been inside, other than to dust the table, fireplace mantel or window seat, but she knew this room was used only for company or important events. As she prepared to face Bishop Atlee, her mouth went dry, her heart raced. She wanted to be respectful, but knowing that her plans for finding meaningful work—indeed, her very future among the Amish—depended on Bishop Atlee's decision made her determined to emphatically state her case. She would not take no for an answer.

She stopped just inside the entrance. Standing at a window, gazing into the side yard, his back to her, was a short, stocky man in black shoes, black trousers and a long black coat with a split tail. Grace took a deep breath and waited. When seconds dragged by without him noticing her, she cleared her throat.

The man turned to face her, a wide-brimmed, black felt hat in one hand. "Grace, it's good to meet you." He tilted his head and smiled sheepishly. "Forgive me.

Have you been standing there long? My wife says I'm getting hard of hearing, but I think I just concentrate so hard I forget to listen. I was going over tomorrow's sermon in my head." His cheeks dimpled as he studied her with warm blue eyes.

Grace swallowed, unsure what to say.

He studied her. "*Ya, ya,* you do have the look of your sisters." He stroked a flowing white beard that made him look like an Amish Santa Claus.

Not that the Amish believe in Santa, Grace thought, glad that he couldn't read her thoughts.

He chuckled. "Jonas's girl, for certain." Spreading open his hands in a gesture of welcome, he said, "Child, we are happy to have you in Seven Poplars."

Relief made her insides somersault. She'd expected a tall, stern cleric, not a jolly grandfatherly type. Was it possible that this man was the senior church elder? Or had she made another of her many mistakes? "Bishop Atlee?" she stammered.

"*Ya. Ya.*" His vest-covered belly quivered with amusement. "What were you expecting? You're white as new lard. Did you think I would reject you for your parents' sin?"

"I...I didn't know. I thought...Old Order Amish...all the rules," she managed, before she ran out of breath.

"We are all human, Grace, none more so than me. Every day, we try to follow God's word, but from time to time we stumble." He rocked his head sideways, one direction, then the other. "Then we must ask forgiveness and do our best to live as He instructs us. That's all any of us can do. It would be a hard heart indeed who could turn away a child for being born."

A wave of relief washed over her. "So, it's all right

if I take the job?" She struggled to find words. "With the animals…at the clinic?"

He shrugged. "Fine by me. Work is always good. Like prayer, for building character. But why are you asking my permission?"

"Hannah said… I thought I had to."

"Ah." The blue eyes narrowed, his expression became serious. "I can see that you don't understand what a bishop does in our church," he explained gently. "I'm an ordinary man, chosen by God to serve our community. I do rule on our members' behavior, because it's my duty to give judgment as best I understand His plan for us. But you aren't one of us, Grace. You would have to be a baptized member of our faith for me to instruct you. You must do as you see fit."

"But that's just it," she said. "I *want* to be one of you. I want to be Amish, like my parents were, to live like you do, to worship and serve God as you do."

He sighed and folded his arms over his broad chest. "So Hannah has told me, child. And I wish you well. We all do. We would like nothing better than to welcome Jonas's girl to our fold, but it is hard. Harder to give up the world than you can imagine. I've seen others try, but never have I known a woman or a man to succeed. The pull of the outside life is too strong."

"But I can try? You won't forbid it?"

"Forbid it?" His eyes widened. "I will pray for you, Grace. We will all pray for you, but…" He shrugged. "I fear your row will be long, rocky and thick with weeds. Try your best and come to talk to me again in…a year, maybe two. Then we'll see."

"But…"

"Two years would be better." Bishop Atlee settled his

hat over a gray-streaked head of thinning hair. "Now, I must get myself to the barn or my friends will think I'm hiding in the house, trying to avoid the work of sorting apples."

A year? Maybe two? Grace watched as the man made his way out of the parlor and down the hall. "Two years," she murmured, half under her breath. She didn't have that long. How could she stand the wait? In a year, maybe less, she'd hoped to be one of them, to have a husband and a home of her own.

She was sure that the bishop meant well, but he didn't know how determined she could be or how many obstacles she'd already overcome. And most of all, he had no idea why she needed this life for herself so badly…why this was the only way. She would show him. She would show them all. She wouldn't fail in this—she couldn't.

"Grace?" Anna's voice penetrated Grace's musing as she appeared in the doorway. "We need your help."

As Grace allowed herself to be pulled back into the noisy hubbub of the kitchen and the preparation of food, she pushed the bishop's warning to the back of her mind. She wouldn't allow his cautiousness to take away any of her excitement and joy over being allowed to take the job…or of the cidering.

She had a plan today. Grace loved a plan. Between working with the other women and keeping an eye on Dakota, she would scout the territory for a new father for him and a husband for her. She hoped he'd be a farmer. It would be good for Dakota to live surrounded by animals and growing things.

And trees…she thought wistfully. She hoped that there would be trees around her new home. Trees were solid. They sank their roots deep into the earth and endured…exactly what she wanted to do.

In the barn, John and his uncle had easily found a place in the cider-making process where they could be useful. Uncle Albert washed apples, while John carried baskets of them to dump onto the hand-crank conveyer belt. The apples dropped into a crusher before moving on to the press. Fresh, sweet juice poured in streams out of the press into a vat and finally into clean gallon jugs.

Around him Amish men and boys laughed and talked, sharing jokes half in English and half in Pennsylvania Dutch, sometimes interjecting German words into an English sentence and vice versa. Not everyone taking part in today's cidering was Amish; a few outsiders had come to share in the work and camaraderie. Uncle Albert knew most of them, either as clients, friends or both, and John watched as he exchanged good-natured ribs with them. A person didn't spend thirty years in a small county without getting to know nearly everyone.

They couldn't have asked for a better day. The sun was out; the air was crisp and cool without being raw, and there wasn't a hint of a breeze. Best of all, the Yoder barn, clean and neat as always, smelled of hay, apples and healthy animals. It was John's idea of what heaven must smell like. He'd been working for the better part of an hour when Bishop Atlee joined them. The bishop greeted Uncle Albert with a grin and a handshake before pulling off his black church coat and hanging it on a nail.

"Let me take over here, John," the older man offered, when he'd been welcomed by the others. "It will do me good to do a little physical work before we sit down to the noon meal. It's quite a spread those women are fixing, I can tell you."

John wanted to ask him if he'd given permission for Grace to come to work at the clinic, but this wasn't the time or place. Over the past few days, it had somehow become important to John that Grace join the practice, and he didn't want to spoil the day if the church elder had given the wrong answer.

John hadn't caught sight of Grace yet, but he had picked out small Dakota, riding in a child's wagon pulled by an older boy. In his straw hat, denim coat and trousers, he looked exactly like every other Amish boy, although his complexion was somewhat darker than the fair German/Swiss faces surrounding him. He couldn't help wondering about Dakota's father, and if he was honest with himself, hoping that the man was out of Grace's life.

John stepped back and handed the bishop an empty bucket, nearly colliding with Rebecca Yoder, who barely managed to avoid spilling the mugs of coffee she carried. "Sorry," John said. He looked around, hoping to see Grace, but was disappointed. There was a girl in a lavender dress with Rebecca, one of her cousins, but John couldn't remember her name.

Rebecca laughed and dodged around him to hand a cup of coffee to his uncle Albert. She offered the second to Bishop Atlee, but he shook his head. Roland Byler accepted it with a nod, and Rebecca smiled warmly up at him. Roland was a brother to Charley Byler, who'd married Rebecca's older sister Miriam.

John had been treating one of Roland's milk cows for mastitis. He didn't know Roland well, but what he'd seen of him, he liked. Roland was a widower with a son close in age to Grace's Dakota. The Amish didn't usually remain single long after the loss of a husband or wife. Roland was a good-looking man, well-spoken and a hard worker. He had a nice little farm. John wondered if there might be something brewing between him and Rebecca. She was young, but not too young to consider marriage to someone as well-regarded in the Amish community as Roland.

One of the young men from Rose Valley called out to Rebecca's companion. "Dorcas! I like coffee. Didn't you bring me a cup?"

Dorcas giggled and held out the mug to John. He shook his head and thanked her.

His uncle Albert used a long-handled wooden paddle to stir the floating apples in the wash tank, and then glanced back over his shoulder at John. "Can you check if we've had a call from the office? I want to make certain that Bernese puppy is still stable."

John nodded. His uncle had performed emergency surgery the night before on the sixteen-week-old puppy that had swallowed a bottle cap. Normally, John would carry his cell phone with him, but he'd just replaced one that he'd accidently dropped into a horse's watering trough. Considering the process involved in making cider, he'd decided to leave his new one in his glove compartment for safety's sake. He crossed the farmyard to his pickup and had just opened the passenger's door when he heard a child shriek.

By the time John pushed through the circle of children crowded around the swing under the big oak tree, Dakota was sitting up on the ground and screaming at the top of his lungs. Susanna knelt beside him, crying, blood on her hands. "What happened?" John squatted down by the injured child. Whatever had happened couldn't be too serious, he decided. No one who could scream that loud could be critical.

Susanna sobbed and mumbled something, but John couldn't understand.

"What happened?" John repeated. He'd located the site of the injury, a cut on a swelling lump on the back of Dakota's head.

Most of the kids stared wide-eyed as John gathered the hysterical child into his arms, but Johanna's son Jonah spoke up. "Swing," he said. "Caleb fell off," he said carefully in English. "The swing hit Kota."

Susanna rubbed her hands on the grass, threw her apron over her head and cried louder.

"Shh, shh," John soothed. "You'll be all right." Dakota clung to John's neck and buried his face in his shirt. The bleeding had already slowed, and John put pressure on the wound with a handkerchief. Dakota howled again. John started toward the house. He hadn't gone more than a dozen steps when Grace came running toward him.

"How bad is he hurt? Lori Ann said…" She broke off as John explained what had happened.

"It looks worse than it is," he said. "Just a bump and a scalp wound. The laceration isn't deep."

Grace put out her arms to take him, but John shook his head. "Let me. We'll take him inside, wash him up and—"

"I can do it," Grace insisted, patting Dakota's back. "It's all right, sweetie, Mommy's here."

"If you want." Reluctantly, John handed over the boy. "If you need bandages, I have some in the truck.

I'd really like to examine him, once you've washed it. I can tell you if he needs to go to the emergency room."

"You think he'll need stitches?"

"If he does, I'll drive you to the hospital. Do you have a pediatrician?"

"No, we haven't had time to find one."

"We have a good medical staff at the hospital, and there'll be one on call."

Women had poured out of the house and were offering advice, mostly in Dutch. Hannah arrived, took one look at the two of them, another at the shrieking Susanna and cleared a path. "Take him into the bathroom," she suggested.

"Is Susanna hurt?" John asked. The King boy had found his way to Susanna and was standing by the tree staring down at her. Oddly, he was crying, too.

Hannah went to her daughter, spoke to her and helped her to her feet. "She's fine," she pronounced. "Just scared of blood and afraid that it's her fault Dakota got hurt."

"He'll be fine," John reassured Susanna, smiling.

By the time they got inside, the bleeding had stopped, and Dakota's sobbing had faded to a faint sniffle. Once they washed the back of the boy's head, he could see that the cut was a small one and the bump didn't seem to be getting any larger. "Put a cold compress on it," he advised Grace.

"Do you think he should see a doctor?" she asked.

"Watch him for any unusual sleepiness, dizziness or nausea. I'd say the swing barely grazed him. Head wounds bleed a lot."

"I think I'd feel better if a pediatrician took a look."

"All right. I'll drive you to the hospital."

"It's kind of you, Mr. Hartman."

"John." He smiled at her. "The Amish don't favor titles. Everyone goes by his or her given name. Even children call adults by their first name. You'll have to get used to that."

"There are a lot of things I have to learn about this life," she said, cuddling Dakota against her. She offered him a grateful smile. "I can come to work for you, cleaning the kennels, if the job's still open. Bishop Atlee said it was all right."

"Great." John grinned. "Now, let's get this boy checked out before we miss out on the wonderful dinner you ladies prepared."

Fortunately, the emergency room was nearly empty, and they were in and out of the hospital in less than two hours. John had been right. A little antibiotic ointment, a couple of butterfly bandages and a superhero sticker completed the treatment. By the time they got back to the Yoder farm, the men were just gathering for the first seating for the meal. Dakota scrambled out of the truck and ran to join Jonah and his new friends as Grace turned to John.

"I can't thank you enough," she said. "For taking us to see the doctor, for offering to hire me, for everything."

"No problem," he said, stuffing his hands into his jeans pockets.

"I want you to know how much I appreciate it. You're a very nice man, John, and I hope we can be friends." She hesitated. "As…as well as employer and employee," she stammered. "I didn't mean…"

John's smile widened and his eyes lit up. "I know

it's not politically correct to say so, but I like you. I like you a lot, and I hope we can get to know each other a lot better. I mean this in the most respectful way. I think you're an admirable woman and a great mother. Would you consider it too pushy if I asked if there was someone…a man in your life?"

"You mean Dakota's father?"

An expression of sympathy passed over his handsome features. "Hannah told me that your husband had…that you're widowed. I'm sorry for that, but is there someone else? You're not seeing someone or…"

"No." Grace shook her head. "No one, but…" She hesitated. John Hartman was a terrific guy: thoughtful, funny, responsible, just the kind of person she'd want in her life…in her son's life. "I can't date you, if that's what you mean," she said. Why was this so hard? Why didn't he wear a wide-brimmed black hat and Amish suspenders? He would be perfect, if only…

"Because you're going to work for me? I can understand—" he began.

"No, it's not that," she said in a rush. "You're not Amish. I want to be Amish," she said. "So you can see, it's impossible…because you're not. But if you were…" Her cheeks grew warm and her vision blurred. "If you were, you'd be the first man I'd set my *Kapp* for."

Chapter Eight

Grace paused on the back step with a pitcher of cider in her hands and surveyed the side yard. A long table, heaped with food, stretched from the cedar tree to the rose arbor. Seated on wooden benches at either side of the table were all the men: the church elders, visitors from other Amish churches and adults from Seven Poplars. Hannah had explained to her that this was the first seating, always all-male. Younger men and teenage boys would eat at the second seating, and women and children last.

When Grace had questioned the custom, Hannah had gone on to explain that baptized men and women were considered equal in the faith, but each had their own duties and responsibilities. Seating the sexes separately at community affairs was simply the way it had always been done and maintaining tradition was a vital tenet among the Old Order Amish.

She looked for Dakota among the preschoolers, didn't see him and had a moment of anxiety. But then, before she could panic, she heard her son's squeal of laughter and saw him chasing Jonah around the corner of the hen house. Dakota was running full-tilt, full of energy, as if the earlier bump to his head had never happened.

"Not to worry," Anna called, carrying a basket of bread to the table. "I told Susanna to keep the little ones away from the swing. And Lydia's big girls are watching them, too." She smiled. "Enjoy yourself. This is a day of visiting."

Grace gave a sigh of relief and smiled back. This was the way things were supposed to be, she told herself: children playing, grandmothers sharing recipes, women singing hymns as they dished up macaroni and potato salads and sprinkled cinnamon on huge bowls of applesauce. It looked like a picture from a calendar that had hung over her foster mother's desk, like a scene out of the past. An entire community had come together for a day of work and fun. This was exactly the life that she and Dakota had come so far to find.

"Grace! Men are thirsty!" Johanna's urging pulled her from her reverie.

"Coming!" Taking care not to spill the fresh cider, Grace moved toward the head of the table. Rebecca placed a bowl of chowchow on the spotless white tablecloth, glanced up and nodded her approval.

As Grace began to fill the oversize drink glasses, her thoughts were still racing. She couldn't help studying the bearded faces, trying to guess which of the men— if any—were possibilities. None of them wore wedding bands. She'd heard that there were several widowers in search of new wives, but she could hardly question her sisters or Hannah as to who they were. Her new family might think her overeager to find a man; she shouldn't, couldn't be so brazen.

There was so much she didn't know about Amish customs. It wasn't that she expected to find a husband today or even in the next few weeks. What she wanted to do, for now, was to find out what her options were. It was part of plan B. Now that she knew she wanted to become Amish, picking a new father for Dakota and a husband for herself would be the next big decision she'd have to make.

She'd hoped that cider-making day would be a perfect opportunity to survey the field, but it was going to be harder than she'd thought. Here at the first meal sitting, all the men had beards. She knew unmarried men didn't have beards. What she didn't know was whether a widower shaved his off. She hoped that they wouldn't be too old. She wasn't exactly over the hill—not yet twenty-eight—but she certainly didn't want to marry a boy barely out of his teens.

This time she was going to choose a husband logically, not because of infatuation, and she knew she was looking for a man she could respect. Friendship would be a good beginning. But when Amish men and women always separated at affairs like this, how did a single girl get to know an eligible prospect?

She smiled at a chubby brown-haired man with a neatly trimmed beard as she filled his glass with newly made cider. Instead of returning her smile, he looked embarrassed. He said something in Dutch that she couldn't understand, crammed a biscuit in his mouth and tried to wash it down with half a glass of cider. Before Grace could get away, she heard him choking.

She wanted to hide under the table. She hadn't been flirting, just being friendly. Had she broken some rule?

She backed away, and some of the cider sloshed onto

her apron. Maybe he was married and he was afraid of offending her. Or maybe he was shy or… Grace's throat clenched. Maybe he didn't find her attractive.

Had she lost the knack of interacting with men? She'd worked as a waitress in more places than she could count, and she'd always gotten good tips, so she couldn't be awful at serving. Since Joe's death, she hadn't dated, but before they met, she'd gone out with lots of guys. She'd never had anyone so turned off that they'd almost choked to death when she'd smiled at them.

The next man was about her age, but he had a coarse black beard, bushy eyebrows, pale gray eyes and thin lips. He appeared dour, and she couldn't imagine making breakfast for him every morning for the rest of her life. When she offered him cider, he didn't speak; he just held out his glass. Grace's heart sunk as she gazed at the other men. Everyone seemed to be avoiding eye contact with her. What was she doing wrong? Why were the men so unfriendly to her? She wanted to turn and run, but she was no coward. Sucking in a deep breath, she plunged on, pouring cider for one man after the next, and having her hesitant smile met with shuttered looks or blank stares.

On the other side of the table, a tall girl with a broken front tooth laughed at something one of the men said. Rebecca had pointed her out earlier as their cousin Dorcas. Rebecca had said Dorcas was single, so that couldn't be her husband.

Grace began to wish she'd stayed in the kitchen and washed dishes. There must have been thirty men at the table, and for all she knew, they were all married except John Hartman at the far end. He sat between an older man in a denim work shirt and ball cap who didn't appear Amish and a pleasant-looking man in his early thirties with a close-cropped beard. John hadn't seemed to notice her, which was fine with her. He was the one unmarried man she had no interest in.

She nibbled on her lower lip. But maybe...maybe John would give her a few hints as to who was who.

Although she barely knew him, the two hours they'd spent together at the hospital this morning had increased her respect and admiration for him. He'd been good with Dakota, easing his fears, and making him laugh. And he'd done pretty much the same for her. Best of all, when the physician on call had backed up John's opinion that Dakota didn't need stitches, John didn't say, *"I told you so."* Leaving the hospital, she realized that she could count John as her first friend in Seven Poplars.

She finished pouring the cider, and when her pitcher was empty, she returned to the kitchen to refill it. She checked to see that Dakota was happily playing under Susanna's watchful eye, and then returned to the yard. This time, she approached the table from the far end, offering cider first to the older man in the ball cap, then to John and then to the Amish man sitting beside him who'd caught her eye earlier. He shook his head. No.

John introduced her to his uncle Albert in the ball cap who was also a veterinarian at the clinic, and to the Amish man, Roland Byler, on his right.

Roland glanced up into her face, and his eyes widened in a look of surprise. "Welcome," he stammered. "You...you have the look of your sisters." He flushed, averted his eyes and reached for a piece of fried chicken.

If this one chokes, I'm out of here, Grace thought, but he didn't. She let out the breath she hadn't realized she was holding. "Pleased to meet you, Roland," she said. He was fair-haired and looked her age.

"Ya." He nodded and fixed his eyes on his plate. "And you, Grace. Good to have you here today. For the cider making."

Roland wasn't quite as handsome as John, but he had nice eyes, and an appealing laugh. Again the thought that it was just her luck that John wasn't Amish rose in her mind and she forcefully pushed it away. She'd married Joe for love, and look where that had gotten her. This time, maybe for the first time in her life, she'd have to use reason alone.

"Are you sure you wouldn't like more cider?" she asked Roland. "It's nice and cold."

"Ne." He shook his head. "Enough already. But it's *gut.* Good," he corrected. "Charley said you look like Miriam, but I think maybe like some of the others more."

Grace smiled at him encouragingly. *He was positively chatty.* She wondered if she could ask which of the women was his wife, which would tell her if he was married or if he was the good-looking bachelor some of the teenage girls had been whispering about—the bachelor with a nice farm. She tried to inspect him without being obvious. *Yes, Roland Byler definitely had possibilities.*

"Atch, sorry," Rebecca said as she rushed up and stepped on Grace's foot. Grace looked up in astonishment, and her sister shook her head. *Not him,* she mouthed silently behind Roland's back.

Grace was confused. She started to move out of the way, but Rebecca caught the corner of Grace's apron and gave a sharp tug. Grace glanced back at Roland.

Thankfully, he hadn't noticed. He was busy consuming a drumstick of chicken, but John was watching her and grinning. *What have I done now?* Grace wondered.

"Mam needs you," Rebecca said loudly. "In the house." She gestured with her hand and hurried away toward the back door. Grace took the hint and followed her. Once they rounded the corner of the house, Rebecca reached for the pitcher. "I'll finish with this," she offered.

"Wait," Grace said. "I don't understand. Did I do something wrong? Is Roland Byler married?"

"Ne." Rebecca shook her head. "Not him. He was, but his wife died. A good woman, so young. The sugar."

"Sugar?" And then it dawned on her. "You mean diabetes?"

"Ya, she had the sugar. And them with a young boy."

"You mean Roland has a son?" *Like me,* she thought. *Both of us. Could that be a sign?*

"Jared. A sweet little boy." She pointed out a chubby yellow-haired child riding a stick horse on the lawn.

"I don't understand," Grace said. "Does he have a…" *She was going to say girlfriend, but did the Amish even have girlfriends? What was the word she'd heard used? Is he betrothed?*

"He's not walking out with anybody," Rebecca answered. "But he's not for you."

"Who's not for her?" Miriam came around the corner with a tureen of corn pudding.

"Roland Byler." Rebecca's eyes twinkled mischievously.

"Ne." Miriam looked like the cat who'd swallowed the canary. "Best you stay clear of him," she advised. And then she glanced at Rebecca and they both giggled.

"Wait," Grace protested. "Roland's single, doesn't have a girlfriend and seems pleasant. What's wrong with him?"

Rebecca stifled another chuckle. "Nothing. Roland is a nice man, everyone likes him."

"He's my husband Charley's brother," Miriam explained. "Ruth takes care of little Jared two days a week."

"Then why—" Grace began. But before she could finish, both sisters strode away toward the table, leaving her completely bewildered.

Roland leaned close to John. "Like Johanna, she looks. Maybe not so tall, but so much. And her voice, too, like Johanna's."

John grinned. "I thought so."

Norman Beachy raised his voice from the far side of the table. "John, wonder if you'd mind stopping by my place later. I've got a sow that cut her snout on the fence. It might need stitches."

"I'd be glad to," John said. "One of your Polands?"

Norman began a long story about the pig, and John nodded, all the while considering what he'd just witnessed. Grace was checking out the men at this table, and she'd shown a real interest in Roland. John liked him. He was a good guy, an honest man, and he showed common sense and affection in dealing with his animals. Roland had even brought his son's cat in to be neutered, which endeared him to John. If country people could be persuaded to spay and neuter their pets, there'd be a lot fewer ending up dropped at the shelter. If Grace were to choose an Amish husband, she couldn't pick a better man than Roland Byler.

"Now that pig can dig under just about any fence a man can build," Norman continued. "I thought if I put down a row of cement blocks…"

John nodded and helped himself to another biscuit. These had to be Anna's. Her biscuits were so light they practically floated off the plate. He appreciated a good meal, and these Amish shared dinners were enough to bring tears to a bachelor's eyes. He'd spent too long suffering under Uncle Albert's attempts at imitating the chefs on television, and he himself was usually too busy to do more than throw together a grilled cheese sandwich and tomato soup.

He glanced over at Roland, wondering what Grace saw in the young farmer that she couldn't see in him. Roland was as much of a stranger to her as he was.

Women were a mystery to John. He liked to look at them, any man did, but he'd never gone out with a lot of girls. In high school, he'd been busy with sports, his part-time jobs and keeping his grades high enough to get into a good college. At university, the competition was even harder.

He'd known he wanted to be a veterinarian since he was ten years old, and his grandfather had warned him that being smart wasn't enough. He had to work hard and never lose sight of his goal. He'd met Alyssa when he was in vet school, and he'd been certain she was the one. But after she broke his heart, he hadn't been serious over any woman until Miriam.

Sometimes he wondered what was wrong with him— if he was too picky. He wanted a wife, kids, someone to share his dream home with, but after Miriam had chosen Charley, he'd let the half-finished log house he was building on the millpond stand locked and empty. He told himself that he was too busy with his practice to deal with contractors, but the truth was, without someone to share his life with, he didn't think he had the heart to complete the project. Because he didn't have the heart to think again about settling down with a woman.

Until Grace Yoder had appeared. Now, suddenly, everything was different, richer...brighter. The smell of the crushed apples today, the green of Grace's dress and the husky-sweet sound of her voice. He told himself that it was his imagination. She couldn't be as attractive as he imagined her, but the time they'd spent together at the hospital had made him all the more eager to see her smile at him. She might not have much formal education, but she was smart and funny and intriguing. By offering her a job at the practice, he was breaking all his own rules, but he didn't care. He wanted to spend as much time with her as he could. And if she was the woman he believed her to be, it might be that he'd want a lot more.

What was it Uncle Albert had said when he was seeing Miriam? A thunderbolt. "You've been hit by a thunderbolt, boy. It comes out of nowhere and knocks you flat. Only one woman ever made me feel like that, and she turned me down. That's why I never married."

Thunderbolt. Being with Miriam had seemed right at the time, but it hadn't been a thunderbolt, and he certainly hadn't felt like this. From the moment he'd laid eyes on Grace, he'd felt disoriented and uncertain around her...and himself. Maybe this was what Uncle Albert had been talking about. Whatever it was, he had no intentions of standing back and watching any Amish man, let alone Roland Byler, walk away with Grace without doing everything in his power to prevent it.

* * *

Two hours later, after the second and third sitting, John noticed Grace and her little boy come out of the house, cross the yard and enter the barn. He didn't hesitate to follow her.

Hoping that no one else was in the barn and that he'd have a few moments alone with her, John opened the door and stepped into the shadowy interior. "Grace," he called. "It's John Hartman."

"Oh, John."

His eyes adjusted to the semidarkness and he saw two figures standing by the cider-making equipment. He approached and stopped far enough away that she wouldn't get the wrong idea.

"Dakota loved the apple cider," Grace said. "He wanted to see how they make it, but…" She shrugged. "I suppose we should have come out earlier."

John crouched down to put himself at the boy's eye level. "How's the head, buddy?" he asked. "Does it hurt?"

Dakota shook his head. "No," he said.

"Good." John smiled at him. "You were brave, even braver than Mom."

The child offered a shy smile in return.

"So you want to know how this works?" John rose to his feet. Again, Dakota nodded. John reached under the conveyer belt and picked up a stray apple, then proceeded to explain how the apples rode up the belt, were crushed and then pressed to make the cider. "Next year, I'll make certain someone brings you out to watch," he promised.

A horse whinnied from a box stall in another section of the barn, and Dakota whipped his head around.

"Can I?" he asked his mother in a small voice. "Can I see the horse?"

"Be careful," she warned. "It might bite."

"Not Molly," John answered, rubbing an apple on his pant leg. "She's a sweet old girl. And she loves apples." He took a penknife from his pocket, unfolded it and cut the apple into four pieces. He offered one to Grace.

She chuckled, accepted it and bit into it. "Delicious," she pronounced.

"Granny Smith. You can't go wrong with Granny Smith. Good for pies, applesauce, eating out of hand."

Grace walked across the straw-strewn floor to the box stall where the dapple-gray mare stood watching Dakota with large, intelligent eyes and cocked ears. Grace slid her hand into her son's small one. "Isn't she beautiful?" She glanced back at John who'd followed three steps behind. "I've always loved horses. I always dreamed of having one of my own when I was a kid."

"Do you ride?" he asked her.

"No, never learned how. Joe…my husband… He always promised to teach me, but the right day never came."

"I'm sorry. About his passing. Hannah said—"

"Joe loved the rodeo. It was his whole life. At least he died doing something he loved."

"Was the accident…" John trailed off. He should have had more sense than to ask for details with the boy present. Grace didn't owe him any explanations, but the way she said it… John looked into her eyes. She seemed sad but not grieving. He wondered how that could be possible. "How long ago?" he asked.

"It will be two years in May." She shrugged. "Dakota doesn't remember him, and sometimes…" She sighed.

"Sometimes I can't remember his face. I try, but it keeps slipping away."

"The boy takes after him?"

She nodded. "Joe was full-blooded Native American." A muscle at the corner of her mouth tightened. "I've always been honest with Dakota. I want him to be proud of his heritage, of his father. He had his faults, but Joe was a great bronc rider. If he'd lived, he might have been a top-money winner, but our relationship wasn't always…" She squeezed Dakota's hand. "Like I said, rodeo meant everything to Joe."

More than his beautiful wife and son? John wondered.

"Some men aren't really meant to be tied down with a family," she added, answering his unasked question. "But if he'd lived, I know Dakota would have learned to ride. His father would have made sure of it."

John knelt down and offered Dakota a section of apple. "You like horses, after…"

Grace grimaced. "Joe's accident wasn't with a horse," she said. "He was thrown from a Brahma bull. It kicked him."

John clenched his teeth. "Were you there? Did you see—"

She shook her head. "No. It was two days before one of his friends remembered where we lived. I thought he had won money and was celebrating. It wasn't unlike Joe to stay away for a week or two after a rodeo. He was in intensive care for four days before…"

"Look!" Dakota pointed at the mare. She was stretching her neck over the railing in an attempt to reach his piece of apple. "She wants some."

John glanced at Grace for permission and then lifted

the boy and settled him on his hip. He gave him another piece of apple and showed him how to hold his hand flat. "Keep your fingers out of the way," he said. "She'll take it from you."

The mare wrinkled her nose and sniffed the apple. Then she lowered her head and gently took the treat between her teeth and munched it until the last morsel was gone. She tossed her head and blew air through her nose with a snort of sheer pleasure. Dakota giggled. "More!" he begged.

John gave him the last section, and the child held it out to the horse. Molly quickly gobbled it. "All gone," John said. "We don't want to give her a bellyache, do we? Hannah wouldn't like that."

"Ne," Dakota answered in a perfect imitation of his older cousin Jonah.

John and Grace laughed. "He's turning into a little Amish man," John said.

"Ya," Grace teased. "He is."

John hesitated, afraid to say anything that would spoil the moment. "I could teach you both," he offered.

"What?" Grace's eyes widened in curiosity. "Teach us what?"

"To ride. I have a horse, Bagherra. He's a Percheron. A really great horse."

"You have a horse?"

John chuckled. "I don't ride him often enough. I keep him at Meg Johnson's stable. She gives riding lessons, and Bagherra earns his keep by being a school horse."

"A Percheron? They're huge, aren't they?"

"Bigger than Molly, but very gentle. He'd be a perfect horse for Dakota to learn on. And I'd be glad to take you both to see him."

"We'd like that," Grace said. "So long as Hannah thinks it's fitting."

John nodded. "We'll do it soon. Just say the day." *And I don't make promises I don't keep,* he thought.

"Can we feed your horse an apple?" Dakota asked eagerly.

"Absolutely," John said. "Two shiny red ones. He's big enough that we'll need to give him at least two."

Chapter Nine

Three weeks later, on a Wednesday afternoon, John and Grace left the side entrance to the veterinary clinic and walked across the parking lot to where John's truck was parked. He opened the pickup's passenger door and helped Grace climb in. "It's good of you to drive me home again," she said. "I appreciate it, but I can't keep taking advantage of you."

"You're not," he answered. He closed the door, went around to the driver's side and got behind the wheel. He'd been out earlier, so the wipers were able to easily sweep the new-fallen snow off the windshield. "I have a call at Martin's, about a mile from the Yoder farm. It was no problem to swing by the office on my way."

Grace wasn't sure that John was being entirely truthful with her. It was the third day in a row that he'd found a reason to *swing by* the office about the time Grace was getting off work, and then *happen* to be heading in the direction of the Yoder farm. She didn't want to give anyone the wrong impression by continuing to allow him to drive her home. Still, she loved every minute of her job and she didn't want to take the chance of losing it due to transportation problems. And she *did* enjoy John's company.

The plan had been for her to ride to work with Melody, one of the vet techs, in the morning and be picked up by a regular driver for the Amish in the afternoon. But the van came past the veterinary clinic around 1:00. If Grace missed that van, she couldn't catch a ride again until 5:30. And because of today's snow, traffic would be slowed and that would make her arrival at the farm even later. She had to work, but she hated being away from Dakota any longer than she had to be.

Grace settled back, fastened her seat belt and stared back at the clinic entrance. Snow had been falling since late morning, early in the year for Delaware, according to her fellow employees. The air was crisp and cold, and the parking lot, remaining cars and yard were draped in a shimmering blanket of white. Like a child, she'd always loved snow. It made everything so clean and fresh.

"Tired?" John asked. "Uncle Albert said the office was crazy today."

Grace had learned that after John's grandfather's retirement the previous year, John had continued to be on-call to care for their large-animal practice, while his uncle had started caring for cats and dogs. They had expanded their office and hired the young female veterinarian and were already thinking of hiring another. Grace got the impression that none of the men in the Hartman family had expected their small-animal practice to take off the way it had.

"I'm a little tired." She rubbed the back of her neck. She'd been up since five-thirty this morning, and they'd been so busy today that she'd barely had time to snatch a sandwich mid-afternoon. Usually, she started work at 8:00 a.m. sharp and finished by 1:00 p.m., but today everyone's schedules were off at the office.

One of the front desk clerks had called in sick, and the office had been mobbed. There had been three scheduled surgeries, a full appointment schedule, two emergencies and a sweet Rottweiler that had lost an encounter with a skunk.

Besides her usual job of cleaning cages, sweeping the kennel, feeding the animals and walking dogs, Grace had taken a turn at the desk. There, she'd answered the telephone, registered incoming patients, made and canceled appointments and collected payment for services.

"Uncle Albert said you were a huge help," John said. "He said he didn't know what they would have done without you today."

A warm wave of pleasure enveloped Grace. "It's what I'm there for, isn't it? To do whatever I can?"

"Yes, as a kennel tech, but that rarely includes the receptionist's job or dealing with skunk-sprayed animals." He grinned. "Poor Mr. O'Brien. I heard he stunk worse than his Rotti."

Grace chuckled. It was a wonder she didn't smell of skunk. Luckily, Melody had insisted she change into a jumpsuit and gloves before taking charge of poor Zeus. It wasn't one of the regular groomer's days, so bathing the animal had fallen to Grace, as well. She really hadn't minded. She loved dogs, and Zeus, despite his size, was as gentle as a lamb.

"Seriously, you're a terrific addition to the staff. Everyone agrees."

Grace smiled but kept gazing out the window. It was difficult for her to remember the plan when John was sitting so close to her. She knew that he liked her, and it would have been easy to like him, and not just as a friend. But that wasn't part of the plan. She had to keep reminding herself of that. He wasn't Amish, so all he could be to her, other than her employer, was trouble.

They were both quiet for a moment. The only sound in the cab was the swish of the windshield wipers and the crunch of the tires on the snowy road.

"You okay?" John asked, glancing her direction.

She nodded. "Fine."

He started to speak, stopped, then went on. "I…I don't want to make you uncomfortable, Grace. If you feel riding home with me…" He cleared his throat and began again. "What I'm trying to say is that you don't have to humor me to keep your job. It just seems silly for you to wait an hour and pay the driver when I can have you at Hannah's back porch in ten minutes."

Grace knew that what he was saying made sense. The van cost eight dollars a trip, and she had to watch her pennies if she didn't want to be a burden on Hannah. It wasn't that she didn't like riding with John. The truth was, she thoroughly enjoyed his company. He was fun and upbeat, and they always found interesting things to talk about. Plus, he usually had the truck radio tuned to the local country music station.

She loved country music. Music was one thing she'd really miss when she became Amish; the Amish, she'd learned, didn't permit using or listening to musical instruments. She'd have to give up her guitar, and she'd played since she was thirteen. She'd never had formal lessons, but she thought she had a real knack for it, and playing had always made her happy.

"You know I'd never do anything on purpose to make you uncomfortable."

"Of course." She turned toward him and placed a hand on his arm. "You've always been a real gentleman...kind to me and Dakota. I won't forget you spending half your day taking us to the hospital."

"It was the least I could do."

"No." She shook her head. "You did more than most people would. You were great. You were patient with Dakota *and* me. You told me it was just a bump, but I was being an overprotective mom. I realized that later." She shrugged. "It's just that he's all I have. I love him so much, and I can't imagine what I'd do if anything happened to him."

"He's a special little guy." He pointed with a gloved finger. "Don't forget, I did promise to give him a riding lesson. Provided it's okay with you."

Grace folded her arms, tucking her hands inside her coat sleeves. The heater was running, but she didn't have gloves, and the cab was still chilly.

She tried to think of a way to keep from hurting John's feelings. Dakota had been begging her to go and see the big horse, and she knew she would enjoy it, as well. But she was afraid that going with John would take her away from the Yoder farm, away from Hannah, her sisters and the Amish community. Not away physically—the place where John stabled the Percheron wasn't that far—but spiritually. It wasn't something an Amish woman would do. Rebecca wouldn't consider going with an *Englishman* for the afternoon. Even with Dakota along as chaperone, it might look like a date. She was still learning the ropes here, but it hadn't taken her long to figure out that the Amish cared very much how things *appeared* to their fellow church members.

Besides, seeing John, one of her bosses, after work

hours might cause gossip at the clinic. And with good reason. She'd always made it a rule not to date people she worked with or for. That was a lesson she'd learned the hard way when she was eighteen and working at an ice-cream shop. She'd taken the manager, Eddy Polchak, up on an invitation for pizza and a movie and later discovered that he expected more than a thank-you for the evening. That had cost her her job, because no way was she going to compromise her sense of right and wrong, no matter how badly she needed money. She might have grown up rough, but she had standards.

Not that John would be like that. She could tell that he wasn't that kind of man.

The sad thing was, John was exactly what she was looking for, or he would have been, if he were Amish. She had a hunch that John would be an easy man to fall in love with if she was looking for love. Which she was. Just not romantic love.

For her, God's forgiveness, faith and the love of family and community had to come first. Becoming Amish was the only way she could see to make up for her past. She had to choose between a life of service and worship over a life of self. She had to choose God over the world; she believed there was mercy and peace waiting if she could step away from temptation.

Finding a solid Amish husband was part of the package, a man who lived simply and put God first in his life, a man who could guide her in the same path. Women married for lots of reasons. Some chose men who could provide them with diamond rings, big houses and fancy cars. Others picked guys for their hot looks and muscles. Grace hoped that she would be wiser. This time, she meant to find a husband best suited to fit into what she believed was God's plan for her, a man who would be a good father to her child, and one she could respect. She knew what she was looking for…a Plain man like…like Roland Byler.

The problem was, none of the Amish men seemed to notice she was alive, especially not Roland Byler. She'd seen him three times since she'd met him at the cider pressing weeks ago, but the most conversation she'd gotten out of him was a brief comment about the weather.

"Did I say something to offend you?" John asked.

"What?" Grace blinked. "I'm sorry. I was thinking about…" She offered him an apologetic smile. "It's not you. Really. I guess I'm under a lot of stress. Not the job," she hurried to say. "Everybody at the office has been great. It's the nicest place I've ever worked. You have a great kennel area. I love the setup and the fenced-in play area for the dogs. I just…"

He turned the truck off the blacktop into a farm lane and brought the vehicle to a stop. "But?" he asked.

Grace supposed she should have been alarmed, his pulling over like this, but it was John, and she wasn't afraid of him. Besides, she had to share her concerns with someone or burst.

"It's not as easy fitting into Hannah's family as I thought it would be," she blurted.

A smile played on his lips. "Or among the Amish in general?"

She nodded, slipping her hands out of her sleeves to rest them on the seat. "True."

"It's tough. I've been working in the community for almost five years and I've made a lot of friends among them. We have a lot in common. I belong to the Mennonite Church, the Amish and Mennonites spring from the same beginnings. We share a lot of the same beliefs."

She waited, sensing a *but* coming. John didn't disappoint her.

"But they *are* apart from the world. It's a tight community. Sometimes I feel welcome, sometimes I don't." He hesitated. "The fact is, Grace, they may never let you in. Not completely."

She curled her legs under her and scooted up on the wide seat. "I know that. But it will be different for Dakota." She couldn't help smiling as she remembered how cute he looked in his little straw hat and high-top boots. "It's already different for him. You should hear him speaking Pennsylvania Dutch. And he knows the rules better than I do. We've been here only five weeks, and he's taken Hannah, Susanna, my sisters, his cousins—even *Grossmama* and Aunt Jezzy—to heart. He and Jonah are inseparable, and Dakota adores Susanna."

"What do you think of the worship services?"

Grace took a deep breath and exhaled softly. "They're long."

He grinned.

"I love the singing—it's almost like chanting. I can't understand the words, but the hymns give me goose bumps. Good ones." She closed her eyes. "You can just feel the joy in those hymns."

He let her go on.

"I understand a little Pennsylvania Dutch, and I'm picking up more every day. But the ministers read from the Bible and quote from it in High German. I'm sure I'll get more from it when my German improves."

He rubbed his gloved hand over the top of the steering wheel. "You're a brave woman, Grace. Not easily discouraged by what some would think an impossible task. Uncle Albert said he'd never heard of an Englisher successfully converting to the Old Order Amish." He shrugged. "But it could be different for you, with Hannah's help, and your sisters. I never knew your father that well, but people speak well of him. You've got that on your side, too."

"I don't know if I'll ever be able to forgive my mother for keeping me from him," she admitted. "I know that we can't expect the Lord to forgive us if we can't find forgiveness in our hearts for others. But all those years that I spent in foster care could have been so different if I'd been able to come here. Of course Jonas might not have wanted me, might have turned me away...."

John reached out and brushed her hand with his gloved one. "He would have wanted you, Grace. Hannah would have wanted you. You're right. It was wrong of your mother to keep you from knowing your father and your family. She robbed you of your childhood, but she must have had her reasons."

"Not good ones. Not from where I sit. I loved her—don't get me wrong. She did the best she could, or at least she did what she thought was best for me. But it hurts so much that I never got to meet my father." She looked through the windshield at the swirling snow. "Not once."

His fingers tightened around hers. "But you have to try to forgive her. Like you said, you have to let it go. Otherwise, bitterness will poison you."

She sighed and looked back at him, pulling her hand from his. It just felt too good there. "I know, but it isn't easy." *And not just Trudie,* she thought. *I have to forgive Joe or I'll never be able to move on.*

She sat up straight and rubbed her hands briskly together. Any more of this, and she'd be blubbering like a baby. "What are you doing tomorrow for Thanksgiving?" she asked, anxious to change the subject to something less emotional. "Are you going to your mother's or spending it at home?"

"Neither. Gramps was invited to a friend's house for the day, and Uncle Albert and I will be helping members of our church serve dinner at a senior center. It's open to the entire community, but we've made a special outreach to those who might be alone or families struggling in this economy."

"That's nice. I helped at a homeless shelter once on Christmas Day. In Reno. Some of the people who came to eat were a little scary, but most were just down on their luck."

"I suppose Hannah's having a big Thanksgiving dinner with her family."

"No." Grace shook her head and sighed. "I thought so, too. The community has chosen a day of prayer and fasting this year instead of the traditional feast. Not for the children, of course. And Hannah said I could fast or not as I wanted. It's fine." She forced a chuckle. "Every day is like Thanksgiving at the Yoder table."

But it wasn't fine...not really. In her heart of hearts, she was disappointed. She expected this Thanksgiving to be like the ones she saw in magazines or on television. Amish-style, of course. Her throat tightened as she remembered the last Thanksgiving she and her mother had shared. There'd been takeout Chinese food in cardboard cartons, a guy named Vick who Trudie had met at a truck stop, a buddy of Vick's and thay guy's girlfriend. The adults had gotten into an argument, then a fistfight, and Grace had ended up hiding in a closet. What had hurt most was that her mother hadn't even missed her, and when Grace finally crawled out of the dark, everyone, including Trudie, had left.

"I'm going to fast with them," she said determinedly. "It's just from after supper tonight until tomorrow night. Then we'll have bread and broth. I'm sure it will be a good experience."

"It is. It's not something my church does often, but I've taken part in fasting before." His gaze met hers. "Did you belong to a church? Before you came here, I mean? I hope you don't mind my asking," he added quickly.

"Not a problem." She gave a wave. "Trudie was never one for churchgoing. But my foster mother, the one with the dogs, never let us miss a Sunday. I got in the habit. I moved around a lot, but I liked to attend church whenever I could. I went to lots of different denominations, but I can't say that I really belonged anywhere."

He hesitated and then backed the truck out of the lane onto the road. "I'd better get you home. They'll be wondering where I am. My appointment, I mean."

"Yes," she agreed.

They rode the rest of the way to the Yoder drive in companionable quiet. As he turned into the dirt lane, John said, "Our church has an open invitation to visitors. We could use help serving tomorrow for Thanksgiving, and naturally, you'd be welcome at any worship service…if the Amish…"

"Thank you," she said, putting her hand on the door handle. She opened the door as the truck came to a stop, just yards from Hannah's back gate. "I would love to help with the dinner, but I couldn't leave Dakota on Thanksgiving Day."

"You could bring him," John suggested, sounding disappointed. "The volunteers from our church always include their kids in our activities."

"I don't think so, but thanks for offering." She climbed out. "Thanks again for the ride home." She didn't look back until she got to the porch. He waved, and she waved back, then stamped her feet to get the snow off before she went into the house.

"I'm home," she called as she stepped into the warm kitchen. She didn't see Dakota or any of the children, but Hannah, Aunt Jezzy, Johanna, Rebecca and Susanna were all there, gathered around the table. Hannah had been speaking, but she bit off her words in mid-sentence.

Everyone looked at Grace.

The nape of Grace's neck prickled as thoughts of John flew out of her head. Hannah's features strained with obvious distress. Not once—not even on the evening she and Dakota had arrived—had she felt so much discord in this room. "What is it?" Grace asked. "Are the children all right? Dakota—"

"Fine." Hannah's voice was uncharacteristically tight. "Playing in the front parlor. Irwin is watching them."

Irwin? What had happened that none of them wanted the children to hear what they were discussing? And what was so important that Irwin would be pressed into babysitting while Grace's sisters, including Susanna, were here? Grace studied the faces she'd come to know so well. Even Aunt Jezzy had traded her sweet smile for pursed lips and a troubled expression. "Have I done something?" Grace asked, afraid they had been waiting for her. Lying in wait even.

"Ne." Hannah shook her head. "Not at all."

"It's private," Johanna said. "Just family."

Grace shrugged off her coat and hung it on a hook. "I am family," she said. Her knees felt weak, but she wouldn't be dismissed so easily. "Whether you like it or not, little sister. I'm here and I care about you all. Anything that worries all of you concerns me."

"Ya," Aunt Jezzy agreed. She motioned to the empty place beside her. "You see that look in her eyes, Hannah, my brother's look." She glanced at Johanna, speaking in English. "Shame on you. Now, more than ever, we must draw close together. And you cannot deny that she is your father's child and your elder."

Johanna's face flushed but she nodded. "I'm sorry, Grace," she murmured. "I'm just upset." She nodded toward their youngest sister. "It's our Susanna. And David King."

Susanna? What could Susanna have done wrong? Grace wondered as she looked across the table at her youngest sister. Susanna's cheeks were redder than Johanna's, and her bottom lip protruded in a stubborn pout.

"Aunt Jezzy found Susanna and David on the stairs," Hannah explained. "Behaving in an inappropriate way."

Grace knew her eyes must have widened in surprise. *Susanna and David King? What had they been doing that upset everyone? Susanna was Susanna, and David, although he was older, seemed even more of a child.*

"Making mischief." Aunt Jezzy lifted her graying eyebrows. "The two of them."

"King David is not bad. He's good." Susanna's eyes

crinkled up. Her pout faded and her chin quivered. "I love him."

"No," Hannah said gently. "David's not bad. No one said that. Neither of you is bad."

Johanna slipped an arm around Susanna's shoulder. "He's not bad. Only unwise."

Hannah whispered to Grace behind her hand. "They were kissing."

But Susanna heard. "I did!" Susanna shouted. "I did kissed King David," she said. "I love him." She nodded vigorously. "King David and me." Her mouth spread into a wide smile. "I kissed him because we're getting married."

Chapter Ten

"There will be no more kissing between you and David," Hannah admonished, waggling her finger. "David is a friend, not family. We don't kiss friends or strangers who are boys. And you aren't old enough to get married."

"Am, too! Ada-Ann said so," Susanna flung back. She threw up all ten fingers. "I had my birthday. I'm nineteen. And...and King David is...is..." She seemed to struggle with her thoughts for a moment. "He's old!"

"He's twenty-three," Johanna mouthed to Grace.

"I know Ada-Ann is your friend," Rebecca calmly told Susanna. "But she isn't your mother. She doesn't know everything. And Mam says you're too young."

"But...I love King David." Susanna giggled. "He kisses good."

"You were kissing David, Susanna?" Grace asked, more to calm the situation than to clarify. "On the cheek or on the lips?"

Susanna patted her mouth with two fingers and giggled again.

"You see," Aunt Jezzy declared, throwing up her

skinny arms. "She's an innocent. Susanna isn't even ashamed of it."

"She doesn't understand," Rebecca told Aunt Jezzy, "but she will if you explain it carefully." She smiled at her younger sister. "*Plain* girls only kiss boys *after* they are married, Susanna."

"Irwin kissed a girl at Spence's Sunday." Susanna bounced in her seat. "An Englisher girl. I saw him."

Grace tried not to laugh. If *that* were true, Irwin was in trouble. But it couldn't have happened on Sunday because the auction was closed on Sundays. Susanna didn't have a strong grasp of the order of the days of the week. When she related any incident, she always said it happened on Sunday.

Hannah rolled her eyes. "If Irwin did kiss a girl, that was wrong. I'll have a talk with him, but we're not talking about Irwin right now, we're talking about you, Susanna. You are *not* allowed to kiss David anymore."

"But...but we're getting married," Susanna insisted. "Sunday."

"Not this Sunday," Grace soothed, rising from her chair to stroke her sister's arm. She glanced at Hannah, who nodded approval, and then back to Susanna. "It takes a long time. First Bishop Atlee has to give his permission, then Mam and David's parents."

"And bans have to be read for weeks at worship service," Rebecca put in.

Hannah looked up at the clock and clapped her hands together. "Goodness, look at the time." She rose. "Girls, set the table. The children must be starving."

"But Mam..." Susanna whined. "I want—"

"You heard Grace. It takes a long time to get married. Now be a good girl and get the knives and forks." Hannah headed for the stove. "Johanna made *ob'l dunkes kucka* and that's your favorite."

"Molasses shoo-fly cake!" Susanna clapped her hands. "King David likes cake!"

The Saturday morning after Thanksgiving, Johanna and Grace sat at a table in the crowded dining area of Spence's Bazaar, a bargain-sale, auction and Amish market, and watched as Rebecca bought Jonah and Dakota ice-cream cones. Katie had remained home with Ruth and Susanna, while the two little boys enjoyed an outing with their mothers and Aunt Rebecca.

The boys loved going to Spence's, and so did Grace. Here in the food building were Amish booths with all kinds of delicious foods, from Lancaster specialty cheeses to ham, bacon, sausage and all kinds of tasty deli meats. There were candies, jams and a bakery where the children could watch Amish girls with muscular arms, red cheeks and starched *Kapps* pull trays of fragrant yeast bread and cinnamon rolls hot from the oven.

The air smelled of hamburgers, apple pie, pizza and gingerbread. Everywhere Amish and non-Amish chatted, ate and shopped, and the guttural Pennsylvania Dutch dialect was as commonly heard as English.

Now that the children were away from the lunch table, Johanna picked up an earlier conversation concerning Susanna and David's kissing incident. "Mam worries," Johanna confided. "We've never expected to have anything like this happen with her. Susanna has always been such an easy child...a good girl."

"And she's still a good girl," Grace defended. "But she's almost twenty. She may have a more difficult time learning than the rest of us, but in some ways, she's a normal teenager." She shrugged. "She must have the same thoughts and feelings as any young woman. Why does your mother treat her differently than she does Rebecca?"

Johanna's mouth firmed. "Because she *is* different."

"Yes, Susanna is different." Grace nodded. "For me, not because she was born with Down's, but because she was the first one to accept Dakota and me. She has such a pure heart."

"I agree with you that our little sister is one of God's special children," Johanna replied, "but realistically, Susanna has limits. One of us will always have to care for her. It's not a burden. We love Susanna, but we know what must be. And she can't go around kissing boys because she likes the way it feels."

"Of course not." Grace took Johanna's hand and squeezed it affectionately. "Rebecca wouldn't be allowed to behave like that, either, would she?"

Johanna's expression softened. "*Ne.* But Rebecca knows what is modest behavior and what isn't. And then, of course, there's an issue of safety."

Grace nodded, knowing all too well that a young woman could get herself into trouble kissing the wrong man. Hadn't she made that very same mistake with Joe?

"Susanna doesn't have the ability to make those kinds of judgments," Johanna added.

"Maybe not, but maybe it's just because she's been too sheltered. When you look at her, what do you see? A little girl?" Grace leaned forward. "I don't. I see a beautiful young woman, not beautiful in the way that Rebecca and you are beautiful, but..." She thought back to the first time she'd laid eyes on Susanna, and how pleasantly surprised she'd been. "I don't know how to put it, but Susanna just glows. Her eyes sparkle with a special inner light."

"Ya." Johanna admitted. "They do. We have all seen it."

"So why can't Susanna do the things that other girls her age do, that Rebecca does? Why can't she go to singings and young people's outings? Properly chaperoned, of course. Why can't she talk to nice Amish boys her own age and share secrets with girlfriends like every other teenager?"

Johanna's flawless brow furrowed and she absently wound a bonnet string around one finger. "Susanna does go to singings and work frolics."

"She told me that she always has to carry the pie basket, sit by the cookies and pour lemonade. Like a *grossmama.* She says that she never gets to play games like the other girls—or ride home alone with boys in their father's buggies."

"Susanna told you that? When?" Johanna seemed genuinely surprised. "When did she say such things?"

"Thanksgiving Day. We were talking when we fed the chickens and gathered the eggs. She confided in me. She said everyone thinks she's a baby and she's not."

"Atch…" Compassion flooded Johanna's eyes. "I never knew Susanna felt that way. She seems so happy, like a—"

"Like a child?" Grace supplied. "But she's not, is she?"

"But…" Johanna scrambled to respond. "She can't ever marry, have children, manage a household."

Grace shrugged. "All the more reason she should have the fun of being a teenager, don't you think?"

"I suppose…"

"Aunt Jezzy never married, did she?" Grace asked. "But I'm sure she had her *rumspringa* years. Probably even had a radio hidden in the hayloft to listen to Elvis."

Johanna's gaze met Grace's, and both started to giggle at the thought of sedate Aunt Jezzy rebelling against her parents' teachings.

"Mam! Mam! I got choc'late!" Dakota dodged an English woman in a blue polka-dot dress and skidded to a stop beside the table. His face was already smeared with chocolate ice cream, and he was grinning so hard that a dimple appeared on his cheek.

"I see you did," Grace answered with a smile. She glanced back at Johanna. "Just think about what is best for Susanna and talk to your mother."

"About Susanna?" Rebecca asked, joining her sisters. Johanna nodded.

"Well, at least Susanna isn't marrying David *this* Sunday. Sadie told Mam that she and David were going to spend a few days at her daughter's house."

Johanna successfully dodged an ice-cream drip as she lifted Jonah and his strawberry cone onto her lap. "The Kings will have their new roof on their house before Christmas and they'll be moving in. I'm sure Susanna will forget all about this getting married to David. You know how she is."

"I do know how she is." Rebecca took a seat. "That's the problem. Sometimes, Susanna latches onto an idea and holds it like a squirrel to a stolen acorn."

Jonah and Dakota both laughed. "I like squirrels," Dakota said. "I want Santa to bring me a squirrel. Not a cartoon squirrel, a real one. And a train, one that blows smoke and has a whistle and—"

"What's a cartoon squirrel?" Jonah asked.

"Secret Squirrel." Dakota licked at a drip of chocolate. "On TV."

Jonah wrinkled his nose and glanced up at his mother. "Secret Squirrel?"

"He's never watched television," Johanna explained to Dakota.

"Ask Santa to bring you one," Dakota urged Jonah.

Rebecca looked uncomfortable. "There was a man dressed up like Santa Claus by the ice cream. Dakota wanted to tell him where he lived now."

"So he doesn't miss me. And forget to bring toys." He waved his cone at Jonah for emphasis. "Last year he brought a Christmas tree and a fire truck with a bell and—"

"Who is Santa Claus?" Jonah tilted his head and looked up at his mother. "Will he bring me a fire truck?"

Johanna's mouth opened and closed. Then she shook her head. "*Ne,* Jonah, Santa Claus is for Englishers. He doesn't come to Plain children, just English houses."

"But I'm English," Dakota protested. "Irwin said so. Englisher, he said."

Jonah nodded. "He did. But Irwin also said there was trolls under the chicken house. And *Grossmama* said Irwin was a *dummkopp* and trolls live far away in Belleville."

"Dummkopp," Dakota echoed with a giggle.

"Not a word for little boys," Johanna chided. "It was unkind to say, even about Irwin. He isn't a dunce, just *verhuddelt.* Mixed up," she translated for Grace. "No trolls here *or* in Pennsylvania."

And no Santa Claus, either, Grace thought sadly. That was a beloved tradition that she and Dakota would have to give up…and that might be even more painful than surrendering her guitar. *I hope I'm doing the right thing. It has to be,* she thought. *I've prayed and prayed, and I can't think of any other way to make up for what I've done.* She was just sorry that Dakota would have to pay the price, too.

Rebecca passed out ham-and-cheese sandwiches that she'd purchased. "I hope you like mustard."

"We do," Grace assured her.

Johanna had found a book of old quilt patterns in one of the thrift shops and was anxious to show it to Rebecca. As everyone ate and talked, Grace found her thoughts drifting away and reflecting on the weeks since she'd come to live at Seven Poplars.

As both Hannah and John had warned, it was a struggle for her to fit into the Amish lifestyle. Dakota had adapted quickly, but as much as she reveled in having family and a warm and joyous home, she was still torn between this new life and her old one. She loved the quiet nights in the snug farmhouse without the blare of highway traffic or the shouts of feuding neighbors. She loved the shared dinners and the animals and the slower pace of life. But she loved her job at the veterinary clinic, as well.

She found being part of the practice exciting. She liked chatting with the drug reps, placing orders for cleaning supplies and socializing with the clients. Lunch with her fellow employees was fun, and she found herself drawn to several of the vet techs, enjoying the camaraderie and the shop talk. She liked the Christian radio station that played in the waiting room and in the kennel area. And most of all, she loved watching everyone caring for sick and injured animals, and the feeling that she was a valuable piece of the puzzle. Every day brought something new to learn, and every day... despite her efforts not to, she found herself watching and hoping for glimpses of John. Even though, as the large-animal vet for the practice, he was on the road much of his day, she never knew when he might stop by for supplies or just to see how everyone was getting along, as he put it.

She had to stop riding home with him. She knew it. The more time she spent alone with John, the worse it would be when she had to let him go. He wasn't part of her future, and becoming attached to him was a wrong turn on the path God had planned for her. Next time John offered, she would simply decline.

"But you can't say no. You'll have to go," Rebecca said, breaking into Grace's musing.

Grace's eyes widened and she blinked. *Had she spoken John's name aloud?* "Excuse me?"

"You'll have to go with Susanna," Johanna explained. "To the corn-husking work frolic at Lydia and Norman Beachy's house next Saturday. To be her chaperone."

"Me?" Grace asked, still trying to catch up with the conversation. "A husking frolic?"

"Ya." Rebecca chuckled. "It will be fun. There will be a bonfire and games. And husking heaps of feed corn for the Beachys. They always have more work than they can manage alone."

"There will be young people," Johanna said pointedly. "A few older couples who act as chaperones, but mostly unmarried. The Amish don't allow their teens and young adults to date, so it's how they meet and decide who to court."

"But you said Susanna..." Grace looked from one

to the other and lowered her voice when she noticed an Amish woman at another table watching them with interest. "She wouldn't be allowed…"

"Susanna will go for the games and the food," Johanna clarified. "But you will go to look for a husband. It's the perfect opportunity."

"A good Amish boy," Rebecca added. "You want one, don't you? This is how we choose."

"Aren't I a little old for boys?" Grace asked.

Rebecca snickered. "Men, then." She glanced at Johanna and then back to Grace. "I'm sure Roland Byler will be there, and he's nearly thirty. Maybe Johanna should go with us, too."

Johanna looked down at Jonah and stood up. "Sticky hands. We'll have to get these two boys to the washroom."

"Of course, if Susanna…" Grace looked from one sister to the other. Rebecca had a positively mischievous gleam in her eyes. "Will Hannah let her go?" Grace asked.

"Probably," Johanna said.

"I'm sure she will." Rebecca spread her hands, palm up and smiled. "What harm could there be with her oldest sister there to watch over her?"

A week later, Grace shared the front seat of the Yoder family buggy with Rebecca and Susanna as they rolled along the blacktop in the brisk darkness. It was a clear, crisp December night, with stars as bright as diamonds and a huge harvest moon. The three of them were well bundled up with scarves, capes and mittens. Rebecca drove the horse called Blackie.

Grace hoped that she wouldn't do or say anything

that made her look foolish tonight. She had no idea what a husking frolic was or how she would tell which of the Amish men were available and which weren't. Maybe the best thing to do was to wait for them to approach her. They all certainly knew who she was.

As they approached the Beachy farm, Grace saw four other buggies ahead of them on the road. "A good lot tonight," Rebecca said, flicking the reins over Blackie's back. The horse broke into a trot, and Grace grasped the edge of the seat. "You know I was teasing Johanna the other day about Roland Byler," Rebecca said as they entered the lane.

"Yes?" Grace urged.

"He won't really be there. Even if he was, he isn't right for you."

"You said that before. But why? He seems nice."

"Johanna and Roland used to walk out together," Rebecca explained. "Before she married Wilmer." She shrugged. "Johanna says the last thing she wants is another husband right now, but who knows?"

"Johanna likes Roland," Susanna said. "Anna said so."

Rebecca chuckled. "And *that,* Susanna banana, is a secret. Don't say it to anybody, especially not Johanna." She reined in the horse near the barn, and a tall, gangly young man came to take the horse's halter. "Vernon, this is our sister Grace," Rebecca said. "You'll have to help introduce her to the others. Grace, Vernon Beachy."

He mumbled something, but before Grace could return the greeting, another figure moved out of the shadows with a familiar rolling gait. Susanna squealed. "King David! Hi!" He laughed and waved, and Susanna scrambled down from the buggy.

"Good luck," Rebecca said with a chuckle. "It looks like you have your chaperone work cut out for you tonight."

Keeping up with Susanna and David should have been easy, and it was while they were all in the barn during the corn husking and the clapping games and singing. Susanna played and won what Grace supposed was an Amish version of musical chairs with hay bales substituted for chairs. But once the frolic moved outside to the bonfire and refreshments, it was almost impossible to not lose one blue dress and black bonnet in a crowd of black bonnets and blue dresses.

There must have been three dozen teenagers, all laughing, jostling and teasing one another amid the roasting of hot dogs and toasting of marshmallows. Susanna and David seemed to be having the time of their lives, but once either of them stepped back from the circle of firelight, they were quickly lost in the shadows and Grace found herself having to gently encourage them to join the others again.

Grace had determined in the first twenty minutes that other than good-looking Mordecai Miller and determined Barnabas Swartzentruber, who were both doing their best to charm Rebecca, there wasn't another unmarried male over the age of twenty-one. Grace's hopes of meeting someone—anyone—had swiftly faded and been wholly replaced by a determination to not allow Susanna the opportunity for any more mischief.

The only person she'd had any exchange of conversation with all evening had been her sister Miriam who'd come with her husband, Charley, to help the host and hostess of the frolic. But there hadn't been much opportunity to talk with Miriam, either, because she had been busy passing out refreshments. Charley, in the meantime, had been busy policing the frolic. He had confiscated two radios, an iPod and a cell phone, and had sent two boys home after he'd witnessed them poking fun at David King.

"Stutzman brothers. Not from our church district," Charley said, as the guilty party drove their horse and buggy hastily down the lane. "But they should know better. Ananias Stutzman is a deacon. Wait until I tell him how his sons behaved. They'll be shoveling manure until Pentecost Monday."

Grace was easing her way into the throng of teenagers around the bonfire when she heard the rumble of wagon wheels and the clip-clop of hooves in the farmyard. She glanced over her shoulder to see a hay wagon pulled by two enormous draft horses. Driving the animals was a man in a black felt cowboy hat and a thick denim jacket. She couldn't see his face, but something looked very familiar about him, so familiar that her heart skipped a beat.

"Look who's here," Miriam said, appearing at Grace's shoulder.

Charley, approaching them, laughed. "I'm guessing that's her ride home."

"Me?" Grace asked, thoroughly confused.

"Grace Yoder!" the man in the cowboy hat shouted, much to the amusement of the teens and young adults gathered around the dying bonfire. "Would you do me the honor?" He swept off the wide-brimmed hat, and there was no longer any doubt as to his identity.

Grace couldn't help laughing. It was John Hartman.

Chapter Eleven

"Grace Yoder! Will you ride home in my courting buggy?" John shouted, to the delight of the audience who all laughed and cheered. He spread his arms wide and swept his cowboy hat dramatically into the air.

Grace wanted to crawl under the nearest bale of hay. Her cheeks burned with embarrassment. Pulse racing, she turned away, hoping to hide in the crowd, but Susanna caught her elbow.

"Look, Grace!" Susanna's round face glowed with excitement in the firelight.

Grace pulled away from her.

"It's John! With…with Samuel's horses! Can we come? Please? Can King David and me ride in the hay wagon?" Susanna tugged at a chubby hand, and David King appeared from the crowd, clutching an unopened two-liter bottle of soda to his chest, his prize for winning one of the clapping games. David rarely spoke, but his eager, smiling face said it all. He wanted to go as much as Susanna did.

"I'm not riding home with John," Grace protested. But, oh, how she wanted to. It was so romantic, John coming for her in Samuel's wagon. And it was fun. Innocent. Unlike much of the Englisher ways of dating. And to think, John would do it in front of the whole young community of Seven Poplars. He must really like her.

The temptation was so great that Grace could feel it urging her toward the wagon. No, that feeling of being propelled forward, she realized, that wasn't temptation. It was Rebecca and two of her girlfriends pushing her forward through the group.

"Go on," Rebecca urged.

Grace planted her feet. "I can't."

Rebecca glanced at her friends and the three giggled.

"Is this a setup?" Grace asked suspiciously. "Did you know John was going to do this?" She'd been chilly earlier, but now she felt as if she'd been standing too close to the fire.

Rebecca shook her head. "*Ne,* but if you take Susanna and David with you, it would be good." She smiled mischievously. "Then, I can ride home with... with someone else."

The two girls beside her, neither of whom Grace knew, chuckled again. "Maybe Barney," the tallest girl said. Her black bonnet shadowed her face, but Grace could see a delicate dimpled chin and pretty mouth.

"Or Mordecai Miller." The other young woman, both shorter and plumper, nudged Rebecca. "They *both* asked her," she whispered.

Rebecca clapped a hand over her mouth and snickered. "Shh. You're not supposed to tell."

"Everybody knows," the tall girl said. "Mordecai told Mahlon that Barney didn't stand a chance of you riding home with him."

Rebecca threw Grace a pleading look.

"Rebecca... Don't do this to me," Grace begged, but it was too late. Charley and Miriam were both urging her to accept John's offer, too. And then the crowd parted, and John was standing in front of her, cowboy hat in hand, grinning sheepishly.

John leaned close to her. "You have to come, Grace," he said softly. "I'll never live it down in the community if you don't. Everyone will laugh at me forever."

"I don't *have* to do anything," she retorted. She couldn't do it. She didn't have the luxury of following her heart—not even for an evening. She had to think of Dakota and what was best for the two of them.

"We want to ride in the hay wagon," Susanna repeated. "Don't we, King David?" David nodded so vigorously that his bottle of soda slid out of his hands and would have fallen to the ground if John hadn't grabbed it in midair and returned it safely to him.

"I'll bet you've never been on a hayride," John teased Grace. "How can you refuse the opportunity?"

How could he know? Grace wondered. A long-buried memory flashed in her mind, a snapshot of her standing at the third-story bedroom window on a Saturday night and watching a hay wagon of singing teenagers roll by the driveway of her foster home.

The hayride was the highlight of football quarterback Bill McNamara's birthday party, and he'd asked her to be his date. It was the first time he'd noticed her, and she'd wanted desperately to go. But even though she begged, her foster mother had refused permission. The 9:00 p.m. lights-out rule was inflexible, and there would be church at 8:30 in the morning, with kennel and house chores and breakfast starting at 6:00 a.m. She'd cried herself to sleep that night, and on Monday, Bill and Amy Pierson were an item. No, she'd never gotten her hayride…and deep inside, it still hurt.

"Ya!" Elmer Beachy shouted. "Go with him!" A dozen other teenagers chimed in, all clapping and yelling. "Ride with him, Grace Yoder."

Would Susanna be as disappointed as she had been if she didn't get to go in the hay wagon tonight? Would Rebecca be upset with Grace if she didn't give her the opportunity to ride home alone with a boy? Was she being as inflexible as her foster mother by putting rules ahead of someone's happiness? Grace glanced at Miriam. "If I agree, I can take Susanna," she said. "But how can I take responsibility for David? His mother might not want him to go. Is he here with someone? It wouldn't be right for me to—"

"It's all right," John assured her. "I already asked his parents. The Kings are sleeping at Hannah's again tonight. Sadie and Ebben gave their permission." John flashed a triumphant grin. "And so did Hannah."

"You mean everyone knows about this ambush but me?" Grace protested. She could feel her resolve weakening. It was only a ride in a wagon with a friend. What harm could it do? She glanced again toward the restless team.

The big horses stamped their hooves, tossed their manes and blew clouds of warm breath into the cold air. What a shame it would be if John had brought them out for nothing. "All right," she agreed. "I'll ride with you *this* time." *But no more,* she vowed. *This is the last time I go anywhere with John Hartman. I'll have my hayride, but after that, I'll find a way to convince John that there's no chance for us.*

The teenagers followed them to the wagon, some clapping, others still catcalling and teasing in Pennsylvania Dutch. But it was all in good fun; nothing was mean or hurtful. Susanna and David followed close on their heels, not wanting to be left behind.

Grace supposed she should have been angry at John. This was preposterous. What was wrong with him that he couldn't take no for an answer? Why couldn't he accept the idea that she wasn't interested in going out with him? Why couldn't he understand that she only wanted him as a friend?

Because it's not true, she thought. A little catch in the back of her throat made her swallow. Coming for her with a hay wagon and a pair of magnificent Percherons was the most romantic thing any guy had ever done for her—like something out of a movie. And how did he guess that she'd always had a thing for men in cowboy hats? John didn't play fair.

"John Hartman, I'll get even with you for this," she whispered as he caught her by the waist and swung her up into the wagon. "You'll be sorry."

"I hope not," he answered.

Young men and women crowded around the wagon. Someone boosted David King up, and then Charley and Norman Beachy helped Susanna. She tumbled into the loose straw, scrambled up, laughed and clapped her hands together.

Rebecca brought an extra blanket from the buggy and wrapped it around Susanna's shoulders. "So you won't catch a chill," she said. And then she leaned close and whispered. "And remember what Mam said. No kissing."

Susanna glanced at David, and hugged herself tightly. "No kissing," she repeated and giggled again.

David, still holding his bottle of soda proudly, plunked himself on a bale of straw and grinned back at Susanna.

Grace saw Mordecai standing behind Rebecca. *I suppose it's only fair,* Grace thought. *Rebecca should be allowed to ride home with the boy of her choice. She shouldn't have to babysit me and Susanna all the time. If doing this made both Susanna and Rebecca happy, it had to be the right thing, didn't it?*

John waved Grace to a bale beside him, tugged his hat down tightly on his head and gathered the leather lines in his hands. Charley backed the team and led the horses in a wide circle. "You and Miriam be good now," John said as he flicked the reins lightly over the Percherons' broad backs. "Remember, married or not, you two need to set a good example."

Charley laughed and called to the team, "Walk on." Susanna gave a small squeal of joy as the wagon lurched forward and rolled across the farmyard toward the lane. "No kissing! Any of you!" Charley shouted, and everyone laughed again.

"Very funny," Grace said to John under her breath. "I hope you've enjoyed your little joke."

"Not a joke," John answered good-naturedly. "How else was I supposed to get a date with you?"

"This is *not* a date," she said.

He chuckled. "You keep telling yourself that, Grace."

Balancing herself with both hands on a bale of straw, Grace turned around so that she was facing the back of the wagon and could see Susanna and David.

Susanna looked up and smiled. "It's wonderful," she proclaimed. David nodded but he didn't take his gaze off Susanna.

Noting that there was a decent distance between the

two, Grace slid around and gave her attention to John. "You weren't exactly truthful with me."

"Me? How so?"

"You told me that it was a hayride," she said with a straight face. "I don't see any hay. All I see are bales of straw."

He groaned and clutched his chest. "You got me. Hayride just sounded better than straw ride. And you wouldn't want hay if you've ever sat on it."

She laughed. "I suppose I can forgive you for that, but I wanted you to know that I know the difference. I did grow up out west. Lots of hay out there."

"And straw?" he teased.

"And straw," she agreed. When they reached the end of the Beachys' drive, they turned right instead of left. "I thought you were taking us home," she said.

"I am, but it would be a shame to get these horses all hitched up and not give them proper exercise. I didn't say what route we were taking." He winked. "An old Amish trick." He guided the team a hundred feet and then crossed the road and took a dirt logging road. "Keep your eyes out for deer," he called to Susanna and David. "Samuel said there have been a lot of them this winter."

"Are you a hunter?" Grace asked.

Joe had been a hunter, and she'd always hated it when he'd brought home a kill. But the game had often been the only meat she could put on the table for the family. Joe didn't work much in winter and her paychecks went for rent, gas and car insurance for both of them. Hunting had kept them from public assistance, and for that she'd been grateful. Still, she'd always felt sorry for the animals.

"I shoot a lot of wildlife," John said. "With a camera,

especially birds. I fish a little, but no hunting. I enjoy watching the animals too much."

"What kind of camera do you use?" She was interested. Joe had bought her an inexpensive digital camera for Christmas one year, and she'd taken pictures of Dakota when he was a baby. The camera had gotten lost in one of their moves, and she'd never had the extra money to replace it. Now, she supposed she never would. The Amish didn't allow photographs to be taken of themselves. Hannah had explained that the Bible warned against making graven images.

John began to tell her about his camera, and her last bit of annoyance at being coerced into riding home with him fell away. They laughed and talked, and when they finally turned into Hannah's lane, she realized that she was sorry the evening was over.

"Thanks for coming with me," John said as he brought the horses to a halt in front of the house. "It was the best first date I've ever had."

"I had fun, too," she admitted, "but it *wasn't* a date."

"Oh yes, it was." He was still teasing, but there was something else in his tone, something she didn't want to contemplate.

"No, it wasn't," she insisted, getting in the last word as she popped up off the bale of straw. But as she jumped down from the wagon without waiting for John's assistance, she suspected that he was right. That was exactly what it was—an unforgettable date that threw a giant monkey wrench into her plans for the future.

The following afternoon, a visiting Sunday, John parked his truck near the Yoders' back gate, got out and walked toward the house. The previous night's surprise hayride had gone better than he'd hoped. Once he had Grace in the wagon, she hadn't held a grudge for the underhanded way he'd landed their first date. She'd laughed and talked, and she'd drawn Susanna and David into the conversation so that they wouldn't feel left out, and, he supposed, they wouldn't do anything of which anyone's mother would disapprove.

Grace's kindness to Susanna and David and her obvious affection for her younger sister had eased the way into his next suggestion. Once a month, on Sunday afternoon, after services, volunteers from his Mennonite church took mentally and physically challenged teenagers bowling. The event ended with pizza at one of the local restaurants. He'd wanted to invite Susanna, and Hannah had seemed open to the idea, but she'd been reluctant to allow her daughter to go because there were no other Amish attending.

This time, he'd asked Grace first, and she'd agreed to speak to Hannah and David's parents. And as he'd hoped, Grace offered to come and help out, so long as she could bring her son with her. Both families had thought that it would be a wonderful opportunity for their children.

Apparently, David had left friends behind in the Kings' old community, and his parents were eager for him to be happy here in Seven Poplars. Broadening Susanna's and David's world was something that John felt good about, but spending more time with Grace was icing on his cake.

The back door to the farmhouse opened and David ambled out, one prong of his battered cardboard crown sticking out from under his straw hat. Susanna came next, with a smiling Grace bringing up the rear.

"Where's Dakota?" John asked as he assisted David into the front seat and the two young women into the one behind. "He's not coming?"

"Toad in his head," Susanna replied.

"A cold," Grace clarified. "No fever, but Dakota was sneezing, and because the temperature is hovering around freezing, I thought he would be better if he stayed home where it's warm."

"I'm glad you didn't wake up with a cold," John told Grace.

"What? And let these two go off on their own?" Grace chuckled. "Hannah made me promise to watch over them like a banty hen with two chicks."

Susanna sat tall and straight on the seat. Instead of her *Kapp,* Hannah had sent her off with a navy blue wool scarf tied over her braided and pinned-up hair. She wore a robin's egg blue dress, a black cape, black apron and black stockings. Her sturdy leather shoes were polished to a high gleam.

"And who is this?" John teased.

Susanna giggled. "You know me," she answered. "Susanna."

David nodded and grinned. "Susanna," he echoed.

John closed the doors and went around the front of the truck. He climbed in behind the wheel. "And you're David King?" he asked, pointing at David.

"King David," Susanna corrected.

John glanced in the rearview mirror at Grace. She shrugged and chuckled. "Right," John said. "King David. I forgot."

David turned on the radio and kept pushing buttons until Christian music poured from the speakers. He nodded and sighed, settling back and tapping time to the music on the door as a group poured forth a joyous song of praise.

John met Grace's gaze in the mirror again, and she nodded her approval. "Perfect," she agreed, as David began to hum along.

By the time they reached the bowling alley, others had already arrived. John introduced Grace, David and Susanna to church volunteers Caroline and Leslie Brown, who were assisting two young people to find the correct size bowling shoes. "These are Daniel's cousins," he explained. "Your sister Leah's husband."

Once introductions were made, Kyle Stoffel, the church youth leader, and his cousin Evan Cho, took charge of David and took him to check his coat and hat and find shoes. Grace offered to keep score, and the group moved to the two bumpered lanes set aside for them.

Susanna quickly made friends with Amelia and Destiny. Susanna's bowling skills were sorely lacking, but that didn't curb her enthusiasm. David, on the other hand, turned out to be the best bowler of the group, easily scoring higher than the girls or the other two boys, much to his delight. His newfound friends admired his crown, as well, and the accolades made his chest swell with pride; he practically strutted up to the lane to take his turn.

The hour passed quickly, and it seemed they'd just gotten there when Grace, David and Susanna climbed in John's truck for the ride to Pizza Palace. There, they were shown to a private room. The owner was another member of John's church, and he had provided the refreshments for the group without charge.

John found a chair next to Grace, and soon they were talking as easily as they had on the afternoons when he drove her home from the clinic. It was just comfortable between them, so easy.

"This was really nice of you," she said as she handed Susanna a straw. "They both had a fantastic time."

"They are invited again next month, if their mothers approve," he said. "And you and Dakota, of course," he added.

"Thank you."

She smiled at him, and his pulse quickened. Grace had tucked her hair up into a knot and covered it with a small prayer cap, much like the ones Leslie and Caroline wore. Grace's dress was green with a white collar and tiny buttons at the throat. He thought she was the most beautiful woman he'd ever seen. Her nose was freckled and tilted up, her face was heart-shaped and she had eyes that sparkled when she looked at him.

She knew he was staring at her, and she blushed prettily and looked away. "Does your church do other things like this?" she said, glancing at the group's guests, eagerly devouring the cheese pizza.

"Plenty," he admitted. "They hold fundraisers to help educate two children in Peru, assist in housing repairs for the elderly locally—I volunteer for that. I put my way through college working at construction, so it's something I'm comfortable doing. And I know Leslie and Kyle help with the local Meals on Wheels program.

"Next Saturday is a Christmas bazaar," John said, "but that's to benefit the Mennonite School."

"You have your own school?"

He nodded. "Some of our members send their kids to public schools, but the majority educate their children privately. The bazaar is great. It gets bigger every year. I'd love to take you and Dakota, if you'd like to come. And Susanna and David, if you think they'd enjoy it. There's food and entertainment. They show movies for the kids that even Bishop Atlee would approve of, and we have our own popcorn machine."

"It sounds like fun. Dakota would love it. I'm not making any promises, but I'll mention it to Hannah and my sisters."

He smiled at her, and a delicious warmth curled in her chest. How easy it would be to let herself fall for John. *If only...* Grace caught herself. Why couldn't he have been Amish? Then all her problems would have been solved.

"You know you're always welcome at our church services, Grace. I know that you attend the Amish ones, but we worship every Sunday. I'd like you to come with me."

"A Mennonite service?" She shook her head. "It's not what I want, John. I don't know how to make you understand. I want to be... I have to be Amish."

"Maybe, but it wouldn't hurt to make certain. Ours is a solid faith. It's given me more than I could ever put into words. Don't forget, your sister Leah chose our path. It's not that far from the Old Amish way."

She shook her head. She could feel tears stinging the back of her eyelids, but she wouldn't let them fall. "No," she said quietly. "It's not what God wants for me."

"Are you certain of that?" John asked. "Or are you just too stubborn to see what's right in front of you?"

Chapter Twelve

Grace, Susanna and David returned to the Yoder house to find the kitchen crowded. After removing their outer garments and hanging them by the door, Susanna hurried to Hannah and began to tell her about the bowling, while a grinning David found his mother. In his hurry to seek her out, he'd forgotten to take off his hat. Sadie whispered in his ear, and he cheerfully returned to the door to hang his hat on the rack with those of the other men and boys. His crown was only a little flattened but still intact. Hanging on to it so that it wouldn't fall off, he went back and squeezed into a seat between his mother and Susanna.

With a squeal of happiness, Dakota ran to Grace and jumped into her arms. She would have liked nothing more than to take him to her peaceful room, close the door and spend the evening reading to him. She didn't want to answer questions in front of strangers about the bowling and pizza, and she didn't want to talk to anyone about John Hartman bringing her home in his wagon. But Grace knew that an evening of solitude with her son was impossible.

This was a visiting Sunday, and Hannah had company: Lemuel Bontrager and five of his eight children. The Bontragers had been invited to take a light supper, and Grace's sisters were busy bringing salads, bread, vegetable soup and all manner of side dishes, cakes and pies to the table. Lemuel, a bearded bear of a man with shaggy salt-and-pepper hair ringing a shiny bald spot on the crown of his head, was seated at the head of the table. His four oversize teenage sons—Clarence, Dieter, Claas and Ernst—lined up on the back bench beside Irwin. The fifth Bontrager offspring, a thin, pinch-faced young woman that Grace judged to be somewhere between seventeen and twenty, sat between Sadie and Aunt Jezzy. Violet Bontrager noisily slurped coffee and complained of what she perceived as loose behavior of the boys and girls who'd attended last night's husking frolic at the Beachy farm. She talked nonstop in a nasally whine, all the while staring at Grace with a disapproving glare. She paid no heed to the dribbles of coffee dripping from the corners of her mouth onto the table.

Grace gave Dakota another hug and seated him on a booster seat beside Jonah. After washing her hands at the sink and greeting the visitors, she began to help Johanna and Rebecca serve the food. Someone had set up a second table so that the Yoders, Bontragers and Kings could all sit together for their meal.

As she placed a bowl of chicken corn chowder in front of Violet, Grace smiled, murmured her own name and said that she was glad to meet her.

Violet sniffed and turned a cold shoulder before continuing her gripe to Sadie on the subject of worldly barn frolics in a respectable Amish community, most especially those including *Englishers*. "When we lived in

Kentucky, we had no truck with the English, and our bishop forbade all clapping games as inappropriate. Would you believe I saw a young woman wearing a fancy dress with flowers on it? She's the one who went off with the Englisher."

Johanna plunked down a yellow crockery bowl of pickled eggs and red beets with such force that it rattled Violet's silverware. "That would be our Grace, and Grace is family," she said, "not an outsider. My sister Grace is *rumspringa*. She may dress as she pleases and she did *not* go alone with the Englisher. Our sister was with her."

Violet's long face flushed and she uttered, "Hmmph. *Rumspringa?* Long in the tooth for *rumspringa*, if you ask me."

Grace knew "long in the tooth" was a reference to an aging horse. What a charming person. Grace's fingers itched to splash the next bowl of soup over Violet's wrinkled *Kapp*. Charity, Grace reminded herself. As rude as Violet was, she was a guest in Hannah's home, and Grace would have to be polite. Maybe she could just drop a bowl of baked beans in her lap.

But Violet wasn't finished sharing her opinion. "I suppose if Grace is *rumspringa*, she's the one who brought the radio to the bonfire and played cowboy music."

"Radio?" Lemuel tugged at his scraggly beard. "Bishop Atlee allows radios?" One thick brow arched in shocked disapproval.

"Ne!" Susanna popped out of her chair and waved her soup spoon at him. "Not Grace. Erb! Erb Stutzman bringed it. Charley took the radio away."

Hannah motioned Susanna back into her seat, and David whispered something to Susanna.

"Erb was mean to King David, too!" Susanna added. "He laughed." Her eyes narrowed. "Not a good laugh. Mean."

"Mean," David echoed.

"I'm glad you would never be mean to anyone, David," his mother soothed. "Erb Stutzman should know better."

"You see, Lemuel?" Hannah passed a plate of corn muffins. "Our Charley confiscated the radio. We are not so loose as to allow our young people to listen to music."

Lemuel grunted and reached for a muffin. He waded through two bowls of soup, several chicken quarters and a mountain of German potato salad before asking Hannah how many quarts of honey Johanna harvested from her beehives the previous spring, the number of quilts she had completed in the past year and how much livestock she owned.

Rebecca rolled her eyes, gathered Katie, Jonah and Dakota and shepherded them off to bed. The rest of the visit passed much as Grace feared it would. After the Yoder women cleared the meal away, they all retired to the parlor where Violet continued her recitation of complaints; the four Bontrager boys stared at the floor, and Lemuel's conversation was confined to inquiring as to the state of Johanna's and Rebecca's health, their ages and how many acres Hannah intended to deed to them when they married.

It was quarter past nine when the Bontrager buggy pulled away from the barn. Grace went to kiss Dakota good-night again, and finding her room empty, went upstairs where she met Rebecca in the hallway.

"The three little ones are all sleeping soundly in Jonah's bed," Rebecca said. "Let him stay there. He'll be fine." She glanced down the wide steps. "Are they gone?" And when Grace assured her that they were, Rebecca grabbed her hand and pulled her into the room she and Johanna shared.

"The martyrs preserve us," Johanna said, waving Grace to one of the double beds. "Sit, sit." She pushed the door shut. "I thought Lemuel was going to ask to see my teeth."

Rebecca giggled.

"What awful people," Grace said. "Who would want to marry one of Lemuel's sons? They never said a word all night. David had more to contribute to the conversation."

"Not the sons," Rebecca said between bursts of amusement. "Lemuel is considering Johanna for his wife, his third."

"He has two more?" Grace asked, confused.

This time it was Johanna who began to chuckle. "*Ne.* He is a widower, twice over, poor man. And he isn't awful. He's a perfectly respectable suitor, if I was looking to marry again."

"Aren't you?" Grace asked. This laughing side of Johanna was one she'd rarely seen. She remembered that Johanna had defended her to Violet, and that she'd been pleasant to her the past few days. But she'd never been in Johanna's room before, and she still felt a little uncomfortable.

Trying not to be obvious, Grace glanced around the kerosene lamp-lit room, taking in the serene white walls, the simple white muslin window covering and bare hardwood floor. There were two beds, two identical dressers and a wash stand with an antique bowl and pitcher. Between the windows stood a blanket chest, and in one corner rested an old quilt stand with an unfinished quilt hanging on it. "That's lovely," she said.

"Star of Bethlehem," Johanna said, clearly pleased. "An English woman ordered it for her daughter's wedding in July."

"All hand work," Rebecca explained. "No machine stitches."

"Your quilts are beautiful," Grace said. "You're a real artist. I don't know how you find the time to make them."

"It's hard some days," Johanna admitted. "And I'm still learning. I just do the old patterns." She kicked off her shoes and sat on the bed, curling her legs under her. "You should know, Grace, that Lemuel and his sons are not bad. They are very respectable people. Good catches, especially Lemuel."

"Lemuel?" Grace grimaced, trying hard not to imagine facing that beard across the breakfast table every morning. "You aren't considering him, are you?"

Johanna shook her head. "*Ne.* I had one husband, and I have no wish to have another." She sighed. "Lemuel has a fine farm and a good herd of milk cows, but Lemuel and I would not suit each other." She smiled. "Either of the oldest sons would make a decent match for Rebecca, though."

"Not me," Rebecca protested, holding up both hands. "I'm too young to get married. I want to have fun for a few more years. No husband and babies until I'm at least twenty-five."

Grace looked from one to the other. "How could your

mother let Lemuel ask such personal questions? It was rude. The Bontragers were all rude, especially Violet."

Johanna nodded. "She was, wasn't she? But marrying Lemuel or one of the sons would not be marrying Violet. She will marry and move to her own home. Maybe you should consider Lemuel, Grace. You want to marry Amish, don't you?"

"Yes, but not…not someone as…" She struggled to find a way to put it that wouldn't sound insulting. "As old as he is."

"You're certainly too old for any of the Bontrager sons," Rebecca put in. "The oldest is Clarence." She pursed her lips. "Or is it Claas? I don't know, I can't keep them straight. Anyway, the eldest is only twenty. He still owes his father another year of work on the farm."

Grace grimaced as she remembered Clarence's long face and the uneven sprigs of sprouting whiskers on his clean-shaven chin. "Definitely too young for me. I need someone who can provide well for my son and be a good father."

"Lemuel could, but he won't consider you," Johanna pronounced. "Not until you join the church and remain faithful for years."

"And learn proper Pennsylvania Dutch," Rebecca said.

"That, too," Johanna agreed. "You are older than me *and* English."

"I'm *not* English," Grace protested. "I was only raised among them. And Bishop Atlee said he would be pleased to accept me into the faith." *He hadn't said that in so many words,* Grace thought, *but it was cer-*

tainly what he'd meant. "There's no rule to keep me from joining the church."

"Few, if any, outsiders succeed," Johanna reminded her. "Our rules are strict. Had your mother remained with her family, she and Dat would have married, made confession, repented of their mistake and been accepted back into the fold."

"People would have forgiven them?" It was a question Grace had asked herself many times.

"We must," Johanna assured her. "If we can't forgive those who repent, how can we expect the Lord to forgive us?"

"Can He forgive anything?" Grace asked. "Could you?"

Johanna sighed. "For me, forgiving comes hard. My Wilmer…he took his own life. I know that I should forgive him. It's something I pray about every day. I can pray for his soul, for him as my children's father, but forgiving him is difficult."

"Your mother told me what happened." Grace traced the pattern of a blue heart on the quilt beneath them. "I'm sorry. It must have been terrible for you and the children."

"My Wilmer was a troubled man. Sick in spirit. In some ways, it will be easier for Jonah and Katie without him. Me…" A shadow passed across Johanna's face. "Sometimes, I go for hours now without thinking of him."

Grace's insides clenched. It was the same with Joe, except sometimes it was days before she thought of him. How strange it was that she and Johanna's lives were so similar.

Johanna smoothed wrinkles from her apron and

looked up. "But if you do stay with us, Grace, you will have to find a husband. And having men come to the house and ask about you is how it's done." She sighed. "And the truth is, it will only be an older widower who would consider you. Maybe even a man much older than Lemuel."

Rebecca nodded. "Or one with nine or ten children to cook and sew for. Could you do that?"

An uneasy feeling curled in the pit of Grace's stomach. "Anna did. Not nine children, but five. Look how happy she and Samuel are."

"Samuel and Anna." Johanna chuckled. "Who would have thought it?"

"She's still the talk of three states," Rebecca said. "Don't expect another Samuel Mast to drop out of an apple tree."

Johanna pressed warm fingers against Grace's wrist. "And you aren't Anna, Grace. Even for her, it's hard to manage so large a household, especially with the new baby coming."

"But having a man look me over like that, like tonight…" Grace said. "I don't know. Don't you find it insulting?"

Rebecca shrugged. "It's the way it's done."

"For Rebecca, who is young and attractive and never married, it will be easier to find a husband," Johanna explained. "While you and I, should I ever want to marry again, must be content to wait for some middle-aged widower to come knocking at Mam's door."

"Are you telling me that the women don't get to choose?" Grace asked.

Johanna considered the question before answering. "We do choose, but we depend on family and community to help in that choice. And we must find a husband from who's available. First, you would want a devout man, a faithful member of the church. And then, as you say, one who would be a good provider."

"Kind," Rebecca put in. "Hopefully, even-tempered."

"Which is why Lemuel Bontrager would not be a bad match for you, Grace. If he would have you—which he won't. By the time you are ready to marry Amish, some other woman will have snapped him up."

"Even with Violet to contend with?" Grace teased.

"Ya," Johanna replied. "Even with Violet and the seven boys." She chuckled. "So, big sister..." Her eyes twinkled. "Don't be so quick to turn away John Hartman."

"John?" Grace felt her throat and face grow warm. "He isn't Amish."

"Neither are you," Rebecca pointed out.

"You don't understand," Grace argued. "I can't consider John. Marrying Amish is something I have to do. I couldn't stand to lose all of you now that I've come to love you."

Johanna stood up. "I suppose you know your own mind better than we do. But..." She hesitated. "As our father always told me, 'Open your eyes, Johanna. Sometimes the thing that will make you happiest is right in front of your face and you're just too stubborn to see it.'"

On Thursday evening, John arrived home in time to share a hot meal with his grandfather and uncle. He'd had another crazy week, and the only time he'd been able to speak to Grace had been a few minutes two days earlier when she had finished work and was waiting for the van to pick her up. He'd offered to drive her home, but she'd refused. Shamelessly, he'd reminded her of the Christmas bazaar on Saturday and had invited her to a potluck supper his church was having afterward. Grace hadn't refused, but she hadn't accepted, either, and he couldn't help wondering if she was still put out with him over the whole hay wagon episode.

"You're just in time," Gramps said as John entered the kitchen. "You're in for a real treat."

John glanced at Uncle Albert and groaned. "What is it? Fish sticks and canned peas again? Or that frozen lasagna that tastes like cardboard with ketchup poured over it?"

"You'll be laughing out of the other side of your face once you taste my one-dish wonder," Gramps said. Uncle Albert made a show of trying to lift the lid off the Crock-Pot and peek inside. "No, you don't," Gramps said, smacking Uncle Albert's fingers with a long-handled wooden spoon. "And it's your turn to wash dishes, Albert."

"It's not," John's uncle protested. "It's John's turn. I washed last night."

John laughed as he retrieved napkins from the counter. "No, you didn't. If you recall, you had that emergency. You had to check the IV pump on Bruce Taylor's poodle. At eight o'clock at night." The animal hospital was right next door, but it was amazing how long it could take his uncle to check on a patient when there were dishes to be washed.

"Never can tell," Uncle Albert replied. "That pump might not have been running properly and then Elvis would have been in dire straits."

"Convenient timing," Gramps grumbled. "Getting you to load the dishwasher is like trying to get a cat to clean its own litter box. Mighty rare occurrence."

Everyone laughed and then the three gathered around the table, sat and held hands while Gramps asked the blessing. He then carried the Crock-Pot to the table. "Behold," he said, whipping off the glass lid. "My masterpiece."

"It's Hamburger Helper with that funny-shaped rice, isn't it?" John teased.

"Be thankful for what you receive," Gramps said. "People in third-world countries would consider this a feast." He scooped out a congealed lump of mystery supper and dropped it onto John's plate.

"I was right," John said, reaching for the hot sauce. "Burger and a box of dried mystery ingredients."

"With peas and canned corn added," Gramps said proudly. "Smells delicious, doesn't it?"

"Smells like a barn that needs to be cleaned," Uncle Albert observed. "Are you sure you didn't add hoof trimmings to this?" He stuck a fork into his portion and left it standing upright. "How many hours did you leave this in the Crock-Pot, Dad?"

"Nine, ten tops."

Gramps sat down in front of his portion, took a forkful and chewed slowly. John and his uncle watched as Gramps washed the first bite down with water, liberally salted the meat, rice and vegetable mix and took another bite. Then, he dropped the fork and began to laugh deep belly laughs. Uncle Albert and John joined in, laughing until tears rolled down their cheeks.

"A masterpiece," Uncle Albert proclaimed between guffaws.

Gramps shook his head, then looked at John. "Well, boy, are you going to call for pizza delivery or am I?" And then they all laughed again.

Uncle Albert pulled his cell phone from his shirt pocket and hit the speed dial. "Albert Hartman," he said. "Yes, the usual. Thanks a lot." He closed the phone. "Twenty minutes." He looked down at the plates. "I suppose we could save this for—"

John shook his head. "Not even the Yoders' chickens could eat this."

"Guess not." Gramps was still chuckling. "But while we're waiting for that pizza delivery, Albert and I want to talk to you about something. It concerns Grace Yoder."

John's stomach clenched. Grace was one subject he didn't want to talk about. "Business or personal?"

"The practice," Uncle Albert said.

John almost heaved a sigh of relief. "Grace is doing her job, isn't she?"

"Absolutely." Uncle Albert gathered up the plates and scraped the inedible meal into the trash can. "Sue came to me this morning. It seems Grace is a wonder. Not only is she the best kennel tech we've ever had working for us, but she's very observant. She picked up on a case of diabetes in the Winklers' cat. It was just here for boarding while the Winklers went on vacation. Sue says Grace is a natural with animals."

"I'm glad she's working out," John said, wondering where this was heading.

"You know Patel's practice at the beach—the big one? Sue says that they're sending a young woman to Del Tech for their vet tech program. It's not a bad idea for us to consider doing the same. You know how difficult it is to find and keep good techs."

"I know," John agreed. "And as happy as Melody

seems here, and as much as we like her, her husband's Air Force. He could get orders and we'd lose her."

"What would you think if we offered Grace Yoder a scholarship?" His uncle rinsed off the plates. "We could work out something where she could stay on, at least part-time while she went to school. But it's a big commitment. Do you believe she'd be interested?"

"I don't know," John answered slowly. "I think she'd make a great vet tech, but she doesn't have a car. We'd have to come up with transportation for her, so she could get back and forth to school." He was so relieved that neither of them had brought up his personal relationship with Grace that he was babbling. "Maybe we could—"

"That's no problem," Gramps interrupted. "Your grandmother's Buick is sitting in the garage. Hasn't been started since she passed, but it's in good shape. Not more than 50,000 miles on it. The girl may as well drive it as have it rust away. I should have sold it three years ago, but there's a lot of things I should do. Grace has a little boy to support, doesn't she?"

John nodded. "He's three years old."

"Well, you tell her to come and speak to me. It's not easy for a woman to raise a child alone. If she's willing to work for us for what we pay, I think I can let her have that car, whether she wants to study to be a vet tech or not. It's a solid vehicle, be safe for the child."

"That's good of you, Gramps." John fiddled with his napkin. "But I have to tell you that Grace thinks she wants to become Amish. She may not accept the car."

Uncle Albert smiled and shook his head. "That's not going to happen. The only person I ever knew around here who joined the Amish from the outside is Hannah

Yoder. And the Old Order Mennonite church she was raised in wasn't much different. I don't think we have to worry about Grace giving up the world."

"So you think it's a good idea?" Gramps asked.

"I do," John agreed. He hoped Grace would accept.

"Need to talk to you about something else, too," his grandfather said, "while we're at it."

By the time John realized where his grandfather was headed, it was too late to make a hasty retreat.

"This relationship you have with this girl. She's an employee, John. Business and friendship don't always make for good partners."

"I've thought about that," he replied, "but I think it's too late. If you want the truth, I think I'm already in love with her."

"You thought you were in love with Miriam Yoder," Uncle Albert pointed out good-naturedly. "What is it with you and those Yoder girls?"

"I thought I was at the time," John admitted. "But this is different—the way I feel about Grace is different. I'm scared. I got my heart broken before with Miriam, and I know I'm taking a big chance. If it happens again with Grace, it will be a lot worse." He looked first into his uncle's face and then met his grandfather's level gaze. "I want to marry Grace, and I want to be a father to her son."

"Sounds to me like you've thought this through pretty good," Gramps said. "Prayed over it, have you?"

"Every night," John said.

"Then you've got to take the chance," Uncle Albert said. "You can't go through life afraid. Sometimes, you have to take a leap of faith and hope for the best."

Chapter Thirteen

Grace gave in and went to the bazaar at the Mennonite School with John. Once there, she was glad she had. It was the kind of Christmas atmosphere that she dreamed of but knew she wouldn't find in the Yoder household. Both she and Dakota enjoyed it tremendously. Familiar carols filled the air as the three of them drank hot chocolate and stopped to admire an elaborate model train display featuring a snow-covered papier-mâché mountain, miniature farms and a Victorian village.

Grace, John and Dakota wandered up and down the aisles of craft tables, tasting samples of brownies and Christmas goodies and chatting with John's friends and clients. Grace was pleasantly surprised to see that many of the shoppers were Amish. She wished Susanna could have come with her, but her sister had decided at the last minute to accompany Rebecca to Anna's to bake cookies. Grace suspected her choice had more to do with the possibility of David's presence there than her desire to bake, but Grace's feelings weren't hurt. In a way, she was proud of the stubbornness Susanna was displaying in regard to her friendship with David.

After walking around for a while, John had to excuse himself to act as short-order cook in the kitchen while a friend took a lunch break. "Not the best choice," John remarked as he donned an apron. "I'm not much of a cook." He flashed a smile at her. "Hopefully, I can manage hot dogs and hamburgers."

"We need him for only an hour," a rosy-cheeked, middle-aged woman with a lace prayer cap called through the open kitchen door. She waved to Grace.

Grace waved back and led Dakota away. She'd drawn Jonah's name in the family gift exchange, and had planned to take this time to search for a special present for him. As with all else, as Rebecca had considerately explained, Amish Christmases were austere and noncommercial. Jonah would receive a few simple items from Johanna, including a new pair of boots, mittens and a toolbox with a small hammer and screwdriver. Other than those, the gift Grace purchased would be all he received.

Christmas fell on a church Sunday this year, but Hannah had explained to Grace that services would be postponed until the following week. December twenty-fifth would be a quiet family day of prayer, fasting and Bible reading. The following day was the Amish Second Christmas, the time for visiting and gift giving. Hannah and the girls would prepare a big holiday dinner for the occasion.

Grace led Dakota around a table and his eyes grew wide and he bounced up and down at the sight of a big Christmas tree. The decorations were all handmade, and instead of lights, someone had strung popcorn and cranberries to adorn the boughs. Beneath the tree, visitors to the bazaar and members of the Mennonite Church had left heaps of wrapped gifts designated for local children of incarcerated parents. "Look! Look, Mommy!" Dakota cried. "Are we having a Christmas tree?"

Grace's heart sank. "No," she said softly. "The Amish don't believe in them." She bent and hugged her son. "But this year, we'll be with family. It will be a wonderful Christmas, I promise you."

They strolled on, lingering near a small stage where a high-school student played "Oh, Little Town of Bethlehem" on a much-loved and battered piano, accompanied by a young man with a guitar. The sweet notes brought tears to Grace's eyes, and she squeezed Dakota's hand tighter. *We're not giving up Christmas,* she told herself. *We're just moving to a simpler celebration of Christ's birth.*

Still, she stood transfixed, listening to the music, unable to keep her thoughts from drifting. A long, long time ago… That year, the highlight of the holiday for her had been the opportunity to play the part of the innkeeper's wife in a Sunday-school pageant. There had been a small pile of gifts for her under her foster mother's tree, but she couldn't remember a single one. What she did remember was the excitement of standing behind the dusty drapes waiting to step on stage and recite her lines.

It had been a bitter night with a foot of snow on the ground and wind that howled around the corners of the building. It was so cold that each breath Grace took sent little clouds of condensation into the air. But when those first notes of "Oh, Little Town of Bethlehem" wheezed from the church organ, she'd been transfixed by the magic and beauty of Christmas.

The Christmas pageant was one of Grace's most

treasured memories, one that had given her pleasure over the years. Secretly, she had always hoped that Dakota would get to experience that same thrill some day. He might even get to play the part of Joseph or one of the three kings when he was older. She smiled at her own foolishness. What she was giving him was far more important: a family, a sense of community and a faith to sustain him when life got tough…. Because it would. Grace wasn't naive enough to think that becoming Amish would solve *all* their problems. Being Amish didn't mean that bad things would never happen to her or Dakota. It simply meant that if they did, she and he would be able to accept God's will and find the strength to carry on.

"I want a guitar," Dakota said. "I want to play a guitar like you."

Grace swallowed, trying to ignore the inner twinge of regret that thoughts of her beloved guitar brought to mind. Musical instruments were forbidden to the Amish, and she'd stored her guitar in Hannah's attic. *I should sell it or give it away,* she thought. *The longer I hold on to it, the more difficult it will be to let it go. Someone may as well enjoy it.*

"Come on," she said, hurrying Dakota away. "We have to find a gift for Jonah. Remember? But it's a surprise. You can't tell what we get him."

"I won't tell," he promised, glancing back over his shoulder at the guitar player as she tugged him away.

"We need something special." Grace glanced around at the booths containing gently used items. "Something that doesn't need batteries."

"Look!" Dakota pointed. Under a table, sticking out

of a cardboard box, was a red roof. "It's a barn," he said. "Like one at my old school."

Grace knelt to pull out the box. Inside was a sturdy plastic barn filled with a tumbled heap of matching animals: cows, horses, chickens, a goat and pigs. There were sections of fence and even a tiny milk bucket and toy bales of hay. "I hope it's not too expensive," she murmured. The toys were well-made and perfect for a small Amish boy, but Johanna had warned her not to spend more than twenty dollars.

The gray-haired lady behind the counter smiled at Dakota when Grace asked how much the barn set was. "For you, young man?" the woman asked Dakota.

He shook his head. "For my cousin. For Christmas." He brought his finger to his lips. "But it's a secret," he warned in a loud whisper.

The woman lifted the box onto the table and examined the barn. "It isn't new," she said. "And one of the doors is cracked on the barn, and there's a little water stain inside. Wait." She rummaged behind the counter and came up with a tiny wagon and a handful of toy sheep. "This must go with it. I've been wondering what to do with those sheep. Would ten dollars be too much?"

"Not at all." Grace was counting out the money when Leslie, whom she'd met at the bowling outing the previous Saturday, approached her. Three small children trailed her.

Grace thanked the woman at the table and turned away, the box with the barn and animals in her arms.

"Hi," Leslie said. "John sent me to look for you. We're starting a movie about the nativity story in the auditorium and he thought Dakota might enjoy it. We're going to have popcorn and apple juice. If you'll let me take him, I'll watch out for him. I promise."

"Can I?" Dakota looked up at Grace with a sweet smile on his face. "Can I go?"

"It's just right through that doorway," Leslie explained. "You can join us, too, if you like."

"All right," Grace agreed. "I just want to get the truck keys from John and put this—" she lifted the box "—into the cab."

Dakota waved as he walked away, holding Leslie's hand.

By the time Grace reached the cafeteria window, John was already finishing his shift. He insisted on carrying Jonah's present to the truck. "I've wanted to get you alone all morning," he said. "I have something important to talk to you about."

"What is it?" Grace asked, fighting an uneasy feeling. She hoped John didn't want to talk about dating again. He was wearing her down with his kindness.

"It's about work." He smiled at her. "Wait until we get outside."

Relieved and intrigued, Grace followed him to the truck. John slid the box of toys onto the backseat, and then opened the passenger front door for her to get in. "It's too cold to stand out here." He went around to the driver's side and joined her in the cab. "Uncle Albert and my grandfather came up with this idea," he said. "It's a great opportunity. I hope you'll at least think about it."

Grace listened as John explained about the vet tech associate's degree the community college offered. A small flame of hope flared in the pit of her stomach. She tamped it down. She couldn't be understanding this correctly. The Hartmans couldn't possibly be offering to send her to college—to pay for her to learn a profession. She loved working with animals, but she'd never imagined that she'd ever have the chance to....

"They believe in you," John continued. "I believe in you. We think that you can do this."

He went on to tell her the solutions they'd come up with for continued part-time work at the clinic and transportation, but she was still stunned by the possibilities. Being a vet tech would mean more money and a real career. She was speechless.

"So what do you think?" John clasped her hand in his. "Is it something that you'd consider?"

She swallowed, trying to dissolve the lump in her throat, and then burst into tears. Mortified, she jerked her hand away and covered her face, unable to hold back.

"Grace, don't," he begged. "Don't cry. What did I say?" He reached for her and she buried her face in his coat and sobbed. "Did I say something wrong? Did I insult you?"

She pulled back, now beginning to laugh through the tears. "No," she managed. "I'm…I'm…just…so happy." She wanted to turn handstands in the parking lot. She shook her head, wanting to pinch herself to be certain this wasn't a dream. She fumbled in her purse for a tissue but couldn't find one.

He pulled a clean red-and-white handkerchief from his coat pocket and handed it to her. "If you're happy, you have a weird way of showing it."

She chuckled and he began to laugh with her as she wiped her eyes and blew her nose on the handkerchief.

"I don't know what to say," she gasped. "I feel like such an idiot."

"But you're pleased?"

She nodded. "Thrilled."

"Great. Fantastic."

She balled the handkerchief and stuck it in her own coat pocket. "I can't believe it. I never thought I'd ever have the chance to go to college. I always wanted to, but…" Her eyes filled with tears again.

"So you'd do it?" he insisted, rubbing her arm. "You're willing to do it?"

"Yes, yes, of course." She looked into his eyes and began to laugh again. "What kind of man carries handkerchiefs in his pocket?"

John groaned. "I know. I know. But Uncle Albert always does, and my aunt kept putting them in my pocket when I was a boy. I guess it's a habit."

"That came in handy today," Grace admitted.

"It did, didn't it?" John's smile widened and she couldn't help thinking how handsome he was.

"So you'll do it?"

"I…" She hesitated, suddenly struck by the thought that it might not be entirely up to her. "Unless…" Her stomach pitched. "Unless it's against the rules… Amish rules. I don't suppose being a vet tech is much different than what I'm doing now," she said hopefully. "But I'll have to ask…ask Hannah."

"You have time. The next session doesn't begin until February."

"I'll talk to her first thing when I get home."

"You and Dakota are still staying for the potluck supper, aren't you? The kids have a great time." He looked into her eyes. "I want you to, Grace. Please say you'll stay."

Moth wings fluttered in the pit of her stomach. She opened the truck door and sucked in a deep breath of cold, fresh air. When she summoned nerve enough to look back at him, she was struck by the vulnerability in his face. "Are you certain I...we'll be welcome?"

She was stalling, wanting to refuse, wanting to keep this as a day between friends...not a date. Letting herself care about John was dangerous. She couldn't have both John and the forgiveness she needed to go forward with her life. No matter how she wished that things could be different, John couldn't fit into her plan.

"Of course you'd both be welcome, but..." He knotted his right hand, pressing it against the leather seat. "I don't want to pressure you, Grace. I don't want you to feel uncomfortable. But I think you know that I'd like us to be more than friends."

She nodded. "It's probably best if you take us home. So that I can talk to Hannah," she added quickly. "This... the bazaar has been great. I've had a good time...really. But..."

He nodded. "All right. I understand."

But you don't, she thought, reading the disappointment in his eyes. *You don't understand at all. And if you knew the truth about me, you probably wouldn't want to have anything to do with me again. Ever.*

Two hours later, Grace stood in Hannah's kitchen staring at her stepmother in bewilderment. "I don't understand," Grace said. "I'll have to work part-time for two years until I finish the program, but I'll still be bringing money into the house. And after that, when I've become a vet tech, my wages will—"

"Ne," Hannah repeated. She laid the rolling pin on the floured board and folded her arms over her chest and shook her head. "I am sorry, Grace, but you cannot do this."

"Is it because of the driving? I could take a van to school if you don't want me to use the car." She hadn't known about this opportunity a few hours ago, and now she wanted it desperately.

"Oh, child." Hannah's expression softened and she dusted her floury hands on her apron. "You can't do this at all."

"But why?" Grace's chest tightened.

"If you truly want to be one of us, you must learn to accept the rules of our community. We do not believe in higher education. It's why our children don't go to high school or to any English school at all. It's why they leave the classroom after the eighth grade. There is no college for us," she added softly.

"But it doesn't make any sense," Grace argued.

Hannah took several steps and extended a hand. "I told you that it wouldn't be easy…for you to make the journey from your world into ours. You must understand."

"Maybe if I went to the elders and explained…"

Again Hannah shook her head. "You heard what the bishop told you. He will make no decisions for you. But if you do this, you will not be allowed to become one of us." She offered a half smile. "Believe me, daughter, no Amish man would consider you as wife if you persist."

"But you work," Grace argued. "You're a teacher. Surely—"

"I had worked as a teacher before I married and returned to it after Jonas died. I did have some studies by mail, but I never went to college. And if...*when* I remarry, I won't be allowed to work any longer."

"How can a higher education interfere with my becoming Amish? With how I serve God?"

"Some things must not be questioned, but simply accepted. Remember, we are a people commanded to remain apart from the world. If you want to continue, you must refuse this offer and keep cleaning the kennels or find another job...a job suitable for an Amish woman. You must do this if you want to be considered for admittance to the church."

"There's no way?"

"None," Hannah replied. "You must choose, Grace. This college or our faith."

She nodded. *She wouldn't cry, she couldn't.* She felt numb inside. *This means that Dakota can never attend college, either,* she realized. *Not even high school.* Slowly, she lowered her head in defeat.

"Your choice," Hannah repeated. "You must learn to accept the *Ordnung,* to submit your will to the laws of our community. Or find a different path," she said softly.

"I have to tell John," she said. "He's waiting outside in the truck. It's only fair. That way, they can find someone else."

"I'm sorry," Hannah said. "I know this seems unfair to you, but it's best. And if you've made up your mind, best to let him know your decision."

Woodenly, Grace left the kitchen, not even stopping long enough to put on her coat. She didn't feel the cold as she crossed the porch and passed through the open gate. John saw her, smiled and waved. She straightened her shoulders, knowing that explaining why she couldn't accept his offer would be hard.

He got out of the truck and came toward her. "What did Hannah say?" he called. "Does she think the bishop will allow—"

She raised a hand, palm up, and a gust of wind hit her hard enough to almost knock her off her feet. "It isn't what you wanted to hear," she said, raising her voice. "I'm sorry, but…" She stumbled through the explanation, repeating the phrases Hannah had used. How could she expect him to understand when he didn't know her reasons?

"No! You can't let them dictate to you, Grace. This is too important a decision for anyone else to make for you. You want it. I know you do."

"I can't fight this," she said, wrapping her arms around her waist. "If I went to college, I couldn't join the church."

"Then don't join the church. Have the courage to make your own life. You have a God-given talent for working with sick and hurt animals. It would be a sin to waste that gift because…"

He was upset, more than upset. John was angry with her. Suddenly weary and heartsick, she stopped listening to him. It wasn't just the job. John still hadn't realized that there was no future for them.

"Stop!" she said. "Just stop talking and listen to me." She tried to sound tough, but her teeth were chattering. It was difficult to be forceful when she was so cold that goose bumps were rising on her arms and legs. "I need to tell you something…something that will…"

"You're shivering," he said, removing his fleece-lined jean jacket and draping it around her shoulders. "Get in the truck."

"Is that an order?"

"*Please* get in the truck."

What difference did it make? Once he knew what she was, she probably wouldn't even have her kennel tech position. But it didn't matter. She was tired of living a lie...tired of hiding.

She was still shivering after she climbed inside the cab. She pulled John's coat around her, raised her chin and looked him in the eye. *God help me,* she prayed. *I have to tell him.*

"Okay," he said, putting his arm on the back of the seat. "Let's have it. You're still married to Dakota's father, aren't you? You're going to tell me that I've fallen hard for a married woman."

"That's just it," she whispered huskily. She made herself look him in the eyes. "There is no husband. There never was."

Chapter Fourteen

John waited. Grace stared down at her hands…small hands, unpolished, but strong and graceful. Like she was, he thought. He loved Grace's hands…wanted to take them in his and hold them and never let go.

Silence stretched between them. "That's it?" he finally asked. "You weren't married when Dakota was born? That's what's making you so unhappy?"

Her answer came in a small voice, the tones almost childlike. "You know what that makes my son?" She looked him in the eyes. "What people will call him if they know?"

"Mean-spirited people. But they won't say it around me or Hannah or your sisters, I can promise you that." He reached for her hand, but she shrank away, hunching against the door, clutching his coat around her. Her shoulders trembled. *Was she crying?* The instinct to protect her that he'd felt when they'd first met rushed back, a hundred times stronger. She was so young to have faced so many obstacles so bravely. But she wasn't alone anymore, not if he could help it.

"Grace, look at me."

She pressed her face against the glass. "I haven't told anyone. Even Hannah doesn't know." A small sob shook her. "When I tell her, I'll probably have to leave."

"That's crazy. Do you think that your family would turn against you for a mistake? That *I* would?"

Her breath fogged the window and she rubbed at it with a slender fingertip. "Because I lied…because I let everyone believe that I was a widow."

"Dakota's father abandoned the two of you?"

"No." Her breath caught in her throat with a small sound. "He *was* a bull rider. He *was* killed in a rodeo accident."

John couldn't help feeling a little relieved that Grace hadn't lied about her husband passing away, that she didn't have an old love who could come back into her life to claim her and Dakota. He tried to tell himself that it was despicable to feel that for the passing of another human being, but all he could think of was that Grace and Dakota—*his* Grace and Dakota were free.

Hope replaced uncertainty as his heartbeat quickened. No matter what it took, he'd convince her that she wasn't meant to be Amish. She liked riding in his truck and listening to the radio. She was friendly and outgoing with the people who came to the office, and she had a special way with animals. And no matter how hard she tried to convince him otherwise, he knew that she desperately wanted to further her education for her future and that of her son.

"Broncs, too."

John snapped out of his thoughts. Grace was speaking to him. Had he been thinking of her so intensely that he'd missed something important? "Excuse me," he said. "Broncs?"

"Bucking broncos. Rodeo horses. He rode them." She half turned. Her voice was little more than a whisper, but huskier than a little girl's. It resonated under his skin. "As I told you, Joe Eagle, Dakota's father, was Native American."

"Dakota's a beautiful child, and his heritage is something to be proud of."

"He looks different than his cousins. He always will."

"He's an individual, Grace, as are you. It's a good thing." He hesitated, and then asked the question that had troubled him the most. "Did you love him—Dakota's father?"

"I thought I did." She shivered, nearly lost in his big coat. "Yes, I did love him at first. I wanted so bad to have someone, a husband...a home. But Joe wasn't an easy man to live with. He had his own demons to fight, and sometimes he took it out on Dakota and me. When Joe died, I think I was more sad than grieving. Such a waste..." Her mouth firmed. "And when—"

"It doesn't matter," John said. "That's all in the past. You don't have to tell me anything you don't want to."

"But I want to." Some of the spunk came back into her and she raised her pointed chin and met his gaze straight on. Her blue eyes glistened with tears. "It was wrong of me to deceive Hannah and...and everyone. You don't know how many nights I've lain awake praying for forgiveness...praying for the strength to tell the truth. I did exactly what Joe did, deceived the ones I should have been the most honest with. But I was so scared..." A single tear welled up and splashed against a pale cheek. "We're all alone, the two of us. I wanted someone...somewhere to belong."

John fought the urge to pull her into his arms, to cradle her against his chest and promise to make everything all right. The desire to protect her, to make her his wife and to become a real father to Dakota was nearly overwhelming. But he could sense that like a terrified filly that had tangled herself in a barbed-wire fence, if he came on too fast or too strong, she'd panic.

Life had buffeted Grace Yoder until she was at the breaking point. If he reached for her, she might run, and he could lose any chance of making her understand that none of it mattered—that he could never judge her for the mistake of having a child out of wedlock. "Grace, it's all right," he soothed with the same tone he'd use on an injured filly.

"No! It's not. You have to listen. I don't know if I've got the nerve to tell this twice."

He nodded, folding his hands to be sure he didn't reach for her. "If you want to, but I'm here for you. Believe me, I know what kind of person you are. If you made a mistake—"

"My mistake was in being stupid. When I first met Joe, I was stranded in the middle of nowhere. I'd been walking for hours, and it was almost dark when he stopped to pick me up in his truck. They can say all they want about cowboys, but he didn't come on to me like I was cheap."

John shook his head. "No one could ever call you cheap, Grace."

"Just listen, *please,*" she begged.

John nodded and Grace went on. "Joe drove me to the next town and introduced me to a retired Baptist minister and his wife who followed the rodeo circuit. Mrs. Bray had broken her hip and needed help. I stayed with them for two months until the season was over. Joe and I dated, but I never did anything to be ashamed of, not with him, not with any man. Then Joe asked me to marry him. I was afraid that he'd leave and I'd never see him again. I knew that it was too soon, that we hadn't known each other long enough, but I said yes, anyway."

"I don't understand," John said. "He asked you to marry him, but then went back on his word?"

"Oh, he married me, all right. Reverend Bray married us and Mrs. Bray witnessed it. I have a license from the State of Wyoming to prove it."

"If you had a marriage ceremony, then…" His shoulders tightened. "This Bray wasn't a real minister?"

"He was the real thing, all right. It was Joe who wasn't the real thing."

"I don't understand," John protested. "How could—"

"Shh." She put her fingers over his lips. "I'm trying to tell you. After…after the accident, things were bad. There were so many bills. Joe had told me he was an orphan, that he didn't have anyone like me. But when I was going through his things, I found a Christmas card from his mother, dated the previous December. I wrote to the address, but I didn't get an answer. For Dakota's sake, I had to try to make some kind of connection with her. I'd had to sell Joe's truck for rent money, and it took me a long time to get enough money for another vehicle. When I did, we drove to the reservation. I just wanted her to meet her grandson."

John winced at the pain etched across her face.

"I found her, but I wish I hadn't. She called me awful names—told me she wished Dakota had never been born. She said that I'd tricked her son, led him to abandon his family—that we should be the ones dead, not Joe." A sob shook her. "You see, I thought I was Joe's wife, but I wasn't. He already had a wife and two children on the reservation. He was married to a woman named Bernadette when he made his vows to me. So... so, I was never really Mrs. Joe Eagle. I was just Grace Yoder."

She reached for the door latch, but John seized her arm. "It's not your fault," he said. "If there was wrong, it was Joe's, not yours, and not Dakota's. How could anyone blame you for—"

She whipped around. "For being stupid? For believing a good-looking rodeo rider with a two-thousand-dollar saddle and a mouthful of lies?" She pulled free. "It's why I have to become Amish, John. It's why I have to do this. If I accept baptism in the Amish faith, God will forgive me—the stain on Dakota's birth will be wiped away."

"Grace, listen to me!"

But it was too late. She flung open the door and jumped out. He climbed out the passenger door and followed her halfway to the gate. "Wait! Can't we talk?"

She stopped and looked back. "Your coat," she said, slipping it off and throwing it to him.

"Grace, listen, I know you're upset. I can come back later. Tomorrow—"

"No." She shook her head. "There's nothing left to say. I've made up my mind, and you won't talk me out of what I know is the right thing to do for me and my son."

"Wanting God in your life is a good thing," he said. "But your father's path isn't the only one."

"It's my business, John! Not yours. No one asked you to interfere in my life."

He felt as though a hard fist had punched him in the gut. He stood there, coat dangling in his hand with the rain pelting his face. "All right, I'm sorry you feel that way. But maybe you're right. Maybe it isn't any of my business. I'll pick you up Monday morning for work, and then we can—"

"No." She started for the house again. "I can see now that I should never have taken the job in the first place. I have to be apart from the world. Being at the clinic—"

"I won't let you quit," he said, following her through the gate. "It's not what you want—not what I want."

"You can't stop me from quitting." She was shivering again. "Tell your uncle that I'm sorry to not give notice, but it's best for everyone if I leave now without a fuss."

"You're making the biggest mistake of your life," he said. "You think about it—about what you're doing. About what's best for Dakota. I'll be here Monday morning."

"Didn't you just hear what I said?" she cried, stopping to turn around again. "I'm not coming. I'm not working for you anymore. Tell your uncle I appreciate the offer of the scholarship, but my new faith won't allow me to accept. Give it to someone else, someone who will appreciate it."

She ran up the steps and into the house, slamming the door behind her. John stood there, wondering what he could have done differently, feeling the woman he'd come to love slipping away from him. He got back into the truck, and tightened his fingers around the steering wheel, using every ounce of his will to keep from punching the dashboard.

Anger rode him as he started the engine and drove out of the yard and down the lane. Anger clouded his thoughts and made him doubt his judgment. Maybe his grandfather was right. Maybe he had fallen too quickly for Grace. Maybe he wanted her because Miriam had rejected him.

The wipers swished back and forth. He wanted to tramp down on the accelerator and put distance between him and Grace, but he didn't. A lifetime of concern for other people was too hard to shake. Instead, he did what he always did when he was confronted with overwhelming problems. He found a safe place to pull off the road, put his truck into park, lowered his head and murmured the Twenty-Third Psalm aloud. And as always, he found comfort in the old words from the St. James version of the Bible. When he was done, he sat in silence for a long time before uttering a simple prayer.

"God, it's John Hartman, again. I'd appreciate it if you could help me out here. I'm in deep water and I can't even see the shore."

When Grace reentered the kitchen, Hannah and Aunt Jezzy turned to look at her. "What were you thinking, child," Hannah said, "to run out in this weather without your coat?"

Grace murmured something and hurried past them into the hallway, but she didn't go to her bedroom. She wanted to be alone, and if she went there, Dakota—who was happily playing with Jonah and Katie—might follow her. Instead, she climbed the stairs to the second floor and then another flight to the attic.

The air was chilly up here, but one section was always kept as an extra guest bedroom. The space was whitewashed and tidy, the antique maple bed and stacks of quilts a welcoming retreat. She wrapped a blue-and-white quilt around her shoulders, removed her shoes and curled up on the bed. Two windows allowed light into the chamber, and even with the rain coming down, Grace could see well enough.

Telling John her secret hadn't worked out the way she expected. Why was it that nothing in her life ever did? He should have been disgusted, repelled by her deceit. Instead, he'd made excuses for her, blamed Joe and tried to talk her out of the only plan that made sense. Why couldn't John see that becoming Amish would cleanse her and secure her salvation? Why was he so stubborn? Why couldn't he accept her decision and her resignation without driving her to say awful things that would end their friendship? And why did he believe that she wasn't strong enough to renounce the world to save herself and her son?

John was the one who was in the wrong here. Why had he ruined such a beautiful day? Dakota had enjoyed the Christmas bazaar as much as she had. She'd loved the music, the decorations, the bustle of holiday shopping, and she'd been so happy with the barn set she'd found for Jonah.

When John had offered her the opportunity to become a vet tech, she couldn't believe her good fortune. She'd forgotten what was important. She'd hoped that she could have both worlds, the peace she'd found here among her father's family and friends, and the excitement of working at a job she loved.

John had meant well. She knew that. If things were different, having John in her life would have been…

No! She wouldn't think about that. John Hartman wasn't for her. All he was—all he could ever be—was a temptation. Letting herself fall in love with John would ruin everything. And she could…so easily…she could. She could imagine the three of them, John, her and Dakota, laughing together over the supper table, cutting down a Christmas tree and decorating it, singing along with the country and Christian artists on his truck radio.

She could choose John and his way of life…even now. She could go to him and say she was sorry, ask him if they could start over. And he would agree; she was certain of it. But in opening her heart to John and his world, she would be closing the door to what mattered most. Forgiveness.

The rainfall intensified, and big drops spattered against the windowpanes. The Lord had brought her this far. It would be wrong to abandon the plan now. Her mother and father had both been born into the Amish faith. She wasn't doing anything radical, not really. She was simply coming home, where she belonged, where she and her precious little son would find peace and happiness. If the price of that was giving up John, so be it. This was her last chance to turn her life around.

Far better to choose a good man, even one like Lemuel Bontrager, and marry him. What had Hannah said? Marriage was bigger than two people. Surely, if she picked a solid Amish husband, one she could respect, love would follow. And if it didn't, she'd married for what she thought was love once before, and that match had turned hollow.

She could never wish that she hadn't met Joe. If not for Joe, she wouldn't have Dakota, and life without her son was impossible to consider. She'd made a foolish decision when she married Joe Eagle, and she couldn't make the same mistake again when it came to picking a husband. The Amish way, thinking of family and community first, had to be the wisest way. Amish marriages lasted. If her father had been alive, he would have wanted her to follow in his footsteps.

Hannah had joined the Amish faith, hadn't she? She hadn't rejected it. She'd had a good marriage and a good life because she'd become Amish.

How much easier things would have been if she, Grace, had been born to Hannah and Jonas Yoder instead of foolish Trudie Schrock. A feeling of guilt made her pause. It was unfair to judge her mother for the mistakes she'd made in her life. Trudie had tried her best. She hadn't abandoned her when she was born, and she'd never been cruel. Grace was convinced that Trudie simply hadn't been mature enough to have a baby, especially not alone, without family or friends to support her. And if Trudie had been unwise in her choice of boyfriends after Jonas, had Grace done any better?

She closed her eyes and prayed fervently. "Please, God, help me to do the right thing. Tell me what You want me to do."

But as hard as she strained to hear His answer, the only sound that came to her was the steady downpour of rain against the shingled roof and windows.

Chapter Fifteen

It was after dark Monday evening and still raining when John got back to the clinic. He pulled his truck into the triple garage and let himself in by a side door. He switched on the overhead lights and went to the supply room to refill the compartments in the back of his truck. He'd retrieved two bottles of lidocaine, a case of bandages, a package of gauze and a suture kit when he heard footsteps behind him.

"John?" his uncle called. Albert halted in the doorway and held out an oversize mug. "Nasty night out," he remarked. "Made you some herbal tea. Lemon."

"Thanks. Hold it for me until I get these in the truck, will you?" He'd hoped to slip into the house and go up to bed without running into either Uncle Albert or Gramps. He was in no mood for talking. All day he'd wrestled with his feelings about Grace, and he kept coming back to a dead end. His uncle was one of his favorite people in the world, and he deserved better than the poor company that John would be this evening.

The older man watched him for a moment. "Why

don't you come to my office? I've been catching up on my reading. There's half a pepperoni pizza left."

John nodded. "Sounds good. I think I missed lunch today."

"And breakfast? Or did Grace feed you some of Hannah's blueberry pancakes before she told you she was quitting?"

John dropped the supplies onto a cardboard box on the table. "Maybe we should talk. I can do this in the morning." He followed his uncle down the hall into what had once been a spacious den in the original house.

This was a man's room, without the hint of a woman's touch: dark paneling, a rough stone fireplace, hardwood floors, bare of even a single throw rug. Two brown leather easy chairs and a small table were arranged in one half of the space; the other end of the room sported an oversize wooden desk and office chair, a fax machine/scanner and a pair of nineteenth-century oak cabinets. The walls were lined floor to ceiling with bookcases, filled to the max and overflowing onto the floor. The only decorations were three English oil paintings of hunting dogs.

John loved Uncle Albert's office. Other than the size and brand of computer, the room had barely changed since he was a boy. He paused for a few seconds, inhaling the scents of burning applewood, cold pizza and Labrador retriever. John had never entered this room without feeling the warm embrace of coming home. The familiar sensation didn't let him down tonight, and in spite of his distress about Grace, he was suddenly glad he accepted the offer of pizza and man-talk.

Travis, Uncle Albert's three-legged Lab, raised his head and thumped his tail against his sheepskin bed in greeting. "Hey, there, Trav," John said to the animal. "Flush any ducks today?" Uncle Albert never hunted, but he liked to take Travis to the marsh regularly so that the dog could swim and flush waterfowl. When John was a boy, those trips to the woods and saltwater marshes had inspired his love of wildlife photography.

John took his usual seat in the chair to the left, facing the hearth. Uncle Albert tossed Travis a biscuit and handed John the lemon tea. The three of them sat in silence for a good ten minutes while the warmth of the crackling fire and the tea drained the chill from John's muscles and bones.

It was John who broke the comfortable stillness between them. "How did you find out that Grace quit?" He hadn't wanted to talk about Grace, but so long as it was the elephant in the room, they couldn't move on to something else.

"She called in about nine o'clock. Spoke to Dad. Said you knew about it." He arched an eyebrow quizzically. "You two have a falling-out? Heard you were pretty cozy at the bazaar on Saturday."

John made a show of scowling, but it was impossible to be out of sorts with Uncle Albert. For a man who'd never married, he was surprisingly knowledgeable about women. And usually as inclined as them to gossip. Very little went on in the Mennonite or Amish communities that Uncle Albert didn't know about. He was never unkind and he was careful with whom he shared his information, but he always knew all the news before it came out in the *Budget* or the *State News*.

"We had a good time together Saturday," John agreed. "And when I told her about the chance to take the tech course, she seemed genuinely excited about the idea."

Uncle Albert opened the pizza box, which had been standing on a section of a cherry log that did double duty as a footstool and table, and selected a generous slice. He pushed the box toward John.

John didn't bother to argue. If he refused the pizza, his uncle would remind him that he couldn't run a motor vehicle without fuel and a man was much the same. Uncle Albert was a stickler for three meals a day, no matter how irregular the fare and what time the food was consumed. John ate the pizza in silence, reserving one round of pepperoni and a bite of crust for Travis, who watched the entire process with eager anticipation.

"No begging," Uncle Albert chided.

John knew the disclaimer was just for show. His uncle would be the first to share his food with the Lab, and fortunately, despite his handicap, Travis had the metabolism of a hummingbird. No matter how much the dog ate, he never put on too much weight.

"She quit because of me," John admitted. "She knows or she's guessed how I feel about her. I guess she'd rather give up her job than be around me." And not for the first time, he wondered if he'd come on too strong…if he had read her wrong about returning his attraction. Guilt weighed heavily on him. If he'd hurt Grace or caused her to feel threatened, he'd done more harm than he'd guessed. That was the last thing he wanted.

"But you said she seemed interested in getting the education." Uncle Albert rubbed at his graying beard. "Hannah put the kibosh on it? Because the Amish don't approve?"

John nodded. "Grace has her heart set on being Amish."

Albert mulled over that statement for a minute. "I suppose she has her reasons."

"She does." John wasn't prepared to share with his uncle what Grace had told him about her marriage. Honestly, it wasn't Uncle Albert's business…or anyone else's, for that matter. "But it isn't realistic. You know her chances of becoming Amish and having it work out are—"

"Less than a snowman's chance in Hannah's oven on baking day." Uncle Albert removed a second slice of pizza and offered it to John. He shook his head, and his uncle settled back and began to eat it himself.

"When she told me she didn't want to take us up on the offer, I tried to make her see reason. I wanted to tell her how much I care about her, but she wouldn't let me. We argued, and she told me that she was quitting. That was Saturday afternoon. I had hoped that she'd change her mind once she had time to think things over. She told me not to come for her this morning."

"You did, anyway."

John nodded. "When she didn't come out, I went up to the back door. Johanna answered, told me that Grace had quit. That she wasn't going to work at the clinic. Not this morning…not any morning."

"How come you didn't give me a call? Let us know what was up?"

"I'm sorry. I should have, but I…I didn't want to…" He tossed the last morsel of pizza crust to Travis. "The truth is, I guess I felt as if telling you might make it real, and I didn't want it to be."

"You still have it bad for her, don't you?"

John nodded. He did, and the disagreement hadn't changed his mind one bit. He wasn't ready to give up on her.... The trouble was, he didn't have the faintest idea how to fix things between them. He didn't know if it was even possible and the idea made him miserable.

"Have you considered that you might be rushing into this? That you don't know Grace well at all? That a few weeks...even a few months' acquaintance isn't the soundest foundation for a marriage?"

John leaned forward and rested his hands on his knees. "I can't explain how Grace makes me feel. It's..." He stopped and started again. "The closest I can come is to say she completes me. When I catch sight of her, the sun comes out, no matter how hard it's raining."

His uncle groaned. "It's a weakness we Hartmans have. We get our heads set on one woman, no matter how unlikely it is that we can win her, and we won't give up."

"I know I told you that I loved Miriam, but this... this is different."

Travis laid his head on Uncle Albert's foot. His uncle reached down to pat the dog's head and scratched behind his ears. "Just the same, I was proud of you, the way you handled losing Miriam. I was afraid it would make you end up an old bachelor like me, and I have to admit, I'm glad to see you interested in someone else."

"It's more than interest," John said. "I understand where you're coming from. If our positions were reversed, I'd be cautioning you. It does sound rash to say I feel like this about Grace when we've hardly ever been alone together." He hesitated. "What I want is a chance to see if we're right for each other."

"And what about her? How does she feel about you?"

John shook his head. "The same, I think. But she won't admit it, not to me, maybe not to herself."

"Because you're not Amish."

"Exactly. She's just being so stubborn about the whole thing. She doesn't want to give us a chance. She doesn't realize that I can give her what she's looking for. The Amish don't have a market on good, old-fashioned courting." He gestured toward himself. "I could court her."

"Take her out in your buggy?" Albert chuckled. "In your truck? Maybe take her to a frolic or two? Or a work bee?"

John nodded. "I'd like to take her to services on Sunday, let her see what our church has to offer. I want to show her what *I* have to offer."

"Grace hasn't been baptized into the Amish church yet, has she?"

"No. There's been no talk of baptism."

"Then, technically, she's not breaking any rules by dating you. So long as you two stay out of mischief."

John felt himself flush. "It isn't like that. I want to marry Grace. I want to be a father to her little boy." He paused. "She's just not seeing the situation clearly."

Uncle Albert waited, giving John time to think.

"I wish it wasn't just me pleading my case," John said. "I wish Hannah would tell her how difficult it will be for her to convert."

Uncle Albert untied one work shoe and pulled it off. He massaged his foot. "And you've talked to Hannah about this, have you?"

"No. I didn't think... No, I haven't. I was afraid Grace would take it the wrong way if I went behind her back to Hannah."

"Fair enough." Uncle Albert reached for the lace on his other shoe, taking his time before speaking again. "But there's nothing to keep *me* from putting a bug in Hannah's ear, is there? Letting her know you could use a little help."

"I suppose not," John answered slowly, "but—"

"But." Uncle Albert broke into a wide grin. "Everybody calls me an old busybody. Might as well have the game as have the name, don't you think?"

The following morning, Grace stood at the door of that same room and knocked. "Dr. Hartman," she called. "It's Grace Yoder. Could I speak to you?" When he answered in the affirmative, she took a deep breath and walked in. "I owe you an apology," she said. "I'm sorry. Quitting without giving notice was wrong."

Albert Hartman turned from his filing cabinet with a folder in his hand. "You've changed your mind?" he asked, not unkindly. "You'd like your job back?"

"No, sir," she answered. This was worse than she'd thought it would be. Her mouth was dry, and her stomach felt as though she'd been riding a Ferris wheel at double speed. "No...I..." She tried again. "I realized what I did was wrong—quitting on you like that. I'd like to finish out the month, to give you time to find someone else to take care of the kennels." She knotted the corner of her apron in one hand. "I don't expect you to pay me. I just don't want to leave you without help— you've all been so good to me. I'm really sorry that this hasn't worked out."

Dr. Hartman's eyes narrowed. His eyes were brown, and his expression was so like John's that she could feel her pulse racing.

"I didn't realize that you were unhappy here, Grace." He closed the drawer on the file cabinet. "We all thought you were doing an excellent job. That's why we offered you the opportunity to enter the vet tech program at Del Tech. Is that why you decided you didn't want to work here anymore? Because we suggested you might be able to use some further education?"

"No, sir. Well, a little, maybe." She looked down at the hardwood floor, then up at him again. "Mostly, it's personal. I don't know if John told you, but I plan to join the Amish Church. The Amish aren't allowed to go to college."

He placed the file on his desk. "So you weren't interested in the program?"

"I would have been if Hannah hadn't..." She stopped short. "It's not fair for me to keep the job when someone else could use the opportunity to attend college. I love it here, I do, but..." She clasped her hands together. "But the truth is, I come in contact with too many people here. Englishers. I need to...*separate* myself. Be less worldly."

Dr. Hartman tapped his pen against the desk, not in an impatient way, but in a manner that she'd seen him do when he was considering treatment for one of his patients. "Are you certain that no one here, no one in particular made you feel uncomfortable?"

"Oh no," she insisted.

"Nothing John or I did to upset you?"

Grace felt her cheeks grow warm at the mention of John's name. "No, really. John's been very kind to me and to my son."

"And Hannah didn't object to him driving you home?"

Grace shook her head. "No, not at all."

"Good. Good. Tell you what," Dr. Albert said. "How about if you go ahead and continue on in the kennel until…let's say after the holidays. We'll just go on as we have been until I can locate a replacement for you."

"But the college? Won't someone have to register for the spring term soon?"

"Nobody else I'd take the chance on. Not at this time. We all think you're special, Grace. If it doesn't suit you, we'll just forget the whole idea." He smiled. "How is Hannah? Well?"

"Yes," Grace answered. "Busy getting ready for the school Christmas party. I understand that the children put on skits and memorize pieces. Rebecca says all the parents and younger brothers and sisters will be there. I know Dakota, my little boy, is excited about it."

"Give Hannah my best, and the girls and Aunt Jezzy. Fine woman, Jezzy Yoder. Makes a great chocolate moon pie." He waved toward the door. "I won't keep you. I'm sure you've got lots to do this morning in the kennel."

"Thank you," she said. She turned away, then back toward him. "I really am sorry for yesterday."

"I appreciate your coming back. I'm sure it wasn't easy for you. You're right, it wasn't the right way to resign your position. But you've made up for it, Grace. Not many young women would have had the nerve to come in and admit a mistake. We'll say no more about it." He offered her his hand. "Friends?"

"Yes," she agreed, shaking his hand. "Friends."

But as she walked back down the corridor to the annex that housed the kennels, she couldn't help wishing that it had been John she'd had the conversation with…and John who had promised to remain her friend.

Losing him… The lump formed in her throat again. She'd been afraid of coming face to face with John after telling him that she'd quit and then not having the nerve to face him when he'd come to the house yesterday morning. She'd hurt him and probably destroyed their friendship forever.

She swallowed, trying to convince herself that it was the only way, that doing anything else would only be encouraging him—making him think that they could continue on the way they had. *Dating.* Yes, she'd ignored what was staring her right in the face. They'd been dating.

Under the circumstances, she'd done what she had to do, but there would be a price to pay. She hoped John would get over it, but she was absolutely certain that losing his friendship would leave a lasting ache in her heart.

Tuesday, Wednesday, Thursday and then Friday passed without Grace and John running into each other. If the other employees in the office wondered why she'd missed a day of work, they were kind enough not to ask. She did her job at the clinic, went home and took care of her son. In the evenings, after supper, she, her sisters, Hannah, Irwin and Aunt Jezzy all sat around the table fashioning Christmas wreaths from live greenery to sell at Spence's Market. The money from the wreaths would go to buy textbooks for the school where Hannah taught.

All day Saturday, Grace and her sisters swept and scrubbed floors and stairs, hung quilts on the clothesline to air. Even Irwin was pressed into service to wash windows and move furniture so that the girls could dust in every corner. Aunt Jezzy and Hannah kept busy in the kitchen, baking dozens of cookies, packing them into clean, shiny lard cans for Christmas and rolling dough for pie crusts. Even Miriam and Ruth came to help make the farmhouse spotless for the holidays.

After the busy day, Ruth and Miriam remained to share a light supper of potato soup and chicken salad sandwiches, but the delicious smells of roasting turkey and baking ham filled the kitchen and wafted through all the rooms. Because even a visiting Sunday was a day of rest, Saturday was the time for making baked beans, deviled eggs, scalloped potatoes, Brown Betty pudding, cranberry sauce and a counterful of pies to satisfy guests at the next day's midday meal.

As Grace bathed Dakota and tucked him into bed, she realized that she was tired, and might turn in early herself. But no matter how weary she was, she was glad that she'd felt a part of the household today. The empty place inside her, left after losing John's friendship, surely, in time, with God's help, would fill. In the days to come, she told herself, she'd find happiness in the small joys of the day: Dakota's laughter, the pleasure of a task well done, the knowledge that she was living her life as her grandparents had. She would find peace here. There was no other choice.

She returned to the kitchen to bid Hannah and the others good-night, but was surprised to find the room empty. Puzzled, Grace looked around. It wasn't quite eight o'clock. The propane lamp over the table was still burning, but there was no sign of any of her sisters. Had Miriam and Ruth left already? Aunt Jezzy never went to bed before ten, and even her rocking chair sat empty, the ever-present bag of knitting standing beside it.

"Hello?" Grace called. "Where is everyone?" She went to the back door and looked out. Still no one.

"Grace!"

She turned to see Johanna in the hallway.

"Come, sister," Johanna said. "We would speak with you."

Even more confused, Grace followed her. Johanna pushed open the parlor door, the room that was never used except to welcome important visitors. There was Hannah, Aunt Jezzy, Miriam, Ruth, Susanna, Rebecca, even Anna. They were all seated in a circle facing one empty chair. Behind them stood the men of the family: Charley, Eli, Samuel and Irwin, arms folded, expressions so solemn that they might have been carved in oak.

"Sit," Johanna said, pointing to the solitary walnut chair. Miriam scooted over to make room for Johanna, and she slid in on the straight-backed settee.

"What is all this?" Grace asked.

"Sit, daughter," Hannah said.

Terrified, Grace looked from one sister to the other. "Have I done something wrong?" she demanded. "Are you sending me away?"

"Sit, child," Hannah repeated. "Open your heart and your ears and listen."

"Ya," Anna said kindly. "It's time to stop trying to fit into a shoe that was made for another woman."

"Don't," Grace murmured, backing into the chair. "I'll do better. I promise."

"You can't," Johanna said softly. "No matter how much you want it, a bluebird can't turn herself into a wren."

"Please." Grace looked from Rebecca to Miriam,

fearing she might burst into tears. She'd been trying so hard. How could they do this to her? "I just want to be Amish like you."

"You are my sister," Ruth said. "But you must know that you are of the world."

Susanna ran to Grace and hugged her. "You are my sister," she whispered, "but you're not *Plain*."

Chapter Sixteen

"What more can I do?" Grace pleaded. Her eyelids burned, but she couldn't cry. The hurt was too deep for tears. She'd found her family, and now they were rejecting her. "I'm already quitting my job. I can't believe that—"

"Hush, child," Hannah soothed. "We need you to listen to what we have to say." She nodded to Miriam.

Miriam folded her hands in her lap and looked at Grace. "We've all been talking and… You need to understand that not everyone is born to wear the *Kapp*." She shrugged. "Our way isn't the way for everyone."

The room was quiet for a moment.

"If Dat were still here, he would agree with us," Rebecca said.

Grace looked from one sister to the next.

"What we're trying to say—" it was Anna who spoke next "—is that, Grace…you aren't meant to be Amish."

Grace rose to her feet feeling as if her heart might break. "So that's it? You're giving up on me?"

"Ne," Hannah assured her. "That's not what we're

saying. Please sit." She paused. "And know that this isn't easy for us, either."

Grace sank back into her chair.

"We've all gotten the impression that you have in your head that we are something we're not," Hannah continued. "That…in seeking our life, you've been seeking something from God." Again, she paused. "We think this might have something to do with your past… before you came to us."

Grace felt her cheeks grow warm. She looked at the floor.

Aunt Jezzy spoke next. "Forgiveness comes to anyone who asks God for it, child. You *do* know that, don't you?"

Grace lowered her head to her hands. "I don't know what I know anymore."

"You know God's been with you all this time," Aunt Jezzy said. "Didn't you see His hand?"

Grace lifted her head to look at them all, not sure what to say.

"Think, Grace." It was Hannah again. "Why did you come here? *Who* guided your footsteps from so far away to this house?"

"I guess I thought God did," she answered.

"He brought you home to Seven Poplars to us, to your father's family, to your Amish roots," Hannah agreed.

Grace nodded. "But I thought He led me here so I could be Amish."

"Maybe He led you here to find us…but also to find a good man of faith, a man who will love you and care for you and Dakota."

Grace blinked. "A man?"

"A good husband." Rebecca smiled shyly. "It's what we all hope for, isn't it?"

Grace still didn't know where this conversation was going, but she had an idea. "But if I become Amish, I can stay with you. Be with you always. I don't want to lose you."

Susanna burst into laughter. *"Snitzeldoodle!"* She covered her mouth with her hands and giggled. "You are our sister. You can't stop being a sister. People don't stop being family."

"Susanna is right. Amish or English, you will always be a part of our family," Hannah explained.

"And you will be welcome here, in my mother's house, in any of our homes," Johanna said. "With *us*. As long as you want to stay."

"We're not turning you away," Hannah continued. "My husband's girl would always be welcome at my table. But…" She rose and crossed to Grace and hugged her tightly. "But we have come to love you for you, not for who your father was. For Grace Yoder, alone."

"Ya," Irwin chimed in. "You're all right for an Englisher."

"I don't know what to say," Grace managed, touching her hands to her temples. She actually felt dizzy. "I…I was so scared. I thought you were sending me away."

"Snitzeldoodle," Rebecca teased. "Susanna has it right. Our Leah is already living far from here. Mam doesn't want to lose another daughter so soon."

Grace closed her eyes for a moment, then opened them. "So…what am I supposed to do now? If…if I'm not supposed to be Amish."

"God will tell, in time." Aunt Jezzy pointed to the

door. "But right now, I think you need to tend to that good man waiting in the kitchen."

Grace stared at her. A man in the kitchen? This…this *Amish intervention* was becoming stranger and stranger. She had thought maybe Hannah was referring to John, but now she was afraid—

"Eli, would you ask him to come in?" Hannah said.

Grace half rose again and Hannah waved her back into her seat. "A man has come to see you, daughter. Sit and receive him."

Susanna giggled and whispered loudly behind her hand. "He wants to court you."

"Who wants to court me?" Grace asked. Shivers ran down her arms. *John. It had to be John. If it wasn't John, she would…she would run out of the room.* Relief that it was not Lemuel or some stern Amish stranger made her giddy as John appeared in the doorway.

Susanna bounced up and down with delight, clapping her hands together.

Grace said the first thing that came to her mind. "I'm sorry, John," she cried. "I was wrong. Can I have my job back?"

"Nope." John folded his arms over his chest and shook his head. "You can't. I got someone else. The scholarship is still open, though." John gazed down at her. "I'd like you to reconsider accepting it, but more importantly…"

"Just spit it out before she gets away," Charley urged.

John took a deep breath and squared his shoulders.

Grace's heart did a little flip-flop as their gazes met. He looked nervous. *Why did he look so nervous?*

"Will you do me the honor of becoming my wife?" John asked. "And before you say anything, I want you to know that I'd like to adopt Dakota. I want him to legally be my son...*our* son."

Grace was glad she was sitting down. If she hadn't been, she knew that her knees wouldn't hold her upright. At the same time, she felt light enough to float up to the ceiling. She tried to think of something to say, but again, she was speechless.

"Say yes," Miriam urged with a giggle. *"Snitzeldoodle."*

Johanna gave her a little nudge. "He'll make a fine father for your son."

"Snap him up before Rebecca does," Ruth teased.

"I know this is sudden." John offered his hand, walking over to Grace. "Come walk with me. We'll talk."

"Don't turn him down until you hear him out," Samuel urged. "He owns land, and he's a good animal doctor. He'll be a good provider."

"And he's a man of faith." Hannah smiled at John and winked at him. "Even if he is Mennonite."

John's strong fingers closed around Grace's. Somehow, she found the strength to rise and go with him. She was vaguely aware of his helping her into her coat, wrapping a scarf over her head and leading her outside into the chilly night air.

"Where are we going?" she asked.

"Just walking. How about the orchard?"

She nodded. She needed to get out into the crisp air to clear her head. "Yes, let's walk." She savored the warmth of his hand as she glanced back at the house. The moon was round and full and as orange as a pumpkin, making the yard almost as bright as early morning. "I'm not sure what just happened in there."

"Are you cold?" Their breaths made gray puffs of condensation in the air.

"No. I like it. It smells like Christmas, doesn't it?" The sweet, pungent scent of fresh-cut evergreens from the unfinished wreaths on tables in the backyard mingled with wood smoke. Giddy with happiness, she squeezed his hand. "They ambushed me, all of them. It was a setup and I walked right into it." She looked up at him. "And you knew, didn't you? That they were going to do this. I should be mad at you for not warning me."

"Don't blame me." John chuckled. "It was Uncle Albert who went to Hannah this week. He picked her up after school, and they hatched this up between them. Hannah told my uncle that you and I were like two goats butting our heads together. Apparently, they decided we needed some straight talk from the family."

She looked at him, suddenly remembering what Hannah had said back at the house about God's forgiveness. "Did you tell them about Joe and me? About our marriage?"

He shook his head. "It's not my place to tell. I don't know that you need ever tell anyone."

She nibbled on her lower lip. "I should tell Hannah. I think I want to," she said in a small voice.

"So tell her when you're ready."

"I thought maybe she knew. The way she was talking about God having forgiven me and led me here."

"All you have to do to be forgiven is ask."

"Hannah said the same thing," she mused.

He squeezed her hand. "Hannah's a wise woman."

She wanted to pinch herself to make sure she wasn't dreaming. When she'd walked into the parlor and saw all the family waiting, she'd been certain that her life was falling apart. Now, in the light of this beautiful moon, with John's hand in hers, with him keeping step beside her, nothing felt beyond her reach. Was it God's forgiveness that had been there all along that was making her feel this way? Was it finally forgiving herself?

"So, no more games between us, Grace," John said. "I love you, and I think you love me, even if you don't realize it yet. And I want you to be my wife." He went on before she had a chance to argue. "You're one of a kind, Grace. It was no accident that we met, and no accident that I haven't been able to think of anyone else since I laid eyes on you."

"Hannah said that," she mused. "She said that if God led me to Seven Poplars, he might have been leading me to you all along."

"Sounds right to me."

Grace walked beside him, feeling his breath in sync with hers. She was in love with him. She really was. "I don't know how to explain it to you, how alone I've felt all my life. Even when I was with Joe, I still felt like I was alone."

"You'll never be alone again. You have me, and you have a family to watch over you. They love you, Grace. Hannah and your sisters and their husbands."

They walked in silence past the barn and the corral, past the brick structure of an old well and a root cellar. The hard-packed dirt lane curved around Johanna's turkey run and led into the orchard. They were beneath the spreading apple trees when John stopped and spoke again.

"Hannah warned me that if I didn't do right by you, I'd have to answer to her." He turned to her, lifted her hand to his lips and gently kissed the tops of her knuckles. "It isn't our custom to wear rings, but if you want one, I'll buy you one."

"No, I don't need a ring. My sisters don't wear one." She looked into his eyes. "But I haven't said *yes,* yet, John Hartman. Don't get your cart before the horse. Susanna said you wanted to court me, and I think I like that idea."

"Just what Uncle Albert said. He thought I should state my intentions, and then we should walk out together, Amish-style." He chuckled. "It seems that that's the way we've already been doing this. I mean, I already drove you home from a frolic in a buggy."

She giggled. "In a hay wagon, not a buggy." She took a breath. "John, this is all crazy. We've got to be crazy. We've known each other only three and a half months. What do you know about me?"

"That I want to know you better." They started walking again, now arm in arm. "That I've never met anyone who makes me feel the way you do."

"Are you sure this isn't too soon to talk of marriage?" she asked.

"I'm asking you to commit to a betrothal and then take all the time you need to be certain I'm right for you," he answered, and the deep timbre of his voice made her shiver with excitement. "We'll marry when you're ready. Three months or three years from now, that's up to you."

"You may change your mind about marrying me when you find out that I can't cook."

"That makes two of us who can't cook. So, either one of us learns or we live on takeout pizza and Hannah's pity."

She ran her hand down his arm. "Be serious, John.

They wouldn't let me be Amish. What if I can't be Mennonite, either?"

"I don't think that will be an issue. It's different with us. With Mennonites. If you come to church with me, if you decide that my faith feels right to you, then you could be baptized there. And I can promise you that you'll be welcomed with open arms. The Mennonites aren't closed off from the world. We believe in doing what we can to bring God's word and comfort to everyone who wants it."

"Like Leah and Daniel in South America."

John nodded. "But I've not been called to mission. At least not yet. I'm content to work in our community, here in Kent County. I want to be the best vet I can be, and I hope we can find time to support my church's charities, especially those that serve children."

"And you think that there would be a place for me?" She slid her hand into his, looking up at him, again. "That I could help?"

"I know you could."

She glanced away into the distant darkness. "It seems like a dream come true, that we could be together, the three of us, and that I'd still have Hannah and my sisters. It's almost too much to hope for."

He stopped and pushed the scarf back from her forehead. "Look around you, Grace, at this orchard. The apples have all been picked and the leaves have fallen, but in a few months, new leaves will form, buds will become blossoms and then bushels and bushels of delicious apples. Maybe our love is like that. It's winter now. We know what's coming in spring, or we think we do. If it would ease your heart, we can take it one day at a time. We can ride in Charley's buggy, attend services together and wait and pray for those new leaves and buds to blossom."

"Betrothed." She smiled up at him. "I think I like the taste of that word on my tongue. John Hartman... my betrothed." And, in spite of herself, tears began to spill down her cheeks.

"What's wrong?" he asked. "Why are you crying?"

"Happiness," she whispered. "Because...because... while nothing I planned worked out, all my dreams are coming true."

John lowered his head and brought his lips close enough to hers that she could feel the warmth of his breath on her face.

"Is that a *yes,* Grace Yoder? Will you do me the honor of becoming my wife? To have and to hold, so long as we both shall live?"

"Ya," she murmured softly. And then he wrapped his strong arms around her and kissed her tenderly. And she knew instantly that at long last, she'd found her way home.

Epilogue

Kent County, ten months later

Grace pulled her car into the driveway and parked under the old Sheepshead apple tree. Ripe fruit rolled and crunched under her feet as she opened the back door and scooped up her books and a bag of groceries she'd picked up on her way home. Glancing at her watch, she let herself into the mudroom with her key.

She kicked off her clogs and walked through the swinging doors into the spacious kitchen. As whenever she entered the new house, a rush of disbelief swept over her. The log house had been completed in September, two months after she and John had been married in the small, white frame Mennonite Church a few miles down the road, the same church where she'd been baptized. No matter how many times she went out of the house and came back in, seeing the warm hominess of the beautiful log cabin still thrilled her. The house John had built for her...*for them.*

She dropped the bag of groceries and her books on the counter and gazed around the great room that featured bare beams, reclaimed barn-wood flooring and a massive stone fireplace. "I must be dreaming," she said to the tabby cat curled up in a basket on the hearth. "I'm afraid I'll wake up and find myself back in the trailer park with a refrigerator that doesn't keep Dakota's milk cold and a stove with one working burner."

Cat, wisely, said nothing but purred in understanding. Cat had seen tough times, as well. Susanna had rescued him from two English boys at Spence's who were attempting to drown the half-starved creature in a bucket of rainwater. Cat had come out of the ordeal with a broken tail, one missing tooth and a tattered ear. Uncle Albert had soon healed her wounds, and sweet John had brought her home to live out her days in the cabin beside the pond.

Grace pulled a sweater on over her dress, turned on the oven and retrieved a family-size chicken potpie from the cloth grocery bag. She had time to stick dinner in the oven and start assembling a salad before she had to run over to Hannah's to pick up Dakota.

Hannah had been true to her word and been supportive, even when Grace had confessed that her marriage to Joe hadn't been real. The whole family had kept their promise, and a year after her arrival in Seven Poplars, Grace felt more like one of the Yoders than ever.

She glanced at the kitchen clock, wondering if she could squeeze in a shower before going for Dakota. Tonight was Wednesday prayer meeting, and Dakota's Bible school class would be packing boxes of school supplies, toys and sandals for Leah's mission school. They had to be there by seven and she wasn't sure how long the frozen potpie would take to bake. She searched for the directions on the back of the box and was about to rip open the packaging when she heard Dakota's voice at the front door.

"Mam!"

She hurried into the great room in time to lean over and catch her son as he hurled himself into her arms.

"Mam! Mam!" he cried. "We're going to do a play at school! A Christmas play. I'm going to be a sheep herd!"

"A *sheep herd?* That's wonderful," Grace exclaimed. She met John's gaze as he walked in the front door carrying their son's little backpack in one hand, a basket in the other. "Dakota's going to be a sheep herd," she repeated.

"I think that's a *shepherd.*" John set the large wicker basket and the backpack on the counter and glanced down at the frozen potpie. "You can put that in the freezer. Hannah sent chicken and dumplings, biscuits and green beans with pecans."

"Bless her." Grace sighed. "She remembered that it was my busiest day of the week."

"Don't knock Wednesdays," he teased. "I had a good day and got off in time to pick up Dakota."

"Mam! Mam!" Dakota jumped up and down. "Jonah and me caught the black hen—the one with the white tail feathers that laid her eggs on the buggy seat."

John grinned, looking at her. "How was your day? Did you get your grade on the test?"

"Ninety-four."

"That's my girl." He put his arms around her and kissed her.

For a few seconds, Grace forgot her grade point average, forgot that dinner would be rushed and forgot that her son was telling her about an escaped hen. Nothing mattered but her dear husband and her sweet son.

When she and John separated, she was laughing and breathless. "And tomorrow we're learning to put in IVs," she managed.

John arched a dark brow. "Hopefully, you had the good sense not to mention to your instructor that you've been doing them since you were fourteen."

"I didn't." She ruffled Dakota's hair as he shot past her, taking his backpack with him.

"I'll make you a deal," John said. "You jump in the shower and Dakota and I can set the table for supper."

"And what do you get in return? Husband of the Year award?"

John's grin widened. "A happy wife makes for a happy house."

"Is this a happy house?" she asked him, taking a step toward him.

"Are you a happy wife?"

Her answer was to stand on tiptoes and kiss him again. "Couldn't be happier," she whispered. "Not even in my dreams."

* * * * *

THE PRODIGAL SON RETURNS

Jan Drexler

To the storytellers in my life, especially
my grandmother, Ethel Sherck Tomlonson Rupel,
and my parents, John and Veva Tomlonson.

To my dear husband and children,
who never stop believing in me.

And to the ladies of Seekerville.net. Without you,
I'd still be typing away, alone in my writer cave.

Soli Deo Gloria

He shall cover thee with his feathers,
and under his wings shalt thou trust:
his truth shall be thy shield and buckler.
—*Psalms* 91:4

Chapter One

~∂~

LaGrange County, Indiana
May 1936

A high-pitched scream forced Bram Lapp's feet into a run even before his mind could identify the source. He raced up the dusty farm lane between a garden and a plain white house at the top of the sloping yard, and when the next scream sounded, ending in a terrified child's voice yelling, *"Ne, ne!"*, adrenaline rushed in, pushing him faster. He knew that sound all too well—a child was in danger, terrified. Grim possibilities flashed through his mind.

Rounding the corner of the barn, Bram's slick leather soles skidded sideways in the gravel. His feet found purchase, and he focused on the little girl crouched in front of him. A chicken flapped at the end of her outstretched arm, but her eyes were on the four draft horses looming over her. He dived toward her, letting his momentum carry him beyond the horses. Grabbing the girl in his arms, he rolled them both past the dinner-plate-size hooves and slid to a halt at the edge of the grassy backyard.

Bram shoved the child off his chest onto the grass, spitting feathers from his mouth, trying to see past the squawking red hen in his face. Where was she hurt? She screamed even louder as he wrenched the protesting chicken out of her hands and tossed it behind him.

Wide brown eyes cut from the horses to his face and then back again, her screams turning to ragged crying. She tried to pull away, but he kept her close with a firm grip on her arm. If she was hurt, or bleeding, the worst thing she could do would be to run and hide somewhere. He'd seen enough of that with kids on the Chicago streets.

He brushed at the feathers caught in her disheveled brown braids. She no longer looked like a copy of the chicken that still scolded him from a distance, but the tears running down her face clenched at his stomach. He turned her to one side and then the other. No blood that he could see. She ignored his touch; her eyes were fixed on the horses behind his shoulder.

The rattle of the harness told him the horses were moving. Her eyes widened even more as she tried to pull out of his grasp, sucking in a deep breath. Before she could let loose with another scream that might panic the horses further, Bram did the only thing he could think of to prevent it. He clapped his hand over the girl's mouth.

"What are you doing?"

The fury in the young woman's voice registered at the same time as the pain in his hand as the little girl sank her teeth into him. He bit back a curse and released her. With a flurry of skirts, a slim Amish woman descended on them from nowhere and snatched the girl up in her arms. Holding the child close, she fixed her blue eyes on Bram, flashing a warning as she watched him scramble to his feet.

He'd rather face the wrong end of a tommy gun than this... *Wildcat* seemed to be the only word for her.

A wildcat who had no business being angry with him.

His answer barked out in *Deitsch* before he thought about it. "I was just saving that girl from being trampled by these horses, that's all. What did you think I was doing?"

Was that a smile that twitched at the corners of her mouth?

"Those horses?"

Bram turned to look at the draft horses and noticed for the first time they were tied to a hitching rail. The near horse flicked a lazy ear at a fly, a movement that did nothing to quell his rising irritation. He spun back to the young woman and the little girl, who stared at him with one finger in her mouth.

"*Ja,* those horses. No matter how docile they seem, she could be hurt playing around them like that. She was screaming so loudly I assumed she *had* been."

The woman caught the edge of her lower lip between her teeth and hitched the little girl around to her hip. The self-righteous soothing of Bram's prickled temper stopped short at her nod.

"*Ja,* you're right. She shouldn't be near the horses at all. She panics like this every time she gets near them, but you didn't know that." She drew a deep breath that shuddered at the end. "*Denki* for helping."

That shaky breath got him. Bram straightened his

jacket and dusted off his gabardine trousers to give his eyes something to focus on. Her steady gaze demanded his apology, but he wasn't about to admit he was sorry for saving the girl, was he?

When he looked up, her gaze was still on him, expectant, her blue eyes a sharp contrast to her brown dress. Even standing on a slight rise above him, her *kapp* barely reached the level of his chin, but he was defenseless.

"I'm sorry. I probably scared her as much as the horses did."

This time he was sure her mouth twitched.

"*Ja,* probably."

Then she did smile, lighting up her face in a way that would make those painted girls back in Chicago green with envy. Bram drew a deep breath. Who would have thought he'd find a beauty like this among these Plain people?

"*Memmi,*" the little girl said, "can I go find *Grossmutti?*"

"*Ja,* for sure." The woman set the girl on the grass and watched her run to the back of the house.

Memmi? Bram's thoughts did an about-face. She was married, a mother, and he had let himself get distracted by a pretty face, and an Amish one at that. He was here to buy a horse, nothing more.

"Is your husband around? I heard he had a horse for sale."

The woman paused, the smile gone in a shadow. "I think you're looking for my father. You'll find him in the barn."

Bram glanced toward the barn cellar door as she

nodded toward it, but by the time he had turned to her again, she was halfway to the house. *"Denki,"* he called after her. She didn't look back.

Ellie Miller fought the urge to run to the safety of the *Dawdi Haus* with four-year-old Susan, keeping her walk steady until she joined *Mam* at the clothesline behind the big house.

She had forgotten. An *Englischer* gave her a crooked grin, and she had forgotten about Daniel. How could something so innocent make her forget her own husband?

Something about that *Englischer* didn't make sense...

Ach, he had spoken *Deitsch.* His suit and hat were *Englisch* for sure, with that bright yellow necktie, but where had he learned to speak *Deitsch?*

And that grin! Her breath caught at the whispery ache that wrapped around her chest. Daniel had smiled at her often, but without a mischievous dimple that winked at her. What was she doing even letting her mind remember that grin? He was just another *Englischer.*

Ellie pulled a shirt from the basket to hang on the line.

Ja, just another *Englischer* who spoke *Deitsch* and made her rebellious heart flip when he smiled.

"Who was that man you were talking to? If it was another tramp, there's a piece of pie in the kitchen." *Mam's* voice drifted to her from the other side of the clothesline, where she was hanging the girls' dresses.

"He wasn't looking for food. He wanted to talk to *Dat.*" Ellie glanced at the barn, glad for *Dat's* ease when it came to talking to outsiders. "There was something strange about him. He was wearing *Englisch* clothes, but he spoke *Deitsch*."

Mam's voice was calm, as if she heard *Englischers* speaking their language all the time. "Maybe he has some Amish friends and learned the language from them. Did he want to buy the gelding *Dat* has for sale?"

"What would he want with a horse?"

"I expect an *Englischer* might want a horse once in a while." *Mam* pulled another dress out of the basket at her feet. "When I see them tear along the roads in those automobiles, I wonder why anyone would hurry that fast just to end up in a ditch."

"Lovina's neighbor only did that once."

"Once is enough, isn't it?" *Mam* pulled the loaded clothesline lower to look at Ellie. "A person can be in too much of a hurry at times. When do you have time to pray, or even think?"

"For sure, I'm glad the church decided to keep them verboten. Not only are they noisy, but they smell terrible. Next thing you know, all the *Englisch* will be buying them."

"*Ach,* not until these hard times are over."

Ellie sighed as she pinned one of her brother's shirts on the line. Would these hard times ever be over?

"I like automobiles." Susan's voice was soft, hesitant.

Ellie looked down at her young daughter. Automobiles? What would she say next?

"Why do you say that?" Ellie shook out the next shirt with a snap.

Susan leaned closer to Ellie from where she squatted next to one-year-old Danny in the grass under the clothesline, her brown eyes wide in her heart-shaped face. "Because they aren't horses." Her words were a whisper as she glanced toward the Belgians waiting to be hitched to the manure spreader.

Ellie pushed the clothespins down firmly. When would Susan get over this fear? Daniel's accident had changed everything.

At this thought, Ellie paused, grasping at the line to control the sudden shaking of her hands. Her mind filled again with the horses' grunting whinnies, the stomping hooves, the smell of fear and blood, Daniel trapped against the barn wall and then falling under those huge hooves… Ellie's stomach churned. That day had left an impression in Susan's mind that affected her even now, months later. It still affected all of them.

Ellie shook her head to brush away the memories and shoved the final clothespin onto the last shirt. What was done was done. She might wish things were different, but her husband was dead. That was a truth she faced every day. She refused to succumb to the stifling blanket of grief that pushed at the edge of her mind, tempting her to sink into its seductive folds.

"All done, *Mam.* Do you want me to help take the clothes in this afternoon?"

"*Ne,* don't bother. I'll have the girls tend to it when they get home from school."

"Come, sweeties." Ellie lifted Danny in her arms while Susan hopped on one foot next to her. "Time to get our dinner started."

Ellie crossed the drive to the worn path between the barn and the vegetable garden that led to the *Dawdi Haus.* The house her grandparents had lived in when she was a child had sheltered her little family during the months since Daniel's death. Susan ran ahead of her along the lane, her earlier fright forgotten.

"Plan on eating supper with us tonight," *Mam* called after her. "I'm fixing a chicken casserole, and there's plenty for all."

"*Ja,* for sure," Ellie called back, then turned her attention to Danny, who was squirming to get out of her arms. "Sit still there, young man." She laughed at the determined expression on his face as she followed Susan.

Ellie watched the little girl skipping ahead, but her mind was full of a queer anticipation. It was as if her birthday was coming or the wild freshness of the first warm air of spring, pushing back the dark clouds of winter....

That *Englischer*'s grin, that was what brought this on. It did something to her, and she frowned at this thought. It didn't matter what an *Englischer* did, no matter how blue his eyes were.

That grin held a secret. What was he thinking when he looked at her?

She hitched Danny up as the thought of what might have been going through his head came to her. *Ach,* why did an *Englischer*'s wicked-looking grin give her such a delicious feeling at the memory of it?

Dat and the stranger stood on the threshing floor between the open barn doors, where the fresh air and light were plentiful, but Ellie kept her eyes on the edge of the garden as she hurried to follow Susan. If she glanced their way, would she see that dimple flash as he grinned at her again?

She had to stop thinking about him. He would talk to *Dat* and then be gone, and she'd never see him again, for sure.

In the backyard of the *Dawdi Haus,* Ellie paused to

pass her hand along a pair of her oldest son's trousers. Dry already. She'd bring in the laundry before fixing the children's dinner. After she put the little ones down for their naps, she could iron in the quiet time before Johnny, her scholar, came home. She smiled, anticipating the quiet hour or so in the shaded house, alone with her thoughts.

Opening the screen door for Susan, Ellie chanced a look at the big white barn behind her. *Ja,* he was still there, talking with *Dat.* She followed Susan into the house, letting the door close behind them with a ringing slam.

Bram glanced at the man next to him. John Stoltzfus was stern, yet quiet and confident. More like the *grossdatti* he barely remembered than the father he had left behind so many years ago. From the clean, ordered barn to the little girl skipping along the lane at the bottom of the ramp, the Stoltzfus farm was a world away from the home he had remembered growing up.

And a world away from Chicago. In the three days since he'd stepped out of his life in the city and walked back into his past, those twelve years had slipped away until even the stench of the West Side was a half-remembered dream. Was he losing his edge already? It was too easy to fall into this simple, Plain life.

Bram's thoughts followed the young woman in the brown dress as she walked past the barn toward the *Dawdi Haus.* When she ran her hand along the boy's trousers on the clothesline, a door opened into a long-forgotten place in his mind. That simple, feminine action spoke of the home he had tried to forget. How many times had he seen his *Mam* do that same thing?

The breeze brought the scent of freshly plowed fields into the barn as the young woman opened the door of the *Dawdi Haus* and then glanced his way, meeting his eyes before disappearing with an echoing slap of the wooden screen door. Why did she live there? And why were there no men's clothes hanging with the laundry?

Movement next to him drew his attention.

"So you're coming home?"

John's unspoken *finally* lingered at the end of the question, hinting at the speculation Bram knew he would be facing as word of his return spread. He could imagine the stir his disappearance had caused, even here in Eden Township.

"*Ja,* I'm coming home." How much information would get him the entrance into this community that he needed without divulging too much? "When I left, I was young and I thought I could always come back, but time got away from me...." Bram sighed and stared across the road at the rich brown corduroy of soil. A flock of blackbirds scattered through the field, picking at exposed seed.

What would his life be like if he had never left? What did he have now, other than lost time and poor choices?

"You left before you joined the church?"

"*Ja,* I was in my *Rumspringa.*" A *Rumspringa* that had never ended. Once he'd left home, Bram had never intended to return.

"What were you looking for out there?"

He glanced back at the older man's expectant face. From what his brother-in-law, Matthew, had said, John was one of the leaders in this district. Bram needed his support if he would ever be accepted into the community, but it wouldn't be easy. The Amish kept tight fences.

"I'm not sure now. Maybe excitement, freedom. I never found it, though." He cast his glance to the side, away from John, as if he was repentant and ashamed. No, he didn't need to do much acting to slip into this role. "I'm ready to come home."

Bram steadied his expression and looked back at the older man's face. He had said it the right way—John Stoltzfus believed him—but Bram didn't know if he'd ever be ready to come home. He wouldn't be here now if it wasn't for Killer Kavanaugh and the contract the gangster had put out on him.

"The *Ordnung* can be hard to live up to." Bram heard a warning note in John's voice.

"Not as hard as the way I've been living." The memory of Chicago's dirty streets clashed against the reality of the fresh spring air outside the big barn door. Yeah, life in Chicago had been dangerous, exciting, risky—and always hard. At least with the *Ordnung,* a man knew where he stood.

"What does your brother think?"

Samuel. Their father's living legacy. His brief stop at the family farm near Shipshewana earlier in the week had let him know what Samuel thought. Where *Dat* had been cruel, Samuel was petty, but that had been the only difference. From the belligerent set of his chin to his bleary eyes, Samuel was *Dat* all over again.

"*Ja,* well, Samuel doesn't believe I'm back to stay."

"You can understand that. You left a long time ago, and much has happened since then."

Twelve years. Yes, a lot had happened, both here

and in Chicago. Bram's stomach clenched. He had to make this work....

He forced his voice to remain quiet, in control. "I hope that with time he'll see I mean what I say." But he wouldn't give Samuel the chance. He could go the rest of his life without seeing his brother again.

"With time," John agreed with a nod. He turned to look back into the shaded interior of the barn, where the horse was tied to a post, the subject closed for now. Bram moved his shoulders against the strain that had crept in without his knowing.

"Partner here should be a good horse for you. He's a little spirited, but he drives well. My daughter Ellie usually chooses him if she's going out, and she won't put up with a horse that won't mind her. She won't take any chances with the children in the buggy."

"Is she the daughter who just went into the *Dawdi Haus?*"

"*Ja.* She and the children have been living there since her husband died."

So the young woman was a widow? Bram tucked that information away as John lifted each of the gelding's hooves for his inspection. The horse twitched his ears but stood quietly during the process. Bram held out a carrot nub John gave him, and the horse took it, eyeing the stranger as he munched the treat.

"I haven't dealt with horses much the last few years, but he seems to take to me."

"He's a good horse."

"Your price sounds fair." Bram pulled his money clip out of his pocket and peeled off a few bills. "Is it all right if I pick him up on Tuesday? I ordered a buggy from Levi Miller's, and it should be ready to pick up that afternoon."

"*Ja,* for sure." John took the money and shook Bram's hand. "I'll be looking for you on Tuesday."

Cool air washed over Ellie as she and the children went into the shaded kitchen. She shifted Danny on her hip, ready to put the heavy load down.

"Can we play with Noah's Ark?" Susan's favorite toy was a new discovery for Danny.

"*Ja,* that will be good. Why don't you set it up in the front room while I change Danny's diaper?"

Ellie took the baby into the bedroom Danny and Susan shared. She used the second bedroom, while Johnny slept on the sofa in the front room. The little house had seemed like such a refuge when they had moved in, but they were quickly outgrowing it. *Dat* had offered to add on another bedroom, but Ellie was reluctant to take that step. It seemed so permanent.

She would be moving back to Daniel's farm as soon as she was able to support herself and the children. The farm belonged to her now. It was the children's legacy from their father and his dreams for their future. When she was ready to make the move, then she would tell *Mam* and *Dat.* No use crossing that bridge yet.

Once clean and dry, Danny was anxious to get into the front room to play with Susan. Ellie put him down on the floor while she took care of the diaper and watched him make his way into the next room, doing his own one-foot-one-knee scooting crawl.

"*Ne,* Danny!" Hearing Susan's cry, Ellie stepped through the doorway to see Danny plowing his way through his sister's carefully set up animal pairs, making a beeline for the cows.

"Just set them up again, Susan. You know he's not doing it on purpose."

Ellie picked the marauder up and set him down on his bottom next to the pair of black-and-white cows. He took one in each hand and stuck a cow head into his mouth. He looked up at Ellie with contented adoration on his face, drool dripping down his chin. She couldn't help caressing his soft hair.

"I think we'll have to ask *Dawdi* Hezekiah to make another set of cows."

"*Ne, Memmi,* Danny can play with those. I still have the brown ones."

Ellie gave Susan a smile. The little girl forgave quickly when it came to Danny. Between the two of them, he was nearly spoiled.

Standing up again sent a twinge through Ellie's back, reminding her of how much work she had done already that morning. She leaned back a bit to ease the strain and caught a glimpse of the strawberry field through the window. She stepped closer to the glass, drinking in the sight of the rows of green leaves nestled in the soil.

Rows of green promising the fulfillment of Daniel's dreams for their children—a home, a future. Giving them what he wanted was the least she could do. She owed him that much.

Ellie rubbed her arms, brushing away the sudden chill that brought goose bumps, and stepped away from the window. Susan chattered to Danny as she walked the wooden animals up the ramp and through the door of the ark. How would she know when she had given the children enough to make up for what she had done?

Brushing the thought aside, she crossed the room to the kitchen. "Susan, I'm going to bring the clothes in. Call me if you or Danny need anything, *ja?*"

"*Ja, Memmi.* I will."

Picking up the empty basket from the back porch, Ellie started with Johnny's shirts, dropping the clothespins into the basket as she folded each shirt. When she reached for Susan's blue dress, the stranger stepped up next to her and took the dress from the line, handing it to her as he dropped the pins with the others.

"I thought I'd check on your little girl before I left."

Ellie froze with the dress in her hands. What was he doing? Asking for *Dat* was one thing, but to speak to her in this way?

"She...she's fine. She's just fine." Ellie concentrated on folding the dress and took Johnny's trousers from the *Englischer* as he dropped more clothespins into the basket. The sleeve of his jacket was gray, with threads of yellow that matched his necktie and the handkerchief in his breast pocket. No one dressed that fancy, not even the *Englischers* in town. Who was he?

"I found your *Dat* in the barn, just like you said. The horse will be perfect for me. John said you've driven him quite a bit."

"*Ja,* I take him when I need to run errands or go visiting." Why didn't he just go? What if *Mam* saw an *Englischer* talking with her?

"My name is Bram. Bram Lapp. And you're Ellie, right?"

Ellie glanced at his face. *Ja,* that grin was there, making a dimple show on his cheek. *Ach,* what a mess! How could she get him to leave and still be polite?

"*Ja,* that's right." Her cheeks were flaming hot under his gaze.

"I'm staying with Matthew and Annie Beachey until I find a farm to buy. Annie's my sister."

Ellie stared at him. "Your sister? But you're..." How could he be Annie's brother? She wasn't *Englisch.*

His grin widened. "Has anyone ever told you how beautiful your eyes are?" He turned away and stepped to the next line to start on the many diapers.

Ellie couldn't pull her eyes away from him, her cheeks burning. How forward could one man be? He ignored her as he pulled the pins off the line and bunched the diapers in his hand. When the line was empty, he dropped the diapers into the basket on top of the clothes.

"I'm glad your little girl is all right." He picked up the basket and started toward the house. He wouldn't just walk inside, would he?

"I can take that." Ellie hurried after him and reached for the basket. He let her grasp the sides as he paused at the porch steps, but he held on until she looked up at him.

"Will I see you again? I'll be around, you know." His dimple deepened, and she pulled the basket out of his hands. Didn't he understand how rude and forward he was being?

"*Denki* for carrying the basket, but *ne,* I don't think you'll be seeing me again."

She left him and went into the house, closing the solid wood door behind her, shutting him out. Leaning her back against the door, Ellie listened. Would he be so bold as to follow her onto the porch?

Setting the basket on the floor, she stepped to the sink and looked out the window. There he was, walking past the barn toward the road, his hat tilted on the back of his head and his hands in his pockets.

Annie Beachey's brother? Ellie squinted her eyes. *Ja,* perhaps if he wore Plain clothes and a straw hat instead of the gray felt one with the yellow band...

Ne. She shook her head and turned to pull a loaf out of the bread box. He was just too *Englisch.* For sure, the clothes made him *Englisch* on the outside, but no Amishman would be so bold with a woman! He was *Englisch* through and through.

Ellie looked up from her task of slicing the bread. She could still see him on the road. He had taken off his jacket and slung it over one shoulder, and as she watched, he did a little skip and kicked at a rock on the road, sending it bouncing along in front of him. He ran up to it and kicked it again, sending it into the ditch. Laughter bubbled up in her throat, and she leaned toward the window to keep him in view as he hunted for the rock in the tall grass at the side of the road. And then he was gone.

Straightening the bread on the cutting board, she cut two more slices for Susan and Danny before she realized she was still smiling. *Ach,* what was it about this *Englischer?* What if he had seen her laughing at him?

She shook her head, putting a frown on her face. *Ne,* that wouldn't do at all. *Englischers* and Amish just didn't mix, especially strange, fancy men. No good Amish woman would let *him* near her and her family.

Chapter Two

Bram kept to the shady south side of the gravel road, letting his pace settle into a steady walk that would eat up the four miles to Matthew's place. It was pure luck his brother-in-law knew about that horse for sale. A week of walking was enough for him. Selling his Studebaker had been a hard sacrifice to make, but it had been a gift from Kavanaugh.

Too risky to keep.

Everything was risky since that night on Chicago's West Side when Elwood Peters had told him his cover was blown.

Bram loosened his tie and unbuttoned his collar to give himself some air. It had been just this hot that April night, but Bram had gone cold with Peters's terse "You've been made."

How had Kavanaugh known he was the source for the feds? He had been with the gangster for nearly all of the twelve years he had been in Chicago, from the time he had hit the streets with hayseed still stuck in his hair. Kavanaugh had taken him in, taught him some street smarts, shown him the ropes during Prohibition.

Man, what a green kid he had been back then—but Kavanaugh liked him, said he had promise. Sure, some of the other guys had been jealous of him, but nobody messed with one of Kavanaugh's boys.

But it was Elwood Peters who had made a man of him. The Prohibition agent had seen his potential and recruited him to be an informant.

Bram shook his head. No, Peters had done more than just recruit him. He had saved his life. Before Peters came along, Bram had been on the same track as the rest of Kavanaugh's boys—just waiting for his chance to take the boss down. Even though he had seen what happened to the guy who made his move and failed, Bram didn't care. What did he have to live for, anyway?

Then he had run into Peters. Over the past ten years, Peters's job had changed from Prohibition agent, to Treasury agent, to the Federal Bureau, and he had taken Bram with him as his eyes on the street. It had worked out well for both of them.

Bram had shared everything with the older man—everything except his past and his real name. Peters knew him as Dutch, the name Kavanaugh had dubbed him with the first time they met. Bram had added a last name—Sutter—and from then on, Bram Lapp had disappeared into the hazy mist of fading years.

Until now.

Peters was sure Kavanaugh had moved his operation to northern Indiana after Bram's information had led to the breakup of his gang in Chicago, but he needed to know where the boss had gone. Bram was supposed to go with Kavanaugh when he left town, but once his cover was blown, he had to change his plans. He'd be dead if Kavanaugh found him, but he couldn't let the gangster escape, either. He'd never be safe until Kavanaugh was out of the way.

Killer Kavanaugh never gave up until he had his revenge.

And then Bram had come up with this new, harebrained idea. It seemed like such a good idea in Chicago—go undercover as himself, Bram Lapp, the green Amish kid from Indiana.

But he wasn't green anymore. He had seen and done things the Amish kid he had been couldn't imagine. He had the skills to keep himself alive on the Chicago streets, but would those same skills be useful to him here as he hunted for Kavanaugh's new center of operations? They had to be.

Bram whooshed out a breath. Meanwhile, here he was slipping away into the life he had left twelve years ago. It wasn't what he had expected. Not at all. The deeper he went into this cover, the more he was losing the edge he needed to keep him alive. But without the cover, without immersing himself into this community, it would be impossible to fade into the background the way he needed to.

And there was only one way to fade into this background: he needed to look and act the same as every other Amishman around. Any difference would make him stick out like a sore thumb.

The list. He ticked off the items in his mind as he walked. He had bought the buggy and horse. Next would be a place to farm, equipment and workhorses, and church every other Sunday. And clothes. This drape suit that helped him blend in on Chicago's West Side stuck out too much around here. Besides, his jacket was ruined after sliding in the dirt with that little Amish girl.

That little girl was something else. So much like his younger sisters at that age…

Bram took off his felt hat and ran his fingers through his hair, trying to get the air to his scalp. Why did remembering his sisters make him think of a wife and a family?

The curve of Ellie Miller's neck eased into his thoughts. He closed his eyes to capture the moment she'd faced him on her back porch. One strand of soft brown hair had escaped from under her *kapp* and fallen softly along the side of her face. She'd have to reach up and tuck it behind her ear. What would it feel like if he did it for her? He saw the smile she would give him as he caressed her cheek….

Bram stopped the direction of his thoughts with a firm shake of his head. He knew a woman like that wouldn't even look at him. Not Bram Lapp. Not with his past. And not with the job he had to do. No, a woman like that wasn't for him. He'd rather take his chances alone.

Wheels crunching through the gravel on the road behind him made Bram sidestep into the cover of some overhanging branches. Buggy wheels and horse's hooves, not a car. He rolled his shoulders as he waited for the buggy to overtake him. He had to stop being so jumpy. No one knew he was here. Even Peters only had a vague idea of the direction he had gone.

"Bram!"

Bram waved as the buggy caught up to him, and his brother-in-law pulled the horse to a halt.

"You'll be wanting a ride." Matthew was a man to get to his point quickly.

"Ja, denki."

The back of the buggy held boxes of supplies, and a frantic peeping rose from one as the buggy lurched forward.

"You bought some chicks?"

"*Ja.* I thought the Yoders might have some to trade for a couple bales of hay." Matthew looked at Bram with a grin. "Annie loves getting new chicks."

Bram let this idea settle in his mind. His sister hadn't asked for chicks, as far as he knew. Matthew had gotten them because he thought Annie might like them. Was that how a real husband acted?

"Did you find the Stoltzfus farm?" Matthew asked.

"*Ja.* John had a nice gelding for sale, just as you said. I'll pick him up on Tuesday."

"I knew John would take care of you. He's a good man."

"*Ja,* he is."

A good man. Bram hadn't known too many of those. He slid a glance at Matthew. His little sister had found a good man.

Matthew pointed ahead with the buggy whip. "Looks like the Jackson place is for sale. It might be the kind of place you've been looking for."

He stopped the horse at the end of the lane. The for-sale sign at the roadside looked new, but the graying barn and leaning fence posts were witness to the toll the recent hard times had taken on the English farmers. Forty acres, the sign said, along with the name of the bank that held the foreclosure. A too-familiar sign these past few years.

"The Jackson place? Do you know why they lost the farm?"

"I'm not sure, but I could see it coming. Ralph Jackson was too quick to spend his money as soon as he sold his crops, and then he'd buy the next year's seed on credit. He only owned the place about five years, but it was long enough to work it into the ground."

"It's vacant. Let's look around."

Matthew pulled the buggy into the lane, and they walked to the barn. Bram examined the siding, the beams and the fences. The barn needed a lot of work, but the structure was sound.

"Forty acres is a good size," Matthew said, looking at the land around them. "There's a creek running through the meadow. Good cropland, too, with the right management."

Bram turned to the house. It might be livable with some work, but he had the time. He needed a farm, and this one fit. All he had to do was go to the bank, sign the papers and hand over the cash, and it would be his. Another item checked off his list.

"The bank on the sign—isn't it in Goshen?"

"*Ja.* I won't be using my buggy tomorrow. You could take it into town if you want to talk to them about it."

"I'll go in the morning, first thing."

Then again, maybe not first thing. This might be another opportunity to get John Stoltzfus firmly on his side, and he wasn't one to pass up an opportunity. He could stop by the Stoltzfus farm before he headed into Goshen tomorrow. A little more grease wouldn't hurt, and besides, old John was pretty savvy. He'd have some good pointers on how to get this farm back on its feet.

It wouldn't hurt to get another glimpse of Ellie, either. Even if she wasn't for him, she was sure a beautiful doll, and looking didn't cost a thing.

* * *

Ellie's toes churned the loose black soil between the strawberry rows, soil that ran in muddy rivers as she splashed water on each plant. Her practiced steps kept just ahead of the mud, and she tipped the watering can in time to an *Englisch* hymn she had learned in school.

"'I once was lost, but now am found…'" The fourth row finished, she stopped to ease her aching muscles and looked back at her work.

Ach, even with daily watering, the plants were barely alive. This hot, dry spell was unusual for May. One good rain would set the young plants off to a good start, but as Ellie glanced up at the clear blue sky, she knew it wouldn't happen anytime soon. Until then, it was up to her to keep them alive. She started down the next row, humming as she went.

A warm breeze carried her sisters' voices to her and told her the scholars were home. Mandy and Rebecca ran up the lane to the big house, but Johnny trudged behind them, his head down. There must have been trouble at school again. Setting the watering can on the ground, Ellie closed the gate to the field and went to meet him as he walked alone to the *Dawdi Haus*.

"Hello, Johnny." The six-year-old looked up at her when she spoke, his face streaked where one tear had escaped and made a track down his dirty red cheek. *What happened this time?*

"Are you all right?"

"Ja." Johnny tipped his head down as he spoke, drawing the word out in his telltale sign that things were far from all right. There was only one way to get him to talk to her, and that was to pretend she didn't notice his attitude.

"Run on into the house and change into your work clothes while I get your snack. *Dawdi*'s waiting for you in the barn."

Johnny looked at the barn, then at his feet. His straw hat hid his face from her, but she knew the look he wore. Daniel had always had the same look when he'd tried to hide something from her, and Johnny was so much like his father.

"Johnny, tell me what's wrong."

"*Dawdi* doesn't need me to help. He has Benjamin and Reuben. They always say I'm too little to do anything."

"You may be littler than Benjamin and Reuben, but I remember when they were your age. They worked with *Dawdi* in the barn just like you do."

"But it's different for them. *Dawdi* is their *dat*."

Ach, Johnny. What could she do for a boy who missed his own *dat*?

"Let's go into the house and get your snack, then you can go out to the barn. Your *dawdi* likes having you work with him."

Johnny took the first bite from his cookie while Ellie poured a glass of milk for him. Susan came out of the bedroom, her face flushed with sleep, and peered into Johnny's face as she climbed into her chair.

"Johnny's been crying."

"Haven't." Johnny's contradiction was muffled by the sugar cookie in his mouth.

"*Ja,* you have. You cried at school again."

"Susan, that's enough." Ellie could see Johnny's tears threatening to start again, so she pulled out a chair and sat next to him. "Were you dawdling again?"

Johnny took a drink of his milk. "I was looking out the window."

Ellie sighed. Johnny was always looking somewhere else, forgetting whatever the task at hand should be, forgetting his schoolwork, his chores… She did the same thing, letting food burn on the stove while she looked out the window, letting the memories of her past drown the reality of the present.

"You have to pay more attention at school." She forced the words out. It was her duty, even though she would rather just gather him into her lap the way she had when he was Susan's age. She wished she could give him what he really needed, but that was impossible. She couldn't erase the past year, and she couldn't replace his father.

Levi Zook's face chose that moment to intrude, but she turned the memory firmly away. The widower had made it clear he wanted Ellie to be the mother for his children. But with his own brood, Ellie knew he would never be able to fit Johnny into his life the way her son needed him to. If she ever married again, it would have to be to someone who would be able to take Daniel's place in her life and her children's lives…and there was no one who could do that.

Bram Lapp's devilish grin popped into her thoughts. For sure, no *Englischer* could ever take her Daniel's place, either.

Johnny stared at her, his eyes dark and distant, and she knew she had failed him again. When had her little boy turned into this sad, sullen child? She couldn't remember the last time he had laughed, the last time she had seen him join in a game.

He stuffed the rest of the cookie into his mouth and went to the bedroom to change his clothes.

Ja, he needed his father. Someone like Daniel, who would give his life to a growing boy, who would teach him, protect him…

"*Memmi,*" Susan said, interrupting her thoughts. "That *Englischer* man that was here? He saved me from the horses."

"*Dawdi*'s horses weren't going to hurt you." Ellie nibbled on a cookie. That same *Englischer* man had been intruding on her own thoughts all afternoon. Only a city man and her daughter would think *Dat*'s gentle draft horses would hurt them. They were too well trained.

"*Ja,* they were. When Henny Penny ran away, that man saved me and her from the horses." Her eyes widened as she rolled her arm in the air. "He catched me and flew to the grass." She took a drink of her milk and then looked at Ellie again. "He's brave, *Memmi.*"

Ach, if she could have Susan's confidence. If only she could just forget that Bram Lapp, but the *Englischer*'s grin danced in front of her eyes. He had really thought Susan was in danger from the horses. What kind of man would ruin his fancy clothes for a little girl and her pet chicken?

"It's good to hear the children playing outside in the evening." *Mam* rinsed another plate in the simple, immaculate kitchen of the big house.

"*Ja,* though I think they'll be disappointed when they don't find any lightning bugs." Ellie dried the plate and placed it in the cupboard with the others. In *Mam*'s kitchen, nothing was ever out of place, from the dishes in the cupboard to *Dat*'s Bible and prayer book on the shelf behind his chair.

Mam chuckled. "Children always start hunting for them much too early in the year." She scrubbed at a stubborn spot on the casserole dish. "What did you think about what *Dat* was telling us at supper?"

"About Bram Lapp? I don't know."

"It isn't unheard of, what he's doing." *Mam* rinsed the casserole dish and laid it on the drain board.

"Just because it happens doesn't mean that it's right." Ellie was surprised at the anger behind her words. "A person shouldn't flip-flop when it comes to *Gott*."

"I've seen others come to their senses after a taste of worldly life." *Mam* swished the water in the dishpan and found a stray spoon.

"Twelve years is a bit more than a taste."

They worked in silence for a few minutes while Ellie wiped off the table, thinking back twelve years. She had been fourteen, just finishing up at school and beginning to notice the boys, wondering which one would be her husband. If she had met Bram then, would he have given her one of his grins? The thought brought a smile to her face.

Bram must be a few years older than her. Since *Dat* had said he had gone to Chicago while in his *Rumspringa,* he would have been around seventeen back then, which would make him twenty-nine now. Amish men usually didn't stay bachelors that long, but she didn't know about the *Englisch.* Maybe their custom was to wait longer before marrying.

"Do you know his mother or any of his sisters?" Ellie straightened the chairs around the big table.

"I knew his mother years ago—we were girls together—but I lost touch with her after she married and moved to the Shipshewana district. I heard she passed on a few years ago, and her husband, too."

"So if he's from Shipshewana, why isn't he settling up there?"

"Maybe he's looking for a wife."

Ellie shot a glance at her mother. For sure, the corners of her mouth were turned up in a sly grin. She sighed. Lately *Mam* thought every unattached man could be a new husband for her, but Ellie hadn't told her that she never intended to marry again.

"We don't know what he's looking for. He could be here to...to..."

"To what?" *Mam's* face was serene, innocent. How could she not know what the plans of an *Englischer* from Chicago might be? She must have heard the stories about gangsters and speakeasies. There were all kinds of worldly evils in a city like Chicago.

"*Ach,* I don't know."

"Daughter, we need to give the man a chance. *Dat* asked us to treat him as a friend. Surely we can do that much."

"*Ja,* I suppose..."

A friend. *Ja,* he was friendly enough, but could anyone trust an *Englisch* man? An outsider?

Chapter Three

The next morning's sunshine brought a promise of another hot day to come. Why was it that weeds always grew no matter what the weather, while the garden plants wilted in the heat? Ellie's hoe chopped through another clump of crabgrass growing between the rows of beans.

"See? This one is a dandelion."

Ellie glanced at Susan and Danny just in time to see the baby put a yellow flower in his mouth.

"*Ne, ne,* don't eat it!" Susan's voice was full of disgust.

Ellie smiled as she watched Susan rescue the flower from Danny's mouth. What a help she was. Daniel would have loved to see how his little dishwasher was growing.

The sound of buggy wheels in gravel interrupted her thoughts. If visitors were stopping by, *Mam* might need some help.

"Who's that?" Susan asked.

"I'm not sure." Ellie straightened up and shaded her eyes from the morning sun as the buggy stopped at the barn. "It looks like Matthew Beachey's, but that isn't Matthew driving."

The *Englischer,* Bram Lapp, climbed out and headed for the barn.

"*Ach,* it's that man who was here yesterday. He must want to talk to *Dawdi* again."

She went back to her hoeing, but found herself working with only half her mind on the weeds.

Why was he here? He said he wasn't going to pick up the horse until next week. And a buggy? It just didn't fit with what she knew of the *Englisch. Ja,* she remembered, he wasn't really *Englisch,* but if he wasn't, then why was he still wearing *Englisch* clothes? But the *Englisch* didn't drive buggies. When they drove a horse it was with a wagon or cart, not an Amish buggy. And if *Dat* was right and he was trying to become part of the community again, then why was he still wearing *Englisch* clothes?

Ellie gave a vigorous chop with the hoe that took out a dandelion and three bean plants. She was thinking in circles again. She stopped hoeing and sighed. *Dat* had asked them to welcome the man, but Ellie's first reaction was to ignore him, just as she ignored all *Englisch.*

Ja, he was friendly and attractive. But so *Englisch.*

She tackled the weeds again.

The *Englisch* were just like these weeds. If you gave them a chance they might choke a person, distract them from the Amish life—the Plain life. She had seen it happen to other people who had opened themselves to their *Englisch* neighbors, but it wasn't going to happen to her family. It didn't matter that this man wanted to become Amish again. The *Englisch* influence was like a dandelion root: you could try to chop it out, but if you left even a little bit, it would grow again and take over. How could a person turn from one to the other?

Ellie moved to the next row. The squash vines were healthier than the beans. Once they grew a little larger, they would cover the ground with their broad leaves, and the weeds would lose their hold. That was what she loved about her life. Peace, order, community—the *Ordnung*—were a protective covering that kept worldliness from taking root. Once she got rid of these few small weeds, the squash vines would grow unhindered through the rest of the summer.

Bram headed to the buggy he had left outside the barn humming "Blue Moon" under his breath. He stopped with a soft whistle. If he wanted to keep on John Stoltzfus's good side, he'd have to forget those songs for a while. In fact, he had a lot of habits from Chicago that would have to go, but that was part of the job.

John had given him some good, sound advice about the farm he wanted to buy. The man really knew his business. He'd answered Bram's questions for almost an hour and never seemed to be in a hurry. The older man's excitement about the prospects the farm held made Bram wish...what? That he wasn't just buying it for a cover? That he could build it into the kind of place he could be proud of?

Bram stopped, resisting the urge to look back at the barn. With someone like John Stoltzfus around, he'd be able to make something of that farm. Who knew— with someone like John, maybe he could even make something of his life.

He pushed the thought away. Too little, too late. With

any luck, he'd find Kavanaugh and be taking off before midsummer anyway.

When Bram reached the hitching rail, the two children at the edge of the garden caught his eye. That little girl was the one from yesterday. She was pretty cute when she wasn't screaming her head off. He chuckled as he watched her try to catch a butterfly that danced among the flowers.

His breath caught when he saw the mother. Dressed in brown again today, Ellie had her back to him. He was glad he wasn't one of the weeds she was hoeing. He'd never survive an attack like that. Her movements were brisk, businesslike, but at the same time Bram found himself caught up in the rhythm of her slim form as she worked.

How did she manage, raising her children without a husband? Bram understood the loneliness of living alone, but to add the responsibility of children to that was beyond him.

Bram found himself drawn to her like a butterfly to a flower. He shook his head. No, he couldn't get involved with a woman like that. A woman like that meant home, responsibilities, commitment. A woman like that deserved better than what he could ever give her. A woman like that would be too hard to leave when his job here was over.

But still, he couldn't ignore her. They were going to be part of the same church, the same community. They could at least be friends.

The little girl's laughter carried toward him on the warm breeze, making his decision for him. He had to get to know her somehow.

* * *

A man's laugh broke through Ellie's thoughts, and her stomach flipped when she recognized the *Englischer*'s voice behind her. There he was again! That man was as persistent as a dandelion and much more dangerous.

He squatted next to the children at the edge of the garden, smiling as Danny held up a grubby fist full of wilted weeds and babbled at him. Susan, usually the one to hold back, had her hand on his knee, ready to add her part of the story.

Ellie gripped her hoe. She needed to stop this now, before he wormed his way into their lives, but how?

Bram turned to Susan, laying his hand on hers as he said something that made the girl giggle. Ellie's breath caught at the rapt expression on Susan's face. Somehow the man had broken through her shyness. She smiled as Susan laughed again and gave Bram the dandelion she held in her hand.

Ellie gave herself a mental shake. *Ach,* what was she doing? What nerve that man had, going behind her back to push his *Englisch* ways on her children!

Ellie dropped the hoe and hurried to the edge of the garden. She scooped Danny up from the ground and took Susan's hand.

"Come, children, it's time to go into the house."

"You don't need to take them in. Susan was just telling me about her pet chicken." He smiled at her daughter, his hand resting on the girl's shoulder. "She likes animals, doesn't she?"

"As long as they aren't horses."

Bram's dimple flashed, and Ellie started to return his grin before she caught herself. His face was so open and friendly, his blue eyes deep and inviting, his smile intimate as he watched her.

As lovely as a dandelion blossom in spring, she reminded herself. Lovely and insidious, with the ability to turn the whole garden to weeds. With an effort she held her shoulders a little straighter.

"I must take the children in now." She kept her voice controlled and polite, then turned and walked away from him. Her face was burning. She hated to seem so rude, but an *Englischer* was an *Englischer,* and her job was to protect her children, wasn't it?

The back door of the little house was safely closed before she let herself look through the small porch window. The man—Bram—stood where she'd left him, watching. Why did she feel as if she had taken the hoe to one of her squash plants instead of a dandelion?

"I like that man," Susan said. "Can he come back again?"

"We'll see. Let's wash our hands, and then you can play with Danny while I make a pie for supper."

Susan climbed onto her stool and pulled at the small hand pump that brought water to the kitchen sink.

"He's a nice man." She wiggled her fingers under the running stream.

"*Ja,* I guess."

"He isn't afraid of horses." Susan's eyes grew large as she said this. "He told me *Dawdi*'s horse isn't scary, and he'll let me pet it."

"When will this be?"

"Next week. He said he'll come back and I can pet *Dawdi*'s horse."

Ellie dried Danny's hands and set him on the floor.

"Susan, take Danny in the front room and help him find the cows."

Ellie rubbed at the spot between her eyes where a headache was threatening. How had he convinced Susan to look forward to petting a horse?

Movement out by the garden drew her eyes to the window over the sink. He was leaving. She watched until the buggy left the drive and turned into the road. How dangerous was he? Ellie tucked a loose strand of hair under her *kapp.* Well, he was *Englisch,* wasn't he?

Wasn't he?

She got out a mixing bowl to make piecrust, then dug into the flour canister with more force than she meant to. Flour spilled onto the counter and floor, wasting it. Ellie bit her lip as tears threatened to come.

Why was a simple thing like making a piecrust so hard? Nothing had been right since Daniel died.

Ellie wiped up the spilled flour. She had to keep everything balanced, normal.

What was normal, anyway?

Just do what needs to be done; keep to the routine. That was something she could do. It was when something unusual happened that her life tilted.

That *Englischer.* He upset everything.

Ne, that was unfair. He was just the little nudge that sent her stack of balanced plates teetering. It wasn't him; it was her own fault.

Ellie crumbled lard into the flour with her fingers and then added an egg and a teaspoon of vinegar.

Her thoughts found their familiar rut and followed it stubbornly. Her pride had urged Daniel to buy the extra land. The extra land that needed more work and new, green-broke horses.

Her pride, her *hochmut,* had caused her to plead with Daniel, to force him to see things her way. She had wanted the larger farm, and she had urged him to buy the new team so he could work more land. If she had just kept to her place, listened to him…but no, she had to keep after him until he agreed to her ideas. If it hadn't been for her nagging, he never would have bought that half-trained team.

The half-trained team that spooked easily. Too easily. A loose piece of harness, a horsefly bite, a playful barn cat… She'd never know what had set them off that day. All she knew was by the time she'd reached the barnyard with Susan, Daniel was already under their hooves, his body broken and bloody.

Her stubbornness had cost her the only man she had ever loved.

She worked the stiff dough with her hands until it was ready to roll. The rolling pin spun as she spread out the crust.

Ach, ja, the punishment for her disobedience had been bitter.

But now, wasn't she sorry? Hadn't she prayed for forgiveness? *Gott* had to be pleased. What more could she do? She went to church, wore her *kapp,* followed the *Ordnung*…

The piecrust was a pale full moon. Ellie eased it off the wooden breadboard and laid it on the pie plate.

She must try harder. The *Ordnung,* the church rules, was there to keep her close to *Gott.* She just had to obey them perfectly, and everything would be all right.

No matter how handsome that *Englischer* Bram Lapp happened to be.

She knew what was most important.

The crust eased into the pan. She trimmed the edge with a knife and then crimped the edges with her fingers. Neat. Perfect. And empty.

Bram swayed with the buggy, letting the clip-clop of the horse's hooves set the pace of his thoughts. He'd known moving back to Indiana wouldn't be easy, but he'd never expected to plunge into a pool with no bottom. Nothing was the way he remembered it. The life he knew as a boy on his father's farm held none of the peaceful order he had found here.

From the simple white house nestled behind a riotous hedge of lilacs to the looming white barn, the Stoltzfus farm was the image of his *grossdatti*'s home, a place he thought he had forgotten since the old man's death when he was a young boy. A whisper of memory rattled the long-closed door in his mind, willing it to open, but Bram waved it off. Memories were deceptive, even ones more than twenty years old. They covered the truth, and this truth was that he had a job to do. *Grossdatti* and his young grandson remained behind their door.

But a question snaked its way up Bram's spine. What would *Grossdatti* say if he could see his grandson now? Bram cast a glance down at the dust caked in the perfect break where his gabardine trousers met his matching two-toned wing-tip shoes. Fancy. *Englisch.* Twelve years as one of Kavanaugh's boys had left their mark.

Was it those long-forgotten memories that kept bringing him back to the Stoltzfus farm? He liked the family. John seemed to be on his side, ready with advice, but the older man was almost too trusting. He'd hate to see what the Chicago streets would do to a man like that.

That little girl. Now, she was something, wasn't she?

Bram smiled. When she wasn't screaming in terror, she was almost as pretty as her mother.

The smile faded. The mother. Ellie. She was worse than a bear defending her cubs. He had to get past that barbed-wire barricade she threw up every time he tried to talk to her. There was something about him that rubbed her the wrong way. If he figured that out, then maybe she'd be more civil.

Something else he couldn't figure out was why he cared so much.

Bram chirruped at the horse to try to quicken its pace, but it had only one speed. The drive into Goshen was slower than he remembered, and it took even longer when he had to stop for a train at the Big Four Railroad crossing. The people in the cars stared at him as the train rumbled south toward New Paris and Warsaw.

Oh, what he wouldn't give to trade places with them. But it would be no use. The mob would find him, even if he went as far as Mexico. No, it would be better to keep on course. He'd run across Kavanaugh eventually, then Peters and the bureau would do their job. Maybe Mexico would be a good place to think about after that.

The train disappeared around the bend, and Bram urged the horse up and over the tracks, then on into Goshen.

Main Street was still the same as it had been when he was seventeen. He let out a short laugh at the memory. He couldn't believe he had once thought of this place as a big city.

There was something new. He pulled the horse to a stop in the shade at the courthouse square and stared. On the corner of Main and Lincoln, right on the Lincoln Highway, stood a blockhouse. A limestone fortress. A cop behind the thick glass had a view of the entire intersection.

Bram tied the horse to a black iron hitching post and then snagged a man walking by. "Say, friend, can you tell me what's going on? What's that thing?"

The man gave him a narrow look that made Bram aware of how out of place his expensive suit was in a town like Goshen. "That's our new police booth. The state police built it to keep an eye on the traffic through town and to keep gangsters from robbing our banks."

"What makes them think Goshen is their target?" If the state police were working the same angle as the bureau, it sounded like Peters had good reason to think Kavanaugh had come this way.

"You remember back in thirty-three, when Dillinger stole weapons and bulletproof vests from some Indiana police facilities?"

Bram nodded. Oh, yeah, he remembered. Kavanaugh had gloated about that coup for weeks, even though he hadn't been in on the heists.

"Well, one of those police armories is east of here a ways, and the other two are just south of here, along State Road 15."

Bram looked at the street signs. He had just driven into town on State Road 15.

"To get to any of those places from Chicago, the gangsters had to drive right through here, right through this intersection and right past our banks. And then when Dillinger and Pretty Boy Floyd hit the Merchant's Bank in South Bend a couple years ago, we decided we had to do something to protect our town." The man nodded toward the policeman in the booth. "All he has to do is radio headquarters, and this place will be swarming with troopers."

"So does it work?" Could one cop in a blockhouse discourage the plans of a gang intent on robbing one of these banks? One lone cop wouldn't stop the gangs he knew.

"It must." The man gave Bram a sideways look before walking on. "We haven't seen any gangsters around here."

Bram had heard enough. He walked across the street and found a spot outside a barbershop on Lincoln two doors from the corner, next to the stairway that led down to the ground-floor establishment. His favorite kind of lookout. Have a quick cigarette, watch for a while, make sure he knew the lay of the land before making his move. He shook his head. He was here legitimately; he didn't need to take these precautions. But still he lit his cigarette, bending his head to the match sheltered in his cupped hand. Habit kept him alive. The bank could wait ten minutes.

He watched the quiet town, pulling the smoke into his lungs. Traffic in Goshen's main intersection rose and fell like the waves on North Beach. Businessmen, lawyers and shopping housewives followed the traffic signals with none of the noisy chaos of the Chicago streets.

He threw the cigarette butt on the ground and screwed it into the sidewalk with his toe. Time to talk to the man at the bank. He took a step away from his cover, but slid back again as a Packard drove by on Main, heading south at a slow cruise. Bram watched the driver. No one he recognized, but he'd know that Packard anywhere. It was Kavanaugh's.

But the big question was, what was he doing here?

Bram waited, watching the cop in the blockhouse. He was no fool. Even though the Packard was out of Bram's sight, he could tell the cop was following its progress through town.

Bram counted to fifty—enough time for the Packard to make a slow cruise around the block and come back. Would he come back, or was he cruising through on his way to Warsaw or Fort Wayne?

The Packard eased into view again, slowing to a halt at the traffic signal. Bram stepped farther into the shadow of the doorway when he saw Kavanaugh clearly in the backseat of the Packard and Charlie Harris in the shotgun seat. They didn't look his way, but kept their eyes on the blockhouse. The cop inside leaned into his radio microphone just as the signal turned green. The Packard roared north, back toward South Bend.

It looked as if that police booth worked. Bram gave a low whistle. He never would have believed it if he hadn't seen it. Maybe Kavanaugh wouldn't think hitting this place was worthwhile. Maybe they wouldn't be back. Maybe Kavanaugh would keep heading east, and Bram could get out of this backwater and leave the past behind him for good.

Bram looked at the two banks, sitting diagonally across the intersection like two fat, stuffed ducks. Kavanaugh leave these two beauties alone just because of some cop?

Yeah, and maybe there were snowball fights in hell.

Chapter Four

Bram backed Matthew's team into place early Wednesday morning, watching as they felt their way past the wagon tongue and stopped just as their tails met the singletree. This was a well-trained team, all right. He'd do nicely to look for one as good. That would be another day, though. Today he was looking at equipment at the auction house in Shipshewana.

The farm's price had been lower than he expected, and he had needed to use only about half of his cash reserves. There was plenty left over to buy whatever else he needed to complete his cover.

He climbed into the wagon seat and then steadied the horses as they shifted, eager to be off. Now he had to wait for Matthew. That man spent so much time with his wife—if Bram didn't know better, he'd think they had been married for only a few days instead of nearly a year.

His *Dat* had never spent more time in the house than he needed to. The house and kitchen were *Mam*'s place, and *Dat* stayed in the barn or the fields. Whenever *Dat* was in the house, *Mam* crept around as if she was walking on eggshells, but it didn't do any good. It didn't matter how hard she tried—she could never do anything good enough for *Dat.*

He rubbed his chin as Annie's laughter drifted through the morning air. *Mam* and *Dat* had never acted like these two, that was for sure. He couldn't remember ever hearing *Mam* laugh, or seeing her smile, but Annie brightened up every time Matthew walked in the door.

"Sorry," Matthew said, finally reaching the waiting wagon.

"You're sure Annie will be all right?" Bram laid on the sarcastic tone in his voice, but Matthew didn't seem to notice.

"I think she'll be fine for the day." He picked up the reins, and the horses leaned into the harness with eager steps. "*Mam* is coming over later to help her get ready for tomorrow's sewing frolic." Matthew grinned at Bram. "Annie's really looking forward to it."

Matthew's excitement was so contagious, Bram couldn't help his own smile. He could do with a bit of whatever made his brother-in-law so happy.

"Giddap there, Pete. Come on, Sam."

"You say this auction is big?"

"*Ja,* for sure it is. Every week, too. It's one of the biggest in the state, and people come from all over."

Bram shot a glance at Matthew.

"From all over? *Englischers,* too?"

"*Ja,* some *Englischers,* especially these last few years with the hard times. But mostly Plain folk—Amish, Mennonite, Brethren."

Bram shifted his shoulders. His new Plain clothes felt comfortable, something that surprised him. He rubbed at the right side of his trousers, where he had inserted a pocket holster under the seam last night after Matthew and Annie had gone to bed. His pistol rested there, out of sight but not out of reach. Who knew who could be hiding in a crowd?

As they drew closer to Shipshewana, the traffic got heavier, and by the time they turned onto Van Buren Street, they were part of a line of wagons, buggies and cars headed for the field behind the sale barn. Matthew pulled the horses up at a shady hitching rail at the edge of the field. Auctioneers' voices drifted out of the barn, quickening Bram's heartbeat with their cadence.

"It sounds like things have started already."

"*Ja,* the livestock auction started at six o'clock. The equipment sale starts at nine, so we're in plenty of time."

"Good. I'd like to look things over before the sale starts."

Matthew led the way to a line of plows, cultivators and other farm equipment outside the sale barn. The first thing he needed to do was to plow his fields, then plant. Matthew said he'd loan Bram his team, but time was pressing. This work should have been done a month ago.

"Here's a good-looking plow."

Bram ran his hand over the seat of the sulky plow. The paint wasn't even chipped. The blades had a few scrapes, but the whole thing looked new.

"This one hasn't seen much use, has it?" Matthew walked around to look at the other side. "It'll go for a pretty penny."

That didn't bother Bram. He had enough money for anything up for sale here.

"Good morning, Bram. Matthew."

Bram turned to see John Stoltzfus heading their way.

John's familiar face sent a pleasant nudge to Bram's senses, and he smiled. He couldn't remember the last time being recognized didn't send him reaching for his gun.

"Are you looking for a plow, Bram?"

Even though John's voice was friendly, his question merely curious, Bram's nerves arose. He did a quick check of the crowd around them. Everyone seemed to be focused on the auction and farm equipment. He turned his attention to John.

"*Ja.* I'm getting a late start on the farm, and I need everything."

"You're planning on buying all the equipment you need?"

"Well, I need a plow first. I'll start with that."

"It looks like you might have found one," John said, taking a look at the sulky plow. "But don't buy everything at once. You have neighbors, you know. I have a harrow you can use."

"And you can use our planter," Matthew said.

John turned to Bram. "All you need to do is let the church know, and we'll have your whole farm plowed, planted, cultivated and harvested before the day is over."

Matthew and John both laughed at this. Bram wanted to join in, but caution nagged at him.

"Why would you do that? Why would you loan me your equipment?"

"You're one of us, son." John's words came with a puzzled frown. "Have you been gone so long that you've forgotten our way? How we work together?"

Forgotten? This wasn't part of his memory of growing up here.

"No one ever helped my *Dat,* and I don't remember

him ever…" His words stopped as he saw the looks on the other men's faces. John and Matthew exchanged glances. Had he said something wrong? Bram gave a scan to the milling farmers around them again.

"Bram, I'm sorry." John glanced at him, then back at Matthew. "I forgot about your father…" He cleared his throat. "You can count on us to give you a hand anytime. Anything you need."

Dat had never had the easy camaraderie with the men in their community that John and Matthew shared, but as a child Bram never knew why. Now he was beginning to figure it out. He swallowed hard as the memories came rushing out of the place where he had shoved them. *Dat*'s stash of moonshine in the barn, the weeks of missed church, the halfhearted repentance that was just enough to keep the ministers from putting *Dat* under the *bann*…

And most of all, *Dat*'s way of always finding something else to do whenever the men gathered together for a work frolic. The Lapps were never part of the community unless it worked into *Dat*'s plans.

He had shoved those memories away and locked the door as he stood on the roadside with his thumb out, heading west. Oh, yes, he remembered the stares, the whispers. This was one of the reasons he'd left.

Matthew put his hand on Bram's arm, and he almost shrugged it off. He wanted to be angry, to shut out their pity, but he stopped himself. That was what *Dat* would have done.

"Let us give you a hand, Bram."

Matthew's face was grim, but there was no pity there, only the determined offer of an alliance.

Bram nodded, trying on the friendship offered. It felt good.

"*Ja,* I'd welcome the help."

"How many quarts of rhubarb juice do you think we'll end up with?" Lovina dumped another pile of cut rhubarb into the bowl.

"Whatever we end up with, you know it won't be enough. *Dat* drinks a cup every day." Ellie eyed the bowl. A few more inches, and it would be full enough to start the first batch of juice. She was glad that even though Lovina lived several miles away she was still willing to help with this chore every year. The two sisters had made the family supply of rhubarb juice for as long as she could remember—ever since they were the same ages as Mandy and Rebecca, for sure.

"The plants at our place aren't growing as well this year. Noah says it's a sign we're in for another bad year."

"And Noah is always right, of course." Ellie looked sideways at Lovina. Even after four years of marriage, that telltale blush crept up her neck at the mention of Noah's name. Lovina still thought her husband was the next thing to perfect.

"*Ja,* of course." Lovina grinned at her, then went back to her cutting. "I do hope he's wrong this time, though. Another year with no rain will be hard."

Ellie's thoughts went to the field of young strawberry plants. There had to be enough rain to keep them alive. She forced her mind in a different direction.

"What does Noah think about the new baby?"

"He's on top of the world with this one. It was a long time to wait after Rachel before we knew this one was coming."

"Not so long. Rachel is only three."

"Ja." Lovina paused.

Ellie glanced over to see a distant look on her sister's face. *Ach,* she should never have mentioned it. Now Lovina was thinking about the one they had lost after Rachel. She always knew what Lovina was thinking, even though they weren't as close as they had been as girls.

Lovina dumped another pile of cut pieces into the bowl. Ellie added her rhubarb and gave the bowl a shake to even it out.

"Looks like it's time to start cooking the first batch."

"Ja. I forgot to ask earlier. Do you have enough sugar?"

"Mam said to use sorghum. Sugar is too dear." Ellie added water to the big kettle on her stove and then poured in a pint of the thick, sticky syrup.

"Not too sweet, remember."

"Ja, I remember. You say that every year."

"If I didn't say it, it wouldn't be right."

Ellie stirred the mixture and smiled at her sister. She was right. They had to do the same things the same way every year. It was tradition. "Do you think Susan and Rachel will make rhubarb juice together when they're grown?"

"That would be sweet, wouldn't it?" Lovina smiled at the thought, then went back to cutting more rhubarb. "How are the strawberries doing?"

Ellie stirred the rhubarb. *Dat* wouldn't let them hear the end of it if she let them scorch. "Truth to tell, I'm awfully worried about them. It's been so dry."

"Do you think they'll last long enough for you to get berries from them next year?"

"I hope so. I can't bear to think what might happen if they don't...."

"What do you mean?"

Ellie looked at Lovina. She could always share everything with her sister, but should she share this problem now?

"Come on, Ellie. I know when you're worried." Lovina gave her a sudden, piercing look. "You spent all of your money on those plants, didn't you?"

Ellie nodded and went back to stirring the rhubarb.

"You're not in danger of losing your farm, are you?"

"*Ach, ne.* As long as the Brennemans continue to pay their rent, I'll be able to keep up on the taxes. It will just delay moving back there. If the plants don't make it, I'll lose the money I spent on them plus next year's income from selling the berries."

"And the year after..."

"I hoped by that time we'd be back home."

Lovina was silent as she sliced rhubarb.

"Ellie, I haven't said anything before..."

Ellie looked at Lovina. "What is it?"

"It's been almost two years..."

"Not yet. It's been only a year."

Lovina's mouth was a firm line as she turned to her. "It's been longer than that. It will be two years in September. You keep talking about moving home as if you think that will make everything the same as it was."

Ellie turned back to the stewing rhubarb. "I just want to give the children what Daniel wanted for them."

"And what is that?"

"You know, we've talked about it before." Ellie turned to Lovina again and gestured with the spoon. "It's what you and Noah have. Daniel never had a home. He was moved around between relatives until he came to Indiana to live with Hezekiah and Miriam. When he bought our farm, he was determined to give his children what he never had."

"Ellie." Lovina's voice was quiet. "You don't have to do it. Things are different now. Daniel is—"

"Daniel is gone. I know." Ellie turned back to the rhubarb. She didn't want Lovina to see the tears that threatened. "But I'm not, and his children aren't. It's up to me to see that his wishes are carried out."

"Have you thought about what he'd want now?"

"What's that?"

"I think he'd want something more important for his children than a farm. Remember, something else he never had was a father. Don't neglect that, Ellie."

Ellie kept her eyes on the pot of rhubarb. She couldn't marry again. How could she bear to risk that again? Besides, her children had a father, didn't they? She'd never let them forget Daniel.

Silence filled the kitchen, along with the sour-sweet fragrance of cooking rhubarb.

"I hear there's a new man in the area." Lovina kept her eyes on her knife as she said this.

"Where did you hear that?"

"*Mam.* Does he have a family?"

"*Ne,* he's single." *Mam* would have told her that, too. She knew what was on Lovina's mind.

"Oh." Lovina put a long lilt on that one word.

Ellie groaned to herself. What else could she talk about?

"Have you met him?" Lovina asked before Ellie could think of anything.

"*Ja,* I have."

"And?"

"And he's very *Englisch*."

Lovina put her knife down and turned to Ellie. *"Englisch?"*

"Well, he dresses *Englisch*. *Dat* says he's been living in Chicago."

"Then what is he doing here?"

Gut, maybe this *Englischer* in their midst bothered Lovina as much as it did her.

"I don't know, but *Dat* says he wants to be Amish again."

"What does *Dat* think? Is he serious about this?"

"Ja. Dat says he is. He came by on Monday and bought Partner, that gelding *Dat* wanted to sell, and he was back again yesterday."

"So what do you think? Is he nice?"

Ellie's thoughts went to his eyes. She had been so rude to him, but those blue eyes had still smiled at her as if he could see right through her. Could he see what she was thinking? She felt her face grow hot. She hoped he couldn't.

"I wouldn't know. I haven't talked to him much."

"Much? Then you have talked to him."

"Ja, a little."

"What does *Dat* say?"

"Dat likes him. He's asked the family to give him a chance to be part of the community." Ellie moved the pot of rhubarb to a cooler part of the woodstove as it started simmering. "But those *Englisch* clothes are so fancy, and he's much too bold." Ellie turned to Lovina. "You wouldn't want an *Englischer* to spend too much time with Rachel, would you? Wouldn't you be worried about how he might influence her?"

Lovina was silent as she cut the next bunch of rhubarb into one-inch pieces. She dumped them into the bowl, then turned to Ellie.

"I'd trust *Dat*. I know he's never been wrong when it comes to a man's character. Don't you remember how everyone else thought Noah was wild and wouldn't amount to anything?"

Ellie remembered. Lovina's husband had almost left the community during his *Rumspringa,* but had returned to be baptized and then married Lovina.

"*Dat* never stopped having faith in him. Noah has told me that *Dat*'s support was the one thing that gave him the courage to come back home after his *Rumspringa.* Without someone believing in him…" Lovina picked up another bunch of rhubarb to cut. "Without someone believing in him, Noah might never have come home. If *Dat* thinks we should give this new man the same support, then I think we need to do it."

Was Lovina right? Ellie cut her rhubarb in silence. Was Bram the invasive weed that would ruin their lives, or was she wrong?

She gave her head a decisive shake. As long as he wore those fancy clothes, she couldn't trust him, no matter what *Dat* said.

"You got this plow for a good price." Matthew ended his sentence with a grunt as he and Bram lifted the final piece of the dismantled equipment off the back of the wagon and onto Bram's barn floor.

Bram lifted the tailgate and fastened the latch. "*Ja,* it didn't go as high as I thought it would."

Matthew took a wrench out of the toolbox behind the wagon seat and started reassembling the plow. Bram held the axle steady while Matthew replaced the bolts and tightened them.

"I saw Samuel while we were in Shipshewana."

Bram didn't answer Matthew. So what if his brother had been there? There had been no sign of Kavanaugh, and that was what mattered.

Matthew continued in his mild tone, "We could have taken the time to see him."

"It would have been a waste." Bram kept his eyes on the wheel he was adjusting.

"I know you have your differences, but it doesn't seem right to ignore him."

"My brother and I don't have anything in common, that's all."

"Except you do." Matthew was persistent. "You share your family, your parents, your history..."

Bram glanced at his brother-in-law. Did he have any idea what it was like to grow up as a Lapp?

"*Ja,* we share our history, and that's the problem." Bram tightened the last bolt and stood up to admire the plow. It was a beauty. He wiped his hands on a rag and turned to Matthew.

"Our *Dat* was an alcoholic. I didn't like it, but that's how he was, and that's what killed him." And what probably killed *Mam,* too, in the end. Bram rubbed a bit of grease from the side of his finger. "My brother is just like him, and if I never see Samuel again, I'll be happy."

Bram waited for the shock on Matthew's face. Any Amishman would tell you that the attitude he had toward his brother was sinful, but Matthew's face only showed sadness.

"*Ach,* Bram, Annie never told me all of this."

"*Ja,* well, it happened when she was a little girl—

and I don't think the girls saw all of it. *Mam* did what she could to protect them."

The silence that followed was as welcome as rain. Bram fastened the barn door and then climbed onto the wagon seat with Matthew for the drive back to their farm.

"How soon do you think you'll be able to move onto this place?" Matthew asked.

"Next week, I hope." Bram was glad to change the subject. "I've been working on the barn, and I'll need to clean out the house before I move in."

"It'll be a good farm when you're done." Matthew slapped the reins over the horses' backs. "You'll be able to count on the church's help with the farmwork, Bram."

"*Ja,* that will be good. I appreciate it." At least he thought he did. He liked to work alone.

Bram glanced sideways at Matthew. What kind of man had his sister married? A good man, for sure, but he was young. Oh, in years he was almost as old as Bram, but he seemed so naive about the world. All these Amishmen did. Compared to the men in Chicago…well, it was a good thing they'd never meet. These poor fellows wouldn't survive on the streets.

Bram rubbed at the grease on his finger. He had survived, but he had been tougher at seventeen than Matthew was in his twenties. Maybe having a father like his wasn't such a bad thing.

"Lovina, you be sure to take some of these cookies home to Noah." *Mam* took another panful of snickerdoodles out of the oven.

Ellie took in a deep breath full of cinnamon and sugar. No matter how old she was, *Mam*'s kitchen would always be home.

"Were the children good for you today?" Ellie couldn't resist taking a cooled cookie from the counter.

"*Ach, ja.* They are always the best when they're with their *grossmutti.* They play so well together." *Mam* slid another cookie sheet into the oven. "Of course, I haven't seen anything of them once the girls got home from school. They're all in the backyard."

"I must be getting home." Lovina found an extra plate and put some cookies on it. "Noah will be waiting for his supper."

"We'll see you at Matthew Beachey's tomorrow?"

"For sure. I wouldn't miss a frolic for anything."

Ellie put down the cookie she was nibbling. "A frolic?"

"*Ja,*" *Mam* said as she put some more cookies on Lovina's plate. "Remember? We're having a sewing frolic for Annie Beachey. It's their first little one."

Ach, how could she forget? The cookie suddenly lost its flavor. She had let this frolic slip her mind, like most occasions that meant facing a crowd of people.

"You're coming, aren't you, Ellie?" Lovina paused, her hand on the door. "It's been a long time since you've been to any of the frolics or get-togethers."

A long time? Only since Daniel's death.

"We'll get her there." *Mam* put her arm around Ellie's shoulders and gave her a quick hug. "We'll see you tomorrow."

Ellie waited until Lovina was out the door before turning to *Mam.* "I don't think I'll go tomorrow."

"Why ever not? And don't try to give me the excuse that Danny's too young. He'll be fine."

"I..." How could she tell *Mam* how it felt to be in a crowd? She had never liked large groups of people, but lately she was more than just uncomfortable. The thought of all the women talking, laughing, staring at her... Church was bad enough.

"I just don't feel like going."

Mam gave her a long look. "I know you don't feel like it, but you've waited long enough. I haven't pushed you, but perhaps I should have. You need to do this, Ellie. You need to be with your church family. The longer you put it off, the harder it will be."

Mam was right, of course.

"*Ja,* I'll go." Ellie sighed, but with the sigh came a stirring of something she hadn't felt for a long time. She would go. She had always enjoyed her friends before, hadn't she? Perhaps she would even have fun.

Chapter Five

As soon as the scholars left the next morning, Ellie and *Mam* were off to Matthew Beachey's in the family buggy.

"Who will be there, *Memmi?*" Susan sat on the front bench seat between them, her legs swinging with the buggy's movements.

Ellie hesitated, her throat dry, and *Mam* answered. "Rachel will be there and most of the children from church."

Susan's anxious face mirrored her own, and Ellie gave the little girl's knee a reassuring squeeze. They both shared an intense shyness around groups of people. Should they have stayed home after all?

Matthew Beachey came out of the barn to greet them as *Mam* drove into the yard.

"Good morning." He reached for Brownie's bridle. "I'll take care of the horse for you while you go on into the house."

"*Denki,* Matthew." *Mam* returned the young man's smile. "You're keeping busy away from the hen party, are you?"

Matthew's natural laugh put Ellie at ease. He was always friendly and ready for fun—no wonder everyone liked him.

When Bram Lapp walked out of the barn behind Matthew, Ellie looked away and straightened Susan's *kapp*. She had forgotten he might be here.

"Good morning, Bram." *Mam's* voice was friendly as usual, as if seeing Bram Lapp in the Beachey's farmyard was an everyday occurrence.

"Good morning." He answered *Mam,* but when Ellie finished fussing with Susan and glanced his way again, he was looking directly at her. His eyes were dark, unsure. *Ja,* he remembered how rude she had been the last time they'd talked. She looked over to *Mam* for help, but she was deep in conversation with Matthew.

Bram stepped closer and reached out to help Susan down from the buggy. Before Ellie could stop her, Susan jumped into his arms, and he gently lowered her to the ground. He lifted his hands up for Danny, but when Ellie held the baby close as she stepped down on her own, he just reached into the back of the buggy for her sewing bag and handed it to her.

"I hoped you would come to the frolic." Bram stood close to her, Susan's hand in his.

Ellie stared at his clothes—his Plain clothes. His brand-new shirt and plain-cut trousers were exactly like the ones all the men in the district wore, complete with the fabric suspenders and broad-brimmed hat. He didn't look *Englisch* anymore, and he didn't talk *Englisch....* Her resolve wavered.

How would she answer him? His nearness was forward and unsettling, but she couldn't help wishing for more. What would she do if he gave her that secretive grin again? The thought brought on a flurry of butterfly wings in her stomach.

"I forgot you'd be here." Her face grew hot as soon as the rude words left her mouth. Why couldn't she talk to him like she would Matthew, or anyone else, for that matter? Every time she spoke with him, her tongue seemed to belong to someone else.

Ellie reached for Susan, but he stopped her with a hand on her arm.

"Have I done something wrong? I know we only met a couple days ago, and you don't know me, but I'd like to change that."

His hand warming her skin through the sleeve of her dress prickled her nerves to awareness of just how long it had been since she had felt a man's touch. She should turn away, let his hand slide off her arm, move to a more appropriate distance, but she was frozen in place.

She glanced up at his face. At her look, a smile spread, flashing the dimple in one cheek and encouraging her own mouth to turn up at the corners. She looked down, her face flushing hot again. What was wrong with her? She was acting like a schoolgirl!

Bram seemed to take her hesitation as an encouraging sign and stepped closer. Ellie found herself leaning toward him to catch the familiar scent of hay mingled with shaving soap, and she breathed in deeply.

Ja, just like a schoolgirl. What must he think of her?

"I've bought a farm." His voice was low, the words for her alone. "It's the Jackson place, just a couple miles west of your father's farm. Would you like to see it sometime?"

The Jackson farm? Ellie knew that farm—it was an *Englisch* farm. A blast of cold reality shoved away all thoughts of dimples and hay and…soap. The telephone lines strung from the road to the house on that farm were the fatal testimony. Her shoulders drew back as her chin lifted, and his hand fell to his side.

"Ne, Denki," she answered as firmly as she knew how. "I'm already familiar with that farm."

She took Susan's hand as Bram stepped away, her face flushing hotter than ever. She couldn't have been ruder if she had slapped him in the face. How could she be so harsh? But an *Englisch* farm? Resolve straightened her spine with a snap.

"Come, Susan, it's time to go in the house."

Ellie followed *Mam* up the path to the kitchen door, anxious to get away from those intense blue eyes. She struggled to regain her composure before she reached the porch steps. How could one man upset her so?

Bram blinked as Ellie walked away. What happened? One minute her arm was lying warm and sweetly soft under his hand as she leaned toward him while they talked, and then those shutters had slammed tight again.

Matthew stood next to him with a grin on his face, watching him stare toward the house. "I don't think she likes you. What did you do to her?"

Bram frowned as he turned and checked the buckle on the harness. "Nothing. We were just talking."

"She's been widowed for almost two years now."

"Ja, that's what her father told me."

"So when will you ask her to go out with you?"

Bram shot a look at his brother-in-law. Matthew's smile hadn't left his face. One thing about married men was that they were usually quick to make sure every other man ended up in the same trap.

"What makes you think I want to go out with her?"

Matthew didn't respond. He just grinned, waiting for Bram's answer.

"All right. I just did. She turned me down flat."

"Oh, I wouldn't worry about that. She'll come around."

Bram took the horse's bridle and started leading him to the hitching rail on the shady side of the barn. "I didn't say I was giving up, did I?"

The problem was he should give up. He should let that prickly woman go her own way. He didn't need her. He didn't want her.

Bram went into the workshop next to the barn and found the broken harness strap Matthew had told him about. He turned the piece over in his hands. It was in good shape other than that one break.

Nothing felt as right as when he worked with harness leather. He loved this peaceful pleasure that came from handling the supple straps and the satisfaction that came with taking something that had been destroyed and making it whole again. Scarred, perhaps, because you could always see the repair, but useful once more and stronger than it had been.

He started in on the harness, first taking his pocketknife and cutting the frayed edges off the broken ends of the leather. As he worked, children's laughter drifted in through the shop window from the backyard, and he shifted to get a view of the sandbox from his stool at the workbench. Girls' pastel dresses and boys' shirts in the same hues filled the yard. Older ones played a game of Duck, Duck, Goose. He looked for Susan, but she wasn't among them.

How long had it been since he'd heard children

playing without traffic noise mingled with their harsh voices?

Almost as long as he had missed the scent of a woman. A real woman, not girls like Babs, with her cloying odor of dying flowers and smoky bourbon. Babs had never looked at him with the cold eyes Ellie Miller used. No, she had been more than willing to press her silken dress against him, batting her heavy black eyelashes.

His eyes narrowed. Babs made sure he knew what she wanted—or what Kavanaugh paid her to provide—and he was glad he had never taken her up on her offer. He had never spent more time with her than an occasional dinner or as a date to one of Kavanaugh's shindigs. Something about the girl had turned his stomach. Not just her—black-haired Cindy before her and Madge before her. Kavanaugh kept his boys supplied with women.

He took a deep breath, dispelling the memory.

Thoughts of Ellie swirled into his mind to take its place. She had leaned toward him, coming within inches of his chest. He could have reached out for her, pressing her slight form against him while he kissed her... but that would have ruined everything. A woman like Ellie would never put up with what the girls in Chicago begged for. He pushed the thought away.

Her arm under his hand had felt alive, firm, capable. Taking another deep breath, he tried to recapture the scent of...what? Just soap and water? Whatever it was, the memory clung to him.

Keep focused.

Bram shaved the two ends of the leather strap with his knife, shaping them to overlap each other. If he did

find Kavanaugh, the last thing he needed was for someone to get in the way. The last thing he wanted was for
someone to get hurt.

Taking the awl from Matthew's tool bench, he drilled
holes through the splices, lining up the shaved ends so
they would overlap in a solid, smooth join.

John Stoltzfus was a good man, and he liked Bram.
That was a step in the right direction. He should spend
more time with him, but that would mean spending
more time around Ellie and her children.

Bram rummaged in a jar for a couple rivets and fit-
ted them into the holes.

That Susan—yeah, she was something. The way she
looked up at him with those solemn brown eyes as if he
was some sort of hero pulled at his heart.

He glanced through the window at the playing children again. Susan had joined the game, her light green
dress and white *kapp* mingling with the other pastels.
She laughed as she played, her face sweet and innocent.

A steel band twisted in his gut. What kind of hero
could he be to a little girl?

He found Matthew's tack hammer hanging on the
wall. A sharp rap sealed the first rivet. He shifted to
the second rivet but stopped.

If Ellie looked at him the way Susan did, what would
he do then?

His world tilted for a brief moment, then righted. He
gave his head a shake and then drove the hammer home
on the second rivet.

Focus. Play the part. Lie low under his cover until his
job was done, then maybe he could…what? Court her?

Forget her. That was what he needed to do. God help
him if he let himself fall for the woman.

* * *

Ellie took a deep breath as she laid her hand on the knob of the Beacheys' back door, listening to the women's voices on the other side. Facing Bram Lapp would be easier than stepping through this door.

"Ellie, you can do this."

Ellie turned to see *Mam*'s eyes filled with understanding. The soft words gave her strength.

The crowd of chatting women parted to welcome them as the door opened. Susan clung to Ellie's skirts as they stepped in. Ellie wished she had somewhere to hide, but it was too late. *Mam* had already set her pies on the table and was greeting her friends.

Annie Beachey came over to Ellie as she lingered just inside the door.

"Ellie, I'm so glad you could come!"

Ellie smiled in spite of her churning stomach. Who could resist Annie's contagious happiness? Although how she could be so merry when she must be uncomfortable with the growing baby most of the time was beyond her.

Annie took her bonnet to the back bedroom, and Ellie stepped farther into the kitchen. Sally, her younger sister, came over and took Danny from her arms.

"I've missed this little man."

Sally's easy confidence was just the balm Ellie's nerves needed. This might be a fun outing after all.

"Well, if you hadn't married last fall, you could have been cuddling him all winter."

Sally looked up from nuzzling Danny's neck. "*Ach,* sister. Then I wouldn't be looking forward to my own *boppli,* would I?" Sally turned to Susan. "The other children are playing out in the yard with Dorothy Ann."

"She'll join them soon, I'm sure." Ellie patted Susan's back, knowing these few minutes of shyness would soon be over.

Sally leaned closer to Ellie, lowering her voice. "I saw the way Levi Zook kept watching you a week ago at Meeting. I think he's still sweet on you."

Ellie's face grew warm with embarrassment. Did everyone know about his attentions to her? "I've told Levi we're not suited for each other. I don't know why he's so persistent."

"I do," said Lovina as she joined Sally and Ellie. "I heard his sister from Middlebury wants him to send his younger girls to live with her, and he's desperate to find a new wife so he can keep his family together."

"*Ja,* well, I can understand why he wants a new wife, but it's not going to be me." Ellie turned to greet Lovina with a smile. "We'll be sewing for your little one next." She nodded at Lovina's expanding waist.

As Sally and Lovina started chatting about morning-sickness remedies, Ellie stepped back, feeling the wall that had risen between them. She and her sisters had been inseparable as girls, and her marriage hadn't lessened that close bond. Not until the past couple years.

Now that she was a widow, and they had their husbands… She crossed her arms in front of her, hiding her slim form. She could have been expecting another baby, too, if—well, if things had been different.

Ne, she had to stop thinking this way. Things were what they were, and it was *Gott*'s will. A faithful, obedient woman accepted *Gott*'s will, didn't she?

And if it was *Gott*'s will that she accept Levi Zook as her new husband? Ellie suppressed a shudder. She still believed two people should love each other if they married, and as kind and faithful as Levi was, she didn't love him.

Ellie followed some of the other women as they moved toward the front room of the house, where Annie had arranged things for the frolic. A table was set up for cutting material, with several lengths of muslin and flannel ready to be cut into the pieces they would sew into gowns and diapers for the new baby. The room was arranged with chairs in a circle for sewing and visiting. Before long, the four women who had taken the job of cutting the material had pieces ready for sewing, and the rest of the women settled in with their needles and thread.

When Susan went off with the other children, Ellie chose a chair near her sisters, where Danny was still happy on Sally's lap. Taking the next available diaper, one of many they would be making today, she started in on the simple hem. Over the hum of conversation, she heard Bram's name mentioned.

"What did you say his name is?" Minnie Garber asked Annie.

"Bram—short for Abram. He's my brother who is staying with us for a time."

What did Annie think of her *Englisch* brother? Ellie hated the thought of one of her brothers jumping the fence, leaving their family and their ways behind. How would she treat them if they had left and then wanted to return?

"I didn't know you had another brother," Minnie went on. That woman was never shy when it came to gossip.

"Bram has been gone for quite a few years—"

"Gone?" Minnie interrupted. The rest of the room

quieted as the other women listened to their conversation.

"Ja." Annie stopped and looked around the room of women waiting to hear what she had to say. "He left home twelve years ago but came back recently. He just bought a farm and will be settling here."

"Twelve years?" Minnie's voice was incredulous. "Where was he all that time? Did he live in Ohio? Pennsylvania?"

"Um, *ne.*"

Ellie's heart went out to Annie. It was obvious that she wasn't interested in gossiping about her brother.

"He was in Chicago," Annie finally said. Her words were met with silence.

"Chicago?" Minnie sounded stunned.

"Ja, but he's home now and wants to be part of our community." Annie looked from one face to another. Most of the women stared at the sewing in their hands, but *Mam* smiled at Annie, encouraging her.

Then Minnie voiced what Ellie had been thinking.

"Won't he have trouble giving up his *Englisch* ways after all this time?"

"He's shedding himself of them as quickly as he can." Annie sounded relieved, as if she was happy to give Minnie an acceptable answer. "When I finished his new clothes yesterday, he wouldn't rest until he had put them on."

"And you say he bought a farm?"

"Ja, the Jackson place on Emma Road. He spent all Tuesday afternoon and yesterday tearing out the telephone lines. He's planning to move there next week."

One of Minnie's daughters joined in the conversation from the other side of the circle.

"So all he needs now is a buggy and a wife!"

Good-natured laughter followed her comment, and the conversation shifted to the coming wedding of Minnie's third daughter. Ellie concentrated on finishing the hem on the diaper, letting the conversation flow around her.

Bram was turning the Jackson place into an Amish farm? Could she have been so wrong about him? From what Annie said, he did mean to give up all his *Englisch* ways. If that was true, then *Dat* had been right all along.

Could Minnie's daughter have been right, too, that he was looking for a wife?

She pricked her finger with the needle, and the pain brought a start of tears to her eyes.

If he was, he wouldn't have any problems finding one. He was no Levi Zook.

But it for sure wasn't going to be her. No man was going to take her Daniel's place.

Chapter Six

"It was a robin. I know it was," said Susan. She nodded to emphasize her certainty.

"It wasn't a robin—it was a blackbird." Johnny's retort was tinged with disdain.

"He had red on him."

"It was a red-winged blackbird. Robins have red breasts, not red shoulders."

Ellie touched Johnny's knee to quiet him before the argument gained strength. She should reprimand them, but on Sunday mornings she just wanted quiet.

The buggy swayed in rhythm to Brownie's trotting hooves. It wasn't as crowded now that Reuben was old enough for his own buggy. *Dat* had agreed he could drive it to Welcome Yoder's for church, and now the two boys were ahead of them on the road, Reuben driving at the same sedate pace. Soon he'd be courting, if he wasn't already, and next Benjamin. At least Mandy and Rebecca were still at home.

Ellie listened to her sisters' chatter. She had been the same way with Sally and Lovina once, their three heads together, sharing their secrets, their dreams. Mandy and Rebecca would have the same sweet girlhood memories.

"There's another robin!"

Johnny looked where Susan pointed. "*Ne,* that one's a blue jay. See how big he is? And his blue feathers?"

Susan didn't argue, but kept her eyes on the side of the road.

Ellie's thoughts went back to Mandy and Rebecca. She'd had that same anticipation when she was their age. Riding to church was an adventure, with Lovina giggling about the boys they would see and Sally bouncing with anticipation of seeing her best friend again. She had looked forward to the singing, even the long sermons, and the fellowship. What had changed?

She never had the urge to kick against the restraints of the church that some people talked about. The *Ordnung* was safe. It provided security against the changing world. Even when her friends tried living outside the protective fence of the *Ordnung* during their *Rumspringa,* Ellie never saw the lure. She knew where she belonged.

Bram Lapp had left the community once.... What would it be like to leave her loved ones behind, to take the children somewhere and start fresh where no one knew her? The thought pressed against her heart, stopping her breath. It would be like dying. *Ne,* she could never leave her home, her family.

Dat turned south at the corner, and Ellie closed her eyes against the morning sun hitting her face.

She must work through this emptiness somehow. Church for her meant nothing more than a long day with a headache. The children needed tending, and every week it was harder to keep them still during the meet-

ing. The hymns were so long, the prayers drawn out.
There had been a time when the singing was her favorite
part of a Sunday. Now she just waited for it to be over.

"Is that one a robin?"

"*Ja,* see his red breast?"

Ellie gave herself a mental shake. Her children
needed her. A pasted-on smile was better than none,
and a kind word to a friend could help lift her spirits.
But how many more church Sundays were going to pass
before the smile became genuine again?

Dat turned the buggy into the driveway of the
Yoders' farm, joining a line of other buggies. When
they approached the sidewalk leading to the house,
Ellie saw the buggy in front of Reuben's stop. Matthew Beachey jumped down, then reached back to
help Annie. He walked with her to the lines of people waiting to go into the house while their buggy
drove on.

Bram must be driving the buggy. What would she
say to him? She had been so rude on Thursday at the
work frolic.

Polite. She could be polite and hope he would forgive her rudeness.

Ellie joined the line of women in the front yard. She
returned the smiles of several, exchanging the brief hug
and brush of the lips on the cheek that was the kiss of
peace. The group was quiet other than occasional murmured greetings. The time for visiting and fellowship
would come later.

Bram couldn't keep his eyes up front. Church hadn't
changed in twelve years. Even here in Eden Township,
the sermons were the same High German as in Ship-

shewana—difficult to follow and meaningless. He tried to listen to the first sermon, but he lost the minister's point and found his mind wandering, just as it had always done. He concentrated on looking alert and interested while all the time his thoughts were elsewhere.

This morning he couldn't keep his mind off Ellie. Glancing her way, he saw the distracted look, the line between her eyes. His years undercover had taught him to read people, and that line was a telltale sign she had a headache. A young boy sat quietly between her and Elizabeth, and Ellie kept Susan busy playing with a handkerchief baby while the littlest boy slept on her lap.

That one strand of Ellie's hair wouldn't stay tucked in her *kapp,* and Bram tried not to stare. The minister's voice droned on, forgotten. Each time he glanced at her, the strand was looser, until it was a curling mist circling her ear. Every movement of her head caused it to droop a little farther. How far would she let it go before she reached up to tuck it in? What would it feel like if he tucked it in for her? Would the soft, silky strand catch on his newly calloused fingers, or would it glide through his hand like smooth water?

She looked up and caught his eyes, holding them for a brief second before she turned to the front again. A red glow started at her neck and traveled up. Bram ducked his head to the floor and smiled. She wasn't immune to him, either.

When *Dat* stood to preach the main sermon of the morning, Ellie shifted Danny's weight to her other arm. He was a heavy load as he slept on her lap.

"*Memmi,* are we almost done?" Susan's whisper carried to the women around them.

Ellie lifted her finger to her lips to remind Susan to be quiet, then leaned down to whisper in her ear, "Almost."

Dat stood with his head bowed. His silent prayer before the sermon was always longer than any other minister's. *Dat* claimed it was to clear his head and discern the Spirit's leading, and maybe it was. All she knew was that it made the sermon last far longer than her back could bear.

Her head pounded. There—Bram was looking at her again. She turned her head to avoid his gaze, but she could still see him out of the corner of her eye. When would this service be over?

"The passage for today's sermon is from Hebrews, the twelfth chapter, the first three verses." *Dat*'s voice broke into her thoughts.

Ellie tuned the familiar verses out. The women on the other side of *Mam* sat with rapt attention, listening to *Dat* as if hearing the reading for the first time.

Dat's voice broke through her thoughts as he started in on his sermon.

"We must take Jesus Christ himself as our example, as the apostle Paul exhorts us in Philippians: 'Let this mind be in you, which was also in Christ Jesus.'"

Of course Jesus Christ should be her example. His humility and sinless life had been held up to her as the goal of every Christian ever since she could remember, but with this thought Ellie shifted. It was her pride that had brought her to this place in her life. She could blame no one but herself.

"Jesus Christ didn't dwell on the trials of his present day. He looked forward to the joy that was set before

Him—the joy of His eternal place at the right hand of the throne of *Gott*."

Not dwell on her present trials when they dragged her down on every side? What was *Dat* trying to say?

"So lay aside the sin, the weight of your sin, that you may run the race set before you. Look forward with joy, and trust *Gott* for the reward He has set before you."

This startled Ellie so much that she missed the rest of the sermon. Trust Him? The *Gott* who took her Daniel? And look forward to what with joy? A life alone, seeking to fulfill Daniel's dreams? She rubbed the spot between her eyebrows where the headache was centered. She could see no joy set before her.

Ellie glanced over to the men's side of the room, where Bram was listening to the sermon instead of trying to catch her eye for once. He leaned forward, resting his forearms on his knees as his gaze fastened on *Dat*. What was he learning from this sermon?

Eli Schrock's testimony followed *Dat*'s sermon, reaffirming everything that had been said, and then he added his own final comment. "You young folk, especially, trust *Gott*'s leading in your life. Follow Him as a sheep follows a shepherd, and then you can hope that He will bring you into His glory."

Follow *Gott?* How could she follow *Gott* when His voice was silent?

The congregation standing for the hymn of dismissal startled Ellie. She had been so caught in her own thoughts that she had missed the closing prayer.

The headache pressed down.

She shifted Danny again to stand with the others, but she didn't sing. She couldn't. She leaned her cheek against Danny's soft hair.

Ach, Gott. She kissed Danny's head, swallowing back the tears that wanted to fall. *Ach, Gott, help me. I can't bear this any longer.*

All through dinner, Bram watched for Ellie among the other women who were serving, but with no luck. He finished his ham sandwich and potato salad, then went to wait under an oak tree while the women cleared the tables.

A group of older boys gathered in the front pasture across the farm lane, a few of them with baseball bats. This was one Sunday afternoon tradition he remembered well.

"Bram, it's good to see you today."

He turned to see John Stoltzfus walking toward him. Bram shook his hand.

"*Denki,* it's good to see you, too."

"How are things going?"

"Coming along." Bram nodded. "The farm is nearly ready for me to move onto it. I pick up my buggy on Tuesday afternoon. I'll be over before then to get the gelding."

John waved his hand in the air, dismissing all that Bram had said.

"I mean the rest of your life. You're still getting on well with your brother-in-law?"

Bram glanced over at Matthew as he stood with a group of other men. Matthew's wiry build made him look as if he'd fit in with the cowboys Bram had seen around the stockyards in Chicago better than in this community of Amish farmers.

"*Ja,* I'm glad Annie married such a good man."

"What about your brother? Have you seen him again?"

He wouldn't have anything to do with Samuel if he could help it, but John wouldn't understand any more than Matthew had.

"I'll leave that up to Samuel. He knows where I am if he wants to see me."

A young boy wandered up to John and leaned against his leg, glancing up at Bram, his brown eyes looking so much like Susan's that Bram placed him right away. It was the boy who had been sitting with Ellie during church.

"Bram, this is my grandson Johnny."

"Hi, Johnny," Bram said. The boy stuck close to his grandfather and eyed Bram doubtfully.

"Johnny..." Bram could hear the gentle rebuke in John's voice.

"Hello." The boy gave his grandfather's leg a quick hug and then wandered to the edge of the pasture to watch the older boys.

"Johnny is Ellie's oldest," John said as he watched the boy walk away. "He misses his father. *Dawdi* here just doesn't fill in that gap very well."

Bram was silent, watching Johnny as he leaned against the pasture fence, his head tilted into one hand. An outsider. Bram swallowed. Yes, he remembered that part of Sunday afternoons, too. A boy with no father to bring him into the game, and no one cared. At least Johnny had his *Dawdi,* even if John didn't think he was enough.

"What happened to his father?" Bram almost bit back the words, but it was too late. What right did he have to ask?

"It was nearly two years ago." John's eyes were on his grandson as he spoke. "I know Johnny remembers that day well. Ellie has said he still has nightmares about it, even though he didn't witness the accident. Daniel— Johnny's father—had a new team of Belgians. They were green broke, and Daniel planned on finishing their training, but he didn't get a chance. Something spooked them while he was harnessing them for work one morning… trapped him against the barn wall."

John paused, but Bram could fill in where he left off. It was obvious that John still struggled with his own memories of that day.

"Ellie was right there with Susan. They saw it all. Ellie had to get the horses away from Daniel, and somehow she was able to do it. She stayed calm enough to move the horses into the pasture, send Johnny to the neighbor's for help and try to save Daniel. He died that evening."

"What a tragedy," Bram said. It was the only thing he could say. He saw Ellie in his imagination, trying to save her husband, to protect her children…. She hid a steel core under that stubbornness.

"It was a hard time, especially for her. She and the children moved to our place. She couldn't stay on Daniel's farm, and didn't want to after the accident, but our *Dawdi Haus* was empty, so it was the perfect place for her and the two children. Little Danny came to live with us eight months later."

Bram looked at Johnny again. The boy kicked at the fence post as he leaned against the boards. That whole family needed a man who could be a real husband and father to them.

But that man wasn't him—not by a long shot.

* * *

Where was Johnny? Ellie paused in the shade of the big maple tree that grew between the drive and the back door of Welcome Yoder's house and searched each group of church members with her eyes. There he was, watching the softball game.

Now that she had found him, what else could she do? Ellie twisted her fingers together at her waist. The children were all occupied, and the afternoon stretched in front of her. *Dat* wouldn't be ready to go home until the ball game was done. At least the headache was easing.

"Ellie!"

Lovina and Annie Beachey had found a bench near the house, and Lovina was waving her over.

"I haven't gotten a chance to visit with you yet today." Lovina grasped Ellie's hand and pulled her down next to her.

Ellie sighed as she took her seat. "It's good to see you, too. How are both of you feeling?"

"Oh, I'm not sure how much longer I'll be able to wait," Annie said. She fanned herself with a handkerchief. "I know the weather isn't hot yet, but I feel like I have a furnace inside me!"

Ellie laughed at the comical face Annie made. "Just be glad you aren't like poor Lovina. She has the whole summer to wait!"

"Oh, but we all know it's worth it," Lovina said. "I would go through this every summer just to hold a wee one in my arms at the end."

Ellie looked away from them as she felt unexpected tears spring to her eyes. What was the matter with her that she couldn't join in a conversation about babies?

She half listened to Lovina and Annie's conversation as she watched the groups of men in the yard. *Dat* was talking with Bram and a couple others, and then Welcome Yoder and Eli Schrock joined the group. It looked as if *Dat* was making sure Bram met them all.

Levi Zook walked over to join them, his ready laugh already carrying to her ears. *Ja,* and he looked in her direction. Ellie turned her gaze away from the men. Poor Levi. She felt for him, bearing the raising of his children alone since his wife died, but not enough to marry him when she felt nothing more than pity.

She waited until she heard him talking with another group, then looked at Bram again. He blended in so well with the other men she would never call him *Englisch* now. His *Englisch* haircut was hidden under his hat, and with his clean-shaven face, he looked like an older bachelor. He joined in the conversation and even stood with the same relaxed posture. If she didn't know better, she would think he really was one of them.

"Ellie." Lovina's voice broke into her thoughts. "Annie wants to know what you think of her brother Bram."

"I've only just met him. I can't say what I think of him yet."

"Well, he's talked about visiting with your *Dat* and being at the farm," Annie said. "And he's mentioned everyone in the family except you. That's a sure sign he's been thinking about you."

Ellie felt her face blush. If he thought about her at all, it for sure wouldn't be romantic thoughts, as rude as she'd been. But now, watching him in deep conversation with *Dat* and the other men, she couldn't remember why he had upset her so. It didn't look as if he was trying to bring his *Englisch* ways to the community; in fact, it looked as if he was trying hard to fit in.

"How soon will he move to his new farm?" Lovina asked.

"He said he wants to this next week, but I don't want him to go yet. That old house is barely livable, and we'll miss having him around when he goes. But he says he wants to get started on the spring work. It's getting late as it is."

Someone in the group of men must have told a joke, because just then they all started laughing. Bram turned and looked straight at Ellie, the dimple on his right cheek making him more attractive than ever. He paused when he saw her looking at him and gave her a smile that started sliding into his grin. Ellie turned away before it did. How could she let him catch her watching him?

"I'd better go look for Danny," she said, rising from the bench. "It's time for his diaper to be changed."

"Oh, Sally can do that," Lovina said, catching her arm and pulling her back to her seat again. "We want to know what you think of Bram."

"What I think of him? Why would that make a difference?"

"You're both single, about the same age. Who wouldn't think of the two of you together? You don't have to be secretive about it like the younger folk are. And since you won't consider Levi…"

Ellie tried not resent her sister's clumsy matchmaking. Of course people would think of them pairing up, and after watching Bram today, she realized it wasn't as impossible as she had thought at first. But she wasn't getting married again, no matter how hard Lovina pushed. If she only wanted another husband, she could have married Levi Zook months ago. *Ne,* marriage wasn't in her plans, was it?

"We hardly know each other. I don't think we've spoken more than five words to each other," Ellie said firmly. "Don't count your chickens before they're hatched, Lovina."

"I'm not counting chickens, Ellie, just trying to get the hen to lay a few eggs."

Annie burst into laughter at this, and Ellie found herself smiling at her sister's joke.

"I'll think about it."

But it was hopeless. Lovina wouldn't give up that easily.

"So Thursday will be good for everyone, then?"

The men all nodded their agreement as John went on. "Bram has seed already." He looked at Bram to get an affirmation. "So bring your teams and equipment."

The conversation drifted away from Thursday's plans to the weather, and when Matthew walked up to him, Bram was ready for some action.

"How about joining the softball game? Those young fellows need to have some friendly competition."

"I don't even remember the last time I played."

"It's something you don't forget. Come on."

He followed Matthew to the pasture, where a group of young men were joining together to make a team. They got some ribbing from the boys on the other team, but it was all in fun.

The boys went up to bat first, and Bram went out to left field. He knew it wouldn't be a rough game with everyone wearing their best clothes, but at least it would get him moving.

The first two batters hit lazy pop-ups to center field. The center fielder missed, and the boys made it to their bases. The next batter struck out. Yes, it would be a quiet game.

Bram looked over to the house between batters and saw Ellie still sitting with Annie and another woman on the bench. She looked preoccupied and was no longer looking at him. What was she thinking about?

The next batter hit a pop-up to center field again, but this time it was caught. One more out before they switched sides.

Bram glanced at Johnny. The boy was watching him. There was something about Ellie's children—first the little girl and now this kid. They had a way of looking at him—how could he ever live up to the trust he saw in their eyes? He glanced over at Ellie again, and the warning bells started going off in his head. He shouldn't get involved.

Just forget it.

The longing look on Johnny's face decided for him.

"Johnny," he said, walking over to the fence, "do you want to play left field with me?"

The boy's face brightened, then fell again. He looked at the ground.

"I don't know how. Benjamin and Reuben won't let me. They'll say I'm too little."

Benjamin and Reuben? That's right, Ellie's brothers.

"They'll have to let you if you're my partner."

"Really?" Johnny said, looking at his face for the first time.

"Sure, come on."

Bram lifted Johnny over the fence and showed him where to stand to wait for the ball.

Johnny turned to Bram as the next batter stepped up to the plate.

"That's Reuben. He always hits the ball."

"If he hits it this way, we'll try to catch it."

Johnny nodded in response, and then he stood with his hands on his knees and his eyes on the batter, in imitation of Bram.

Reuben let the first two pitches go past him and then swung at the third. The big softball hit the bat with a muffled *thunk* and flew toward left field.

"Catch it!" Johnny yelled to Bram.

Bram caught the ball on a bounce and passed it to Johnny.

"Throw to second!"

Johnny tossed the ball to the second baseman, who picked it up as it rolled along the ground toward him, then tagged the runner from first out.

Bram gave the boy a smile and nod. "Good job, son."

The grin on Johnny's face gave him a start. He didn't look anything like the forlorn kid who had been leaning on the fence. John was right; the boy just needed a man's attention, someone closer to his own father's age.

The afternoon wore on, and more boys Johnny's age joined in the game with their fathers and older brothers. There were more than a dozen players on each team, but no one minded. All too soon the afternoon ended, and it was time for the families to make their way home.

"I hope your *mam* isn't too mad that I let your clothes get dusty."

Johnny looked down at the dirt on his knees in surprise. Bram did his best to brush it off with his hand, but the boy's Sunday pants were still stained when he was done.

"Do you think she'll whip me?"

Bram's heart stopped at the thought of someone whipping this kid. The unsought memory of a hot, dusty barn and a horsewhip in his father's hand rose before he could slam the door shut on it again. He couldn't bear to be the cause of Johnny's suffering.

"I'll explain. She'll have to whip me to get to you."

Bram looked into the boy's eyes. They glowed with merriment.

"I'd like to see her try to whip you!"

"Now, Johnny." Bram's head snapped up at the sound of Ellie's voice. "Have I ever whipped anyone?"

Johnny laughed as he caught hold of his mother's hand. When Ellie's mock frown softened into a winsome smile, Bram understood. He was being let in on a family joke. Nestled against Ellie's left hip, even little Danny drooled a gap-toothed grin. What kind of family was this?

"*Dawdi* has our buggy ready. It's time to go."

Ellie spoke to Johnny, but her eyes were on Bram. Her usual guarded expression had disappeared. She looked more relaxed. Calm. Willing to talk.

"Thank you for including him in the game." Voice soft, she stepped close while Johnny and Susan dashed for the stone drive. Danny reached out to pat Bram's shoulder, and the baby's touch soothed the prickled feelings of old, dredged up by Johnny's teasing words.

"I haven't seen him have so much fun since..." She stopped and caught her lower lip in her teeth. Why did he think about kissing her right then?

"My brothers forget to include him in what they're

doing. They still think of him as being Danny or Susan's age, I guess. You made him very happy."

"It was fun for me, too." Bram cast about for something to say to keep the conversation going. He didn't want to break this better mood, this more friendly approach. "He's a fine boy."

Goodbyes were exchanged as families sorted themselves into the waiting buggies. Ellie should join her family, but she still stood next to him.

She finally looked at him. "I need to apologize to you." Her clear blue eyes held his.

"There are no apologies needed."

"*Ja,* there are. I…well, I was mistaken about something. I was wrong to be so rude to you."

Bram pushed further, in spite of the cacophony of warnings in his head.

"Does that mean that you might go riding with me sometime?"

She cast her eyes away from his. "I…I would have to think about it."

"I'll be at your place on Tuesday. I'll ask you then."

The look she gave him was uncertain, wavering. She nodded a goodbye and then headed to her father's waiting buggy.

Bram's heart started to follow, but he stopped it with a frown. Strong and stubborn he could handle. Vulnerable and unsure? A woman like that would grab him and never let go.

Chapter Seven

"Walkin's for chumps."

Kavanaugh's words echoed in Bram's mind with every step he took toward the Stoltzfus farm on Tuesday morning.

"You're one of my boys now, and my boys have wheels." Then Kavanaugh had given him the Studebaker.

Puffs of dust rose each time his foot landed on the edge of the gravel road. Man, he missed that Studebaker.

But he didn't miss it enough to risk Kavanaugh finding him first. In this game, he needed every advantage he could get, and his biggest advantage was that Kavanaugh had no idea where he was.

A rising blister on his left heel reminded Bram to shorten his stride. He'd bear a thousand blisters before he'd give up that advantage.

When he reached the crossroads, the trees gave way to a view of John's white barn and outbuildings, and Bram's pace quickened. He was only anxious to get his rig so he wouldn't have to walk anymore, right? He hadn't given Ellie Miller a thought all morning.

But he scanned the garden and the yards before heading to the barn. She wasn't anywhere in sight.

Bram found John on the threshing floor, currying the gray gelding he had purchased last week.

"Good morning," Bram called to him.

John nodded his greeting over the horse's back. He gave a final stroke with the currycomb and then picked up a brush.

"He's almost ready for you." The horse stood quietly while John brushed him.

"There's no big hurry. I'm not due to pick up the buggy until midafternoon."

"You'll eat dinner with us, then?"

Bram hesitated, but the invitation wasn't really a question. If he was at the farm during the noon meal, he would be expected to eat with the family. It was the Amish way. Would Ellie and her children eat with her parents, or did they eat at the *Dawdi Haus?*

"I'll be glad to stay."

"It's too bad today is a school day. Johnny will be sorry he missed you. He chattered away about that softball game all the way home on Sunday."

"It was a lot of fun." Bram rubbed the back of his neck. Johnny's trusting face, that gap-toothed grin, had haunted him ever since he watched the Stoltzfus buggy drive away Sunday afternoon. The whole family had wrapped themselves around his heart somehow. "He's a fine boy."

John stopped his brushing and leaned his arms on the horse's back.

"He's been a sad and moody boy. I've been at a loss

as to how to make things better for him and haven't been able to reach him. You did, though. I haven't seen that boy so lively since his father died."

Bram didn't know what to say. He had enjoyed the ball game, too, but he hadn't expected to enjoy the kid. Things were getting complicated.

The sound of a dinner bell drifted into the barn.

"Dinner's almost ready." John gave the horse another pat. "He'll be fine here until this afternoon."

As the two men walked to the house, Bram looked toward the *Dawdi Haus*. Still no sign of Ellie. Just as well. He'd be polite, have dinner and be on his way.

After washing up at the bench outside the back door, Bram followed John into the large kitchen. He took a deep breath. The tantalizing odors drew him in. Potatoes, fried chicken... Bram's throat was suddenly tight when he saw Ellie pouring peas into a serving dish. He took a deep breath.

A tug on his trousers pulled his gaze down.

"I helped set the table."

Bram crouched down to Susan's height. Her brown eyes were shining as she smiled at him.

"*Denki,* I'm sure your *memmi* likes the help."

"I put a fork by your plate."

Bram stifled the urge to take her in his arms. He satisfied himself with stroking her hair. Funny. He had never liked children before, but this little girl...

"Susan, come sit down."

Ellie blushed when he caught her eye, and she gave him a brief smile as Elizabeth directed Bram to a seat and the family took their places.

When they bowed their heads for the silent prayer, the ticking clock in the front room was the only sound, propelling him back to his *grossdatti*'s table. He could almost hear *Grossdatti*'s voice reading from the *Christenpflicht,* the book of prayers, after the meal. What would his life have been like if the old man hadn't died when Bram was so young?

As the prayer ended with a soft "amen" from John, he looked up, directly into Ellie's blue eyes. Her face reddened as she turned away to help Susan choose a piece of chicken.

"What do you have left to do on your farm before you can move in?" John asked as he passed Bram the bowl of potatoes.

"The house isn't livable yet. I thought I might be able to use one room, but then I found a family of skunks living under the floor. They put up a fuss when I tried to get them out of there."

"How did you do it?"

Bram looked around the table. Reuben had asked the question, but everyone was staring at him, including Susan.

"I used a trick I learned from my *grossdatti.*" Bram's mind flashed back to the day he had watched the old man trap skunks. He must have been Susan's age.

"I took a box—the right size, of course. It had to be low enough so the skunk couldn't lift its tail." The little girl's eyes got even bigger. "I put a dead fish in it and waited. Sure enough, right about moonrise, here came a mama skunk and her four babies out from under the house and into the box."

"What did you do?" Benjamin asked between bites of potatoes.

"I had an old horse blanket that I threw over that box and wrapped it up tight."

"Didn't they spray you?"

"*Ne*. Remember, the mama skunk couldn't lift her tail."

"What did you do with them?" Susan's voice quavered.

Bram hesitated. Susan's eyes were wide and trustful. He couldn't tell her he had drowned the entire lot.

"I took them out to the woods."

Reuben and Benjamin nodded at each other. *Ne*, he hadn't fooled them.

"What about their *dat*?" Susan asked.

"I caught him the next night and took him out to the woods with his family."

Bram glanced up at Ellie and grinned. The corners of her mouth twitched as she tried to keep herself from smiling. She had enjoyed the skunk story.

"Did I hear they had electricity on the Jackson farm?" John asked.

"I didn't find any electric lines. I don't think the power company has gotten that far yet. There were telephone lines, but I took those down." That had been hard. He could think of a hundred reasons to keep a telephone, but there was still one big one to get rid of the lines. No Amish farmer would have them.

He glanced at Ellie again. She caught his look, her blue eyes smiling. He could drown in those eyes if he wasn't careful.

What had he gotten himself into?

Ellie took as long as she dared washing up after the noon meal. Bram and *Dat* were on the front porch, visiting. How long was he going to stay? How long could she stall? But he was waiting to talk to her, to ask her to come see his farm, to go riding with him.

It was tempting. To have such a nice-looking man look at her the way he did—she hadn't felt that for such a long time. But what if...what if she gave in to him?

Resolve straightened her back like a rod of cold steel. She wouldn't give in to him. Let him be charming, let him be good for Johnny, let him bring a smile to Susan's face. He wasn't going to get to her. She wasn't going to risk that loss again.

When Danny and Susan began fussing in the next room, she couldn't put off taking them home any longer. It was past time for their naps. *Mam* sat with her feet on a stool, taking a much-needed sit-down while she watched the children play in the front room.

"Thank you for dinner, *Mam*." She helped the children put the blocks away.

"It was nothing. You did most of the work." *Mam*'s voice was relaxed, content. She'd take a rest, too, if it kept her as serene as *Mam*.

Susan yawned as they walked along the path to the *Dawdi Haus,* and Danny was already nodding on her shoulder. Ellie kept her face toward her destination. She hated this feeling. She longed to see Bram again, feel his gaze on her and enjoy just being with a man again, but she couldn't let herself give in to that pleasure. What if she enjoyed it too much? What if she got used to it and then...

Why didn't he politely ignore her so they could both go about their business?

After seeing Susan and Danny to their beds, she wandered back to her kitchen to look out the window.

"What are you looking for?" her whispered voice scolded. As if she would be looking for someone.

Ellie gathered her sewing from the front room. She had a bit of handwork to do on Johnny's new pants and hated to sit inside on such a beautiful day. The glider under the tree in the side yard was out of sight of the big house and the barn. She always enjoyed this shady, secluded spot where she could lose herself in her thoughts. No one would know she was there.

She threaded her needle and began to finish up the hem of the trousers. It needed to be good and deep, with plenty of room to let it out as Johnny grew.

"This is a nice place to sit."

Bram's voice came so suddenly that Ellie jumped.

"I didn't mean to startle you. I saw you come around this corner of the house, and I wondered where you had gone."

Ellie didn't answer. His voice was quiet, almost intimate. She slid over on the seat as he sat down beside her. Her mind was whirling—what could she do now? His weight made the glider rock back as he sat and he let it swing forward again. Could she just tell him to leave her alone without sounding too rude?

He pushed the glider back again with one foot. The motion pulled at her mind to relax, to enjoy the feeling of his strong presence.

"That was a good dinner you made."

"Denki." She took another stitch.

Bram kept the glider moving. How long would he sit there if she didn't help keep the conversation going? Did she really want him to leave? It was one thing to tell herself she didn't want him around when she was alone in *Mam*'s kitchen, but it was quite another when he was sitting next to her, smiling at her, as he was when she glanced at him.

"Did I hear you say you're going to pick up your new buggy this afternoon?"

"*Ja,* that's right. I'll need to leave in a little while to get there on time, but I wanted to talk to you first."

"Talk to me?" Ellie's sewing slowed, then stopped.

"To ask you to try out my new buggy with me sometime. I'd like to get to know you better."

"I…I don't know…." Ellie could feel her face blushing. She was acting like a girl with her first beau. What was wrong with her? She should just tell him no.

"Why not?" Bram was persistent. "Is it because I'm new? Or because I lived *Englisch* for so long?"

"*Ne.*" That wasn't what she meant. "Or *ja,* it was at first, but not now."

"Then you just don't like me."

"*Ach, ne,* it's not that…." Ellie turned to him. How could he think that? Had she gone too far? But he grinned at her with that same cocksure grin, the dimple winking at her. She couldn't help smiling back at him, and then she looked away. What a tease he could be!

Bram turned in the glider so he was sitting sideways, facing her. He put his arm along the back of the seat, his hand brushing her shoulder. Ellie almost sighed with the comfortable pleasure the light touch gave her. It was so tempting to spend time with this man….

"Ellie." Bram's tone was serious now. "I know I shouldn't… I mean, I can't help feeling that…well, there's something about you that I…I think if we spent some time together, we could learn to be friends."

Ellie looked at him. He was teasing again, wasn't he? His eyes held hers. She knew. As she looked into his blue eyes, she knew she could never just be his friend, and as quickly as that thought came, fear followed on its heels.

"I can't." She whispered the words, tears filling her eyes. She couldn't look at him anymore.

"Why not?"

"When I lost Daniel..." Ellie stopped, took a deep breath and let it out to steady herself. "It hurt so much. I can't go through that again." She turned to him, willing him to understand. "Don't ask me to risk that."

Bram looked toward the barn, the muscle in his jaw working. Was he angry?

"I can't promise that you won't be hurt." This time he was the one who whispered. Not angry. He was afraid, too, but of what?

Ellie blinked back the unshed tears. Where had that steel rod of resolve gone? The sensation of this man sitting next to her, encircling her within the shelter of his arms with a bare touch, had banished her determination in a single moment. What would an afternoon or evening with him do?

"I...I can't..."

Bram looked at her, but she turned her face away. She was too close to giving in to risk looking at him. He didn't speak, didn't move.

After a long minute she turned toward him, ready to say that he should leave, but the look on his face arrested her. She had never seen him so open, so vulnerable, so tender. He lifted his hand to her face and touched the strand of hair that always came loose. He let it run through his fingers and then tucked it behind her ear. He leaned closer, his eyes locked on hers.

"You're right." His voice was hoarse, strained. "I know you're right. I can't let you risk this."

Then, abruptly, he was gone, striding toward the barn. He didn't look back.

Ellie's hand shook as she picked up her sewing again, her mind following after Bram as he disappeared around the corner of the house. Her eyes blurred.

The tears that had waited at the edge for so long threatened again, pushing to be released. She hadn't cried when Daniel died, not even through the long months of that winter. She hadn't cried through all the lonely evenings of the spring and summer, or even during Sally's wedding the past fall.

Even when Levi Zook had come courting, even when the temptation of joining their families together had enticed her, she hadn't given in. She had stood firm, holding on to Daniel's dream, keeping the tears walled up.

But now, after this one man showed a hint of tenderness, a crack threatened to burst the dam. Slow, hot tears wet her cheeks as her thoughts raced.

What was it that battered against her defenses? Was it Bram's gentle touch?

She went over their conversation in her mind. It wasn't anything he had said; it was what he did. With his arm around her she had felt sheltered, protected. She hadn't felt so cherished since Daniel had held her last.

The memory of her own helplessness as she had willed Daniel to live, to breathe, to open his eyes assailed her.

"No, no, no!" she whispered to the air, to someone… to *Gott?* "Don't ask me to do that again."

Dat's words during the preaching on Sunday came

back to her. What was it he said? Trust *Gott?* A sob rose in her throat at this thought.

She furiously stopped the tears that threatened to overwhelm her again. She needed to think this through. He had hit the center of her whole problem. The layer of cotton fog that lay between her and the sisters and brothers at church, her fear of loving again, the way every day was a hard chore to get through… The trust was gone. *Gott* had betrayed her.

Trusting Him had been so easy once. Joy had been part of her life before, and she longed to have that feeling back. She had done all the right things, lived the right way, but there was more she needed to do.

Gott knew she had closed her heart to Him. The tears fell freely again as she considered this. She had closed her heart tightly against the loving Father of her childhood.

It wasn't my fault.

The protest rose against a flood of accusations. It *was* her fault. Could she ever be forgiven?

Trust Him. Was it as simple as that?

A phrase from *Mam*'s favorite Psalm echoed in her mind: "He shall cover thee with His feathers, and under His wings shalt thou trust."

Even her? Did He cover her with His feathers? Even though she was the one stubborn chick who must poke her head out from under the shelter?

The words were simple enough. *Gott* could be her refuge, her protection. He would lead her in the right way, if only she could trust Him enough to follow— allow Him to forgive.

Tears streamed down her cheeks as the dam ruptured. She buried her face in the bundle of Johnny's trousers, letting the tears flow. Long minutes passed until the wrenching sobs left her empty of every feeling, drained and exhausted.

She had nowhere else to turn except to hide under His wings. She must trust Him.

Bram struggled to shut the door in his mind. A lesson he had learned in Chicago was to never show your feelings to anyone. Keep thoughts, memories and emotions behind mental doors. That was the only way to survive. But this door refused to shut.

What was his problem? She was just a girl. He had known plenty of girls before, girls who were a lot prettier than that Plain woman sitting on the other side of the house. Even as he tried to convince himself, he knew that his arguments didn't work. Babs's brittle brightness didn't compare to the gentle womanliness of this one.

She was just a girl! He hammered mercilessly on that imaginary door, willing it to close, shutting away the urge to rush back and crush her in his arms, to kiss her and keep kissing her until she yielded to him and promised to be his.

He stopped short at the barn door. John Stoltzfus would see right through him if he walked into the barn like this.

He took a deep breath, willing the mask to fall across his face. Emotionless, unaffected. He had to get that mental door shut, and quick.

Stop thinking about her.

If he wasn't careful, he'd find himself trapped in a marriage he didn't want, slogging through every day following some horse around a field...

It doesn't have to be like that.

No, it didn't have to. He saw that in the way John Stoltzfus looked at his wife. Even after all these years, they had something his *mam* and *dat* had never had.

But that life isn't for you. Stop thinking about her.

That blasted lock of hair. He rubbed his fingers on his pants to get rid of the silky softness and felt the revolver in his pocket. The unyielding metal stopped him short. Letting his breath out with a whoosh, he felt the door slam shut. Cold, hard reality had done it. If he got too caught up in a girl, it could be the end of him.

Not just him. Cold water ran through his body at this thought. He looked back at the *Dawdi Haus,* sheltered close under the maple trees that filled the yard around it. If the mob had any idea he cared about someone, it would be their first weapon against him. He'd have to keep that door closed and locked, no matter how tempting it was to open.

Ellie pumped water onto a towel and held it to her eyes, glad the tears had finally stopped. The cool water felt good against her hot face. Susan would be getting up from her nap soon, and she didn't want swollen, red eyes to be the first thing she saw.

The ache was gone. Ellie dropped the towel from her face and stared out the kitchen window. The crying had washed away the pain in her chest, arms and throat that had become so normal she barely noticed it. But now it was gone.

She rinsed the towel in fresh water and held it to her face again.

The door of the children's bedroom opened quietly. Ellie put a smile on her face as she turned to greet Susan—a smile that didn't need to be forced. The little girl yawned.

"Did you have a good nap?" Ellie sat down in one of the kitchen chairs and pulled Susan onto her lap.

Susan nodded as she leaned against Ellie. Ellie held her close for a minute, and then she straightened her up so she could rebraid Susan's mussed hair.

"We're going to work in the garden until it's time to make supper." Ellie combed her fine hair with her fingers and then started braiding. "Will you help me?"

"*Ja.* Danny can help, too."

"*Ja,* when he wakes up."

The beans that needed thinning were at the end of the garden closest to the main house. Susan skipped along the path in front of her.

They hadn't gone far when Ellie heard Danny's cry. He hadn't slept long, either.

"Susan, I'm going in to get Danny. I'll be right back."

Susan nodded and stopped at the foot of the ramp leading to the barn to wait. Ellie hurried into the house.

All was quiet as she looked in the door of the bedroom where Danny was sound asleep. He must have had a dream.

As she stepped back out to the porch, she saw Bram leading the big gray gelding down the ramp to the lane. The horse was skittish, prancing sideways and pulling on the halter while Bram talked to him, calming him.

Then she saw Susan. The little girl stood like a statue at the bottom of the ramp, staring at the horse's dancing feet as they came closer and closer. Bram hadn't seen her—couldn't see her as the horse moved sideways, blocking Susan from his sight. The girl didn't move.

With her heart pounding, Ellie ran toward her daughter, but she couldn't move quickly enough. The horse kicked and danced—he would step right over Susan; she would be hit by his hooves.

"Bram!" She screamed his name as she ran. "Stop!"

Thank *Gott* in heaven, he heard her.

Bram halted the horse, calming him with his voice and hands. She saw his face when he noticed Susan just a few feet away. He turned white, then gray. He looked at Ellie, and his eyes reflected her horror of what might have happened.

Ellie reached for Susan, but he held out a hand to stop her.

"Let me." He smiled at her, his face changing in an instant, as if he had slid on a calm mask, and then knelt in front of Susan. The horse shook his head, watching Bram, but stood quietly.

Ellie waited, trying to catch her breath. What was he doing?

"Hello, Susan," he said, his voice quiet and controlled.

Susan's eyes were wide, staring at the horse, and tears ran down her cheeks. At the sound of Bram's voice, she looked at him as he knelt at eye level between her and the horse.

"I just bought this horse from your *dawdi*." Bram went on in the same quiet tone. "Do you want to say hello to him? His name is Partner."

Ellie's instinct was to grab Susan, take her away from the horse. Why torment her like this? But Susan relaxed at Bram's words and even took a step closer to him. He gave her a reassuring smile and picked her up. A rush of warmth flowed through Ellie as she recognized the same step she had taken toward *Gott* just a little while earlier. Susan placed her trust in Bram.

"Partner is so happy to go for a walk with me that he was dancing down the ramp. Did you see him?" Bram's even voice was quiet, inviting.

Susan nodded and leaned against Bram's shoulder, as far from the horse as she could get, but she smiled.

"Do you want to say hello to Partner?"

Susan nodded again.

"Then talk like this." Bram started saying nonsense words in a singsongy voice that made Susan laugh. She imitated him in the same tone of voice.

"Have you ever felt how soft a horse's nose is?"

Susan shook her head, staring at the horse. He was still calm, watching Bram.

"Take your hand like this."

Ellie watched him take Susan's hand and stroke the horse's nose. She shook her head in disbelief. How did he do that?

Bram turned toward her, and Ellie stepped forward to take Susan from his arms.

"Denki," she said, "Susan has been so frightened of horses ever since—"

"I know," Bram interrupted her. "Your father told me about it."

They stood close together, Susan reaching for Partner while Ellie held her.

"I've been thinking…"

Bram didn't say anything, wasn't even looking at her. He held the horse's head still while Susan patted the whiskery nose.

"I've been thinking that I would like to go riding with you."

Bram shot her a quick look. What was that in his eyes? Fear? *Ne,* longing. Longing that matched her own. He nodded, his Adam's apple bobbing as he swallowed.

"I'd like that, too. How about Sunday afternoon? There's no church that day, right?"

Ellie nodded. "Sunday afternoon will be fine."

Bram gave her a quick smile, but it was a smile that never threatened to slide into his grin. Did he regret asking her? He tucked that stray strand of hair back behind her ear again with a shaky hand.

What had she gotten herself into?

Chapter Eight

Thursday at noon Ellie ate a quick lunch with *Mam* while *Dat* and the boys were at Bram's farm with the other men. Dishes were done in no time, and Ellie settled the last plate into the cupboard with a quiet clink. She closed the door and turned to survey Mam's kitchen. Were they finished already?

"Doesn't take much to *redd* up after such a small meal, does it?" *Mam* wiped the crumbs from the oil-cloth on the table.

"*Ne,* with *Dat* and the boys away, it was a quiet dinner."

"Why don't you put Susan and Danny down for their naps here, and you can help me finish up my new quilt top."

Susan loved taking her afternoon nap at *Grossmutti*'s house, sleeping in the big upstairs room that Ellie had once shared with her sisters. Danny was already asleep by the time she laid him down on the bed next to Susan. She smiled at her daughter as she pulled the door closed, and Susan responded by putting her own little finger to her lips in a sign that she would be quiet. Susan would be asleep by the time Ellie reached the room off the kitchen that *Mam* used as her sewing room.

Mam had most of the blocks already pieced and was arranging them on the sewing table.

"Who is this quilt for?" Ellie asked, picking up one of the blocks. From the colors, it looked as if *Mam* had used leftover scraps from making men's shirts. She had arranged the blocks on her worktable to form the Tumbling Blocks pattern.

"I'm hoping it will be for your brother Reuben."

"A quilt for Reuben? Then he's serious about someone."

Mam's eyes twinkled as she switched blocks around to work out the best order for them.

"You know your brother. He won't tell us for sure, but he's out every Saturday night with someone. And he spends most of Saturday afternoon cleaning his courting buggy."

"It will be fun to have another wedding in the fall."

"*Ach, ja,* it will." *Mam* looked at Ellie. "Maybe two weddings? Wouldn't that be fun?"

"But who else would be getting married? Benjamin is too young…." Suddenly Ellie realized what her mother was hinting at. "Now, *Mam,* don't be getting any ideas."

"Not get any ideas from the look in Levi's eyes when he sees you?"

"I've already told him *ne*. I feel sorry for him, but that's no reason to marry."

"He needs a wife." *Mam* sighed as she switched another block around. "*Dat* and I thought it would make a good match last fall, you and him. Both of you needing someone, and his little ones need a *memmi* for sure."

"*Mam,* we've talked about this already."

"*Ja,* I know." *Mam* waved a quilt block in the air. "But some time has passed. I thought perhaps you had changed your mind."

"*Ne, Mam.* Nothing has changed." Her mind brought up the image of Bram, the tender look on his face as he had let that stubborn lock of hair glide through his fingers.… Her cheeks grew hot. Something had changed, but not with Levi. Levi had never made her blush.

Mam gave up any pretense of working on the quilt and looked directly at Ellie.

"It's time I spoke plain to you, Ellie Miller. You need a husband, and your children need a father. The Bible tells us that young widows should marry, and it's time for you to be thinking about it."

Ellie sat down in one of the small rocking chairs, still holding two of the blocks in her hands, forgotten.

"*Ach, Mam,* I know I should marry again, but I just don't feel ready."

"Daughter, you'll never feel ready."

"But what if…"

"What if you lose him, too?" *Mam* finished the sentence for her quietly. "Is this what has been holding you back? And I'm not just talking about marriage—I've noticed it with the family and with the church family. You're holding yourself at a distance from everyone."

"*Ja.*" Ellie nodded. "I've just come to realize that when Daniel died…" She stopped and wiped away a tear. Tears came every day lately. She took a ragged breath. "When Daniel died, it was like my whole world stopped. I just haven't been able to go on.… I've been so afraid that *Gott* will take someone else—one of the children, or you or *Dat.* If I married again, I'd have to risk losing a husband all over again. I'm just not sure I'm ready to do that—to take that risk."

Mam came to sit in the other rocking chair, next to her. She laid her hand on Ellie's arm. The touch was comforting, warm, familiar.

"*Ja,* I've seen your struggle. But you can trust *Gott.*"

Ellie gave her mother a small smile. "That's just what *Dat* said in his sermon."

"Well, he's usually right."

"*Ja,* he is."

"What about Levi? I've seen him with his children. He's a good father, and he would treat your children as if they were his own."

Ellie nodded, tears threatening again. Levi was a good father, but the look on Susan's face as Bram held her, helping her to overcome her fear of the horse, tightened her throat.

"Don't let your pride stand in the way of *Gott*'s plan for you and your family, Ellie."

Mam's words interrupted her thoughts like a burst soap bubble.

"Pride?"

"Pride is a terrible sin. It can make us think that we know better than *Gott* does. It can make us afraid to trust Him and His plan for our lives."

There was that word again. *Trust.* It should be easy, shouldn't it?

"But how do I know what His plan is?"

Mam smiled as she patted Ellie's arm and went back to the worktable.

"Do you remember when you told me you and Daniel had decided to marry?"

Ellie's mind flew back to that long-ago time. Had it really been almost nine years?

"You told me that you knew Daniel was the one for you because you were so happy."

Ellie nodded, unable to trust her voice. That had been such a joyful time, full of bright promise.

"Listen for *Gott,* Ellie, and look for that same feeling of peace. When we are in *Gott*'s will, He gives us peace. Whether Levi is the right one for you or not, *Gott* will lead you to the right decision."

Levi? That decision had already been made. Levi was a nice man and a good father. Someone would love to be his wife, but not her. Marriage to him would mean not only submitting herself to his will, but it would also mean burying Daniel's dreams for his children. Johnny, Susan and Danny would become part of Levi's many children.

And Daniel's legacy would be buried forever.

Bram leaned on the top rail of the pasture fence. It had been a long day, but now ten acres were plowed and planted to corn. It would be a good cash crop to start out. He pulled out his handkerchief and wiped the sweat off his face and neck again.

Matthew joined him at the fence. "We're heading home, Bram."

"I don't know how to thank you."

"*Ach,* don't worry about it. It's what we do."

Was it really as simple as that? Eight men had taken an entire day of work, a day they needed for working on their own places, and had spent it here on his farm. Bram swallowed. A farm that he'd be leaving behind as soon as he found Kavanaugh. With any luck, he'd never even see this corn harvested come November.

Bram thanked each of the men as they left his farm. When he reached Bishop Yoder, the old man took Bram's hand and held it in his own frail ones, but his voice was strong.

"I haven't officially welcomed you back. I hope you're feeling at home here."

"*Ja,* Bishop. The church has made me feel very welcome."

"There's a baptism class starting next week. You're welcome to join it."

Bram's first instinct was to give a pat reply—assure the bishop that he'd be there—but lying to the elderly man didn't come easy.

"I'll have to let you know...."

Bishop nodded, reached up to pat him on the shoulder and then turned to climb onto the seat of the waiting wagon with his two grown sons.

As tired as he was, Bram tried to feel elated over the bishop's words. This meant he was accepted, that they were willing to talk to him about joining the community. But going through baptism and everything that went with it? He was already misleading the church by making them think he was settling here permanently. Bram shifted his shoulders. Lying to that kind old man didn't feel right.

Bram joined John as he stood looking over the newly planted fields. He could hear Benjamin and Reuben hammering in the barn. They had volunteered to repair the box stall and manger so it would be usable.

"A lot of work got done today," John said, his voice tired.

"It sure did. The men really helped out. Getting such a late start as I did, I would never have been able to do this on my own."

"You know you're not alone. When you become part of the community, they help you out." John scraped his boot on the bottom fence rail. "They know you'll return the work when it's needed somewhere else."

Bram rubbed his face, feeling the late-afternoon stubble of his beard. "My *dat*...well, you know what he was like. I don't remember him ever helping out like this."

The sun rode high in the sky, even though suppertime was near. The world he had lived in growing up— that world where his *dat* avoided the other men of the church as much as they avoided him—was far away from this place.

"I saw you talking with Bishop Yoder."

"*Ja.* He invited me to join the membership class."

"That would be a good step, but it isn't something to take lightly."

Bram looked out across the field again, his gut twisting uncomfortably.

"*Ja,* I know. I'm not sure I'm ready yet." Would he ever be ready to join the church? Maybe, if he was able to stay around long enough. For the first time in his life, the thought appealed to him.

"It's better for a man to wait, if there are things in his past that need to be dealt with first."

John's voice was easy, companionable, but his words went straight to Bram's heart, leaving him gasping for air. He had this man figured out, didn't he? He shifted his eyes to John's and then back to the field. Why did he have the feeling John saw right through him?

* * *

Bram stood in the center of the drive, between the barn and the house, alone at last. His farm. His fields. His frogs croaking by the stream. It was almost ready for him...ready for a family. He could almost hear children's voices calling from the barn, could almost smell supper cooking on the stove.

Bram stared at the kitchen window of the empty house. A family? What if he had found someone to marry all those years ago? What if he had never left? Would he have the kind of life Matthew and Annie had?

Probably not. He would have become his *Dat* all over again, just like Samuel, drowning himself in moonshine and anger.

Those years in Chicago weren't wasted. Peters had made something of him—but what? He was good at what he did, and bringing criminals to justice was the right thing to do. So why did his life still feel so empty?

The west-facing window was golden with the reflected setting sun. Dappled shadows played across the surface. If Ellie were there, she'd watch for him through that window. She'd wave and smile; the corners of her mouth would upturn in anticipation of the long summer evening stretching before them.

Ellie. She wasn't in his plans. He had no business getting involved with a woman, especially her. If she was hurt because of him...

He didn't know what he'd do.

And yet, what if she married someone else? Someone who could take care of her, be a father to the children. He shut his eyes at the thought of Johnny's delighted face, Danny's drooling grin, the memory of Susan's shy, sweet smile. So much like her mother.

He rubbed his face with both hands, looking around him. He was still standing in the middle of the barnyard, mooning around like some lovesick teenager. What was happening to him?

The back door of the house stood open. He'd opened both the front and back doors earlier in the day. That skunk smell was fading, but it would need a few more days of airing before the house was livable. He walked through the house to the front bedroom and slid the window closed. The window faced north, and a lilac bush half covered it, throwing the room into shadow. He faced the room, leaning against the windowsill.

Bram buried his face in his hands. The thought of what he should do wrenched his gut. He should keep his distance. Shut every thought of Ellie Miller away. Why did he ever have to meet her? He couldn't marry her. Why had that thought ever entered his head?

But the memory of the few close moments they had shared on her glider the other day came roaring out of the sealed place in his mind. He groaned with the thought of never letting himself be alone with her again. But that was what he should do. He had to forget her. He had to. He could never be just her friend.

If the mob ever found out about her…

He forced his thoughts to obey. Shut the door. Lock Ellie away. *Keep her out of your thoughts.*

He tried to remember Kavanaugh's narrow face, the noise of the city, Babs's platinum bob, to bring something—anything—else to his mind, but the only image that came was a stubborn lock of hair that escaped its confinement under a pure white *kapp*. Ellie again. It would always be Ellie.

He wrenched his thoughts away. Why couldn't he forget her?

With a dash of cold clarity, he knew. God was doing this. Tempting him. Destroying him. What was He doing, meddling in this? It had nothing to do with Him! Bram had spent his entire life ignoring God; why couldn't He do the same?

Trust Him. Trust Him. Trust Him.

The memory of John's sermon played like a record needle caught in a groove. John had said that was what he was supposed to do.

Trust God? The way his life was going, he couldn't trust anyone, especially God.

What if he did? What if he trusted God to take care of Ellie, and then He failed?

Did God fail?

What if God trusted him to take care of Ellie, and Bram failed? He'd try his hardest, but he had failed before, and he would do it again. He couldn't bear the thought of being responsible if something happened to Ellie or the children.

Trust Him.

Did he dare?

Sunday morning Ellie woke with a dream still haunting the edges of her memory. Daniel. She sat up, trying to clear the lingering remnants of the dream. What time was it?

Amid the predawn clamor of the birds, the dream became clear. She was at a Sunday meeting at the Troyers', and Daniel stood at her shoulder. She had turned toward him—what a joy it was to see his dear face once more—but his expression turned to reproach.

"What about the children?"

He had spoken softly, urgently, and then said it again. "What about the children?"

Then he had turned and walked away from her.

Was he disappointed in her? What had he meant? The children were fine, weren't they? She was trying to keep his memory alive for them.

But Daniel's plans for his family were dropping in the dust with her struggling strawberry patch. They were dying, and she was doing nothing about it. She couldn't let that happen, could she?

Ellie turned on her stomach, burying her face in the pillow so her crying wouldn't wake the children. Grief and regret pulled long sobs from her throat, cries of anguish that were swallowed by the pillow. She had failed Daniel while he was alive, and she continued to fail him now that he was dead.

Her heart burned.

"Ach, Gott." Her voice was a cry of anguish in her head, but only a hoarse whisper escaped into the pillow. *"Ach, Gott,* help me. Why is this so hard?"

Maybe she didn't want to fulfill Daniel's dreams. The thought tore another sob from her throat. How could she think that? She was Daniel's wife. She had promised to work with him in life, and as he lay dying all that long, hot September day, she had promised to continue what they'd started.

What about her own dreams? Had they died with Daniel?

The sobs turned to deep sighs, and Ellie turned to look out the window. Through the top pane above the curtain, she could see the pink-and-yellow streaks of the coming sunrise.

For months she had devoted every thought, every decision to the children, to making sure they received the legacy their father had wanted to give them. Daniel's words from her dream thrummed once more.

Ellie rose from her bed and peered out the window at the lightening world. An uncomfortable shadow in the back of her mind demanded attention. She had to face it. Her dreams? They were for her, not for the children. Stubborn through and through. Would she ever learn her lesson?

What she wanted wasn't what they needed. *Mam* was right, Lovina was right, even Levi Zook was right.

Ellie wiped a hot tear from her cheek. She needed a husband. Her throat tightened. *Ja,* and the children needed a father, a strong man who could teach them the right way to live through his example.

Across the road, the woodlot stretched to her right. When she was a little girl, she had seen a deer there once, the first one she had ever seen. *Dat* had been as excited as she was, and he had told her how the deer had been hunted for so long that they were very rare, and she was especially blessed to have seen one. *Dat* shared that special memory with her, something that belonged to the two of them.

Her own children had no *dat* to share anything with. Had she been selfish to try to keep Daniel alive for them? Who would they go to when they needed something only a father could give them?

Who would she go to when she needed something only a husband could give her?

Ellie leaned her head against the window frame, turning this question over in her mind. As she watched the birds flit from the trees of the woodlot down to the bit of brackish water in the ditch where the frogs lived, a deer stepped out of the cover of the trees. The doe paused, watching, listening, then took another step and lowered her head to drink. Ellie's breath caught as she watched two fawns follow the doe, mimicking every movement, their long ears flicking at every sound.

She had been doubly blessed by the presence of these beautiful, elusive creatures.

Her eyes filled with tears again as she caught the significance of her thought. *Gott* could also bless her twice by giving her two men to love in her life. Loving another man didn't take anything away from her love for Daniel. How could she have been so blind, thinking that choosing another husband meant she had betrayed Daniel?

The tight band around her throat loosened further, and she took a deep breath, smiling up at the sky, pale yellow in the imminent daybreak.

"Denki," she whispered.

Chapter Nine

Mam helped Susan into the family buggy Sunday afternoon. "Ellie, you're sure you don't want to come with us to Lovina's? I hate for you to miss out on the visit."

"*Ja,* I'm sure. I know you'll have a good time, but I have other plans. Bram will be here soon."

As Ellie handed Danny up to Mandy in the back of the buggy, she saw the look that passed between her parents. Well, let them think what they would, but her plans for this Sunday afternoon were simple. Bram was going to take her to see his farm and get her opinion on what needed to be done in his kitchen. It wasn't as if they were courting!

Once the family buggy was gone, the farm settled into a quiet that Ellie seldom heard. The early-summer sun was hot, and the cows had all sought the shade of the pasture. One pig's grunting echoed through the empty barn, keeping rhythm with the thump and clatter as he rubbed against the wooden planks of the sty.

Ellie wandered to the lilac bushes that surrounded the front porch of the big house, and she buried her face in the blossoms. They were nearly spent, but the scent still lingered. On either side of the front walk, *Mam*'s peony bushes held round pink-and-green buds. Another day or two, and they would burst into bloom.

Sitting on the front step, Ellie was enveloped in the fragrant lilacs growing on either side. She leaned back into the shaded seclusion and pushed aside one of the branches. *Ja,* even after all these years, her very own playhouse still waited between the leggy branches of the bushes. Lovina's had been on the other side of the porch steps, while Sally's had been around the corner.

Was that a cup? Ellie leaned farther into the bush. For sure, there were a cup and a plate, with carefully arranged leaves for food. So Rebecca and Mandy had found the playhouses, too. Had they shared that same thrill of discovery that she and Lovina had the day they found these secret places?

The measured clip-clop of a horse's hooves on the gravel road brought her to her feet. What if Bram found her here? The thought brought heat to her cheeks. They would be alone, hidden from the road by the trees, in the cool shade of the lilac bushes. He was so bold— would he try to kiss her? Did she want him to kiss her? She rubbed her hands on her apron. Friends didn't kiss, and friends didn't think about the feel of his touch on her shoulder.

She hurried to meet him in the lane at the end of the front walk.

"Good afternoon." He smiled as he greeted her, the dimple winking in his cheek. It would be so much easier to be his friend if he didn't have the kind of smile that made her knees feel like jelly.

"Hello, Bram." Ellie climbed into the front seat of

the buggy as he brought it to a stop. "It's certainly a nice day for a drive."

Bram reached out a hand to help her, but she ignored it and sat as far from him as possible on the seat to still keep a friendly distance. A sidelong look told her the smile was still there. He truly looked happy to see her. Would she ever figure this man out? The last time they were together, he had hardly looked at her, had hardly talked to her. Men. She had never figured Daniel out, either.

Bram drove the buggy toward the barn and turned around in the circle drive. Partner shook his head with a nicker as Bram guided him back down the drive to the road.

"Sorry, fella. You don't live here anymore."

"He was good friends with Billy, Reuben's goat. You'll have to bring him over sometime to say hello."

Bram looked at her. "You're saying I should bring my horse over here just to say hello to a goat?"

Ellie laughed at the disbelieving look on his face. "If he starts feeling bad, you might try it. It wouldn't be the first time animals missed their friends."

Bram just shook his head and then laughed along with her. "*Ja,* I might just try it sometime."

The laughter started the afternoon out on a friendly note. When Bram reached the end of the drive, he turned right, the opposite direction from his farm.

"I thought we might go down to the lake. The road along there is shady, and it's cooler next to the water."

Bram was right. As soon as they turned onto the county road that led them past Emma Lake, the dappled shade and water-cooled breeze tempered the unusually hot last day of May.

"Look at those kids play." Bram pointed the buggy whip in the direction of some boys laughing and playing in the water. "Kids in Chicago don't have places like this."

"No lakes to swim in?"

"Lake Michigan is close, but for kids on the West Side it might as well be on the moon. On really hot days the fire department will open a hydrant for them to play in the water. With this depression going on, there's nothing for them. No jobs, no money. It's a rough life for a kid."

Ellie tried to picture children with only streets to play in. No trees, no grass—just automobiles and noise. She had to ask him. "Do you miss the city, Bram?"

Bram was silent while he used the buggy whip to shoo deerflies away from Partner's ears. "I did when I first left. There's a certain excitement about the city. Always something going on. Vendors in the streets shouting, the shoe-shine boys trying to make a penny or two, the streetcars clanging by…"

Ellie stole a look at his face. Did he wish he was still there?

He returned her look. His face was serious, but then his smile crept back, filling his eyes with a light she hadn't seen before. "I don't miss it at all."

Bram went back to flicking away the flies.

They turned west for a mile, the overhanging trees still giving them some shelter from the sun. Bram rode without talking, but every few seconds Ellie caught a tune that sounded under his breath. She let herself relax into the rhythm of Partner's hoofbeats, watching the lake as they drove past.

She was on a buggy ride with a man—a man who

wasn't her husband. If anyone saw them, there would be talk that they were courting. The look that had passed between her parents told her they were thinking it might be true. There was already speculation about them, just like there had been about Levi in the months after his wife's death. But she and Bram were friends. Nothing more. She knew how to keep her distance.

When they reached Bram's farm, she was surprised at how much it had changed. The run-down place she remembered looked like a true Amish farm now. The house looked almost new with a coat of white paint and the shutters removed. Lilac bushes flanked the front porch, just like at home.

As they drove into the barnyard, Bram motioned to the new boards on the barn that contrasted with the weathered gray of the old siding.

"Next week I'll be painting the barn. Still have a few more boards to replace on the other side." He pulled his horse to a stop at the end of the brick path that led to the back door of the house. "You go on in while I water Partner. Make yourself at home and think about what needs to be done yet."

Ellie let herself in the back door. The back porch had been enclosed at some point, and it held a sink with a pump, handy for washing up after working out in the garden. She opened the door to the kitchen and stepped in.

All of the cabinets were brand-new, and the smell of fresh lumber filled the room. She ran her hand over the wood of the nearest cabinet. Smooth oak planks were joined together with a nearly invisible seam to form the cabinet doors. Bram had taken care with their building.

She turned to take in the rest of the room. As large

as *Mam*'s kitchen, it had room for a big family table. Bram had left space for a stove on the wall opposite the sink where the chimney would go up through the center of the house, warming the upstairs bedrooms. Even the wood floor looked as if it had been recently refinished.

This was a kitchen a wife could work in. Ellie ran her hand along the countertop. Plenty of space for baking, canning, preparing food for her family... *Ja,* any woman would be happy in a kitchen like this.

Ellie turned to the view out the window over the sink. Between the plowed fields and the road was room for a garden, and she could see apple trees in the yard to her right. A big maple tree stood next to the brick walk, with a low branch that was just right for a swing. Wouldn't Susan love a swing like that!

In her imagination Ellie could see her children playing in the yard—Johnny running out to the barn to help with the chores, Susan shooing the chickens into their coop at night, Danny learning to walk in the soft grass...

Bram stepped out of the barn and closed the door behind him, smiling when he saw her watching from the window.

What was she thinking? This was Bram's farm, and she had no right to be imagining her children living here. Her children didn't belong here. Their farm was waiting for them. Daniel's farm, his dream—that was where her children belonged. She owed that to Daniel. It was his legacy to them.

The morning's dream echoed in her mind.

If *Gott* saw fit to bless her with another husband, it surely wouldn't be Bram, would it? Not a man who had spent so much time among the *Englisch,* a man who hadn't even joined the church yet. To marry an unbeliever would weaken her own faith and only confuse the children.

Ne, Bram Lapp was not the man for her.

She dried her wet cheeks when she heard Bram open the back door.

Bram's heart stopped at the sight of Ellie in his kitchen. Like a bolt shot home, it was right.

But it wasn't. Was she wiping away tears?

"Ellie, what's wrong?"

"Nothing." She shook her head and gave him a bright smile. "It's a beautiful kitchen. I haven't looked at the rest."

She glanced toward the door that led to the front room.

"I haven't worked on that part of the house yet." Bram moved to put himself between her and the disaster that was his front room and bedroom. The former owners had left everything from peeling wallpaper to overstuffed, ratty furniture, and he wasn't about to let anyone see his house in that shape.

"What do you think about the kitchen?" He turned her attention back to this room, where every cabinet door had been finished and mounted, every drawer built, every floorboard sanded with thoughts of her. "Does it need anything else?"

"Paint. And a stove and a table."

And her. It needed her. Here. Every day.

Bram drew his palm across the back of his neck. That was just a dream. A pipe dream, but he didn't pull his mind away from the image.

"What color paint should I use?"

Ellie swept her gaze around the kitchen, and Bram couldn't take his eyes off her. Her small, slim form twirled on one foot as she turned.

"Yellow, I think. But not a bright yellow. Soft, like butter."

"*Ja,* yellow would look just right." He took a step closer to her, but she turned away from him. She had been acting as skittish as a barn cat all afternoon. How could he get back to that closeness of last week? Had that one afternoon on her glider scared her as much as it had him?

"I don't know about the stove. What kind should I look for?"

"*Ach,* every woman has her own likes and dislikes."

"I know. What would you choose?"

She gave him a sideways look that made him catch his breath. She looked perfect standing there. Longing was an ache that filled his chest.

"If I were choosing, I'd want one just like my mother's. It's the one I learned to cook on, and I like it." She turned toward him. "But I'm not choosing, Bram. It isn't my home. You need to get a stove you can use."

Bram held her gaze, letting himself indulge in the dream for a few seconds longer. When he had found Kavanaugh and his job was done, he'd be leaving all this, but the sight of Ellie in his kitchen would belong to him forever. A picture to linger over during the lonely nights ahead.

If he could bear to leave it behind...

"I like *Grossmutti* Miriam's cookies."

"What if she didn't make any?"

Johnny loved to tease his sister. Ellie supposed all big brothers acted like that.

"She always has them."

"But what if she didn't make them this time?"

Susan paused, her face clouding as she considered this. "But if she doesn't make them, what would *Dawdi* Hezekiah eat?"

Ellie broke in. "I'm sure the cookies will be waiting for you when we get there."

"Maybe..."

"Johnny, that's enough."

Johnny looked up at her with a grin, his brown eyes shining with fun. Ellie caught her breath. Every month that passed, Johnny looked more like his father, but the change in the past few weeks made her see Daniel in every movement and expression. Ever since Bram had come into their lives....

The children started a game of Twenty Questions to pass the time on the long drive. Danny slept in a make-shift bed on the floor in the back, leaving her free to handle the reins and her mind free to wander. She had started these monthly visits to Daniel's aunt and uncle soon after Danny was born. The older couple grieved as much as she did. When they lost Daniel, and Ellie moved to *Mam* and *Dat*'s, they also lost their daily contact with Daniel's children, the only grandchildren they would ever have.

"There's the creek!" Susan shouted.

Ellie looked past the creek, the landmark the children used to know they had arrived, and saw Miriam and Hezekiah waiting for them in the drive. Their smiling faces told her she should consider bringing the children more than once a month, but when would she fit in another day for this trip? Once a month allowed her to stop by Daniel's farm and collect the rent from the tenants.

"*Ach,* the children!" Miriam held out her arms as the buggy stopped in the drive.

Susan and Johnny jumped out and raced to Miriam, almost knocking over the short, round woman in their enthusiasm. Hezekiah limped over to the buggy to take a sleepy Danny from Ellie.

"Hello, Hezekiah. How are you today?"

"*Ach,* I can't complain." He didn't look at Ellie, but he smiled as he rubbed his beard on Danny's head, making the toddler giggle.

Ne, he never complained, but from the way he walked, his arthritis was bad today.

"Good morning, good morning," Miriam called to her over Johnny's head. "Come in. I have coffee ready, and cake."

"And cookies?" Susan was still fearful that Johnny's teasing might come true.

Miriam leaned down and took the little girl's cheeks between her hands. "Of course there are cookies! What would a visit to *Grossmutti* Miriam's be without cookies?"

Hezekiah handed Danny to Miriam as he took Brownie's bridle. Ellie would have taken care of the horse, but the one time she had tried to ease the older man's work, he had shooed her out of his barn with a frown. He would keep working until the arthritis made his joints so stiff he couldn't move. If he could handle things on his own for a few more years, then Johnny would be old enough to help him.

Once Susan and Johnny had helped themselves to a soft sugar cookie from Miriam's cookie tin, they headed out to the barn to see the animals. Miriam put Danny in the high chair she kept waiting in the kitchen and broke up a cookie on the table in front of him.

"It won't be long before this one will be running out to the barn with the others." Miriam patted Danny's arm as if she couldn't get close enough to him.

Ellie remembered *Mam* telling her once that ever since her only daughter had died as an infant, Miriam's arms always seemed to be hungry to hold babies, and it was true. She loved being near the children.

She helped herself to the coffee, pouring two cups, while Miriam cut large pieces of cinnamon-laded coffee cake for them.

"How are your parents?" Miriam asked as she took her seat next to Danny.

"They're doing well." Ellie joined her at the small table. "*Mam* is working on a quilt for Reuben."

"Not Reuben! Already? Who is the girl?"

Ellie smiled. "He hasn't told us yet. He's been very secretive about the whole courtship."

"As he should be. It must be someone from another district. I haven't seen him paying attention to any one girl at our church."

"I don't know. It could be. I know he was sweet on Sarah Yoder at one time, but that was when they were both quite young."

Miriam's face was suddenly serious, and she leaned toward Ellie across the table. "I know I shouldn't say anything. Hezekiah would say it's none of my business, but I have to wonder. Have you ever considered marrying again? I know Levi Zook is ready whenever you are."

The memory of being within the circle of Bram's arms came to Ellie, but she pushed it away.

"I'm too busy with the children to think of marrying again, and there's the farm. We still plan to move back to it when we can. Daniel would want us to."

Miriam stroked Danny's arm. "You're too young to hold on to the past. Don't let yesterday's memories rob you of tomorrow's dreams."

The elderly woman drew a shuddering sigh and took a sip of coffee, then studied the cup carefully as she spoke. "For many years I prayed to *Gott* to give me another child after we lost our Abigail. I wanted so badly to give Hezekiah a son." She stopped, caught her bottom lip between her teeth and rubbed her thumb along the rim of the cup.

Ellie waited for her to go on, blinking back tears.

"I've wished my life away, always looking back to our poor daughter." Miriam looked up at Ellie. "I have spent my life grieving, crying for what was lost instead of looking at the gifts *Gott* has given me. Don't make the same mistake."

Miriam's eyes were wet as she smiled at Danny. He grinned at her, squeezing the soft cookie between his fingers.

"Daniel was the closest we will ever have to a son. When he came to live with us, I resented him at first. I had prayed for a baby, not a sixteen-year-old young man." She turned to Ellie with tears pooling in her eyes. "But he blessed us with his presence, then with you, then with the children. *Gott* answered my prayers more completely than I ever imagined."

She grasped Ellie's hand in her own, her soft, papery skin cool and dry. "Don't make the same mistake,

Ellie. Don't try to bring the past alive again. *Gott* has other plans for you, better plans than you can imagine."

Ellie smiled back at Miriam, unable to trust her voice. Wasn't that just what she had been thinking? That it was time to move on from the past? But to think *Gott* had better plans for her than Daniel and their family? *Ach,* that couldn't be.

By midafternoon Ellie and the children said goodbye to Hezekiah and Miriam. The drive to Daniel's farm was short, just to the end of the mile, then the first farm on the right. Daniel's land joined Hezekiah's small farm in the middle of the section.

The house needed painting. The paint Daniel had used had faded from the gleaming white, and in places it was peeling. It couldn't be that old, could it? Ellie counted back. It was almost ten years ago that Daniel had bought this land and built the house. He had worked so hard and insisted everything had to be perfect before their wedding.

She could still hear his voice. "This is my family's house, and it will last for generations."

How sad he would be to see his house now. It wasn't just the peeling paint. The lawn was ragged, and the barn door sagged in one spot. Mr. Brenneman wasn't a farmer, although he tried. At least his job in town provided money for them to pay the rent, and they were good tenants, in spite of being *Englisch.*

Ellie saw a rusty black automobile parked near the barn like a dusty beetle as she pulled the buggy up to the hitching post by the back door of the house. Shouldn't Mr. Brenneman be at work on a Monday? Could he be sick? Or was today a holiday for the *Englisch?*

Mrs. Brenneman came to the kitchen door before Ellie got out of the buggy. The young woman looked as if she had been crying, and two children clung to her skirts as she stood on the top step.

"Good afternoon, Mrs. Miller," she said. Something in the *Englisch* woman's voice caused Ellie to stay seated. Something was wrong.

"Good afternoon, Mrs. Brenneman. How are you today?"

The other woman ignored Ellie's question. "We can't pay the rent today. My husband has lost his job."

"When did this happen?"

"Two weeks ago. I wanted to send you word, but James thought he'd be able to find something by the first of the month." Mrs. Brenneman's face was desperate. "Could you let us pay you later? It's only one month. He will surely find work soon, and the crops are already in. I told James we could sell the cow to pay at least some of the rent."

"You can't sell your cow." Ellie refused to think what the delay of the rent would mean to her family, but then, her children weren't in danger of going hungry. "You pay me when you can, Mrs. Brenneman."

The other woman held herself straighter. "We don't take charity, Mrs. Miller."

"And I don't give it, Mrs. Brenneman, but you have your children to think of. You will pay when you can. I know you will."

The other woman's smile trembled. "Thank you for understanding."

"These are hard times for everyone, Mrs. Brenneman. Please send word with the Millers when Mr. Brenneman finds another job."

Ellie turned Brownie toward the road as Mrs. Brenneman went back into the house. Without the rent money, she wouldn't be able to pay the taxes on the farm when they came due next month. If she had only known about this before she bought the strawberry plants! She had counted on the Brennemans paying their rent, and she never thought he would lose his job.

All three children napped on the drive home, giving Ellie plenty of time to think. Too much time. She was thankful the Brennemans wouldn't lose their home again—they had lost one farm to foreclosure already—and besides, it wouldn't help her to turn them out for not paying the rent. At least this way someone was living on the farm.

But where would the money come from for the taxes? The strawberries wouldn't start paying until next year, if they survived that long.

She could ask *Dat* for the money, but she knew what his response would be. He had told her more than once that she should sell the farm and let go of the responsibility. But she couldn't. From the time Daniel had first bought that farm, he had meant it as a legacy for his children. To let the farm go would be letting Daniel's dream die. She couldn't let that happen.

Would the church help her? *Ja,* but Bishop Yoder had already talked to her once about marrying again. The help would most likely come with the condition that she obediently sell her farm and marry Levi Zook or one of the other widowers in the church. She shuddered at the thought of the other two men the bishop had mentioned as possible husbands for her. Both of them were old enough to be her father.

Then there was Bram. He must have money. He had

already spent so much on his farm, but where did he get it? He'd come from Chicago with nothing, but he now owned a farm, horse and buggy, and she had seen a brand-new hay rake and a plow in his barn. Most people she knew weren't spending money—they didn't have it. But Bram did. More than enough, it seemed, and he was planning to spend more on a new stove. Was he just going into debt for everything? *Ne,* even she knew banks wouldn't lend money for nothing. So he must have brought it with him from Chicago.

The question circled through her mind: Where did he get his money?

Chapter Ten

A red sliver of sunrise pierced through the clinging mist of predawn coolness, promising another hot, dry day. Bram glanced at the sky above. The early-morning gray had given way to clear blue in a sweep from east to west. Not a cloud in sight. A good Saturday morning for a barn raising.

Partner's steady trot echoed in the morning stillness as the road led through a stand of sugar maples. The only other noise came from the treetops, where birds chirped and whistled, their predawn singing already done.

Bram settled back in the buggy seat. How long had it been since he had heard a car horn? Did he miss it?

He could come up with a whole list of other things he missed. Smoking. He hadn't had a cigarette since that day in Goshen. An electric refrigerator with cold cuts and cheese for his sandwiches. Telephones. Movies. Music. He missed going to the jazz clubs. That music spoke to his soul.

But staying in Chicago hadn't been an option, not with Kavanaugh's contract out on him. He could have gone west, taken on a new identity, a new job. He could have been enjoying electric fans on hot days instead of sweltering in this breathless humidity.

No, he would never have felt safe, always leery of someone recognizing him when he least expected it.

And he would never have met Ellie. The sound of her name caressed his mind with the soft flutter of wings, opening the doors that contained memories of her. He held each one in turn: standing in his kitchen, talking with her as they rode in his buggy, the light touches she let him give her.

Would she be at today's barn raising? John and the boys would, but would Ellie come?

The dark red shadow hovering at the edge of his mind pulsed. Kavanaugh. Was he still a threat? Bram hadn't seen any sign of him for more than two weeks, even though he had made the rounds through the surrounding towns. His hand slipped down to feel the gun in his pocket. He couldn't let his guard down, not yet.

Another buggy turned onto the road in front of him, and from behind he could hear the sound of a third one. He must be getting close. John had said to go west to County Line Road, then north and follow the buggies. The quiet of the morning was broken.

The barnyard was full of straw hats and black bonnets as families arrived. Bram found a place for his buggy among the others. He tied up Partner, loosened his harness and got his toolbox out of the back. Bram caught the eye of a young boy with a water bucket, and the boy nodded. Partner would be well taken care of by the crew of hostlers too young to help with the carpentry.

He made his way to the spot where the men were gathering.

"Good morning," he said, nodding to several men he didn't know, and then he joined John and the other men from his church.

"Good morning, Bram," said John. His greeting was seconded by nods from several of the others. "There are coffee and doughnuts over by the house."

"That sounds wonderful," said Matthew as he joined the group. "But at least I had a good breakfast this morning. How is that bachelor cooking these days, Bram? Did you even have breakfast?" He smiled as he shook Bram's hand.

"My toast and coffee were just fine this morning." Bram set his toolbox on the ground. "Both of them black."

The men all laughed. Bram gave them a grin as he headed over to the long tables set up in the yard outside the house.

Plates piled high with fresh doughnuts filled one table, while several women filled coffee cups. Ellie wasn't one of them. Was she even here? How could he ask John without sounding too obvious?

Bram scanned the crowd as he headed back to his toolbox and caught sight of his brother, Samuel, talking with some men from the Shipshewana district. Samuel at a barn raising? This was something new. What was he doing here?

When Samuel looked up, Bram nodded to him, but Samuel turned his back. Well, had he expected anything else?

"Levi Zook is here." Lovina spoke low into Ellie's ear, but every woman in the crowded kitchen heard her.

"Did he bring his children?" *Mam* was across the

table from Ellie, where they both worked at rolling out dough.

"*Ja,* all ten of them."

"His Waneta is a big help, isn't she?"

"She and Elias are sixteen years old already. She'll make a *wonderful-gut* wife for some lucky young man in a few years."

Ellie let the talk swirl around her. Levi and his large family took everyone's attention wherever they went. Just as well for him. There were plenty of young women ready to mother his little ones.

She rolled the dough until it filled her half of the table, then picked up the doughnut cutter.

If she had married Levi, her own little ones would be lost in that crowd. Levi's children were older than hers, at least most of them. Her Johnny and his Lavern were together in school, and he had one younger, Susan's age. His little Sam.

Ja, her heart went out to those poor motherless children, too, but not so much that she wanted to be part of that family.

The dough on the table filled with empty circles as the cut doughnuts went to the women frying them up. Circle after circle, blending together into an unbroken pattern.

She'd be lost in Levi's family. Daniel would be gone forever.

She gathered up the leftover dough and rerolled it into a smaller round, ready to be cut again.

If she married again... Her thoughts flitted to Bram and then back. She could marry again, and when she did, it would have to be because it was a man, not his children, who loved her and needed her.

"That's the last of the dough." *Mam* emptied the final bowl onto the table and started rolling it out.

"How many have we made?"

"I counted fifteen dozen," said a dark-haired woman at the sink.

Ellie took a deep breath of hot oil and sugar. She loved sweets, but after this morning she for sure wasn't hungry for a doughnut.

She poured herself a cup of coffee and stepped out onto the back porch to get some fresh air. Lovina joined her, carrying plates piled high with delicious-smelling doughnuts ready to take to the serving table.

"Do you know that man over there?" She nodded to a heavyset man helping himself to a handful of doughnuts.

"*Ne,* I don't think I've ever seen him before. Why?"

"He was asking about Bram. He asked me if I knew him and which district we lived in."

"Was he just being friendly?"

"*Ne,* I don't think so. He was very unpleasant."

Ellie's fingers turned cold around her coffee cup. Was Bram in some kind of trouble?

"It's probably someone who knew him from before. It's really none of our concern."

Lovina stared at her and then leaned close, her voice quiet.

"You don't fool me, Ellie Miller. You ignore Levi Zook, a man who's had his eye on you for months, but then you turn all shades of red whenever Bram's name is mentioned. Don't act like you don't care."

Lovina was right. She cared more than she wanted to admit.

* * *

"Isaac Sherk has built more barns than anyone else in the area." Matthew moved next to Bram, ready to team up with him. "He'll divide us into crews, and then each crew will work on a section of the barn."

Isaac moved from group to group, assigning work. Bram and the rest of the men from the Eden district were given the west wall, and they headed in that direction. Bram loaded his tool belt with his hammer and chisel and then grabbed a handful of nails from a nearby keg.

"First we put the frame together," Matthew said, "then we raise that up to join the other frames. After that, the rafters are raised, and then we start on the walls and roof."

"How many of these have you been to?"

Matthew grinned. "Only one, and I was a little shaver then, but I remember how it went. Once you've been to a barn raising, you never forget."

Bram looked around at the other teams. There were nearly a hundred men here from the surrounding districts. He looked from face to face. Habit. It was hard to break. Kavanaugh wouldn't be here, not in a million years.

As the groups organized themselves and started pulling the lumber they needed off the pile of waiting saw beams and planks, the sounds of building started. The hum of voices in the cool, moist air was punctuated by the echoing slap of wood hitting wood, the rhythmic sighing of saws and the occasional thwack of a hammer sounding like a car backfiring in the early-morning air. The work progressed as the men warmed up, a shout or two could be heard, and then the hammers started in earnest. Finishing the framing for the walls became a friendly race between teams, and soon there were shouts of triumph as the first wall was raised into place.

Bram kept busy working with his team. As the oldest and most experienced among them, Eli Schrock fell into the lead position for the crew, and Bram watched him carefully. Fitting the big beams together was easy with such an experienced foreman, and their wall was soon up.

When they started hammering the planks onto the frame to enclose the barn, Bram was on more familiar footing. It seemed that most of the men were, because the level of conversation increased and the rhythm of the hammering settled into a steady series of *thwack, thwack, bump* from each man's hammer. Bram was enjoying the repetition when he caught the words of a conversation from the Shipshewana group. It was Samuel's voice.

"*Ja,* you're right about that. I'm just not sure how far we can trust him."

"Does he think he'll just fit in again, after living in Chicago all those years?" This was from the man working next to Samuel.

"I don't see how he can, but I know one thing. He isn't going to waltz in and take what's mine."

"Your old *dat* gave you that farm, not him."

"*Ja,* but he's always had his own way. It would be like him to try to buy me out with that money he brought back from Chicago. Don't you have to wonder where he got all that money?"

Bram looked around the portion of wall he was working on. Samuel had a hammer in his hand, but he wasn't using it. He moved from one man to another a few feet away and started talking to him. A troublemaker, just like he was as a kid. Just like *Dat*. The gossip Samuel was spreading made his stomach grind. All he needed now was for Samuel's rumor to reach the wrong ears. The reward for leading the feds to Kavanaugh's gang had been a hefty one, enough to let him live comfortably for years, but he still had to lie low until his job was finished and Kavanaugh was out of the way for good.

Forget it. Forget him. Bram bent the next two nails under his hammer and gave up. He motioned for Reuben to come over to take his place, then he sat down on a pile of shingles.

Bram let his hands dangle between his knees and stared at the ground. What could he do about Samuel's gossip? The thread of truth in Samuel's words was just enough to hang him, and what if those words got around to Ellie?

"Worn-out, Bram?"

Matthew was next to him, holding out a dipper of water. Bram took it, downed half of it in one gulp and handed it back to Matthew.

"I guess I'm not used to this work yet."

"I volunteered to make a trip into Goshen. The sawmill there has donated another stack of lumber, and I'm going to pick it up. Do you want to go with me? I could use the extra hands."

"*Ja,* for sure." Any excuse to get away from his brother.

Matthew drove the patient horses through the middle of town on Lincoln, past the courthouse square. Bram spotted a policeman still watching the intersection from the police booth. The day he had come into town to buy his farm seemed like a lifetime ago. Had it really only been a few weeks?

Traffic picked up as they neared the industrial district along the canal on the west side of town. After the quiet of the Amish community, the noise of the factories was deafening. Matthew threaded the borrowed team and wagon between parked dray wagons and trucks to the sawmill. They loaded the lumber and were soon heading back through town.

"It's good to get away from those factories," Matthew said as he turned the horses onto Main Street.

"When I first got back from Chicago, I thought I'd go deaf from the silence in the country, but now..."

Bram stopped. He had been letting his gaze move from face to face as they drove by the storefronts when he saw what he had been looking for. Dreading.

Habit paid off.

Bram didn't move, but he let his eyes slide across Kavanaugh's face and ahead to the next corner. He saw Kavanaugh's reaction, though. A flash of puzzled recognition, the faltered step.

Don't panic. Bram took a breath, then another, keeping them even and controlled. His mind raced. Did Kavanaugh suspect it was him? He couldn't risk a glance back. Up until now, Kavanaugh had had no idea he was in the area, but if the gangster saw through the disguise... He forced the muscles in his neck to relax. *Just ride.*

His ears roared. He resisted the urge to jump from the slow wagon, to run as fast as he could. Any second now, he'd feel the pluck of Kavanaugh's hand on his sleeve. He'd turn around, look into the gangster's eyes and then who knew what would happen, what Kavanaugh would do. Bram put his hand in his pocket, grasping the comforting butt of his pistol.

Matthew's voice filtered through the roaring in Bram's ears.

"...getting married in the fall. He's already started his beard..."

What was he talking about?

"...says it makes him feel married already. How about you?"

"What?"

"I was talking about my brother. He's starting his beard now. Says he's old enough. What do you think? Should he wait until after the wedding?"

"I guess he could start it now. It'll make a difference in how he looks, won't it?"

Ja, that was what he needed. A beard. He needed to work himself into the community even deeper. A man his age without a beard stood out. He'd stop shaving today. He'd blend in so well his own brother wouldn't be able to pick him out of a crowd.

The roaring in his ears eased, and he swallowed. It might be enough. Bram risked a glance back down Main as Matthew turned the team onto Lincoln heading east, out of town. Kavanaugh had turned to follow the wagon, weaving through the other pedestrians to keep it in sight. He was watching Bram, but the puzzled look was still there. He wasn't sure. Yet.

Desperate for some way, any way, to keep Kavanaugh off his track, Bram's mind raced. Would a beard be enough of a disguise? A cold wrench clamped around Bram's gut. What if it wasn't enough? What if, by some freak chance, Kavanaugh found him anyway? He knew too well what the gangster would do to him. To Ellie… to the children.

"Are you all right?" Matthew's voice made him jump. Bram fought for control.

"*Ja,* I'm fine. I just thought I saw someone I knew."

Maybe he should run today. Bram watched the roadside pass by without seeing anything. Leave Indiana, leave Ellie, leave everything. He'd call Peters in the morning, tell him he quit. It was too risky.

Never see Ellie again.

Or stay and risk Kavanaugh using her to get to him.

He couldn't bear either one.

Once the wagon crossed the railroad tracks, the sounds of the city faded. Bram risked a look behind them. The road was empty. No Packard followed. Maybe Kavanaugh hadn't recognized him.

Would he even hear the soft purr of the Packard before it was too late?

A wash of cool silk flowed through his mind, giving him the calm he needed.

Bram looked behind him again. Nothing but dusty gravel.

What should he do? The cool-silk feeling flowed again.

Stay, watch, listen. If he stayed, at least he could try to protect Ellie. If he ran, there was no guarantee Kavanaugh would follow. He'd never know if Kavanaugh had recognized him until it was too late.

The cool silk folded around the tight feeling in his gut, loosening it. It was as if someone had been listening to his thoughts and guiding him to the right decision. Whatever it was, it had helped.

Ja, he'd stay.

* * *

At dinnertime, Ellie volunteered to help with drinks for the workers, even though the job of keeping the men's water glasses filled would let her mingle with them. The thought of seeing Bram made her hands shake, but she had to see him. She couldn't shake off the feeling that something was very wrong.

A sea of muted color swirled through the space between the house and the tables. Hurried snatches of conversation filled the air as the women flew in and out of the house, bringing out the food. Bowls of stewed chicken and noodles, mashed potatoes and jars of chow-chow filled the tables. Sliced loaves of bread sat next to crocks of fresh butter, jars of last year's jam and apple butter. Pies filled another table made of sawhorses and planks, causing the boards to bow precariously in the center.

The whole group of more than two hundred men, women and children fell into silence during the blessing pronounced by Mordecai Miller, bishop of the Forks church, and then the crowd of men lined up at the table and began filling their plates.

Ellie kept the glasses full, nodding to the men she knew as they passed through the line.

"*Ach,* Ellie, this looks *wonderful-gut.*"

Levi Zook smiled at her, his round face red from the morning's work in the sun.

"*Denki,* Levi. I hope you enjoy it."

"Are your children here today?" Levi lingered at the table. Ellie glanced at the row of blue, black and brown shirts waiting for him to move on.

"*Ja,* they're playing with the other children." She moved a cup within reach of the next man in line.

Levi shifted to the side to let the man pass. "You know, I think about you a lot."

Not here, not now.

"Levi, I can't talk right now." She tried to keep a pleasant look on her face as she filled another glass with water.

"*Ach,* between your children and mine, there's never a time when we can talk."

Ellie put the pitcher down on the table, ignoring the water sloshing over the sides, and looked straight into Levi's eyes. "We don't have anything to talk about. I told you before—I don't plan to marry again. You need to find someone else."

Levi leaned in close, ignoring the men waiting for him to move on. "You need me as much as I need you, Ellie." His voice was laced with desperation. "Please say you'll consider it."

Suddenly aware of the silence around them, Ellie realized her voice had risen. She and Levi were the center of attention. She turned from Levi to serve the next man in line and looked up into Bram's face. He looked from her to Levi, and his eyes were a stormy gray. How long had he been standing there? Her stomach clenched and unclenched at the thought of the conversation he had just overheard…the conversation everyone had just overheard, she amended as she realized that her brothers and Matthew Beachey were standing right beside him.

She dropped everything and ran—away from the talk, away from the questioning eyes, away from Bram. Blind steps took her to the field where the buggies sat in a row and found *Dat*'s. Climbing into the back, she curled up on the seat. Tears filled her eyes.

How would she ever face him again? How would she

ever face any of them again? Not only had she had a conversation with Levi in front of everyone that should have been private, she had drawn attention to herself. Nothing could be more humiliating.

"Ellie?"

Ach, ne, it was Bram. Ellie froze. He must have seen her coming this way. Maybe he had missed her scrambling into the back of *Dat*'s buggy.

"Ellie?"

Bram's voice sounded louder, and she heard footsteps in the grass next to the buggy. She curled up tighter, then jumped when Bram's face appeared in the door.

"I thought I saw you go in here. What are you doing?"

Ellie hesitated at the demanding tone of Bram's voice. Was he angry? She cleared her throat.

"I'm fine. I'm just resting for a bit where it's quiet."

"What were you thinking, talking to Levi Zook like that in public? Do you know how many people heard you?"

She nodded, unable to look him in the eye. Ellie waited for him to leave, but he didn't move. It was a mistake to come to the barn raising today. She should have stayed at home, but she had wanted to be with her friends... *Ne,* why try to lie to herself? She had been hoping to see Bram today, but she had for sure made a mess of everything.

"What is he to you, Ellie? Have I been making a fool of myself these past few weeks?"

"*Ach,* Bram, there's nothing going on between Levi and me."

"He seems to think there is."

"That's because he won't take *ne* for an answer."

Bram sighed, his shoulders slumping as he leaned against the buggy door.

"What am I, then?" His voice was nearly a whisper. Did he want her to answer?

How would she answer? What was Bram to her? He raised his eyes to hers, shadowed steel-gray.

Her voice whispered back, "You're no Levi Zook, Bram Lapp."

Chapter Eleven

Mercifully, Bram left her alone sitting in the back of *Dat*'s buggy. Alone to think about what she had said and done.

Her hands wouldn't stop shaking, even when Ellie clenched her fists, leaning against the buggy wall. She took deep breaths, forcing the threatening tears to stop.

She must face them again, all those people who had heard her outburst, whether she felt like it or not. They would forgive her, of course, but would they ever forget? The longer she stayed hidden in *Dat*'s buggy, the worse it would be.

Ellie smoothed her apron with her hands, bringing back some control. She reached up to tuck any loose hairs under her *kapp* and wiped her cheeks once more. Taking a deep breath, Ellie stepped out of the buggy.

As she rounded the wheels, the heavyset man Lovina had pointed out earlier stepped into her path. He stopped Ellie with a hand on her arm and leaned in close, reeking of unwashed clothing. Why wasn't he working with the other men?

"I'm looking for Bram Lapp. I saw him follow you over here, but then I lost track of him. Where did he go?"

Ellie pulled her arm away from his clumsy fingers. "He went back to work. Why do you want him?"

The man grinned, turning his face into a distorted reflection of Bram's. "I'm his brother. I just wanted to have a chat with him. If you see him, tell him I'm looking for him, all right?"

"*Ja,* I can do that, but you'll find him over at the barn."

Bram's brother winked at her. "*Ne,* I don't need to bother him there. I'll find him. You just give him the message." Ellie started walking away, but the man's voice followed her. "You tell him I want a piece of whatever he has going on, you hear?"

Ellie hurried toward the house, glad to leave Bram's unpleasant brother behind. What could he mean, that he wanted a piece of what Bram was doing? Bram wasn't involved in anything more than getting his farm going, was he?

She stepped into the kitchen, intent on gathering her things and finding her children so they would be ready to leave as soon as *Dat* said it was time. Relief washed over her when she found *Mam* there, sitting at the kitchen table with a whining Danny on her lap. When she was younger, *Mam* would listen to all her sorrows—now it was enough to just sit near her, drawing in her quiet strength.

"*Ach,* Danny, here's your *memmi.*"

At *Mam*'s words Danny turned and lifted his hands to her, and Ellie took her tired boy, letting him bury his face in her shoulder. She sat in an empty chair and settled Danny on her lap. He would be asleep in no time.

Being with *Mam* as she held Danny's small body close comforted her raw nerves. She laid her cheek against Danny's soft head and closed her eyes as she rocked him gently back and forth. If only she could stay like this forever. Forget about Bram, his brother, Levi...everything.

The kitchen was quiet now, or as quiet as it could be during the after-dinner cleanup. Most of the work was being done outside under the shady trees, with women coming into the kitchen now and then to put dishes away. The sounds of the children's games drifted in from the yard.

As Danny's body relaxed into sleep, Ellie opened her eyes and sat straight, adjusting the baby into a position that was comfortable for both of them.

"Do you want to lay him down somewhere?" *Mam* asked, her voice quiet so she wouldn't disturb Danny.

"*Ne,* I'm ready to sit for a while, and I don't want to risk waking him by laying him down in a strange place."

Mam nodded. She waited until the kitchen was empty and then said, "I didn't see you at dinner. Did you have a chance to eat?"

Ellie shook her head. "I'm not hungry."

Mam gave her a worried look but went on. "The men have been working hard. The new barn is almost done."

"That's *wonderful-gut.*"

If the men were almost done, they could go home soon. Ellie longed for her own kitchen, her own bed. Why had she thought joining the barn raising would be a good idea?

"I saw you talking with Levi earlier."

Did she miss Ellie's humiliating behavior? She must have. "*Ja,* he wanted to visit for a bit."

"He does so well, alone with all those children."

Ellie shifted Danny a little higher on her lap.

"*Mam,* I'm not going to marry Levi Zook."

Mam shook her head. Ellie knew that expression on her face. She wouldn't give up until either she or Levi was married, but she did know when to change the subject.

"I heard some talk about Bram." Ellie nodded, and *Mam* went on. "You know I don't listen to gossip. If what is said has any truth to it, then it should be said openly."

"I don't know if there's any truth to what's being said."

"Have you asked Bram about it?"

"Well, his brother said Bram was involved in something, but I don't know what he meant."

"But what did you hear Bram say?"

A trio of women came into the kitchen just then, laden with clean dishes. With the interruption, Ellie couldn't answer *Mam*'s question. How would she even respond?

Bram swung his hammer in a precise, measured blow. Set the next shingle and set the nail, a swing of the hammer, another nail. Once you learned to shingle a roof, you never forgot. He stopped to straighten his back and wipe the sweat from his forehead.

Below him, women were gathered around a quilting frame that had been set up for the afternoon. He couldn't see Ellie anywhere, but she must still be here. Her brothers were nailing in their shingles on the opposite end of the roof from him.

He returned to his work. It wouldn't do to let those boys get ahead of him. He'd never hear the end of it.

Shingling took concentration and attention, but it was repetitive and allowed his mind to wander. Why hadn't Ellie told him about Levi Zook before? Why did he have to find out about the man's intentions this way?

He hit a nail too hard, and it bent under his hammer. He pulled it out and pocketed it, then put a new one in its place. Precise, measured blows.

He forced himself to concentrate, but the look on Ellie's face as he had left her in the buggy haunted him. She had faith in him, but had she heard the gossip Samuel was spreading? And then there was Kavanaugh. He had to talk to her—he had to warn her.

Warn her about what? To watch for a rat-faced man in a maroon Packard? All he had to go on was that maybe, just maybe Kavanaugh had recognized him and might be looking for him along the back roads of LaGrange County. That wasn't enough for her to take him seriously.

As he reached the peak of the barn roof, Bram took a quick glance at the Stoltzfus boys. They had finished their part of the roof and were filling in the space between him and them. He put his last nail in just as they reached him. "Is that the last?" Bram asked.

"Everything except the rail," said Reuben.

Bram followed the boys down the ladder and watched another crew finish up the ridge. The final nail went in with a cheer, and the men scattered to gather their tools and families.

Trying to keep track of the Stoltzfuses in the milling crowd, Bram lost sight of John and his boys. He made his way toward the house. Ellie must be here somewhere, gathering up her children. Or maybe avoiding him.

"Bram, hold on."

He cringed inwardly at Samuel's call—his brother's call. Did Samuel have anything to say he'd want to hear?

Bram kept his expression calm when Samuel stepped in front of him, a triumphant grin on his face. He looked as if he was satisfied with his day's work.

"I was surprised to see you here today," Samuel said.

"You shouldn't have been. A barn raising is a time for the whole community to come together." Bram waited. Samuel wanted something, and sooner or later he'd get around to it, but Bram would rather get it done with. He looked past Samuel to where the women were busy gathering up their things and calling their children together. Ellie stepped out of the house carrying Danny.

"I hear you bought yourself a farm."

Bram turned his full attention to Samuel. He was a loose cannon and needed to be dealt with. He could only hope that Ellie wouldn't leave too quickly.

"*Ja,* it's down near Emma. I'm settling there now."

Samuel grinned. "It makes me wonder where you got that kind of money, after being away in Chicago all those years. I've heard the only people in Chicago with money are gangsters."

"I know you've been spreading rumors, Samuel, and there's no truth in them."

"That's not the way I see it. The way I see it, there might be people back in the city willing to pay to find out exactly where your money is. You made a big mistake coming back here."

Bram fought for control, but he knew how to handle a man like Samuel. He drew himself up to his full height, laid his hand on his brother's stocky shoulder and drew him close. He put a pleasant smile on his face, but his words, whispered so only Samuel would hear them, carried the punch he wished he could put into his fist.

"You're the one making the mistake, Samuel. Don't try to threaten me. You don't know anything about any money. As far as you know, I saved up while I was working in Chicago and now I've come back." He leaned closer to Samuel and put one arm around him in a brotherly hug. "I don't need to tell you what might happen if you keep spreading rumors, do I?" he breathed in the other man's ear.

He drew back. Samuel's dismayed face told him his words had carried the right weight. He patted the dirty shirtfront. "I'm glad we had this talk."

Bram pushed past his brother, hoping he hadn't made a mistake leaning into Samuel like that. Hopefully, throwing around a bit of muscle was all he needed to keep him quiet. Even so, he'd have to be careful. Samuel was just the kind of man Kavanaugh loved to use.

Once he reached the back door steps, Ellie was nowhere to be seen.

Standing on the back porch, Bram scanned the crowd, hot with impatience. Samuel had delayed him just long enough. He looked toward the field where the buggies were parked, but in the milling crowd he couldn't tell one family from another.

There, a young woman with a boy walking beside her. He started after them, but before he was even halfway across the yard, he could tell it wasn't her. He shot a glance toward the parked buggies again and swallowed a curse. The Stoltzfus rig was gone.

An endless line of buggies stretched in both directions up and down the road. They were in there some-where, but he didn't have a chance of catching up with her—not unless he could pull off the impossible.

Partner greeted Bram in his usual way, mouthing the front of his shirt with rubbery lips.

"No time now, boy. We've got to get going."

Bram checked the horse quickly and then reached for the harness. One of the reins was broken. A word from his Chicago past almost made it to his lips at the delay. He couldn't drive Partner with it hanging loose, but how did it get this way?

When he found the two ends, a cold chill ran down his back. They had been cut. This wasn't an accident. He flashed a quick look into the trees of the fencerow. Could Kavanaugh have followed him all the way from Goshen? But the trees weren't hiding anyone—the early-summer growth was too sparse.

He tied the ends so the rein would hold together long enough to get home, slipped the bit into Partner's mouth and tightened the harness buckles. That cut edge was clean. Whoever had done it had used a very sharp knife. Could Samuel have cut the rein? That was the kind of petty crime the brother he knew twelve years ago would have pulled off.

Ja, Samuel was the same today as when they were growing up. They had been alike back then, as alike as brothers could be, but he wasn't the same as he had been at seventeen. Seeing Samuel now was like look-ing into a shadowy mirror…at what he would have be-come if he hadn't left home.

So what had happened to change him? Life in Chi-cago, living on the streets? *Ja,* that was part of it. But there was something else. Something had made Samuel's life repulsive to Bram.

Something had given him a new way of looking at what he had been.

That silken coil flowed through him again, and the answer pressed on his mind. God. The same God he had ignored for years was doing something to him...no, for him. Protecting him from being like Samuel, providing Ellie for him. Had that same God brought him back to Indiana and to a new life here?

Would God do that for someone like him?

Bram slowed Partner down to a walk. He'd give Ellie time to settle the children in for the night. But then he had to talk to her.

The sun lowered, turning the whole sky into a deep blue bowl with a fiery red rim to the west. He tilted his head back to find the first star and spied it high in the eastern sky, just above a pale, full moonrise. He let himself relax as he watched more stars reveal themselves one by one, diamonds against deep blue velvet.

Ja, he had to talk to her.

Echoes of her footsteps whispered in the quiet house as Ellie walked from room to room, willing her mind to settle so she could sleep.

Johnny's body sprawled on the front room sofa, tangled in his sheets already. She straightened his legs and lifted his arm back onto his makeshift bed from where it dangled over the floor. He didn't wake, but rolled onto his side.

The children had all fallen asleep quickly after a supper of bread and butter. Ellie wished she could join them; she was ready to put this day behind her.

Stepping onto the back porch, she took in the summer night. Every night of her life, as far back as she could remember, she had taken the few moments this ritual required, even in the cold or rain.

The dusky air was warm for June. The sky still held the light of the setting sun, but to the east a full moon hung over the trees. One bright star shone, hanging in the sky above the moon. As Ellie's eyes grew used to the moonlight, she could see more stars dusted across the darkening sky.

An owl swooped out from under the barn's eaves, the first of several trips back and forth to the nest in the barn loft. Frogs croaked from the bog across the road, the bullfrog's guttural *gunk* contrasting with the peeper's *creak*.

Then a different sound intruded—a horse and buggy on the road. Who would be out this time of night?

The horse slowed as it came closer and turned into the drive by *Dat*'s house. Even in the dusk she could see the pale gray of the horse well enough. It was Bram. Her heart plummeted into her stomach, knowing she must talk to him. She must face him.

He drove past the big house and barn toward the *Dawdi Haus* and pulled Partner to a halt in her yard. When he climbed out of the buggy, he stood watching her. She waited, returning his steady gaze. The silence stretched between them until Bram's feet shifted in the dirt at the bottom of the steps. He leaned on the handrail and looked up at her, his eyes soft in the moonlight.

"Come down here, Ellie. Sit on the step with me."

A warning bell went off in her head. Sitting next to him in the dark would be too close, too intimate.

Any more intimate than feeling his arm encircle her on the glider in her yard?

She sat on the top step, and he joined her in the shadowy dusk.

"I have something important to tell you, but I want you to trust me."

Was he about to tell her what his brother had meant—what was it he had said? He wanted a piece of what Bram had going on. Would she ever be able to trust Bram?

Bram reached for her hand. She let him take it, turn it in his hands, stroke her palm with his finger.

"I need to tell you about…" He stopped, stroked her palm again. "How can I tell her?" he murmured, as if speaking to himself.

Her mouth was dry, but she had to know the truth.

"Your brother told me he wanted something from you—that you have something going on. Is it something illegal, Bram? Did you come here to hide from the police?"

He looked at her, his face unreadable in the moonlight.

"*Ne,* Ellie. I don't know where Samuel came up with that idea. I'm not hiding from the police."

His hand stroked each of her fingers in turn. She longed to give in to his touch, to lean against his body in the darkness, to feel his strength. She had been fooling herself saying they were just friends. Friends didn't lean this close, mingling their breath, their thoughts.

Bram put an arm around her waist and drew her closer to him. His cheek brushed her cheek, the whiskers scratching against her soft skin. If she turned her face slightly, if she moved at all, his lips would find hers and she would lose herself in his kiss. She didn't move and felt a butterfly-soft kiss on her cheek.

He straightened, putting a few inches between them, but kept her hand covered with his. She should pull it away, disentangle herself from this temptation, but she was too comfortable to move. With one arm around her waist and the other holding her hand, she felt as safe as a nestling bird.

"I need to tell you why I'm here, but for now it needs to be just between the two of us, all right?"

She nodded. A secret? What could he tell her but not *Dat* and the other men?

"I'm not on the run from the police—I'm working with them. Well, with the bureau, at least."

"The bureau?"

"*Ja.* I'm working with the FBI, tracking down a gangster."

A cold chill made Ellie shiver. Gangsters, the FBI, secrets… What kind of man was this?

"Bram, I don't understand. If you're working with the police, why are you here?"

He didn't answer; he stared at her hand caught in his.

"You've been lying to us? Pretending you want to be part of the community, but all the time lying to *Dat,* to your sister…to me?" Her voice dropped to a whisper. How could she even talk about such a thing?

"I…I didn't mean to mislead you." Bram let go of her hand and rubbed his face. "It's gotten out of hand. I meant to just put on a disguise—hide in the community while I tried to find out what Kavanaugh was up to. But it isn't that simple…."

"Lying never is."

"I never planned for this to happen, Ellie." His

voice was soft velvet against the night sounds. "I never planned to meet you, your *dat* and *mam,* the children... I never thought I'd find a home."

Ellie's mind spun. Just when she was beginning to trust him, to think he was one of them. "What did you plan?"

"I thought it would take just a few weeks to find Kavanaugh, and then I was going to start over—maybe out west somewhere."

"So you never meant to settle here? What about your farm? What about..." She couldn't ask him. She had no right to ask him what his plans were concerning her. He was just a fancy *Englischer,* and she was Amish. They lived in two different worlds.

"I don't know, Ellie. Everything has changed now."

His body went stiff as a sound drifted toward them from the road. They both turned to watch an automobile, its headlights glaring in the pitch-black of the road under the overhanging trees. It drove slowly, as if the driver was looking for something. The engine roared as the driver picked up speed at the Stoltzfus farm. Ellie heard it continue down the road to the east.

He stood suddenly, putting distance between them.

"I'll watch out for you, Ellie, try to keep you safe. But don't trust anyone, all right? Promise me? I need you to trust me."

He needed her. He needed her to trust him, an *Englischer.* An *Englisch* policeman. His eyes were nearly black in the moonlight, pleading silently with her. This wasn't just any *Englischer,* a stranger. This was Bram. Could she trust him?

From the depths of her soul, it came. Peace.

She did. In spite of her doubts, she trusted him.

She nodded, and he was gone.

The buggy whip popped as Bram urged the horse to a fast trot when they turned onto the road. Ellie held her hand, still warm from his touch, to her cheek as she listened to the fading beat of the horse's hooves in the empty night.

She went back into the dark house and wandered through the kitchen to the front room. She could see up and down the road from her front window, but it was empty.

The room was close. Hot. She opened a window and stood in the fitful air, watching the silver-white moonlight on the strawberry field. A mosquito whined against the cheesecloth screen.

Just…trust him? Do nothing else?

Could she do that?

That elusive peace struggled and was gone, driven away by her nervous fears. He wasn't who she thought he was—a wayward Amishman coming back home. He was an *Englischer,* an outsider, a stranger. How could she have let him into her life? How could she trust him?

How could she love him?

She couldn't love him…she mustn't love him.

Mam's words came back to her. She hadn't said anything about how to trust a man; they had talked about trusting *Gott.*

Panic rose like a frantic butterfly trapped in her closing fingers, but instead of letting the wings beat her into senseless fear again, she tightened her grasp, holding it, examining it.

What was she afraid of? If she trusted *Gott,* what was the worst that could happen?

She could lose Bram. The sweetness of his touch,

the soft kiss on her cheek, even his insistence that he trust her all told her they would never be able to be just friends again. Could she bear to take that risk?

What if, in spite of everything, she gave her love to Bram and then... She wiped at the tears that flowed down her cheeks. What if he went through with his plans and she was left alone again? Could she bear that?

The peace she was searching for came back, filling her with a calm that stopped her tears. *Ja,* for Bram she could bear even that.

Chapter Twelve

A scared rabbit, that was what he was.

A few months ago, he would have gone after that Packard. His own car would have followed that rat to his hole and finished this business, and that would have been the end of it. But here he was, stuck in this backward place.

Bram slammed his hand against the side of the buggy in frustration, making Partner jump into a panicked gallop.

"Whoa, boy, it's okay."

The horse settled down, but Bram's nerves still jangled.

He had let himself get into the worst position he could imagine. No car, no backup, no telephone, a woman to worry about…

At the thought of Ellie, he cast a glance backward along the road, where the moonlight stretched its silent way behind him. No lights cast a glow under the overhanging trees, and no motor sound echoed in the still night. Would she be safe?

If anything happened to her…

The rising heat found a focus. Kavanaugh. The man loved killing, whether he pulled the trigger or ordered one of his men to do the job, and he struck without warning. No open spray of hot bullets from a tommy gun for him. The snake preferred to kill with a derringer.

Bram pressed against the lump of the pistol in his pocket. With luck, he could protect himself if Kavanaugh found him, but what about Ellie and the children? What about her parents?

The heat against Kavanaugh was quenched in a dash of ice. Before he'd come, they had been safe. Yeah, sure, the gangsters were in the area, but they never would have thought of searching among these peaceful farms if it wasn't for him. He was the one who had put them in danger.

Rising irritation hammered against his tactics so far. He had established his cover, but now he needed to use the cover to do more than just hide. Kavanaugh was around, for sure, but it was time for Bram to be on the other side of the table. No more scared rabbit for him. He would become the fox and hunt out that snake.

Should he put a call in to Peters? The FBI agent would love to know he had found Kavanaugh, but then what? All Bram could tell him was that he had seen Kavanaugh in Goshen. Peters wouldn't be able to act on such a slim lead, not when things were so hot in Chicago.

Besides, if he contacted Peters, he'd increase the risk that his location would be known, and it could get out to the wrong people.

Bram shifted on the buggy seat, his skin crawling. Kavanaugh wasn't his only enemy, or his worst. Someone had tipped off Kavanaugh about the raid in April, and it had to be someone in Peters's office. If he was premature in contacting the Chicago office, he'd have to leave the area quickly and quietly. No goodbyes, no explanations, no contact…not even Ellie.

The scent of her as he had held her close filled his mind, and he shut his eyes against the memory. Why had he dared to kiss her cheek like that? Her sweet face enticed him until he nearly turned the buggy around to get one more look at her. How could he bear to leave her?

He couldn't. The only thing he could do was to start hunting.

Ellie woke with a start in the hot bedroom, the early-morning sun at work already. If she hurried, she might have a chance to water the strawberries before fixing breakfast.

Benjamin was already at her pump, filling a bucket.

"*Denki,* Ben, I slept late this morning." She grabbed a second bucket to fill.

"When I finished my chores early, *Dat* said you might need a hand."

They walked through the gate, each carrying a full bucket of water. Ben had already finished two of the rows, so Ellie started on the third. As she reached each plant, she tipped the bucket to splash water onto it. The ground was dry and dusty, even though she had done this same chore the morning before.

"It's so dry."

"It's bad for your strawberries. Look at this one." Ben stopped watering and knelt down to show Ellie the next plant. "It's hardly grown at all from when you planted it a month ago."

Ellie reached out to lift up the stems of the heat-stressed plant. The seedlings were still green, but the papery leaves and stunted growth told her they were just barely alive.

"If we can just keep them going until it rains…"

"It doesn't look like it will, at least not for the next week."

"Well, it has to rain sometime." Ellie chewed on her lip, remembering the days and weeks without rain two years ago. It couldn't happen again, could it?

"Maybe we're in for another drought. *Dat* said the pond is lower than he's ever seen it."

Ellie shot her brother a glance. He had no idea what a drought would do to her plans. She went back to watering her row. Every farmer knew that weather went in cycles. They had just gone through years of drought, but last year's normal rainfall was the end of that cycle, wasn't it?

"The pond is spring fed—it won't dry up. That will help us, won't it?" There had to be hope somewhere.

"*Ja,* that's what *Dat* said. But it gets low in drought years, just the same."

Low water. But she had a well, and there was another one for the big house and the barn. There would be enough water for them all.

There had to be.

She continued down the row, giving each plant a splash of water.

Ellie straightened for just a minute to ease her back, and her mind flitted ahead to the rest of the day. It was a church Sunday. Would Bram be there?

She tipped the bucket at the next plant.

The thought of seeing him again sent her heart beating fast. Did she even want to see him, after what he told her last night?

Ja. When he grinned at her, that secretive grin meant just for her, it drove all other thoughts out of her head. And then last night when he had kissed her cheek! Ellie stopped with the bucket in midair, remembering that delicious, tender kiss as he had held her close. He made her feel...

Ellie smiled to herself as she finished one row and turned to start the next one. He made her feel like a girl with a beau instead of a widow with three children. Even if he was *Englisch,* even if he was leaving soon, it was a *wonderful-gut* feeling.

"*Ach,* Ellie. What are you smiling about?"

Ben passed her with his bucket, heading back to the pump.

"Today's a meeting Sunday, *ja?*"

"For sure it is. We'd best be hurrying on."

Bram opened the back door of the house quietly, last night's caution still weighing on him. He reached into his pocket to let his hand close around the reassuring grip of the gun while he surveyed the barn and fields. Nothing out of place.

It was early, but he had a harness to mend before church. That cut rein had haunted his dreams. Was it a warning, or was it just Samuel's spiteful way of delaying him?

Bram shifted his shoulders and stepped onto the back porch. He was letting himself get spooked. Caution was one thing, but panic could kill him.

In the quiet of the barn, with Partner's munching the only sound, Bram concentrated on splicing the ends of the harness together. The task of tapering the blunt ends so they would fit together smoothly was so familiar that he did most of the work by touch.

Was this what God was doing to him? His own blunt edges were being shaped to fit into this community, conforming in a way that he never had during his childhood. God's presence was with him, molding and shaving off the rough edges, taking away his past more cleanly and completely than shutting it up behind a door.

Growing up, he had never felt part of the people, but now God was taking the rough, blunt mess of his life and working it into the community bit by bit, just as he was taking this piece of leather and binding it to the other. Nothing he had ever done gave him the satisfaction that his life here did, even if he did face the frustrations of living without modern conveniences when he needed them. Sometimes conveniences were necessities.

Bram stopped working and looked out the open door of the barn to the quiet lane and the road beyond. If Kavanaugh ever found him, all he had gained would be lost, just as quickly and cleanly as this strap had been cut.

Ellie. Knowing she was close, just a few miles down the road, was like money in the bank. He grimaced at that thought. Not like money, something much more secure, fixed, immovable, like the North Star. No matter where he went or what he did, she would be his center.

Bram tried the strength of the splice, and it held. Time to harness Partner and then get cleaned up for Sunday meeting.

Taking the brush from the wall, he moved into Partner's stall. The horse looked at him, his brown eyes calmly accepting whatever Bram wanted him to do. The horse trusted him.

Ellie's nod last night was her acceptance of him, the one thing he needed. The one thing he craved. She trusted him.

That thought whooshed through him like a north wind, and with weak knees, he leaned against Partner, the brush dangling from his hand. How could he ever live up to her trust?

There was one big problem, though. He couldn't live up to her trust. He knew that and God knew that, so why had he even asked it of her? All he could do was his best. He prayed it would be enough.

Deacon Beachey's sunny farmyard emptied quickly after families finished the Sunday dinner of cold-cut sandwiches and potato salad. The sweltering heat made activity impossible, and families left early to find some relief in their shaded yards. *Mam* came out of the house with her empty dinner basket hanging from one arm.

"*Dat*'s ready to go home, Ellie. Are you?"

Ellie shifted Danny in her arms. "*Ja,* I'm ready. The children are so hot, and Danny is ready for his nap."

"*Ach,* let me take the sweet boy. I'm sure heat rash is bothering him." *Mam* reached for Danny and then nodded past Ellie. "Besides, I think you might have plans for the rest of the afternoon."

Ellie didn't have to turn around to know Bram was walking toward them; she could see that by the smile on *Mam*'s face. Bram had gotten on her good side when she saw him working so hard at the barn raising yesterday.

"I'll see to the children. They can nap at our house in

the downstairs bedroom. It will be cool for them there. You won't need to worry about getting home soon."

"*Mam, ne.* You don't need to…" But *Mam* took Danny to the family buggy, rounding up Johnny and Susan as she went.

"Is she stealing your children?" Bram was smiling as he walked up to her.

"*Ja, Mam* and *Dat* are taking them home. It will be cooler for them there."

"So you're left on your own?"

"I'll be able to get a ride from someone, I'm sure. Lovina and her family are still here."

"You don't need to ask them as long as I'm here."

Bram's eyes dropped as if he had said more than he meant to, and Ellie felt her face heat even more as she remembered the last time they had spoken and how close he had held her. Was he thinking the same thing?

"Will you let me take you home? We can drive around by the lake again. It will be slow, but we're not in a hurry, are we?"

"*Ne,* I'm not in a hurry. It would be a nice drive."

As Bram headed off to get his buggy, a niggling feeling told Ellie he was worried about something, but she had promised to trust him. She let herself watch his shoulders move easily beneath his Sunday coat as he walked. He was a handsome man, pleasant to talk to, and his smiles made her heart flutter. Any woman would be pleased to have his attention. *Ja,* any woman, so why would he think she was special?

"Ellie, do you need a ride home?" Lovina joined her at the edge of the drive with Rachel.

"*Ne, denki.* Bram is taking me."

Noah drove up, and Lovina helped Rachel climb into

the buggy, giving Ellie a knowing smile. "Then you'll be busy the rest of the day, *ja?*" Lovina made sure Rachel was settled next to Noah, then stepped closer to Ellie. "Is he taking you somewhere special?"

"*Ne,* just home."

Lovina gave her shoulders a squeeze. "You've been looking too happy lately for this to be just a ride home. I think Bram Lapp is good for you."

"Get yourself on home and take care of your family." Ellie gave Lovina a quick hug before she climbed into Noah's buggy.

What did Lovina mean, Bram was good for her?

Bram's buggy stopped beside her and she looked up at him, smiling as he held the horse quiet so she could climb up to the seat beside him. His dimple winked under his whiskers, making her heart flip as he held out one hand to help her.

Ja, Bram was good for her.

Bram kept Partner at a walk. He could smell the lake as they got closer. Emma Lake stretched away to the north from the road, the low water exposing black, silt mud. Lily pads covered the water at this south end, but the rest of the lake was a mirror under the flawless blue sky.

Turning north onto Emma Road, the black silt gave way to a sandy shore separating the lake from the road. Bram pulled Partner over to a spot where someone had placed a bench under a lone tree.

"Do you mind if we stop here for a bit?"

"*Ne.* We can sit in the shade."

Bram helped Ellie settle on the bench near the shore where the overhanging trees made a shady cover.

"This is a great fishing spot."

Ellie didn't answer. She looked out over the quiet lake with that worry line between her eyebrows again.

"Last night..." Bram stopped. He had never felt like this before—as if he was one man torn in two directions. He wished Kavanaugh would just disappear.

"Last night you told me you never intended to stay here." Ellie kept her eyes on the far side of the lake, where a heron stalked in the shallows. "I know I said I'd trust you, Bram, but I don't know what to think. You're like two different people sometimes—sweet and tender one minute, and then harsh and almost frightening other times."

"*Ja,* I know, and I'm sorry." Bram paused, his own eyes on the motionless heron. The bird was nearly invisible in the shadow of the trees, his gray-blue coloring a shadow within a shadow. Living undercover. How did a man stop living a lie?

"I want to stay, Ellie. But I don't know if I'll be able to." He took her hand in his, and she looked at him.

"Even if you stay, we can never be more than friends." Her voice was soft, almost a whisper, her blue eyes reflecting the water.

"Aren't we already more than friends, Ellie?"

Her face flushed and she turned away again, drawing her hand out of his grasp. "Just because you kissed me once doesn't mean anything. I'm not a woman you should be courting."

Bram picked up a stone from between his feet and threw it into the water. She was right. She wasn't the woman he should be courting, especially now that he knew Kavanaugh was in the neighborhood, but why did she think so?

"You know I can't marry outside the church, Bram."

She said it softly but firmly, as if she had rehearsed the words again and again. He wrestled with the overwhelming desire to prove her wrong, but she was right. He couldn't marry her, at least not now.

"You're going to marry someone else, aren't you?"

Even though she kept her face averted, he could see her eyes filling with tears. "*Ne,* Bram. There's no one else."

"So you plan to remain a widow and raise your children by yourself?" Should he tell her she was crazy for thinking she could do such a thing or admire her for her courage?

"*Ja.* I have to."

"And where will you live? With your parents?"

Ellie swallowed hard. The tears had stopped, leaving her face mottled in the afternoon heat. "I still own Daniel's farm. Our farm. There are tenants there now, but…" Her face paled.

"What's wrong?"

"*Ach,* I try not to think about it, but the tenants haven't paid their rent and I can't pay the taxes."

Who would leave a widow without an income? Bram had a brief flash of what he would do to that faceless man if he ever saw him. "Tell me who they are. I'll get them to pay."

She laid her hand on his arm. "*Ne,* Bram. You can't do anything. Mr. Brenneman lost his job. The family has no money."

The faceless man had a name, a family. Bram's anger disappeared like sand washed away by a wave. "Have you thought of asking John?"

"*Ja, Dat* would help if he could, but he doesn't have

that kind of money. And the church would help, but Bishop wants me to marry Levi Zook. He wouldn't say so, but I know he'd expect me to obey his wishes if I took their help."

Levi Zook? The man's round face danced in front of his eyes. Would Ellie consider marrying him? Could he stand by and watch that happen?

"I can help you. When are the taxes due?"

Ellie looked at him, her eyes wide. He'd do anything for her to see her look at him like that again.

"I can't let you do that. It's a lot of money."

"We're friends, aren't we? Can't you let a friend help? You can pay me back after your tenants pay you."

She shifted on the bench. She was considering it, but he knew she had run out of options. Bram prayed she would let him help her. He longed to do so much more than just give her some money.

Ellie turned to face him. "I have to know one thing, Bram. Where did you get your money?"

That wasn't the response he was expecting. "What do you mean?"

"I know you paid cash for your farm. You've spent a lot of money fixing it up, plus buying your buggy, the horse, equipment for the farm… Bram, where did you get that kind of money?"

Bram felt cold in spite of the summer heat. If Ellie was wondering, who else had listened to Samuel's attempt at rabble-rousing yesterday? Would Kavanaugh hear rumors about an Amishman spending cash when no one else had any?

"I earned it working in Chicago. It was a reward for…" For ratting out his friends? *Ne,* for getting murderous scum off the streets. "It was payment for some work I did for the FBI."

Ellie nodded, the line between her eyes relaxing. "All right. I'll let you help me, but only if you don't tell anyone."

That suited Bram perfectly. He'd rather keep any money transactions as quiet as possible.

It wasn't until after he was home and settling Partner in for the night that he remembered he had forgotten to warn her about Kavanaugh.

Chapter Thirteen

Streaks of lathered sweat covered Partner's flanks by the time Bram turned him into the Stoltzfus family's drive on Thursday afternoon. Today's trip to Goshen, through Middlebury and then to Shipshewana had been exhausting and fruitless. Another day of hunting with no sign of Kavanaugh.

He should go home, but he couldn't pass this close to the Stoltzfus farm without seeing Ellie. Four days had passed since their Sunday drive, four days with thoughts of her crowding every moment. He craved one glimpse, one sure confirmation she was safe.

Tying the horse to the corral fence next to the barn, Bram loosened his harness and made sure he stood in the shade of the tall maple trees. He filled his cupped hands with water in the nearby trough and wet the horse's nose and mouth. Partner was too hot yet to let him drink his fill.

Bram removed his hat and wiped his forehead with a sleeve. The yard was deserted, but that wasn't surprising. In the middle of the afternoon he expected the children to be napping. Ellie and her mother were probably working in the cool house.

The metallic squeak of a pump handle rang through the heavy air, the sound coming from near Ellie's *Dawdi Haus*. Bram turned that direction and then pulled up short at the sight of Ellie and her two brothers carrying buckets of water to the field beyond Ellie's house.

What was she thinking, working like that in this heat?

He met her as she returned to the pump for another trip, and her pale face and bleary gaze told him he hadn't come any too soon. She tried to wave him off as he took the bucket out of her hands, but she let him steer her toward the shaded glider in the side yard.

"The strawberries," Ellie said. Her voice lacked strength, as if she was falling asleep. Bram's stomach clenched, and he hoped he wasn't too late.

Ben and Reuben were at his side.

"We tried to get her to stop," Reuben said, "but she said she'd do the whole field by herself if we didn't help her."

"I can believe it." If he had ever seen a more stubborn woman… "We need a bucket of water and some towels."

While Reuben ran to fill Ellie's abandoned bucket, Bram started to unfasten Ellie's dress at her neckline.

"What are you doing?" Ben reached out to stop him.

"She's suffering from heat exhaustion. We have to keep her from having a heatstroke."

Ben didn't argue; he ran into the house for towels.

"I have to water the plants before they die." Ellie tried to refasten her dress, but her movements were uncoordinated and slow.

"Ellie," Bram said, "we have to cool you off first. You shouldn't have been working out in the heat."

Reuben set the full pail of water next to Bram as he knelt on the ground. "Will she be all right?"

"*Ja,* if we can get her cooled off. Where's John? And your mother?" Bram took the towels Ben brought and plunged them in the cool water.

"They took the girls over to Lovina's. They're making jam, and *Dat* was going to a sale with Noah."

Ben had brought a dipper, and after Bram gave Ellie a drink, they all took turns.

"The children?"

"In the house sleeping."

Bram took one towel, wrung most of the water out of it and draped it over the back of Ellie's neck. Her eyes were closed, and her breathing was rapid. He took another wet towel and began sponging her face. It wasn't enough.

Bram took handfuls of water and poured them over Ellie's feet and lower legs. He wet his towel again and went back to sponging her face, hands and arms.

Ellie caught the towel in one hand and took it from him.

"I can do that, Bram. *Denki.*"

Her face was returning to a normal color. Her eyes looked tired, but the glaze was gone. Bram's stomach unclenched, and he sat back on his heels. He glanced from Ben's flushed face to Reuben's. Ellie wasn't the only one suffering from the heat.

"Do you boys have a swimming hole?"

"*Ja,* but what about Ellie?"

"I'll take care of her. She's out of danger now, but you need to get cooled off, too."

Ben looked at Reuben. After a long minute of inde-
cision, Reuben nodded.

"You're right. We'll take care of your horse before
we go."

Bram nodded. *"Denki."*

"If I were a different man, I'd throttle you right now."
Bram's voice was gentle as he sponged her cheeks with
a wet towel.

Ellie didn't answer, but sniffed back threatening
tears. He sounded angry with her, but why? She was
only taking care of the work that needed to be done.

Bram took the towel off the back of her neck and
rinsed it in fresh water before handing it back to her.
She held it to her face and neck. The cool cloth felt
wonderful-gut on her bare skin.

"What were you thinking, working out in that field
in this heat?"

"The strawberries. I watered them early this morning, but this afternoon I saw they were dying." She
was too weak to stop the tears that fell. "I can't lose
those plants."

Bram sat on the glider and offered her another dipper of water. She drank it slowly, the water seeping into
her body in cool swallows.

"Those are your strawberries?"

She nodded. "That's why I don't have enough money
to pay the taxes on the farm. I used my savings…" Ellie
glanced toward the dusty field dotted with shriveled
bits of green. "But I'm going to lose them all, aren't I?"

"I'm afraid you've already lost them. It's just too hot.
My corn is drying up, too."

Ellie reached a hand to the front of her dress where

it hung loose. How did she get this way? She started to refasten it, but Bram stopped her by taking her hand in his.

"Not yet. You haven't cooled down enough."

"But I must look a sight."

When Bram twitched the corner of his mouth into that secret grin reserved just for her, any resistance she had to him melted away to nothing. *Ja,* she trusted him, and more. Much more.

"You sure do. Are you feeling better?"

"*Ja.* I didn't realize how exhausted I was until I sat down."

Bram still held her hand in his. He reached up with his other hand and tucked some damp hair behind her ear.

"You don't have to worry about the money, remember? I said I had enough."

"But how will I pay you back?"

He squeezed her hand with reassuring pressure. She let the tension drain out of her shoulders.

"You will somehow, but I'm not in a hurry."

Ellie closed her eyes. Bram put his arm around her and pulled her close to him.

Resting in his embrace, Ellie let herself lean into him, giving way to the comforting strength of his presence. Long minutes went by before she thought about moving, but she should.

Sit up, she told herself, but instead she opened her eyes to see Bram's face just inches from her own, his expression unreadable, his eyes locked on hers. He bent his head slightly and then paused, his eyes flickering with doubt.

Ellie put her hand up to his cheek, bridging the gap

between them. His blue gaze stilled and darkened. He was going to kiss her and she longed to let him, but she couldn't. To kiss him would be a step into a sin she would never be free of.

Forcing herself, she lowered her hand and shifted away from him. A hot breeze played between the two of them on the glider.

Bram wanted to pursue Ellie as she drew away from him. She had wanted his kiss, but she was right to stop him. With an inward groan, he loosened his hold on her soft, yielding form, his arms already aching with the loss. He kept her as close as he dared with his left arm around her shoulder and closed his right hand around hers. It was small, soft and cool from the wet towel as it lay in his larger one. Relaxed. Trusting. Fragile. A bird in his hand.

His throat tightened as he turned her hand over and stroked her palm with his thumb. What reason had he ever given for her to trust him? How could he ever keep her safe?

He opened his mouth to speak, to warn her about the man he was hunting, but the look on her face stopped him. She was watching their hands together, a small smile turning up the corners of her mouth. A slight breeze had dried a few hanging strands of her hair, and they drifted across her forehead, making her look like a young girl. The worry line that usually strained her features was gone. When had it disappeared?

He couldn't tell her. Not yet. This wasn't the right time to let her know about the violent past that continued to dog his footsteps. Kavanaugh had been close, but even though Bram had spent the past week hunting for him through the neighboring towns, he hadn't seen any sign that the gangster was still around. As long as he kept to his plan, he would be safe.

Bram tightened his hand, enfolding Ellie's in his own. They would both be safe.

"Will we buy ice cream?"

Susan heard her brother. "Ice cream? Will there be ice cream there?"

"Ice cream costs too much money." The disappointed looks on the children's faces pulled at Ellie's heart, but they didn't argue with her. "I think we can buy a treat at the grocery store, though. How about some chocolate to make brownies?"

Johnny and Susan grinned at each other with delight. Trips to town were rare, and even though Daniel would have said the trip was enough of a treat, the chocolate would make it extra special.

"I hear Bram's buggy." Johnny raced out the door to meet him.

"Wait, Susan. You need to wear your *kapp*."

"Just like *Memmi*." Susan smiled up at her, the stiff white *kapp* framing her sweet face as Ellie fit it over her braids.

"*Ja,* just like *Memmi*. Now, you go on out with Johnny. We don't want to keep Bram waiting."

Ellie settled her bonnet over her own *kapp* before picking up Danny. Bram's greeting to the children drifted in through the open window, sending her stomach rolling and heat flooding to her cheeks. Bram was here to take them to LaGrange, to the county tax office.

It was a trip she had been dreading, but Bram had lifted a sore burden from her when he'd offered to loan her the money she needed. She would pay the taxes this morning, and then she didn't need to worry about them for another year. Surely by then Mr. Brenneman would be working again, and she would be able to pay Bram back as well as pay next year's taxes.

Another reason for her light mood filled the field next to the house. At least half of the strawberry plants still survived, in spite of yesterday's heat. Perhaps she would have berries to sell next spring after all.

From Bram's animated conversation with the children as they waited for her in the back of the buggy, it sounded as if he was looking forward to this trip as much as she and the children were. When she stepped out of the house, he came to meet her.

"Good morning." He leaned so close to her she was afraid he was going to start the day with a kiss on her cheek, but he only gave her a grin as he took Danny—that secret grin meant just for her.

"Good morning, Bram. *Denki* for driving us into town."

He helped her into the buggy and then held her hand until she looked at him. "I wouldn't let you go alone. I'm here for you, Ellie." His voice was low, intimate. Her cheeks flushed hot.

Taking Danny from him, she waited as he climbed in on the other side and chirruped to Partner. Her heart fluttered like leaves catching a passing breeze, and she resisted the urge to thread her hand through his elbow as if they were courting. How long had it been since she had felt like this? Bram's strength gave her a security she hadn't known since she was a girl.

Even when Daniel was alive… *Ach,* had she really been the proud, stubborn woman she remembered? She never let him care for her, cherish her. Their lives together could have been even happier if she had learned to be content with what Daniel—and *Gott*—provided for her. She shied away from the thought that perhaps their lives together could have been longer if she hadn't insisted that he expand the farm. How had Daniel ever put up with her? How did *Gott* ever put up with her?

She stole a glance at Bram and caught him watching her, a quiet smile on his face. *Ja,* she could get used to this.

When they arrived in LaGrange, Bram drove Partner to a hitching rail in the shade on the courthouse square. Their footsteps echoed in the vast entrance of the limestone building, cool and dark after the blazing sunshine. Bram found the tax office, and Ellie signed the papers while he handed the money to the clerk.

Bram shepherded them outside again and steered them to a bench on the shady lawn.

"Now I think we need to do some shopping."

"*Ja,* I hoped we could stop at a grocer's."

Bram cleared his throat, watching the children as they played a hopping game on the cement walk. "I was thinking of a dry-goods store."

"I don't need anything there."

"I think you do."

Ellie thought of the few coins in her pocketbook. Some baking soda, flour and the chocolate would use all her money.

"Bram," she said, lowering her voice so the children wouldn't hear, "I only brought enough to buy the groceries I need."

"You need a new dress." His lowered voice matched hers, and he held her gaze with his own.

He was right, of course. The brown one she was

wearing had been mended many times, but it would still do. The children's clothes came first when she had money to spend on fabric.

"I don't need a new dress, even if I could afford it."

"Ellie, let me buy you the material. Enough for Susan, too."

Her face flushed hot as she glanced at Susan playing tag with Johnny. The little girl's dress was much too short. Watching her, Ellie knew she had lost the argument, but only part of it.

"I'll let you loan me some money for a new dress for Susan."

"Enough for both of you. And it's not a loan. It's a gift."

Ellie started shaking her head.

"Ellie, please." His eyes were pleading. "I have more than enough money. Let me do this."

A cold thought fluttered in the back of her mind. His money again. She was coming to depend on him too much.

He lifted her hand from her lap and held it entwined in his solid, capable fingers. He leaned close to her, letting Danny pat his short beard.

"Let me take care of you." His whisper was carried off on the breeze, but not before it reached her ears.

Tears stung her eyes as his words destroyed any argument she had left. She nodded without speaking.

Bram glanced in the windows of the empty building next to the dry-goods store as they came back onto the sidewalk. Another closed bank was a common enough sight these days, but this one meant he didn't have to worry about Kavanaugh showing up here. He could relax his guard a bit and enjoy the day.

The stop in the store had been a success. He had persuaded Ellie to choose several pieces of fabric. One was green, perfect for weekdays, and another was a deep blue that matched her eyes. That would be for Sundays. A couple lengths of black and white for aprons and other necessities hadn't been hard to convince her to add in. He had also bought a new straw hat for Johnny and one for himself.

"If I cut carefully," Ellie said, her eyes glowing, "I'm sure I can make some shirts for Johnny and Danny out of the blue. And there is enough of the green to make dresses for both Susan and myself."

Bram had never seen Ellie so animated. If he had known new fabric would make her this happy, he would have made this trip weeks ago.

When they reached the buggy, he checked on Partner while Ellie helped Johnny put the bundles in the back of the rig. He wasn't ready to take them home. Ellie would immerse herself in her work again, and he'd have to make another round of the nearby towns, looking for some sign of Kavanaugh. There must be something he could do to make this day last longer.

Activity at the drugstore caught his eye. *Ja,* a lunch counter would be a *wonderful-gut* treat for Ellie and the children.

He took Danny from Ellie's arms and stopped her before she climbed in the buggy. "Are you ready for lunch?"

"Lunch? I didn't pack anything. I thought I would make dinner at home."

He pointed toward the drugstore and then reached

for Susan's hand. "There's a lunch counter over here. Have you ever eaten at one?"

"You mean buy a meal?"

Her voice was incredulous. If she only knew how many hundreds of meals he had eaten at lunch counters just like this one.

"*Ja,* buy a meal. I'm sure the egg-salad sandwiches here are almost as good as yours."

She looked at him with suspicion. "You've never tried one of mine, so how do you know?"

Bram laughed at this. "Let's just go in and eat."

Watching Ellie enjoy the new experience of eating out made everything he had done to earn that money worth it. Johnny and Susan swung their legs as they sat on their stools at the counter eating their hot dogs while Danny ate bits of a grilled cheese that Ellie cut up for him. She had been nervous at first, but she had relaxed at her first bite of a chicken-salad sandwich.

To top off the treat, Bram ordered ice-cream cones. He was sure Johnny's eyes would pop when the clerk handed his to him. Life didn't get much better than this.

The final stop was at the grocer's around the corner from the drugstore. Ellie bought her supplies, and Bram filled a box with groceries for himself, making sure he bought plenty of sugar. Ellie was probably using sorghum in everything she baked, since sugar was expensive. He'd slip the sack into her box later.

Finally, Bram couldn't put it off any longer. Their errands were done, and the tired look on the children's faces told him it was time to go home. As Bram led them to the buggy still tied at the courthouse, he exchanged a glance with Ellie. Was this what a family was supposed to feel like? He would give anything for more days like this one.

Out of habit, he scanned the streets surrounding the square while he boosted the children into the back of the rig. LaGrange was a much smaller town than Goshen, in the next county over. There were a few cars and several buggies, but the county seat wasn't crowded.

Then Bram saw it. A maroon Packard purred up State Road 9 from the south and passed by just half a block away. The fragile buggy was all that stood between Bram and the car, and his stomach plummeted to his feet just the same as if he had been standing exposed on the curb as the car drove slowly by. He gripped the sides of the buggy with cold fingers as he watched the Packard cruise through the small town, then on to the north.

"Bram, are you all right?"

The black tunnel of his vision cleared. Ellie was staring at him, and all three children looked at him with solemn faces. He took a deep breath, forcing his fingers to release their hold.

"*Ja,* I'm all right. Just thought I saw someone I knew."

Ellie kept her eyes on him but didn't say anything more. That worry line had shown up again.

Bram turned Partner toward the south, heading down Hawpatch Road before turning west, toward the Stoltzfus farm. His mind raced, matching the pace of his heart. If he took a roundabout way, there was a chance they'd be able to get home before Kavanaugh found them.

He worked the reins in his sweaty hands, trying to get a better grip. He felt like swearing, but the words stuck in his throat. He had let his guard down and had made the fatal error of underestimating Kavanaugh. Worse yet, Ellie and the children were in danger. He was trapped by his own stupid mistake.

Glancing behind them at the empty road, Bram adjusted the reins again and took a deep breath, forcing himself to relax.

He had panicked, and panic was deadly. Kavanaugh, if it was Kavanaugh, hadn't seen him. He gave himself a mental shake and checked the road again. He just had to get Ellie and the children home safely.

Ellie watched Bram as he leaned forward on the buggy seat, the reins tight in his hands, his jaw set. What could have gone wrong this time? Ellie cast her mind back over the morning, but she couldn't think of anything that would have made Bram angry. It had been a fun family outing.

Catching her breath at this thought, she turned her face to the dusty roadside. With Bram beside her, she could pretend they were a complete family. How could she have let him worm his way this far into their lives... into her heart? Bram had been honest with her, letting her know his future plans. He wasn't Amish, in spite of his upbringing. He had turned his back on the Amish once, and he would do it again as soon as his work here was done. He wasn't a man she could count on being there for her children. He wasn't a man to fall in love with.

She turned to check on the children in the back of the buggy. Susan had fallen asleep, lying on the narrow seat. Johnny sat beside her, his new hat on his head, watching the roadside. His face was the picture of little-boy contentment. She had grown used to his sullen expression and downturned eyes, but ever since Bram had taken him into that ball game, Johnny had been a different boy. Bram's attention had brought back the boy she knew before Daniel's accident.

Danny sighed on her lap and turned his sleeping, sweaty face upward. She leaned closer to him to catch his sweet baby scent. Why did they have to grow up?

A sudden thought stopped her. Danny would grow up, and he would never have any memories of his father, only the stories she could tell him. Susan had been so young—did she remember anything about Daniel? And Johnny's memories were already blurred. He told stories of going fishing with his father, or traveling with him, but Ellie knew he had never done those things. Daniel was just a dream to him.

Ellie would never forget her husband, his plans. He had longed to give his children the home he had never known as an orphan, handed off from relative to relative until he ended up with Hezekiah and Miriam. His only goal had been for his children to know a life he had never lived, but now she was the only one left to keep his dreams and his memory alive.

Her mind flitted over the morning. Bram had been so loving and caring, making the children laugh at his jokes and surprising them with ice cream. The memories of Daniel she tried to keep fresh for her children would never bring them the same joy.

Bram turned in the seat and took a long look down the empty road behind them. When he turned back to the front again, his jaw was clenched. Maybe he regretted taking them to town and the time it had taken from his work. Whatever it was, he was acting as if this morning had never happened. Was it something she had done that brought this change?

"*Denki,*" she said. Her voice felt muffled in the hot air.

Bram turned to look at her, his body jerking as if he had forgotten she was there.

"*Denki* for what?" His words were clipped, sharp. Was he angry? She really didn't know him well enough to tell.

"*Denki* for driving us to LaGrange, and for the material…and for lunch…" Her voice faltered. He wasn't listening.

Bram nodded, his eyes hard, and then he turned and chirruped Partner into a faster trot, although the horse was already covered with sweat.

"Bram, I'm not in a hurry to get home."

He looked at her again, then behind them. His face was a blank, stony mask. He licked his lips and glanced behind them once more.

"*Ja,* you're right." He pulled Partner to a walk but shifted in his seat with a restless kick of his feet against the dashboard.

Would he tell her what was wrong? She had to know if she had done or said something to make him act like this. It had happened before, this abrupt change from tender and attentive to hard and angry.

Trusting *Gott* was one thing; she could rest in His all-powerful care. But trusting a man? Ellie glanced at Bram's face, still hard and closed. He looked back at her, and his eyes softened. Without a word he transferred the reins to one hand and put the other on top of her hands enfolding Danny. He gave them a gentle squeeze while the corners of his mouth turned up in a reassuring smile.

Ja, she could trust this man.

Chapter Fourteen

Susan and Danny were both still sleeping when they reached the Stoltzfus farm, and Johnny's head was nodding.

"I'll carry Susan in for you." Bram followed Ellie into the *Dawdi Haus*. She nodded toward the bedroom on the left as she took Danny into the other one. The dim room was cool after the brassy sunshine, and Bram laid the little girl on the bed with the blank-faced doll leaning against the pillow.

Johnny followed them and crawled up on the other side of the bed, his eyes closed already. Bram took the boy's new straw hat off his head and smoothed the brown curls. Johnny's face was flushed but peaceful. No cares troubled him.

Bram swallowed, a stone of regret lodged in his throat. Had he ever been this innocent?

"They'll all sleep for a while after the excitement of the morning," Ellie said as he returned to the kitchen.

"*Ja,* you're right." He stood in the center of the small room that spoke of Ellie everywhere he looked, from a jar of flowers on the table to the neatly folded dish towel draped over the pump handle. The serene order soothed the panic slamming around in his head ever since he had seen that Packard in LaGrange.

Every time he came to the conclusion that it couldn't be Kavanaugh's car, another part of his mind convinced him it was. It was as if the car was following him, haunting him with an unseen presence.

Ellie opened a cabinet door and got out two glasses. "I have some ice down in the cellar. Would you like some mint tea?"

"That sounds *wonderful-gut,* but if I'm going to stay for a while, I have to take care of Partner."

"*Ja.* I'll bring the tea to the glider. It's shady out there."

As Bram unharnessed the horse, his thoughts went to that maroon Packard again. There had been something about it that wasn't quite right, and the answer hovered on the edge of his thoughts. He let Partner take a quick drink of water at the trough by the pump and then tied him to a tree in the side yard, where he could crop the grass along the shady side of the fence.

The sparse rows of strawberries caught Bram's eye. Some of the plants were still holding on, and they had better survive, for Ellie's sake. Her heart was set on making money from those berries, and any other year it would have been a sure thing, a good investment. But the way this summer was turning out, it looked as if she was going to lose everything.

He met Ellie at the glider and took the glass full of ice and green mint tea that she handed him. He breathed in the scent of mint as he took his first swallow. It gushed down his throat, cool and sweet.

"*Ach,* this is good. Where did you get the ice?"

"Years ago my *Grossdatti* built an icehouse. All the neighbors harvest the ice on Emma Lake in the winter, and we store it for them. Ben and Reuben brought a block for me yesterday, and I keep it packed in straw in the cellar."

As Bram kicked at the grass under the glider, setting it in motion, his thoughts went back to that Packard. What could he do if that had been Kavanaugh? He had made the mistake of convincing himself they were safe in LaGrange, but he could never take Ellie's safety for granted. He hated ruining the end of their day together, but he had to warn her about the danger.

"Are you feeling better?"

Ellie's question interrupted his thoughts.

"What do you mean? I feel fine."

"I just thought… I mean, ever since we left LaGrange you've seemed like you were upset about something."

Either she knew him better than most people, or he was losing his touch at controlling his feelings.

"I'm sorry. It's nothing to do with you or the children." He had to tell her. He hated to have her living with the same caution he did, but if Kavanaugh came around, she had to know enough to protect herself from him.

"Ellie, I have to tell you—" He stopped, looking at her profile as she sat quietly, waiting for him to speak. What he had to tell her would ruin that trusting innocence. Wasn't there another way?

Ellie wiped a thumb-wide swath through the condensation on her glass, waiting for Bram to continue.

"When I lived in Chicago, things were pretty rough." She glanced at him. He sat with his forearms resting on his legs, dangling the cold glass between his knees. She didn't want to hear about his *Englisch* days, but he still belonged to that world.

"What do mean?"

He shrugged his shoulders and sat up, taking a drink of his tea. "You know, the mob, the cops." He looked at her. "I did some things that you wouldn't like."

"Does it matter, what I would approve of?"

He took another swallow, his Adam's apple bobbing as he watched Partner crop the grass along the fence. When he looked back at her, his eyes were dark with regret.

"*Ja,* Ellie, it matters. More than I ever thought it would."

She looked away. *Ja,* it mattered.

"A man in my kind of work makes some enemies, and I made one of the worst kind."

"*Ach,* Bram…" Ellie cast about in her mind for an answer, her heart breaking. "Our way is to love our enemies and to pray for them."

"Not this kind of enemy." Bram's voice was harsh, his eyes focused on his glass. He upended it, draining it, and then turned to her. "I grew up hearing the teaching of the church, with the 'love your enemies' and all that, but I don't think the church fathers dealt with the kind of men I've seen."

"*Ne,* they didn't have gangsters in the old country, but you know the stories of how our ancestors were persecuted and hunted down like criminals, and yet the doctrine of nonresistance stood the test during that time."

"And how many died? Maybe they should have

fought back. Maybe sometimes there are things worth fighting for."

"Nothing is worth disobedience to *Gott*."

"Even the safety of your children?"

Ellie choked down a sob in her throat. She didn't know how she would act if someone threatened her children, but the church's teaching was clear.

"We are not to resist those who are against us."

Bram put his empty glass down in the grass as he stood, sending the glider rocking. He paced over to Partner and ran his hand along the horse's neck and then abruptly turned back toward her.

"This man I'm looking for is evil, Ellie. He has killed before, and he'll kill again without a thought. He would hurt you and the children only because I care about you. He has to be stopped."

"With force? With violence?"

"He doesn't understand any other way."

Ellie shifted her eyes from his. Were there really such evil men in the world? Men beyond the reach of *Gott* Himself?

Bram knelt in front of her, capturing her hands in his, spilling her tea.

"Ellie, promise me, if you see an *Englisch* stranger hanging around, or if he comes to the farm..." Bram stopped. He wiped one hand across his eyes as if trying to erase a nightmare. "If you see anyone, tell me. Don't talk to him. Don't tell him anything." Bram tightened his grasp on her hands. "Don't...Ellie, don't trust him. This man, his name is Kavanaugh, and he's dangerous. If you see him, send someone to get me—Ben or Reuben. Can you do that?"

Ellie stared into his eyes, seeing her own fear reflected there. What would she do if this stranger came around? If she sent word to Bram, the way he asked, would he use violence against this gangster? On the other hand, if she warned Bram, perhaps he could escape from this man and save himself.

"*Ja,* Bram, I will, but only so you can avoid him. I don't fear for myself, only for you."

Bram reached one hand to that stubborn lock of hair that never stayed put and tucked it behind her ear.

"I'll try my best to keep you safe, Ellie. You have my word on that."

Bram kept Partner at a walk all the way home from the Stoltzfus farm. He had rushed out of LaGrange so fast that he had risked his horse's health. Well, better risk the horse than Ellie and the children.

But then, really, what good would it have done? No matter how fast he pushed Partner, a car could overtake them. His mouth went dry as the scenario played itself out in his mind—he could have lost everything.

That Packard. One elusive detail flicked at the edge of his mind. He closed his eyes, trying to capture a picture of the car in his memory. Chrome. That car in LaGrange didn't have any chrome trim. Bram laughed out loud in his relief. What kind of idiot was he to be jumping at every car he saw?

But just as quickly, the memory of his panic sobered him. It could have been Kavanaugh just as easily as someone else. The gangster was in the area, and Bram was almost certain he had been recognized in Goshen that day with Matthew. As long as he stayed here, he would be haunted by his past.

Should he leave, then? Get back to his original plan

and keep moving on? He had known he shouldn't get tangled up with a woman…. Now it wasn't just his safety he needed to worry about. This whole affair could cost both their lives.

In all his years of working and living undercover, living the lie that had become his life, he never thought he would let himself get ensnared like this. But this time was different—this assignment had been screwy from the beginning. Who ever heard of going undercover by being yourself? And now he was in trouble. Big trouble. Not only had he been spotted—maybe—but for the first time in his life, he wanted to stay in this cover.

For the first time in his life, he had something to work for, a life to build. If he was free of Kavanaugh, free of his past, he could turn his farm into something worthwhile, something for a family.

Bram rubbed his palm over his face.

Ja, in any other job he would say it was time to get out. But where would he go? Mexico was the only option he could see.

What about Ellie and the children? That morning's trip had given him a glimpse of the family they could be together, but now that vision was slipping away as quickly as a piece of ice melting on a hot afternoon.

He loved her.

He couldn't love her; he wouldn't love her. Loving her would only make her a target for Kavanaugh, and he wouldn't be foolish enough to risk that.

But it was too late.

He loved her.

He felt that now-familiar upsurge of calm, like a cool-silk breeze. God knew he loved her.

But what could he do? If he stayed here, they would

all continue to be in danger. Kavanaugh was too close. If he had recognized Bram in Goshen that day, he wouldn't give up until he found him. There was nowhere he could hide.

If he left...

If he left, he would be leaving Ellie behind.

Ellie and every hope for his future.

A sudden idea sent a chill through him. What if she went with him? He could buy another car. She and the children could come with him to Mexico. They could start a new life there and never have to worry about Kavanaugh again.

Partner turned into his lane and stopped at the barn door, but Bram didn't move. He had to follow this thought through....

If Ellie came with him, they'd have each other. He'd take care of them. They'd have a ranch down there, and Johnny would love being a cowboy.

Partner tossed his head, pulling on the reins in Bram's hands. They were home.

But as Bram climbed out of the buggy and opened the barn door, he knew it was useless. He couldn't uproot Ellie from the only home she had ever known. If she came with him to Mexico, they'd have to leave more than just her family. Everything she knew and loved was here. Her home, her family, her faith, her heritage.

He knew now what he hadn't known twelve years ago—his own identity was defined here, among the Amish. His heritage. He might be able to survive away from it, but he could never ask Ellie and the children to bear that burden with him.

But could he bear leaving without her?

Bram unhitched Partner and took his harness off.

The horse was warm but not too hot. The time in the shady grass at Ellie's house and then the slow walk home had been good for him. Bram got the currycomb and brush and began giving him a good grooming.

Bram tried to let his mind go blank as he concentrated on the familiar task, but the thoughts kept swirling.

"God, what should I do?" he prayed out loud, leaning on Partner's back.

The idea came so suddenly, so clearly, Bram knew it couldn't be anything but the answer to his prayer. His search for Kavanaugh had been fruitless so far—but he had been an Amishman hunting for an *Englischer*. To find an *Englischer*, he needed to be one. To find a gangster...

Ja, if he went deeper undercover, inserted himself into the seamier side of these towns surrounding him, he could track down that snake in the sewers where he lived, places no Amishman would go. He would need to use every skill he had honed during those years in Chicago. It would be dangerous, but there was no other way to find Kavanaugh.

And once Kavanaugh was arrested, he'd have no reason to leave.

Chapter Fifteen

Sunday's weather was pleasant, and after the meeting at Deacon Beachey's home, the men moved church benches into the shady backyard for the fellowship meal and visiting afterward.

Ellie sat with Annie Beachey watching the children play while Annie tried to calm her new baby, Micah. Ellie took the crying baby when his mother offered him to her.

"See if you can help him. After trying to keep him quiet all through the meeting, I'm exhausted."

"Oh, I'm sure you are." Ellie held the wee bundle in her arms and rocked him. "It's been so hot. Could it be heat rash?"

"*Ja,* he has heat rash and a terrible diaper rash. I just can't seem to get rid of it."

"Has he been eating well?"

"*Ja,* and your *mam* told me to give him some water, too, since it's been so hot." Annie stroked the baby's head.

Ellie turned the baby so his stomach was pressed against her hand. He gave a loud belch.

"Do you think that's what was wrong with him?"

Ellie smiled at her friend as the baby's cries subsided. "*Ja,* I think so."

She continued rocking little Micah. *Ach,* holding a baby was a sweet joy.

"I haven't seen much of Bram lately," Annie said. "Have you been able to talk with him often?"

Ellie looked across the shady yard at Bram, conversing with *Dat* and Matthew. She knew what Annie was really asking, but what could she say? Bram had become so important to her, but didn't he still belong to his *Englisch* past? Did she have any right to think of him as more than a friend?

"*Ne,* I haven't seen him for a week or so."

"*Ja,* well, he must be busy with his work."

"*Ja,* probably." She didn't tell Annie about the fears that kept her awake at night, the fears of a strange *Englischer* coming in search of Bram.

"*Ach,* Annie. There's Miriam. I want to see how she's doing."

Ellie and Annie made their way to the bench where Miriam was sitting on the shady side of the house.

"I'm so glad you were able to come to church this morning," Ellie said, rocking Micah back and forth.

"*Ja,* me, too," Miriam said. "The rheumatism keeps Hezekiah in his chair so much that we don't get out often anymore. Some days, he doesn't even get out of bed."

"I didn't know it was so bad," Ellie said.

"*Ach,* he didn't want to burden others with our troubles, but I tell him it's time. He can't do everything on his own anymore."

And if Daniel had lived, he wouldn't have to. The

thought made Ellie hot with shame. They shouldn't have to ask for help; she should have offered sooner. But when would she have time to work on their farm?

"What can I do to help?"

"You don't need to worry about us. Mr. Brenneman helps when he can."

Just as Daniel would have.

"But when Mr. Brenneman finds another job, he won't have the time."

Miriam patted her hand. "The good Lord will take care of us. Hezekiah will find another neighbor to hire."

Verna Bontrager, one of Miriam's longtime friends, joined them on the bench. As the two older women visited, Ellie thought about Miriam's words.

She should have seen this earlier. Hezekiah's arthritis was worse every month, and yet it hadn't occurred to her that he couldn't do his work. Daniel planned that his farm and Hezekiah's would be joined together, with the older couple's small house as a *Dawdi Haus,* while Daniel and his children farmed the land. But none of them had foreseen Hezekiah's advancing arthritis or Daniel's death.

But what could she do? She had no money to pay for a hired hand and neither did Hezekiah. And yet if he didn't hire someone, the crops would be ruined.

The strawberries should have brought her some security by next year, but now there were barely a dozen plants in each row that were surviving. It would be at least two more years before she could count on income from that source, and that was only if she could afford to buy new plants next spring.

She rubbed the line between her eyebrows. Her headache was coming back.

Gott, what am I to do?

"So you're getting used to having a new baby in the house?" John Stoltzfus winked at Bram as he asked Matthew the question. Bram grinned back at him. Matthew hadn't been able to talk about anything else all day.

"*Ja,* I am. I've gotten used to the night feedings, even. I've been able to get plenty of sleep." Matthew's face was serious as he started another lengthy discussion about his new son's eating habits. John listened patiently, but Bram's mind wandered to Ellie.

He had the perfect vantage point under this tree. He watched Ellie and Annie join some older women, Ellie holding Matthew's new son, his nephew. The sight made his throat tight. What would it be like to see her holding his baby one day?

He shook his head and shut that thought behind a door. Not yet.

Can't think about that now, not until Kavanaugh is taken care of.

He glanced her way again. She looked *wonderful-gut* in her new dress. She was visiting with Annie and an older woman he had never seen before, but that worry line was back again. Something was bothering her. Was one of the children ill?

He scanned the crowd from his spot under an oak tree. Johnny and Susan were playing a game of tag with some other children. It took a while to find Danny, but Bram finally spotted him on Sally Yoder's lap as she sat with Elizabeth Stoltzfus. He let out a sigh of relief.

Everything seemed all right, but something had caused that crease to appear again.

Bram made his way through the maze of benches until he stood next to her. She looked perfect, graceful, feminine. He ached at the sight of her.

"Ellie, would you like to take a walk with me?"

He spoke softly, but Ellie had heard him. The older woman next to her looked on with interest.

"*Ja,* I would like that." She turned to give the baby to Annie, and then the older woman grasped Ellie's hand for a moment. A silent message of some kind. The two exchanged a smile. He would never understand women.

He took Ellie up the lane that passed by the barn and went toward a farm pond. It would give them a nice walk, not too far, and they would remain within sight of the rest of the congregation.

"Is something wrong?" he asked.

She looked at him, surprise on her face.

"*Ne.*" She looked away. "Well, *ja,* but it's nothing you need to worry about."

What a stubborn woman—didn't she know he would worry about anything that affected her?

"Tell me."

She walked in silence until they reached the pond. A frog jumped into the water as they approached the edge. They stopped, and Bram watched the ripples from the frog's splash until they disappeared on the opposite side of the small pond.

"It's Miriam and Hezekiah Miller."

"Who?"

"Daniel's aunt and uncle. They're the only family he had, and they had no other children."

"Hezekiah Miller?" Bram searched his memory of the names he knew. "The man with the cane?"

"*Ja,* that's him. His arthritis is getting worse, and without Daniel to help them…" She stopped as if she was staggering under a load too heavy for her to bear.

"Won't the church step in?"

"*Ach, ja,* with the heavy work. But it's the day-to-day chores that are hard for him, too."

Bram understood. In any other family the older folks would retire to their *Dawdi Haus,* helping with the chores they were able to do and enjoying the quieter days with their children nearby. But with no family, Hezekiah didn't have that option, even as frail as he seemed.

"I'm the only family they have left, but I don't know what I can do to help them right now. Maybe in a year or two I'll be able to hire some help for them, until Johnny's old enough."

She was counting on the strawberries.

"I told you I'm here for you, Ellie."

"But this isn't your responsibility. It's mine."

"I want to bear this burden with you, if you'll let me." He would bear all of her burdens if she'd let him.

She shook her head, looking at her feet. She chewed on her bottom lip, but that worry line was easing. Good. At least she was thinking about it.

"What could you do?"

"My farmwork is caught up, thanks to the church, and I don't have a family to take care of. I could drive over to help out." It would add some hours to his day, but he could still continue canvassing the area towns in his search for Kavanaugh.

"They live over by Topeka. That's at least four miles."

"Well, I won't be able to go every day, but often enough to help ease the work. Maybe some of the younger single men could do the same thing. There are enough of us that it wouldn't be too great a burden for anyone, and yet Hezekiah would have someone to help every day."

Bram was rewarded with a grateful look.

"Thank you. I never thought of anything like that."

He reached up and rubbed away the last of the crease between her eyes, letting his finger fall to caress her cheek.

"I told you, I can help you bear your burdens. All you have to do is ask. I'll talk to your *dat,* and between us we'll take care of it."

If only all *his* problems could be solved so easily.

A week later, Bram left home at dawn for his second turn at Hezekiah's farm. The older man appreciated the help, and Bram had found him to be cheerful the week before, in spite of his crippling disease. A morning spent working with him had flown by, and during the dinner with Miriam afterward, he had come to know Ellie through their eyes. She was as dear to them as any daughter could be.

The rest of his week hadn't been as pleasant as he became Dutch Sutter again, complete with *Englisch* clothes, and worked on sounding out contacts in Goshen, the most likely place to find any sign of Kavanaugh.

The suit he bought for the job was uncomfortable, although it was almost identical to the one he had worn in Chicago just a few months ago. When he put it on, it was as if Bram Lapp had disappeared. Daily shaving had completed the image, erasing the Amish look altogether.

He never thought going undercover could be this complicated, but it was effective. He had found just enough information to narrow Kavanaugh's activity to somewhere around Elkhart or South Bend, although he still had no idea where the prey was holed up or how many men he had working for him. Even so, it was time to find a phone and call in.

Partner's hooves clip-clopped on the cement road that took him through downtown Topeka. When Bram caught a whiff of bacon frying, his growling stomach reminded him he hadn't taken time for anything more than a cup of coffee before he'd left home. He took a deep breath of the mingled odors from the café. He'd have to stop in for some eggs and bacon before going on to Hezekiah's. He took another deep breath. *Ja,* and a few doughnuts.

Coming out of the café with a bag of doughnuts twenty minutes later, Bram noticed the telephone exchange office was open. This would be a good time to call Peters.

He stepped into the office and closed himself in a public booth. He picked up the receiver and watched the bored-looking operator through the glass until she answered.

"Number, please."

"I'd like to place a long-distance call to Elwood Peters, FBI, Chicago Division."

He wasn't surprised to hear her gasp on the other end, but he hoped she wasn't the kind to listen in on calls.

* * *

Ellie lifted one foot to rub it over a new mosquito bite on her other leg. Sunburn, mosquito bites and twenty quarts of strawberries from the Mennonite neighbors down the road, all before eight on a Thursday morning.

"Don't forget to keep stirring the jam, Mandy," *Mam* said as she set the last jar in the large pot to sterilize. She turned back to the table where Ellie was cleaning the final basket of this morning's picking of strawberries.

"Whew. Wouldn't it be nice if canning season was in the winter when a hot kitchen feels welcome?"

"*Ja, Mam,* you say that every year, but you're right. At least today is a little cooler than last week."

Mam nodded as she picked up her knife. Her fingers flew as she took the stem off each berry and sliced it.

The berries were small, making the work take even longer. A drought summer made even something as simple as strawberry jam more work.

"We're going to have strawberry shortcake for dinner, aren't we?" Mandy stood at the stove, as far away from the heat as she could and still stir the jam.

"Do you really feel like eating strawberries after spending the morning with them?" Ellie said, scratching a mosquito bite on her other leg.

"Well, maybe not the strawberries, but shortcake would be good."

By dinnertime three dozen jars of strawberry jam were cooling on the counter, and one of *Mam's* sweet, flaky shortcakes had just come out of the oven.

Johnny burst through the door, slamming the screen against the wall.

"*Memmi,* the cows are in the strawberry field!"

Ellie rushed to the back door to look. Her heart

turned cold at the sight of the family's two milk cows and the yearling heifer in the field next to the *Dawdi Haus*. She grabbed *Mam*'s corn broom from the back porch and ran to the field. Johnny and Mandy were close behind her.

"You two go around them to the other side and get them to go toward the barn."

Ellie stayed near the gate and used the broom to guide the cows toward the hole in the fence on the other side. She groaned as the splayed hooves of the animals churned the dusty soil, uprooting row after row of plants. When Buttercup stopped to pull one of the remaining green survivors up with her teeth, Ellie swatted her bony rump with the broom.

"Get on there, you miserable cow! Get in your own pasture!"

Mabel, the heifer, was in no hurry to return to the shady grass. She danced around Johnny's and Mandy's efforts to get her to follow the others, scattering bits of strawberry leaves and roots with every jump. Ellie added the broom to their efforts to corral her, but it wasn't until Benjamin joined them that they were finally able to get all three cows through the hole in the fence.

Ellie turned to survey the damage. The field had looked pitiful before, but now it was gone. The money she had invested, the hours watering them, the worry... Any hope of seeing Daniel's dreams fulfilled lay trampled in the dust.

Ellie felt *Mam*'s comforting arms around her shoulders and wanted to bury her face against her and cry, just as if she was Susan's age, but she wasn't a four-year-old.

Dat and Reuben joined Benjamin in the task of

mending the fence. They finished the quick patch, and then *Dat* joined Ellie.

"*Ach,* Ellie. This is too bad."

Rebecca stood at the gate with Susan and Danny, while the rest of the family gathered around Ellie. Whatever came of this, she wasn't going to have to bear it alone.

"What will you do?" Benjamin's voice was subdued. He had to be almost as disappointed as she was after all the work he had put into this project.

Ellie shook her head. "I don't know."

Mam squeezed her shoulders. "The Lord will provide. You'll see."

"*Ja,* I know."

But when? How would she ever pay Bram back now?

Bram spent Friday morning in Elkhart after taking the Interurban from Goshen. A larger town than the county seat, and closer to South Bend and Chicago, Elkhart had much more to offer someone like Kavanaugh. He had found some evidence of criminal activity—duly noted and passed on to the local police—but no sign of the gangster.

He changed his clothes in the public restroom in Goshen and turned Partner toward the Stoltzfus farm. It had been more than a week since he had seen Ellie. The desire to talk with her had grown into an aching need. How had he survived before he met her?

He had called Peters again before heading home from Elkhart, letting him know what he had found. The FBI agent would put his findings together with the information other agents had been able to gather on the Chicago end. They were closing in, squeezing a tight circle around South Bend. That had to be where Kavanaugh's new headquarters were. Peters told him the feds would be making their move soon, and then Bram's job would be over—as long as the cops were thorough this time and the gangster didn't slip through the cracks. Another day or two and he'd call Peters again, just to see what progress had been made.

Meanwhile... He smiled, enjoying the thought. *Ja,* meanwhile, once they got Kavanaugh out of the way, he could stay right here. No more FBI, no more Mexico on his horizon, no more running, just the sweet anticipation of courting the most beautiful woman he had ever met. He'd start by asking her to a picnic with the children at Emma Lake.

The first thing Bram saw when he turned Partner into the Stoltzfus barnyard was Reuben working in Ellie's strawberry field with a singletree plow. What happened to the strawberries?

Ellie came out of the *Dawdi Haus* to greet him as he tied his horse to the hitching rail.

"Good afternoon, Bram."

It was all he could do to keep from taking her in his arms, but he settled for a brief touch on her shoulder.

"What's Reuben doing with the plow?"

"*Ach,* the cows got into the field yesterday and ruined anything that was left."

Her voice was flat with discouragement.

"You're not planting more right away, are you?"

"*Ne.* I can't buy more plants now, even if I thought they might survive. *Dat*'s planting buckwheat."

Bram nodded. Buckwheat grew quickly, and they'd be able to harvest it before frost, even with this late planting. He glanced at the clear blue sky and amended his thought—they'd get a harvest if the rain came.

"The worst part…" Ellie lowered her voice as she walked with him into the shade of one of the maple trees. "The worst part is that I won't be able to pay you back as soon as I hoped."

"Don't worry about that."

"But I do. I hate being in debt. I have to save for next year's taxes, but I will pay you back."

"Ellie, I said don't worry about it. I'm not worried. Everything will work out."

"That's what *Mam* always says." Ellie looked away from him, watching the dust cloud behind Reuben's plow.

Bram reached up and turned her chin toward him. "Your mother is right, as usual."

Her expression was solemn. He longed to kiss her cheek. Maybe that would force her into a smile. He dropped his hand and cleared his throat.

"I came to ask if you'd like to have a picnic on Sunday—you and the children. We could drive over to the lake, and the children could go wading…" He stopped as she looked away from him again.

"I don't want the children to be a burden to you."

"Your children are never a burden." He waited until she looked at him again, then smiled and stroked the line of her jaw with his thumb. "I never regret any time I spend with you or the children. Being with the four of you for a day is the nicest thing I can think of." He took Ellie's hand in his and turned it over, stroking her palm with his finger. "I want to take you on this picnic. Please come."

She hesitated for a long minute. He enfolded her hand in his, longing to be able to pull her into his embrace.

He stole a glance to her face. The worry line was there, her lips drawn into an expression of doubt. Confusion. Something still stood between them.

"I…I can't, Bram. It isn't fair to…" She stopped, biting her bottom lip between her teeth.

"It isn't fair to whom, Ellie?"

She whispered the answer. "To me. To the children. The more time we spend together, the more they like you, and the more they'll miss you when you're gone."

"What if I told you I wasn't going anywhere?"

"What?"

"My job is almost finished, and I thought maybe I'd stay on." He smiled, anticipating the pleased look of surprise he'd see in her eyes, but instead her worry line deepened farther.

"Stay on? Do you mean as part of the community?"

"*Ja,* sure."

"Become a member of the church?"

Bram shifted and looked away. He hadn't thought about joining the church since his brief conversation with Bishop Yoder. Was he ready to take that step?

"I…I don't know. Maybe."

Ellie pulled her hand out of his and took a step, putting distance between them.

"I've let myself become too close to you, Bram. I can't keep being friends with someone who's a nonmember."

"And if I never joined the church?"

She lifted her eyes to his, her voice a whisper. "Then I can't see you anymore."

Bram swallowed and looked to the sky. How was he supposed to handle this?

"Give me some time, Ellie. I need to take care of this thing with Kavanaugh."

"And then what?" She gave him a trembling smile. "After you take care of this problem, what comes next? You look like you're Amish, Bram, but you've never left the *Englischer* behind. What if you're never ready to submit to the church?"

Bram tore his gaze away from her clear blue eyes. She was right. He felt like swearing, but could only accept her words. If he couldn't submit to the church, everything he had come to treasure here would slip through his fingers. Even Ellie. Even the children.

But to join the church, to agree to live by the *Ordnung,* to give up his freedom, his independence…

Did she know what she was asking him to do?

"If it was Levi Zook standing between us, I'd fight for you. I wouldn't give up until you chose one of us, and then I'd abide by your decision. But this…Ellie… You're asking me to give up everything." He stopped and rubbed the back of his neck.

She looked at him, her eyes wet. "Sometimes *Gott* asks us to give up what we hold dear in order to give us the better thing He has for us."

Bram shook his head. "I don't know if I can believe that."

"You can trust *Gott,* Bram."

Could he trust God that far? He wasn't sure.

Chapter Sixteen

Bram left the house the next morning with a check of the clear blue sky. Another day with no rain meant the crops would continue to suffer. He glanced at the corn-field on his way to the barn, but there was little change. The seeds had sprouted, but by now the plants should be almost a foot high, with bright green leaves reaching upward. Here it was nearly the Fourth of July, and the plants were barely six inches high, dull leaves hanging from the fragile stalks.

He harnessed Partner and hitched him up to head to the telephone exchange in Topeka. He was itching to find out if Kavanaugh was in custody. If the gangster was out of the way, he'd be able to settle into his life here—but what kind of life would it be?

Little spurts of dust rose with Partner's hoofbeats in the empty road as the relentless question echoed in his mind. Ellie was right—if he stayed here, he'd have to make a decision to either join the Amish church or leave it. How could he make a decision like that?

At the corner ahead, a buggy turned onto his road, trotting fast. As it drew closer, Bram saw that Matthew was driving. He pulled Partner to a halt when the two buggies met.

Bram's gut wrenched when he saw Matthew's haggard face. Something was wrong. Terribly wrong.

Ellie…

"Matthew, what's happened?"

"It's Hezekiah Miller. He's missing."

"What do you mean, he's missing?" Elderly Amishmen didn't just disappear.

"Amos Troyer went this morning to help out and found Miriam beside herself. Hezekiah never came in from doing his chores last night."

"I'm on my way over there. Where's Ellie?"

"She and Elizabeth went to Hezekiah's as soon as they got the news. I've got more families to tell, and then I'll be down there."

Bram gave a brief nod goodbye in return to Matthew's and then slapped the reins on Partner's back. The gelding set off at a fast trot.

Taking a deep breath to steady himself, Bram thought of all the possible reasons for Hezekiah's disappearance. If it was any of the other farmers, he might have thought the old man had decided to take a walk around one of the fence lines in the evening, but as crippled as Hezekiah was, he wouldn't go farther than the barn itself. Not alone. Not willingly.

He chirruped to Partner again, even though the horse was keeping up his steady, fast pace. Where had they looked already? Bram went over the farm in his mind, glad he had been there often enough in the past two weeks that it was familiar. It was only ten acres, not so large that Hezekiah could get disoriented and lost. The creek had steep banks—could he have slipped

down them? He'd make sure someone looked there.
The woodlot wasn't big, but it was dense with under-
growth. Another place to make sure of. The barn itself?
It was fairly small, but there were still places to look.

Bram pulled into the small farmyard, glad to see it
crowded with buggies. The people had come together
in this crisis, as they always did.

A couple boys had been given the job of seeing to
the horses. Bram handed Partner's reins to one of them,
then strode to the house, where he saw the men and
older boys gathering around the back porch.

John Stoltzfus nodded as Bram joined the group,
his mouth set in a firm line. Almost every man from
the church was here. Bram nodded to Jim Brenneman,
Ellie's *Englisch* tenant, while John organized the searchers.

"Amos already searched the barn and farmyard this
morning, before sending for help. We'll divide the rest
of the farm between us. Look in all the fencerows,
ditches, anywhere he may be lying hurt."

John sent a grim look around the circle of faces and
then nodded to Bishop Yoder, who stood at the edge
of the circle. The old bishop lifted his hands, shaking
with palsy, to bless the men as he prayed. The rhythm
of the *Deitsch* words flowed over Bram, giving him
strength and confidence. With God's help, they were
sure to find Hezekiah.

Before joining John and his boys as they headed to
the east fence line, Bram glanced toward the house.
Ellie stood in the doorway, holding on to the frame as
if it were her lifeline. He caught her eye and nodded,
giving her a smile that he hoped would be reassuring.

She returned his smile with a worried one of her own and disappeared into the kitchen.

Ellie turned back to the kitchen and joined *Mam* at the counter, where she prepared chicken casseroles for the men who would be hungry at dinnertime. Ellie prayed it would be a celebration dinner as she chopped stalks of celery for the casseroles.

Miriam stood at the counter next to her sink, where she could watch the fields through the window while she kneaded bread dough. She seemed calm, but her movements lacked the smooth efficiency that was normal for the older woman.

Ellie remembered her own panic when Daniel was lying in bed, hurt, while she sat helpless at his side, waiting through that long day only to face his death at the end. Miriam must be feeling the same thickening of her throat, the same telescoping of sight to that last glimpse of her husband, and yet she continued to knead the dough until it was nearly overworked.

Ellie's eyes blurred as she concentrated on the knife and the celery. What would any of them do without Hezekiah?

Mam put two large casseroles into the oven and went over to Miriam while Ellie washed up at the sink.

"Come, Miriam, the bread has been kneaded enough. Let it rest now."

Mam took Miriam's hands in her own and handed her to Ellie. The older woman's eyes stayed fixed out the window, but she was as compliant as Susan when Ellie washed her floury hands at the sink while *Mam* covered the dough with a damp towel.

"Let's have another cup of coffee while the dough

rises." *Mam* got three cups from the cupboard. "Ellie, can you pour us all a cup?"

Ellie led Miriam to a chair at the kitchen table. She had seen *Mam* do this same thing many times during a crisis. Keep things as normal as possible. Keep the conversation going. Anything to keep Miriam's mind off what the men were doing, what they might find or if they never found anything.

"I won't be able to go on without him." Miriam's voice was edged with tears, and Ellie stifled a sudden sob. The last time she had heard Miriam's voice like that had been the evening of Daniel's death, when the waiting at his bedside finally ended. Ellie's heart chilled at the thought of the lonely night vigil Miriam had just spent waiting for her husband to walk through the door, a vigil that had only ended with Amos's arrival in the morning.

"*Ja,* you will. *Gott* will give you strength." *Mam*'s words were solid ground in this miserable morning.

"They're sure to find him soon, with all those men searching." Ellie tried to sound hopeful, but Miriam didn't seem to notice she had spoken.

"*Ja,* Ellie's right. They're sure to find him soon."

Miriam got up from the table to look out the window over the sink again. "*Ach,* if only I could help them."

Whatever happened with Hezekiah, Ellie knew she couldn't let Miriam stay on the farm without some help. The men of the church had been faithful in coming to help with the work, but even that hadn't prevented this accident.

Ellie looked at Miriam over her coffee cup as the older woman stood at the window watching the searchers for the first sign that her husband had been found. She rose to stand next to her, a woman as dear to her as her own *mam*. She put her arm around Miriam's shoulders and supported her as the elderly woman leaned into Ellie's strong embrace. They would share this vigil together.

Bram made his way to the woodlot growing on either side of the fence that separated Hezekiah's farm from Ellie's, the farm the Brennemans were renting.

He eyed the brambles that grew at the sunny edge of the lot. Yellow jackets buzzed hungrily at the stunted black raspberries that covered them. It would take a determined man to break through that mess, and he would leave a trail. Hezekiah certainly didn't have the strength to do it.

Bram followed a path through the grass as it skirted the brambles and then stopped where it disappeared in a narrow tunnel leading into the trees. Could Hezekiah have gone in there?

Looking around, Bram spotted Benjamin ten yards behind him.

"Ben, over here."

"What did you find?"

"Look here," he said as Benjamin leaned down to look through the narrow opening. "Could he have followed a cow through there?"

"*Ja,* I think so." Benjamin pointed to a deep, cleft-hooved print in the long grass just outside the opening. "That's not a deer print. If he was following a stray cow, he might have tried it."

Benjamin ducked and started down the narrow tunnel. Bram waited, listening to the sounds of the other searchers, praying they would find Hezekiah alive.

"Here! Bram, in here. Hurry!"

Bram echoed Benjamin's shout to the other searchers, then followed the trail into the woods, ignoring the brambles that snagged at his clothes. He paused just inside the shadowed cover of the trees, letting his eyes adjust. The close, humid air pressed against him and hummed with mosquitoes.

"Bram, he's over here. I found him."

Benjamin knelt next to Hezekiah's prostrate form; the old man's body slumped over a fallen log. Adrenaline shot through Bram when he saw blood-matted hair on Hezekiah's face. Kneeling next to him, Bram checked for a pulse. He thanked God it was there, faint but steady.

"Is he…"

"He's still alive."

"We need to get him to the house."

"Not yet. We need to see where he's hurt first."

The thick air of the woodlot filled with voices as the other searchers joined them. One by one, the men fell silent as Bram checked Hezekiah's arms and legs. The old man groaned when Bram turned his head to find the source of the bleeding. A cold shock went through him when he found the wound. That ugly bruise didn't come from a fall—he had been hit by something hard.

Bram spoke to John hovering at his shoulder.

"We can move him, but we need to make a litter out of a blanket or something."

Two of the boys left the group. They would take the news to the house and fetch the blanket.

"Will he be all right?" John's voice was raspy as he looked down at his longtime friend.

"I don't know. It looks like he has a concussion, and spending the night on the ground hasn't done him any good. He's been eaten up by mosquitoes." Bram looked at John. "He'll need the doctor. Can someone fetch him?"

"I will." Mr. Brenneman spoke up. "I'll take my car."

Bram supervised as Hezekiah was moved onto a blanket, but he stayed behind as the group took the elderly man into the house. There had to be clues to tell him what had happened here last night.

He looked around to get his bearings. The fallen tree was in a low spot, near a ditch that might be a small stream in a rainy year. Bram walked around the log, outside the perimeter of where the group of men had been standing. He found the cow's prints in the soft ground of the ditch and the print of Hezekiah's work boot.

Following the ditch farther along, Bram found what he dreaded. There had been two men in the woodlot, and judging from the footprint in a muddy spot at the bottom of the ditch, they weren't Amish. That print had been made by someone wearing shoes, not work boots. Bram slipped his hand inside his pocket and grasped the reassuring handle of his pistol.

Following the faint signs on the disturbed floor of dead leaves, Bram arrived at the edge of the woodlot about fifty feet from the trail. Here he found a cleared space littered with discarded cigarettes and a couple of empty bottles that told him one or two men had spent several hours here—maybe even several days. A short log had been stood on its end. From the number of cigarette butts on the ground around it, it looked as if someone had used it as a seat for a long time. Why?

Bram sat on the stump. What he saw made his stomach clench. An opening had been cleared in the brambles, just big enough to give him a perfect view of the barn, house and fields. Someone had sat here watching the farm.

Hezekiah must have found them, surprising them as he followed that stupid cow. Bram could see how the scene played out: two gangsters overpowering the old man, cracking his skull with a gun butt and then leaving him for dead.

He leaned down and picked up an empty cigarette packet, not wanting to believe what he saw. They were Jose L. Piedra cigarettes from Cuba, Kavanaugh's favorite. The only reason for Kavanaugh being here was that they had somehow tracked him down. Bram's mouth went dry. He never thought his efforts to help out would put the old man in danger, but if Kavanaugh had found him here, at Hezekiah's farm, who else had he unwittingly set up as a target?

Turning slowly, his eyes pierced the shadowy depths of the woodlot. Surely with the crowd of searchers that had been on the farm that morning, the gangsters would have cleared out, but there was still a chance they could be hiding in the underbrush, waiting. Hand on his gun, Bram made his way to the path through the bushes and headed to the house, the spot between his shoulder blades itching the whole time.

Ellie stood with Miriam and *Mam* at Hezekiah's bedside, listening to the doctor's advice.

"He has a concussion, which can be dangerous." The *Englisch* doctor pulled the light summer quilt up to Hezekiah's shoulders as he rose to his feet and gave Miriam's hand a reassuring squeeze.

"Keep him warm and quiet, and I wouldn't let him get out of bed for a couple days. If there are any changes, or if he falls asleep and you're not able to wake him, send for me right away."

Miriam nodded as the doctor snapped his black bag shut and followed *Dat* out of the room.

"I'll stay with you tonight, Miriam," *Mam* said. "I know I can count on Ellie and the girls to take care of things at home for a day or two."

"*Ja,* of course," Ellie said. She helped Miriam to her small rocking chair next to the bed and then stepped out of the room and headed to the quiet front porch. The creak of the front screen door as she pushed it open was a comforting reassurance that everything was going to be all right, in spite of the day's turmoil.

Her stomach did a flip when she saw Bram sitting on the porch swing. If yesterday's conversation had never happened, she could have found some comfort in his presence. As it was, she folded her arms in front of her and stood in the gap between the front door and the swing. How could she mend this rift between them?

"I thought everyone had gone home," she said.

Bram's face was set in a worried frown, but why? Hezekiah was going to be fine.

"Not yet," he said. "I want to make sure everything is going to be okay."

"You heard the doctor. Hezekiah has a concussion, but he'll recover." Thanks to Bram.

He didn't answer, just looked toward the barn. His hands gripped the edge of the porch swing. Something more than Hezekiah was worrying him.

"Bram, what's wrong?"

He slid over to make room for her next to him on the swing. Ellie sat, waiting for his answer.

"Hezekiah's injury wasn't an accident."

"What do you mean?"

"He came across that man I told you about—Kavanaugh." Bram swallowed, his Adam's apple bobbing in his throat.

"But how would he? I mean, what does that man have to do with Hezekiah?"

He turned to her, his eyes dark. "Me. He must have tracked me here one day and then waited for me to come back. He's been hiding in the woodlot, and Hezekiah must have surprised him last night."

"Where is he now?"

Bram shook his head, his face stony. "I have no idea." He sighed, looking toward the barn and the fields beyond it once more.

Ellie felt the thrill of fear that tales of wolves had given her when she was a little girl. She would look into the trees and imagine them lurking there, waiting to pounce when she wasn't looking. But this fear had a name. This wolf was real.

Bram took her hand, running his thumb across the back of it, and then with a sudden groan, he gathered her to him. Ellie clung close, pressing her ear against his chest, his steady heartbeat reassuring her of his strength. He would protect her, if he could.

He pressed her closer to him and kissed the top of her head. "Ellie," he whispered, "I couldn't bear it if he hurt you."

"He won't, Bram." She tried to smile as he released her enough to lift her chin and look into her face. "Between you, *Dat* and my brothers, I'm very well protected."

"I'd like to believe that." He stroked her cheek with

his thumb. "I'm sorry about what I said yesterday. I've been miserable ever since then, knowing we disagree."

She nodded. That same disagreement still hung between them.

"I won't rest until I find Kavanaugh. You know that."

A cold screw twisted her heart.

"That isn't our way, Bram. Vengeance belongs to the Lord."

"This isn't vengeance, Ellie. This is my job." His hand lingered on her cheek, and then he rose so abruptly he sent the swing rocking. "I'll see you tomorrow?"

Ellie nodded, regretting the rift that widened between them.

"*Ja,* tomorrow at church."

Bram drummed his fingers on the desk in the telephone booth at the exchange as he waited for the operator to make the connection.

"Peters here."

"It's Dutch."

"Dutch, are you all right?"

"Yes, I'm fine, but I'm worried about Kavanaugh. Do you have any news?"

"The information you gave us so far was right on the mark. Kavanaugh has been expanding operations into South Bend, Fort Wayne, Toledo and Detroit. We were able to track down one of his boys in South Bend, and the thug sang like a canary."

Bram wiped his face with his handkerchief and propped the door of the telephone booth open to let in some air. If Peters had done his job, then who had attacked Hezekiah?

"So you got Kavanaugh?"

"That's just it. We rounded up a dozen of his men, but he was nowhere to be found."

Bram rubbed his palm on his pant leg. So he was right about Kavanaugh hunting for him. The gangster was getting desperate.

Peters went on. "That stool pigeon told us Kavanaugh went out west. That he is working in Los Angeles now."

Bram's mouth was dry. "He's not in California—he's here. He almost killed an old man last night, a man who owns a farm I've been working on."

There was silence on the other end, and then Peters cleared his throat.

"It looks like your cover is gone, Dutch. You need to get out of there."

Bram leaned his head against the wooden side of the telephone booth. Peters was right. *"Ja, es richtig...."*

"Dutch? Are you still there?"

"Yes, I'm here. I said you're right. I'll call if I need anything, but I hope you don't hear from me."

"Right. And, Dutch, take care of yourself."

Bram hung up the telephone. The tables were turned again, and he was no longer the hunter. As long as the snake was still around, he couldn't risk staying here.

He sighed and slumped against the side of the telephone booth. Just when he had begun to hope...but no. Home and family? They weren't for him. He was a fool to think his life could be anything more than hunting down men like Kavanaugh. Ellie deserved more than that, much more.

But there was one thing he could do for her. He could draw Kavanaugh away from here, away from Ellie and this community. Once he drew him far enough away, he'd make sure the gangster never got a chance to come back.

Bram rubbed the back of his neck, suddenly aware of how long this day had been. And it had been the last day. He had no illusions about what could happen when he offered himself as bait, but he couldn't hope to get rid of that snake without sacrificing himself.

There was one last risk he would take, though. If Kavanaugh hadn't found him by morning, he'd attend the Sunday meeting. He couldn't bear to leave without seeing Ellie one more time.

Chapter Seventeen

Mornings on church Sundays usually started early, but this one was even earlier for Ellie. Since *Mam* had stayed with the Millers last night, Ellie took on the task of getting the entire family ready for Sunday meeting. She was thankful for the long ride in the buggy to Amos Troyer's. The children rode quietly, making up for their lost sleep after an early breakfast.

Watching the passing fields, Ellie tried to quell the sinking feeling in her stomach. What would she say when she saw Bram? Was he still set on taking revenge for Hezekiah's wound? He had said it wasn't vengeance—but could it really be anything else?

"We have much to be thankful for today, knowing Hezekiah is safe," *Dat* said. He seldom spoke on the drive to meeting, using the time to pray about what he would say if he were asked to give the sermon.

"*Ja,* we do, but I can't help worrying about them. How will they live on their farm?"

Dat reached over and laid his hand on hers. "*Gott* knows their needs. Reuben is going to live with them for the rest of the summer and into the fall, and after that, we'll see what *Gott* has planned. Keep trusting Him."

Caution still dogged Bram as he tended to his few chores before church. If Kavanaugh knew where he was, what was keeping him from showing his face? Driving through the still, morning air, he kept his eyes and ears open, but there was no sign of the Packard.

Bram set a mask over his frayed nerves as he drove into the Troyers' crowded farmyard. No one could suspect this would be his last time with them.

As he drove past the congregation lined up outside the barn, he caught sight of Ellie greeting another woman. She glanced toward him and gave him a smile, making his heart soar in spite of the thoughts of Kavanaugh hovering on all sides.

He joined the line of men just as the congregation started into the barn, and he chose a seat where he wouldn't be tempted to glance at Ellie during the service. She was by far the most beautiful woman there, but Bram grew cold every time he thought of what could happen if Kavanaugh knew about her. His gut twisted as he remembered the bloody gash on Hezekiah's head, but instead of the old man's matted gray hair, he saw Ellie's fine brown hair and *kapp*.

As Bishop Yoder and the ministers rose to go to an upstairs room for prayer, one of the older men started the first phrase of *Das Loblied,* and Bram joined in the familiar hymn with the congregation, his mind still on the gangster. If Kavanaugh was looking for him, wouldn't it be smart for him to lie low? But then how long would it take for him to stop feeling as if danger was stalking him? He would never get there. He'd always be looking over his shoulder. How long could he live that way?

Then, as he looked up between hymns, Bram saw Ellie lean forward slightly, right into his field of vision. Her lips were parted in a smile as she whispered something to Susan, and her face held a look Bram hadn't seen before—joy, contentment. He couldn't stop staring at her. Longing for her filled his heart.

Bram knew what he had to do, in spite of the ache in his chest. Or because of it. As soon as Sunday meeting was over, he would leave. He'd leave Partner and the buggy at Matthew's, along with what was left of the cash he had. He could leave a note telling Matthew to give everything to Ellie. From there it wouldn't take long to walk to the highway, and then he could hitch a ride somewhere. Anywhere but Chicago. Anywhere but here.

Kavanaugh would follow him, with any luck—he'd leave a big enough trail—and it really didn't matter where the gangster caught up with him, as long as Ellie was safe.

He forced his eyes away from Ellie and her family. He was aware of the service continuing as one of the ministers prayed, but his mind was occupied in a war. He knew what he should do, but could he do it? He had never met a woman like Ellie. The thought of leaving her, of never seeing her again, pulled his heart in one direction, and then the knowledge of what could happen if Kavanaugh knew how much he cared about her sent cold fingers yanking him in another.

Bram forced his hands to unclench, willing himself to relax. He had to remember where he was. Matthew was sitting in front of him; Reuben and Benjamin

Stoltzfus were to his right. Welcome Yoder was two benches in front of him, sitting next to Eli Schrock. These men had accepted him into their community, helped him on his farm and given him their time and advice. Could he turn his back on them? In the past few weeks he had gotten a taste of what the church could be, what his heritage could give him, and all he planned to do was use them and throw them away.

As soon as the service ended, Bram made his way through the men to the side of the barn. He glanced behind him as he slipped out the door, but the milling crowd cheated him out of one last look at Ellie. He closed the door, ignoring the sinking feeling in his belly.

She's just a woman.

Who was he kidding? There wasn't another woman like her.

He rounded the corner of the barn, heading toward the parked buggies, but stopped short when he saw John Stoltzfus waiting for him.

"Good morning, Bram."

"Good morning, John."

"I was hoping to talk to you."

Bram quelled the retort that came to his lips—words from his own anxiety. He couldn't speak to this man like that. Now that John had stopped him, he wouldn't be able to make his quick escape anyway. He mentally closed the door on his plans and forced himself to turn his attention to the older man.

"I was watching you during the meeting." John paused, pretending to study the buggies lined up in the field.

Bram waited. He knew John well enough to know that he would get to his point sooner if he let him do it in his own time, no matter how anxious he was to get going.

"Is something bothering you? You seemed distracted."

Bram almost choked. *Ja,* he was certainly distracted, but he thought he was better at hiding it than that. One thing Bram had learned over the past several weeks was just how deep John's perception of people went.

"*Ja,* I've been worried about Hezekiah, just like everyone else. It kept me from paying attention to the meeting as I should have." If he gave John a partial explanation, maybe he would leave it at that. Once Bram was out of the area, Kavanaugh would be old news.

John turned to look at him.

"You've been on my mind a lot lately. Your name keeps coming to me at odd moments, and I always pray for you when it does." Bram didn't know what to say. Had anyone ever prayed for him before? "It can't be easy leaving your old life behind."

He doesn't know the half of it, Bram thought, but without the bitterness of a couple months ago. He felt an urge to confide in John—to warn him about Kavanaugh, about his part in the gang and the danger he had brought to this community—but the calm acceptance in John's eyes stopped him before he even started. He couldn't talk about the sordid things he was involved in. Not here, not now, not among these people. Once he left, it would all be over for them anyway.

"*Ne,* it isn't," Bram said. "I lived that way for many years, and old habits are hard to get rid of."

John nodded, waiting for him to go on. How much could he confess? John deserved to know.

"I've seen an old acquaintance around."

"Someone from Chicago." John's words were a statement, not a question. "Someone you don't want to run into again."

"I did some things there that...well, that I'm not proud of." Bram swallowed. He had already said more than he should, but he felt that silken coil again, urging him on. "I want to just leave them behind me, along with the people I knew there."

John's eyes were piercing. Could he see the details Bram was leaving out? Bram wasn't sure how much this man had already guessed.

"If you left any unfinished business, you should resolve that before trying to move on. Otherwise, you'll never be free of your past."

Bram rubbed the back of his neck as John paused.

"I heard an automobile go by our farm last night. A big, powerful one. No one around here owns a machine like that." John looked at him again. "It went by twice."

Bram's hand automatically went to the pocket where he carried his gun. He closed his cold fingers around the grip.

"You don't need your gun."

He shot a glance at the older man. How...

"*Ach, ja,* I've known about it for a long time."

Bram dropped his pretense. It looked as if John knew everything.

"John, this guy is dangerous. I need my gun."

"We are a people of peace, Bram. Guns have no place in our lives."

Bram looked away, anywhere but into the older man's face. John had no idea how violent life could be outside this community. Violence had to be dealt with or else innocent people would be hurt, people like Hezekiah.

"I need to protect myself. I need to protect the people around me."

"Do you believe *Gott* can protect you?"

Did he believe that? *Ja,* up to a point…but at what cost?

"I don't know," he answered John truthfully. "I'm not convinced that *Gott*'s protection works against bullets."

"Perhaps bullets aren't what you need to worry about." Not worry about bullets? What could be worse? What was he talking about? "Put your trust in Him, Bram." John paused until Bram looked at him. "Your very soul is in danger, and, more important, the soul of the other man. If he commits a heinous sin because of your actions…" John shook his head at his own words. "There are things more important than our lives."

Bram looked away again. He wished he could have that confidence, but he knew too much. He had seen too much.

"I have to go."

"Bram." John stopped him with a hand on his arm. "I'll still be praying for you."

Bram nodded his thanks and then continued to his buggy.

By the time Bram was within sight of his farm, his plan was set. He had to protect Ellie at all costs. If he survived somehow, could he come back eventually? And see Ellie married to another man? Someone like Levi Zook? The thought made his hands clench. No, he had to leave for good.

As he turned the horse into the barnyard, he saw it. The maroon Packard sat along the side of his barn, out of sight until he turned into the drive. The knot that had been growing in his stomach all morning exploded.

He sawed on Partner's reins, trying to get the horse to turn, but it was too late. Kavanaugh sauntered out of the barn, followed by Charlie Harris's lumbering form. Kavanaugh's face was stony, but Charlie's grin turned Bram's feet to ice. Running was out of the question. Bram couldn't pray. He put all his strength into keeping his voice steady.

"Hello, Kavanaugh. I didn't expect to see you around here."

The gangster's thin face twisted into a sneer as he gave Bram a cold smile. "I was surprised—but very happy—to see you while I was doing some business in Goshen a couple weeks ago."

Bram put an amazed look on his face. "I didn't see you there, but then, I've been busy."

"I can't help being curious to know—" Kavanaugh took a drag from his cigarette, measuring his words "—what you would be doing in that hick town, dressed like some—" he gestured with his cigarette toward Bram, the buggy, his Plain clothes "—like some *farmer*." He emphasized the last word with derision and then took another drag. Bram waited. Kavanaugh's right hand was tucked under his suit jacket, where he would have quick access to his gun.

"And then when I happened to see you at that old man's farm—" the cigarette smoke plumed from Kavanaugh's mouth and nose as he spoke "—I couldn't believe my luck."

He pulled another lungful of smoke from the cigarette.

"I didn't like it when you slipped away from us last

night, you and that buggy." He exhaled the smoke. "I'm glad we finally tracked you down." The gangster paused and tapped some ash off the cigarette with a flick of his finger. "What happened to the Studebaker, Dutch?"

Bram was silent. He knew better than to respond when Kavanaugh was trying to bait him. Charlie, off to Bram's left, still grinned and flexed his hands.

"You left Chicago in a hurry and didn't tell anyone where you were going, and around that same time some G-men showed up, knocking on our door. That makes me wonder what you're up to. I wasn't sure where to even begin looking for you until I saw you on that farm wagon a few weeks ago."

Bram still didn't answer. Anything he said to Kavanaugh now would only make things worse for him.

Kavanaugh stood at the horse's side, eyes even more narrow than usual, staring at Bram. He threw his cigarette butt on the ground and twisted it into the dust with his heel. Without taking his eyes off Bram, he beckoned to Charlie.

"Get him down."

Charlie wasn't the type to be gentle at his work. He reached up and grabbed the front of Bram's coat, then pulled him off the seat as easily as a kitten. Charlie held him up; his feet brushed the dirt of the drive.

"Shall we go into the barn?" Kavanaugh's polite words mocked the desperate situation Bram was in. Unless a miracle happened, he was a goner.

Without waiting for an answer, Kavanaugh turned and led the way as Charlie dragged Bram after him. Dust motes swirled in the sunbeams, throwing bars across the shaded interior. Charlie backed Bram into the support beam with a shove, holding him with his arm across Bram's chest. Cigarette butts littered the dirt floor. They must have been waiting for him all morning.

Bram looked toward the roof as Kavanaugh closed the barn door. Thank *Gott* he had been able to see Ellie one last time.

Charlie patted him down, finding his gun. The thug stuck it in the waistband of his pants. When Bram eyed it, Charlie saw the direction of his gaze and slammed an elbow into his ribs.

"I wouldn't have taken you for a churchgoing chump," Kavanaugh began, lighting another cigarette. After taking a puff, he turned the burning end around, staring at it as if he had never seen the glowing tip before. "We don't like stool pigeons, Dutch. You know that. You betrayed me, and no one gets away with that. Want to tell us what you told the feds?"

Ellie watched *Dat* closely. Ever since the meeting ended and the women started preparing dinner, he'd paced at the edges of the crowd. When she glanced his way, he was often looking toward the road, where Bram's buggy had disappeared.

She hadn't noticed Bram leaving until he was already on the road, his horse trotting away at a fast pace. She couldn't remember the last time someone had left Sunday meeting early, before the meal and fellowship afterward. But if something had been wrong, wouldn't he tell her?

Not long after the meal ended, *Dat* found Ellie as she talked to yet another concerned woman about Hezekiah and Miriam. "It's time to go." His voice was gruff, short, and Ellie knew she shouldn't delay. *Dat* was never in a hurry without a reason.

By the time Ellie had gathered her children, *Dat* was waiting with the buggy. Mandy and Rebecca followed.

"But why can't we stay and come home with Reuben?" Rebecca asked as they climbed into the buggy.

Ellie turned to help Susan settle in the backseat between the girls. "Because the boys aren't coming home until late, after the singing."

Even as Ellie spoke, she gave *Dat* a questioning glance. *Why the hurry?*

Dat didn't speak, but started the horse off at a quick trot. When he reached the end of the lane, he turned west, instead of east toward home. *Now what?*

"Dat," said Ellie, leaning close so the children in the back didn't hear, "is something bothering you?"

"I had a conversation with Bram earlier. I'm a bit worried about him, and I thought we'd drive past his place on the way home, just to check if things are all right."

Ellie felt a cold chill, even though *Dat*'s voice was calm. She trusted her father's judgment. He was able to read people so well, some thought he had a gift. If he felt this concerned after talking with Bram…

Had Bram found that man he was looking for? Fear wrapped its icy fingers around her heart. Bram was in danger.

The girls hadn't caught *Dat*'s tension. They chattered like birds as they played a game with Susan and Johnny in the backseat, Rebecca holding Danny on her lap.

Did that man, Kavanaugh, have something to do with why Bram had left church so early? In fact, he hadn't even looked at her all through the service. Ellie worried the inside of her lip. It wasn't like him to ignore her completely.

When *Dat* turned onto Bram's road, Ellie saw Partner in the lane between the gravel road and Bram's barn, but why wasn't he tied? For some reason Bram had just left the horse unattended, and Partner had pulled the buggy partway into the grass. As she watched, Partner took another step toward the long grass at the edge of the cornfield and the buggy tilted, along with her stomach. Where was Bram?

Dat pulled to a stop at the end of Bram's lane and handed the reins to Ellie. "You take the children home. I'm going to check on Bram."

"I'm coming with you."

Dat looked at her, weighing his decision. Finally he nodded. "Mandy, you drive the buggy on home and look after the children."

Mandy gave Ellie a mystified look as she obediently climbed into *Dat*'s place and took the reins.

"We won't be long." Ellie smiled at her little sister as she climbed down. "It will be fine."

Dat waited until Mandy had driven off before turning to Ellie.

"There's something going on, and Bram may need help. I'm going to check the barn."

Ellie followed *Dat* as he walked toward the barn, glancing into Bram's buggy as he went.

Ellie crossed the lane to the other side, where she'd have a clearer view of the barn door, and stopped short. There was an automobile parked alongside the barn, out of sight until she'd seen it from this angle. What was going on here? Her mind flashed back to Bram's face when he had first told her about this man, this Kavanaugh. Could the automobile belong to him?

Dat reached the barn and paused, leaning against

the wall next to the door as if he was listening to something. What? Was there someone inside with Bram? Ellie's stomach clenched.

She could hear indistinct sounds from inside the barn. Men's voices. She had to hear what they were saying.

She slipped up next to *Dat,* and they both listened to the men inside the barn.

"You're tougher than I thought." Ellie didn't recognize the voice, but she didn't want to meet the man it belonged to.

"It's no use, Kavanaugh. Peters knows where you are." Bram sounded weary but not afraid. "I talked to him yesterday. He's on his way here right now."

"Charlie, stand him up again."

There was a scuffling noise as Charlie obeyed the first voice.

So there were at least two men in the barn with Bram.

"Work him over some more. I have to know how much he told the feds."

A sickening sound filtered through the barn wall— the sound of something hard hitting flesh. Ellie's head pounded, and the icy fingers tightened around her heart. That was the sound of Bram being beaten. *Dat* knew it, too. He gave Ellie a hard look that ordered her to stay back and then rammed his shoulder against the barn doors, forcing them open with a crash of splintered wood.

The two men looked up, surprise and anger twisting both of their faces. Ellie took in the whole scene in one glance through the open door. Bram was pinned against a beam by a huge man, his face bloody and raw. He looked straight at Ellie, and fear filled his eyes when he recognized her. *Dat* walked into the barn, his hands outstretched in an effort to calm the situation, watching the big man.

Then Ellie saw the smaller man, his clean, tailored suit a stark contrast to Bram's torn and bloody clothes. His eyes on *Dat,* he threw a cigarette down and in one fluid motion pulled a pistol from beneath his suit jacket.

Ellie's feet were lead. She must keep that man from using his gun. She ran forward and grasped the cloth of his sleeve. He spun around, swinging the gun toward her face, his eyes sharp with evil intentions. The blow caught Ellie on the side of her head as she turned away from him, then he had no more regard for her than a fly he had just swatted away.

As she fell to the floor, Ellie was horrified to see him raise his gun again, pointing it toward *Dat.*

Chapter Eighteen

The crash of the barn door brought Bram to his senses. Was he dreaming? No, the sharp pain in his ribs was all too real. John strode into the barn between Kavanaugh and Charlie, holding out a hand toward each, a gentle smile on his face. Bram sent a quick prayer for *Gott* to protect this brave, foolish man. Charlie froze, his suspicious eyes on John.

"Surely, brother, we can talk about our differences without resorting to violence," John said, his voice calm in the charged air.

Bram looked past him to Ellie standing in the barn door, and the fog cleared out of his mind with a rush.

No, she can't be here!

Charlie turned toward John, readying a ham-size fist at shoulder level. Without the thug's hand pinning him against the supporting beam, Bram swayed. The air around him turned black. Staggering, he shook his head, trying to clear his sight. When he looked up again, the first thing he saw was Kavanaugh backhanding Ellie. He gathered what strength he had to go to her aid, but when Kavanaugh's hand lifted, the snub nose of the pistol pointing straight at John, Bram changed direction and sprang to his left, shoving John over just as Kavanaugh's finger squeezed the trigger of the gun.

He and John skidded to the floor as Kavanaugh's gun roared in the small barn. Bram rolled to his knees—Ellie was still in danger—and stopped as he faced Charlie's prostrate form on the dirt floor beside him, a bloom of red blood soaking his shirt's shoulder. Bram's pistol was still tucked in Charlie's waistband, right in front of his eyes. He grabbed it and turned to face Kavanaugh, every nerve focused on his target.

The gangster's face was calm, his eyes like steel. Bram had seen that look before—the man was determined to kill. Deliberately, Bram raised the gun in his hand to meet Kavanaugh's stare.

"Drop your gun." His voice croaked, but he was able to force the words out. Blood ran into his mouth from a split lip, and he spit it out.

Kavanaugh's lip curled in the sneer that was his trademark. "No cop is going to take me."

The snub nose of Kavanaugh's gun steadied as the gangster's finger tightened on the trigger. Bram shot at the same time. His body jerked as Kavanaugh's bullet hit his chest, and he fell into blackness.

The small man fell to the ground, but Ellie didn't look at him as she flew to Bram. *Dat* reached him first, turning him on his back. The wound was just a blackened hole in Bram's shirt, but as Ellie watched, blood began spurting out of it.

"Good," *Dat* said as he propped up Bram's head. "He's still alive."

Stars whirled around Ellie, the icy grip on her heart

squeezing mercilessly. *Dat* gripped her arm, covering it with Bram's blood.

"I need your help, Ellie. We need to get him to a doctor."

Ellie swallowed. Bram's face was pale, and blood was everywhere. Just like Daniel.

"What do I need to do?" Her voice cracked in a whisper of breath.

Dat removed his jacket and tore off his shirt. Wadding it up, he pressed against the wound.

"Keep pressure on this."

Ellie pressed her hand against Dat's shirt, Bram's warm blood pulsing against her cold fingers.

"We need to get him to town. We'll take that automobile outside."

"The automobile?"

Dat looked at Ellie, his eyes grave. "This is a matter of life or death. It's here, so we'll use it."

Ellie kept pressure on Bram's wounds, walking beside *Dat* as he carried him to the big maroon machine. She sat on the backseat with Bram's head in her lap as *Dat* returned to the barn and carried the small gangster to the automobile. The man was barely conscious as *Dat* set him in the front seat, and he slumped against the door.

Dat sat in the driver's seat, pausing to study the controls.

"Can you make it work?"

Dat gave her a grim smile as he turned on the motor. "*Ja*, I drove an ambulance during the war, remember? It wasn't too much different from this."

"What about the other man?" Ellie tried to remember if he was dead or only hurt.

"He'll be all right. I tied him to the barn post, and I'll send someone to get him when we get to the hospital."

Once *Dat* figured out the controls of the automobile, the trip into Goshen was faster than Ellie had ever experienced. *Dat* knew more about driving than Ellie imagined, but the machine still bucked and stuttered as he tried to make it speed along the dusty road.

Bram lay deathly still for the entire trip, his head resting in her lap. Ellie watched his pale face as she leaned over him, keeping her fingers pressed against the makeshift bandages. She tried to pray, but the words didn't survive the icy grip on her heart. Memories of Daniel flooded her mind. Once again she was helpless, hopeless, watching the man she loved as he lay dying. With every breath that made his chest rise beneath her fingers, she took a breath herself. Which one would be his last?

Ellie blinked back tears, watching Bram's face. She loved him. Her mind embraced what she had feared all along. Could she love him? Love meant risking her heart, risking loss again. Could she bear that?

As *Dat* pulled up to the hospital, the car's engine sputtered and died. Ellie stayed with Bram as *Dat* ran into the building, her numb hands pressed against Bram's wounds. The automobile's door swung open, and a man in white looked in.

"We'll take it from here, ma'am."

As they took Bram and put him on a wheeled cot, Ellie's hands fell uselessly into her lap. She watched the small man, Kavanaugh, being wheeled into the hospital behind Bram. What could she do now?

Dat opened the door next to her.

"Come, daughter. We'll wait for news inside."

Ellie looked down at her bloody hands and dress. *Dat*'s Sunday coat was just as bad.

"Like this?"

Dat smiled at her, but the smile didn't change the worried look in his eyes.

"*Ja.* This is a hospital. They're used to these things here."

Ellie let *Dat* help her into one of the chairs lining the hall just inside the door of the hospital. *Englischers* were everywhere, even on a Sunday afternoon. *Dat* went to the desk to use the telephone while she sat. Her hands shook as she stared at the blood that covered them. Bram's blood.

She barely noticed when *Dat* took the seat next to her.

"I called the Wrights," he said. "They'll take the news to Eli's, and it will be passed on from there."

As the afternoon wore on, people started showing up at the hospital. Annie and Matthew Beachey were among the first, and Annie had brought some fresh clothes for them both.

By the time Ellie changed her dress, the corridor was filled with Amish. Friends and family surrounded them. She numbly returned to her seat and heard *Dat* relating the news to some recent arrivals.

"The doctor said they would have to operate. He said it didn't look like the bullet had hit his lung, but it broke his shoulder blade. He wasn't sure what other damage had been done."

Dat's words sank in slowly. Was Bram still alive?

Mam sat down, and Ellie found herself clinging to her. She gave way to the tears that she had dammed up. Her failed promises to Daniel, her doubts about

Bram, her own miserable pride all caught up in tears that flowed like a spring flood.

Bram gunned the engine, Kavanaugh's breath hot on the back of his neck.

"Go, go, go!" The gangster cursed at him, and Bram put all his weight on the accelerator, but his foot couldn't reach the floor—the Packard didn't move. Bram risked a look over his shoulder. Kavanaugh's face disappeared in an explosive flash.

Bram's eyes shot open. Ellie was in danger. He struggled to sit up, fighting against the pain that seared across his shoulder and down his back.

Ellie's face came into view.

"Bram, don't try to move."

But Kavanaugh would kill her; he had to move. He fought against the black fog in his mind.

"Bram, it's all right. You're in the hospital."

Ellie's voice pierced the thick layer. The hospital? Pieces of the events in the barn fell into place in his mind like shattered glass shards, arranging themselves into bits of memory. He lay still, watching her face. Her blue eyes were red-rimmed and wet, as if she had been crying. A tear made its way down her cheek, and he tried to lift his hand to brush it away, but the only thing that moved was his index finger. His right arm, shoulder and chest were covered in bandages. Kavanaugh... Where was he?

His eyes sought Ellie's again. "Wh...wh..."

"Shh. Don't try to talk."

Ellie moved away as a nurse bustled in. Quiet shoes whispered on the wooden floors.

"Lie still, young man." The middle-aged nurse spoke

in a no-nonsense tone, and he couldn't fight her. His chest felt as if a heavy weight held it down. The nurse gave him a sip of water after checking his pulse and temperature.

"He's doing fine so far." The nurse shook the thermometer and placed it in her pocket. "You may stay only a few more minutes. He needs to get his rest."

The nurse left the room as Ellie came into view again. Behind her were John and Elizabeth.

"Tell me what happened to Kavanaugh." His voice was stronger. The water had helped.

Ellie glanced at John. The older man looked down at his feet, then back at Bram. "You shot him."

"Is he dead?"

John shook his head. "*Ne,* praise *Gott.*"

"Where is he? You can't let him get away."

"He's here in the hospital, along with that other man."

Bram closed his eyes, exhausted. He had to let Peters know where to find them, but not now.

"We'd better go."

Bram forced his eyes open to see John ushering Elizabeth out of the room. Ellie stood by his feet.

"I need to go, too."

"*Ne,* wait."

She moved to his side and rested her hand on his as it lay outside the covers. Her mouth quivered as she looked at him.

"If you and your father hadn't come… I still don't know how you got there."

"*Dat* had a feeling there was something wrong."

"*Ja,* he was right." Bram closed his eyes, but he opened them again as he heard Ellie start to move away. "Don't go."

Ellie shook her head. "I need to. The nurses won't let me stay." Her hands shook, as if she was trying to bear up under a great strain.

"I'm not going to die, Ellie. I'm here for you."

Ellie smiled at him, a quick, tearful smile, and then turned and followed her parents out the door as the nurse came in again.

"Now, no arguing. You need your sleep." The nurse adjusted his pillows, checked his IV and took his pulse again. Her eyebrows rose as she looked at him. "Your pulse is up a bit."

"I need you to do something for me."

The nurse didn't answer until he had swallowed the pills she gave him.

"Will it help you rest?"

"*Ja*...I mean yes. I need to make a phone call."

"No phone calls for you, young man." She moved to the end of his bed to adjust the sheets.

"Is there someone who could send a wire for me?"

"I can send a telegram for you, but you have to promise to go to sleep then. All right?"

Bram nodded, and the movement made his head ring. He gave the nurse Peters's information.

"Tell him where I am and that I have some of his friends." He moved his head toward her too quickly and winced from the pain.

"None of that. I'll send your message."

"One more thing. I have to talk to the police." His voice was getting weaker. Making an effort to rally his strength just made him sink further. Whatever drug she had given him was taking effect.

"Sure. They'll be here first thing in the morning to talk to you if you're feeling up to it. They always do for a shooting." She unfolded a blanket over his legs. "Although what Amish folk are doing involved in a shooting…" Her voice faded.

"Those other men…" But she was already out the door, beyond hearing. He was helpless against the sleep that claimed him.

Ellie sat alone in the back of the buggy while *Dat* drove home. Brownie's hooves kept up their tireless cadence on the road while lightning bugs hovered above the fields in the growing darkness, floating in the hot breezes that carried the scent of acres of cornfields.

Exhaustion made her head thick, numb, so much like the days after Daniel's death….

But Bram wasn't dead. Ellie choked back a sob before *Mam* could hear it. This was what she had been afraid of, wasn't it? That if she let herself care for another man…

Bram wasn't dead, but that didn't mean he felt anything for her. That man in the barn… Ellie shuddered as she remembered his cold eyes, the blow that had sent her reeling to the ground. This was Bram's world—violence, blood, death. Did *Gott* have any place in a world like that?

Mam turned in her seat and reached back, resting her hand on Ellie's knee. "Bram seems to be doing well after his surgery, doesn't he?"

Ellie nodded, not trusting her voice.

"Annie said they would move him into their house after he's released from the hospital. We'll have to be sure to get the women together to can her garden, since she certainly won't have time." *Mam* paused, looking carefully at Ellie's face in the growing darkness. "It will be all right, daughter. Bram will come back to us."

"It doesn't matter, though, does it?" The words came before Ellie could stop them, strident in the night air. "He's never been one of us. He's *Englisch,* and he'll be going back to his *Englisch* world now that he's caught those two criminals." She ended with a choked sob.

Mam glanced at *Dat* and then turned around to face the front again. Ellie's face burned. Her words and her tone had both been hateful.

"I'm sorry *Mam, Dat.* I shouldn't have said that."

"We don't know Bram well." *Dat*'s voice was soft, tender, almost sad. The things he had seen today had shaken him, too. "But I do know this, Ellie. He's an honorable man, but his past followed him here. We'll have to wait and see how today's events will affect him."

"*Ja,* you're right."

Mam and *Dat* lapsed into silence, and Ellie let the swaying motion of the buggy calm her. Could Bram ever come back and be one of them? His words as he had spoken to that man in the barn had been as cold as death, and the determined look on his face as he had fired his gun haunted her memory. She saw no reluctance to use violence in his actions, only the same set look she had seen on *Dat*'s face when he killed a snake. But this Kavanaugh wasn't a snake; he was a man, and violence against another man was against the *Ordnung.* Against the Bible. How could Bishop accept him into the church after this?

Bram woke with every temperature and pulse check through the night. If these nurses were so concerned about him sleeping, why didn't they leave him alone so he could do it?

Dawn brought a shift change with a visitor. Elwood Peters walked into his room as soon as the nurse had finished with the temperature check.

"I'm glad to see you're still with us." The older man's clothes were rumpled, his face gray and unshaven.

"You look worse than I feel." As he tried to smile, Bram concentrated on keeping his body still. Every movement sent a shot of pain through his chest.

Peters pulled a chair over to Bram's bedside and sat heavily on it, tossing his hat onto the blanket covering Bram's legs.

"Yeah, sleeping on a train will do that to you."

He reached into his pocket for his pack of cigarettes, tossed one out into his waiting hand and then stopped with a mild curse.

"I forgot. No cigarettes in here." He gestured his hand toward the oxygen tank sitting next to Bram's bed.

Bram found himself cringing at Peters's language. When had cursing become offensive? It hadn't been that long since he had talked the same way.

"What about Kavanaugh?" Bram had to know.

"Kavanaugh is still here, just a couple doors down the hall. He's in worse shape than you are. His goon—"

"Charlie Harris."

"Yeah, Charlie. He had a flesh wound in his shoulder, and he's in the city jail this morning."

Bram's muscles released their tension with Peters's words. He sank into the softness of the hospital bed. Ellie was safe. How soon would he see her again?

"With those two in custody, Kavanaugh's gang is finished." Peters leaned back in his chair, tapping his cigarette against his knee. "It's a good feeling, Dutch, and we couldn't have done it without you and your work."

"Yeah, well, just keep that part to yourself."

"Are you sure? There's a reward. It would set you up for life."

"I don't want money for this. Give it to the policemen's fund or something."

Peters tapped his cigarette against his knee and stared out the window. He had something on his mind.

"Now that this business is over, we could use you back. The gangs are all moving out west. California, Nevada. We made Chicago too hot for them. You could work for us out there. Become an agent, not just an informant." He shifted his eyes to Bram's. "You show real promise. You have a gift for this kind of work."

Bram couldn't look at Peters. He moved his gaze toward the window. No clouds. They sure could use some rain.

What Peters was offering...wasn't that what he had always wanted? He knew he would be a good agent. It would be a hard life and probably a short one—agents didn't have a very long life expectancy. But the thrill of getting his man! He had felt something like it when he had faced Kavanaugh in the barn. How many crooks could he get off the streets? How many innocent lives could he protect in that kind of work?

The hollow clip-clop of an Amish buggy on the street outside drifted up to his open window. The measured beats of the horse's hooves slowed his thoughts, brought them back to Ellie, the children, his farm, the church. He felt that fluid, silken movement again, caressing his mind.

That unseen presence had never left him since he'd

first felt it—since he'd first come back. Would it be with him if he took Peters up on his offer? Even if it was, his heart would be here.

The sounds of the buggy faded off into the distance. He knew where he belonged.

Chapter Nineteen

After three weeks of lying in a hospital bed, Bram was anxious to get out of there, although he'd hate giving up the electric fan that cooled the ward. The end of July could be stiflingly hot in northern Indiana, but this year the temperatures felt like a blast furnace, and still no rain in sight.

He leafed through a copy of *Look* magazine. The headlines spoke of the coming Olympic Games in Berlin, a civil war in Spain, the heat wave two weeks ago that had claimed nearly five thousand lives across the nation. And Adolph Hitler's picture was everywhere.

Bram let the magazine fall closed and pushed it away, along with the news. He was so weary of the world and its problems. Was John right when he said believers were to keep themselves separate from the world? John was confident in his belief in *Gott* and the brotherhood of the believers—but where did his confidence come from? The older man centered his world on his church and his family, not the cares of the world.

Not that he wasn't concerned about the people in

the world—Bram had heard the killing heat and the violence in Spain mentioned in his prayers—but they weren't his utmost concern. John's greatest desire, he had said, was to see his children and grandchildren close around the family table, in fellowship and love.

A fitful breeze fluttered in the leaves of the maple tree outside the window, catching Bram's eye, and he watched them turn one way and then the other, limp and ragged in the dry heat. "Blown by the cares of the world," John had said once.

John's words described Bram perfectly. Tossed and turned by events and ideas that had no place in the Amish life, but where did they fit into his life? What was his greatest desire?

Memories of the day he and Ellie had taken the children to LaGrange came to his mind. Family. Home. The bright laughter in Johnny's eyes, Susan's shy smile, Danny's downy-soft hair. And Ellie.

Could he be to them what John was to his family? Could he be the one to pray for them, discipline them, lead them to a life of obedience and joy?

The window disappeared as his eyes grew wet. Could this be why *Gott* had brought him home to Indiana?

The large ward was quiet in the afternoon heat, with most of the men dozing or reading. Sitting up slowly, Bram waited for the gray fog in his head to clear. He had been given bathroom privileges just yesterday, but he was still too weak to walk down the hall alone. The young, pretty nurse who worked the day shift glanced up from her charts and walked toward his bed.

"Now, Mr. Lapp, you aren't going to try anything dangerous on your own, are you?" Her voice was light, but the set of her mouth told him she still wouldn't put up with his efforts to take care of himself.

"I just wanted to go down the hall for a bit." The gray was clearing, and he tried a smile. It worked.

The pretty nurse smiled back at him and felt his forehead in a way that was half professional check, half a caress. "I'll get a wheelchair and take you myself."

He eased into the chair she brought, glad he had the use of one hand to help steady himself. As soon as he was settled, the nurse wheeled him toward the hallway.

"I hear you're going home today," she said as the cumbersome chair rolled along the narrow hall. Bram searched through his mind for her name but came up empty.

"That's right. The doctor's letting me go to my sister's house. She'll take good care of me."

"We'll certainly miss you here." She gave him another smile as she opened the door of the bathroom for him and helped him to his feet. "You'll be all right on your own?"

Bram steadied his shaking knees. He hated being so weak, but there was no chance he was letting the nurse help him in the bathroom. "Sure, I'll be fine."

Once he finished, he was glad to sink into the wheelchair again. Who knew a man could lose his strength so quickly?

As the nurse started wheeling him back to the ward, he kept his gaze on the door at the far end of the hall. He'd be going through that door soon, free to get his life started again. Free to see Ellie again. As if his thoughts had beckoned her, the door opened and Ellie walked into the hallway, followed by her father.

At the sight of her slim form with her black bonnet

and a lightweight black shawl covering the blue dress, Bram's eyes grew moist again. He leaned toward her. Couldn't this chair go any faster?

"It looks like you have visitors," the nurse said.

John stepped forward. "We're here to take Bram home, if he's ready to go."

Home. Bram sought Ellie's eyes. She glanced at him once with a tentative smile and then looked at the floor.

"The forms still need to be signed by the doctor," the nurse said. "But you can wait on the sunporch until they're ready."

"I'll wait with them," Bram said, watching Ellie. He hadn't seen her since he had woken up after his surgery—he hadn't seen anyone except John. The older man had stopped in to visit a couple times a week, taking the time to talk with Bram about nothing in particular, and always giving Bram guidance, sharing his faith and answering his questions.

After the nurse wheeled Bram to the screened-in porch that overlooked the street outside, she disappeared to find his doctor. Ellie sat in a chair near Bram, still silent, while John walked to the screened window and looked out.

"Well," he said, clearing his throat, "I think I'll go find a drink of water."

The wink he gave Bram as he left the room made Bram smile, in spite of Ellie's silence. John would be gone for a while, giving them a chance to talk.

Ellie sat with her hands folded in her lap, her eyes on the trees outside the window. Bram reached his left hand out to touch her, brushing her arm with his fingers. At his touch, she turned to him.

"I've missed you," he whispered.

Her gaze pierced him. "Are you all right?" she asked and then caught her bottom lip between her teeth.

"*Ja,* I'm feeling better every day."

"*Dat* said you were on the mend."

"*Ja.*" He had to ask her. "Ellie, your *dat* came to see me often. Why didn't you come with him?"

She looked away. "I wasn't sure you wanted me to."

Didn't want her to?

"Why would you think that?" His voice rose louder than he meant, and Ellie jumped at the sound.

"I'm sorry." Bram dropped his voice. "I only meant that I wanted to see you. You could have come. I...I need you."

Ellie scooted her chair closer to his and laid her hand on his arm as it rested on the wheelchair. He pulled her hand into his lap and held it.

"Now that you've found that man, you'll be leaving, won't you?"

Bram's hand stroked her fingers one by one. "*Ne,* I won't be going back. I have a few loose ends to tie up in Chicago, but then I'll be here to stay."

Ellie turned her head away, pulling her hand from his. Chicago? Once he left, he would never come back.

"You believe me, don't you, Ellie?"

She hesitated. She had trusted him once, but now? Before she could answer, the nurse swept into the room, followed by an orderly.

"Here we are, Mr. Lapp. The forms are all signed. Mr. Stoltzfus has paid your bill, so everything is taken care of."

* * *

A week later, Bram couldn't wait any longer. He was going to see Ellie if it killed him, and if Matthew hadn't helped him harness Partner and hitch up the buggy, it just might have. He drove slowly, easing the horse around the rougher sections of the road, and made it to the Stoltzfus farm without too much pain.

As he drove up the lane, Ellie waved to him from the middle of the garden. He pulled Partner to a halt by the trough and eased down from the buggy. Ellie met him at the edge of the grass, lugging a bushel basket full of tomatoes. He started to reach out to take the basket from her, but the pain in his shoulder reminded him he was still too weak.

Ellie set the basket in the grass and gave him a smile. "You must be feeling better, to make the trip over here." She shaded her eyes with her hand, her tanned face and sun-bleached hair telling him how many days she had worked out here in the garden.

"*Ja,* I am." Bram stepped closer to her and wiped a smudge of dirt from her cheek. "Why don't you have any help today?"

Ellie shrugged. "Benjamin is working in the fields, and *Mam* and *Dat* took the children to Lovina's. These tomatoes need to be picked, whether I do them alone or with help. It isn't hard work, but I'm ready for a rest. Would you like some tea?"

"*Ja,* that sounds good."

Bram walked with her to the *Dawdi Haus,* listening to her talk about the children, the garden, the weather... It all went over his head as he watched her expression change with each new subject. She was more beautiful than he had remembered.

He let himself down into the seat of the glider with careful movements while Ellie went into the house to fetch the tea. The walk had exhausted him. He leaned his head back and started the glider moving with his foot. Insects hummed in the sultry air, and a slight breeze played with the leaves above his head. How many nights had he lain awake in the hospital thinking about sitting on this glider with Ellie?

By the time she brought his tea to him, Bram had gotten his breath back and took the glass from her with a smile.

"Denki." The first swallow was as delicious as the feeling that went through him when she sat next to him.

Silence hung between them. There were so many things he wanted to say to her. He had practiced them in the buggy all the way here, but now his tongue clung to the roof of his mouth. He took another swallow of tea.

"We haven't had a chance to talk." He stopped as he felt Ellie stiffen next to him. She moved slightly so that their arms no longer touched.

"You're going to Chicago."

"Ja. I have to, or else Kavanaugh will go free."

"I understand that, but…" She stopped.

He turned to look at her, shifting his weight as he moved to ease the pain in his shoulder. Her eyes were wet as she steadily looked toward the barley field, the barn, the fence. Anywhere but at him.

"Ellie, what's wrong?"

"I know you miss your life in Chicago. You were only here to do your job, and you never wanted to come back to the Amish life. Once you're gone, I'll never see you again."

How could she think that?

"After I give my deposition, I'll be back."

"Your deposition? Do you mean a court trial?"

"Ne, not quite. The lawyers wanted me to testify against Kavanaugh for his attack on Hezekiah and for shooting me, but the Amish don't bring lawsuits against people. John helped me understand that."

Ellie looked at him. *"Dat?"*

"Ja. He helped me sort through how I can keep my commitments to my job and still stay faithful to the church. Bishop approved the deposition, since I wouldn't be appearing in court to do it."

"And since you haven't taken the vows of baptism." She turned her head away from him again.

"Ne, not yet, but I will when I get back. Once all the ties to my past life are cut, I'll be free to commit to the church and to you."

She shook her head. "Don't lie to me again, Bram."

"I'm not lying. I never did lie to you, Ellie."

Then she looked at him, the pain in her eyes unbearable. When had she stopped trusting him?

"How can I believe you? I want to, but I can't."

Bram rubbed his forehead. This wasn't the way he wanted this conversation to go.

"What can I do to make you believe me?"

Ellie's voice was soft, strained through tears. "I don't know."

Bram reached out his hand to touch her cheek, feeling its soft warmth. He ran his finger along her jawline and caught the stray hair in his fingers. That stubborn lock of hair that never stayed in its place. Stubborn like her. He twisted it softly around one finger and then moved his hand to the back of her neck, drawing her to him. He held his lips on her cheek, breathing in her scent, and then released her.

"When I get home from Chicago, then you'll know I'm here to stay. I'll never leave you, Ellie."

Chapter Twenty

"*Memmi,* look! Look!"

Ellie turned from the sink full of dishes to see Susan holding Danny's hands as he walked from the front room into the kitchen.

"Danny's walking!"

"*Ja,* almost." A walking Danny would be twice as much work to keep track of, but she had known this day was coming. Time never stood still.

Susan let go of one of Danny's hands to brush some stray hair out of her face, and the baby plopped down on the floor.

"He'll need a bit more practice before he's ready to take off on his own."

"Can I take him outside?" Susan helped Danny stand again.

"*Ja,* but stay in the grass."

"Can we go to *Grossmutti*'s house?"

"*Ja,* sure. I'll be coming soon. Walk at the edge of the garden so Danny will have a soft place to land when he falls."

Danny crawled after Susan to the door and scooted

down the porch steps. Ellie watched as Susan helped him to a standing position, and they started the tedious journey to the big house. Back at the sink she could see their entire route through the window while she finished washing the breakfast dishes. They were both growing up too quickly.

As thoughts of Bram crowded into her mind again, she scrubbed at a spot of dried egg yolk on a plate. Why couldn't she stop thinking about him? He had left for Chicago more than a week ago, and she needed to put him out of her mind. She had feared losing him to death, but losing him to the world wasn't any less painful.

The dishes done, Ellie took one last glance out the kitchen window. *Mam* had seen Susan and Danny coming and was holding the door open for them as Danny climbed up the back-porch steps toward her. She had probably already finished one canner full of tomatoes this morning, and it was time to get over there to help.

Ellie rubbed the crease between her eyebrows, easing her headache a bit. A buggy coming up the lane to the big house caught her eye and she paused. Who would be visiting this early in the morning? Matthew Beachey got down from the buggy, and then he went around to the other side to help someone else out. Had Annie come for a visit? *Ne,* it was a man.

Dat came out from the barn to meet them, Johnny running behind. When the man stepped forward to shake *Dat*'s hand, Ellie saw he was wearing *Englisch* clothes.

Bram. He was here.

Johnny stopped in front of him. She could almost see the shy hesitation on his face before Bram bent down to gather the boy to him with one arm. Johnny flung his arms around Bram's neck.

The sight of Bram and Johnny's reunion held her captive at the window. Why hadn't she seen how completely Bram filled the empty place in Johnny's heart? Her son didn't just need a father; he needed Bram.

She needed Bram.

Ellie wiped tears from her cheeks with quick motions. If he meant to stay, then why was he back to wearing his *Englisch* clothes? He had to be here to say goodbye.

How could she bear that?

"Bram, I missed you."

The boy's words, whispered in his ear, brought tears to Bram's eyes.

Ignoring the ever-present pain in his shoulder, Bram held Johnny to himself for a moment with his good arm and then pulled back far enough to look into his face.

"Have you been taking good care of your *memmi?*"

Johnny nodded, his eyes shining. "*Ja,* Bram. I always take good care of her."

"And your sister? And Danny?"

"*Ja,* Bram."

"That's my boy." Bram half choked on the words.

Would Johnny be his boy? He hoped so. It was what he had been praying for.

Before he could stand again, Susan appeared at his side. Her shy smile told him just how much she had missed him, too. He wrapped his arm around her small frame and held her close, her little-girl body as fragile as a newborn chick. He wished he could lift her up in both arms, but that would have to wait until he had healed more.

He stood to greet Elizabeth as she came out of the house carrying Danny, but he couldn't help glancing beyond her through the screen door. Where was Ellie?

"Come up to the porch," John said, ushering them all toward the shaded front of the house. "We have some tea, don't we, Elizabeth?"

"For sure we do. I'll bring it out."

As Bram hesitated, John turned to him with a smile. "We'll wait for you on the porch, Bram. Why don't you go to the *Dawdi Haus* and tell Ellie you're here?"

Bram grinned at John, thankful the older man understood. He wished he was strong enough to run along the lane, but he had to content himself with a slow walk.

At the edge of the garden, Bram paused to straighten his jacket. The *Englisch* suit was uncomfortable, but he had insisted that Matthew bring him straight to the Stoltzfuses' from the train station. He had to see Ellie.

Movement at the *Dawdi Haus* kitchen window told him she knew he was there, but he still hesitated. What could he say to her? Just blurt out how much he loved her? That he wanted to marry her?

Ne, he had to take it slow, win back her trust. He took a deep breath and whooshed it out.

Even when he'd faced Kavanaugh straight on, he hadn't been this scared. The worst Kavanaugh could do was shoot him.

Ellie could sentence him to life without her.

Swallowing hard, Bram adjusted his hat. The distance to the back porch wasn't long, but before he reached it, the kitchen door opened. Ellie. She stood in the doorway watching him, her face unreadable.

"Good morning, Ellie."

"Hello, Bram." Her voice was cool.

His mouth was as dry as cotton.

"I've missed you." He tried smiling at her, but his face refused to obey. "Will you come sit on the glider with me?"

"*Ja,* I will."

Bram brushed a couple fallen leaves off the glider as they sat. Ellie gripped the edge of the seat on either side of her skirt, betraying how nervous she was. Somehow the thought comforted him.

The summer locusts began their daily serenade in the trees at the edge of the field.

"Six weeks till frost." He felt like kicking himself. Where had that come from? He wasn't here to talk about insects.

"What?"

"Something my *mam* used to say when she heard the locusts in August. There's six weeks until frost."

"*Ja,* you're right. My *mam* says the same."

They fell into silence again. Bram moved the glider with his foot. Where should he start?

"I've been—"

"*Dat* says—"

They both stopped.

"You go on, Ellie. What were you going to say?"

"Just that *Dat* says your farm is doing well."

"*Ja.* I'm thankful John and the other men kept it going for me."

"With Partner over here, you had no animals for them to tend to, so it wasn't too much work."

More silence.

Bram pushed his foot against the ground, setting the glider into motion again.

"I have to tell you something."

She tensed, but didn't look at him.

"I've requested to be baptized." Her head shot toward him, her eyes round. "Bishop has been coming to Matthew's for my instruction, and I'm joining the community next Sunday."

Ellie waited for his teasing grin. He wasn't serious, was he?

"You're joining the church?" she asked, watching his face.

Bram smiled, his eyes warm and sincere. "*Ja,* at the next Sunday meeting."

Ellie gripped the edge of the glider seat harder, willing her trembling hands to still. A thin shaft of light pierced her thoughts. He wasn't saying goodbye; he was staying.

"But I thought…well, your trip to Chicago, your *Englisch* clothes…"

Bram reached up, pulled off the necktie and stuffed it into his pocket.

"I didn't let Matthew take me home to change. I had to see you."

"Bishop is allowing you to join the church even though you shot a man?"

"I had to shoot him. He had hurt you, and he intended to kill all of us. It was my job to stop him, one way or another. He didn't leave me any choice."

"But won't you keep working for the FBI?"

Bram's left hand closed over hers, warm, strong and confident.

"Ellie, that life is behind me now. I've confessed everything to the Bishop and your father. What's more important is that *Gott* knows everything. When Kavanaugh found me, I was on my way to find him and have it out with him, once and for all." He squeezed her hand. "I knew I wasn't going to survive. I knew I'd never see you again. But I did survive. It's like I have a new life, and I don't want to waste a minute of it."

His clear, steady eyes told her more than his words, but she had to ask...

"If it happened again—if you run across someone from your past like that—would you do it again? Could you shoot a man?"

Bram looked at the ground, his grip on her hand tightening. "I can't say for sure unless I was in that situation again." He looked back at her, his eyes moist. "But I hope I would act as *Gott* desires, that He would give me the strength to do the right thing. I still believe I need to protect my family, my friends, but I hope I would be able to do it in a way that protects the other person also. That's all I can promise."

"And Bishop believes that's enough?"

"*Ja.* He says desiring to obey *Gott* and praying for His help is as much as any man can promise."

Bram leaned across her lap, taking her other hand from the edge of the glider. He cupped her two small hands in his large one. Ellie let them rest there, birds surrounded by a protecting hedge.

"I know this is where I belong, Ellie, with you and with this community."

The small shaft of light widened, plunging into her soul with the dawn of understanding.

"You're really staying?"

"*Ja,* Ellie." He rubbed his thumb along the side of her finger, his touch sending tingles up her arm. "I've done some terrible things, Ellie, but I've never lied to you."

She looked into his eyes, meeting the hope she saw there.

"I was wrong not to trust you, Bram." *Ja,* she should have known she could always trust him.

Bram raised his hand to her face, catching the stray lock of hair.

"Ellie, I couldn't bear to live without you." His voice was a whisper as he drew her close.

"You don't have to."

Bram's kiss was gentle, tentative. He brushed her lips with his and then drew her to him in a close embrace. Ellie lost herself as he held her with his good arm, pressing her ear against his chest to listen to the reassuring beat of his heart. She could rest here forever.

Two weeks later, Bram sighed as he pushed away his empty plate and leaned back in the chair. Miriam's sugar-cream pie was the best he had ever tasted.

"There's another piece left," Miriam said, pushing the dish toward Bram.

"*Ne, denki,* I couldn't eat another bite."

"I'll take it." Reuben reached for the dish and dug into the last piece as if he was starving. He shouldn't be. He had been living with Hezekiah and Miriam since the accident, and Miriam had doted on him with her cooking.

Hezekiah chuckled. "I sure like that young man's appetite."

As Miriam started clearing the table, Bram turned to the older man. "I've told you what I have in mind, and you've looked at the house plans." Miriam paused to listen to Bram, and he glanced up at her. "What do you think?"

"Well," Hezekiah said, reaching for Miriam's hand, "it was hard to hand the work over to Reuben this summer, but I have to admit the rest has done me good. I feel better than I have in a long time. I know Miriam has worried about what would become of us when I couldn't work anymore, especially after we lost Daniel." He looked at Bram, his eyes bright and sure. "We'll move in as soon as you're ready for us."

Miriam squeezed Hezekiah's shoulder. "*Ach,* and I have to thank you, Bram. To live so close to Ellie and the children..." She smiled as she busied herself with the dishes.

"Now, don't say anything to Ellie yet." Bram looked at Reuben. "She doesn't know anything about this, and I don't want her to until I get a chance to tell her."

Reuben grinned at him as he got up from the table to head back to his chores. "You had better let her in on the secret soon, then. I know my sister. If she hears a rumor about a new *Dawdi Haus* being built at your place, she'll ferret out the truth faster than anybody."

Bram went out to his buggy, leaving Miriam and Hezekiah to discuss their packing. He hoped to get the *Dawdi Haus* built before winter, but he had one more thing to do first. It was time to let Ellie in on his plans.

He couldn't believe he hadn't thought of this solution before. Having Hezekiah and Miriam close would help ease Ellie's mind, and he was looking forward to having the older man's help to build up his farmland. Hezekiah may not be able to walk behind a plow anymore, but his knowledge of farming would never go to waste.

Partner pranced and blew a couple times before he settled into his steady trot, enjoying the cooler fall weather as much as he did. Bram settled in for the drive to the Stoltzfus farm, watching the corn crops in the fields he passed.

It had been a long, hot, dry summer, but it looked as if the farmers would have enough of a harvest to survive. His own crop would give him enough to use for the winter and enough seed for next spring, but nothing extra to sell.

It didn't matter. Bram still couldn't shake the feeling that he had opened a door and discovered a wonderful new world. Now if he could only convince Ellie to share it with him.

He had spent nearly every evening with her since coming home from Chicago. He would meet her on her glider at dusk, after the children had gone to bed, and they'd sit for an hour or more.

Sometimes they talked. Bram thought they'd run out of things to talk about, but they never did. He grinned to himself. They wouldn't run out of things to talk about in a hundred years.

Other times they sat quietly, holding hands, or with Bram's arm around Ellie's shoulder, while he kept the glider swinging with one foot. He wouldn't get tired of that in a hundred years, either. He'd have to make sure he built a glider like that for their own place.

Their own place.

Bram chirruped at Partner, suddenly anxious to hear Ellie's answer to his question.

The tomato plants had started producing again with the onset of cooler weather. Ellie pushed aside the old, dry stems from the summer to find the tomatoes that grew amid the new, green leaves. A second chance at life brought new fruitfulness to the tomatoes.

Ellie glanced toward the glider at the side of the *Dawdi Haus*. The tomatoes weren't the only things with a second chance. She couldn't keep a smile off her face at the thought. How would she ever have known love could be so sweet a second time? She couldn't bear the thought of waiting until this evening to see Bram again.

"*Memmi,* help!" Susan's cry came to her ears yet again.

Ach, there was Danny, heading for the cow pen at the side of the barn. Ever since he had learned to walk, the cow pen was his favorite destination. Until school started last week, Susan had helped Mandy or Rebecca watch the toddler while Ellie did her chores, but now that Susan was on her own, Danny was proving to be a handful.

Ellie caught him just as he reached the fence and swung him up in her arms as he giggled. The little stinker! He liked being caught as much as he wanted to see the cows. She tickled his belly to hear him laugh again as she carried him back to the toys Susan had set up in the grassy yard.

"*Ach,* Danny, you play here with Susan for a little while longer while I pick the rest of the tomatoes."

"Won't he just run away again?" Susan tried to get Danny to play with a toy cow.

"*Ja,* probably. Just do like you've been doing. Call me when he does."

Buggy wheels in the lane caught her attention.

"*Memmi,* look. It's Bram." Susan ran to the hitching rail by the *Dawdi Haus* to wait for him.

Ellie forgot the tomatoes when she saw Bram. He glanced her way with his crooked grin as he pulled Partner to a stop, then turned his attention to Susan while he tied the horse.

"This is a nice surprise," Ellie greeted him as he held Susan up to give Partner a pat on the nose.

"I have another surprise for you," he murmured in her ear as he gave her cheek a kiss. "Do you think your *mam* can take care of Susan and Danny?"

Bram wouldn't wait for her to change out of her work dress or even wash her hands. As soon as the children were taken care of, she was in his buggy and they were heading down the road.

Ellie sat close to him, her hand tucked in his arm.

"Where are we going?"

Bram leaned over and kissed her *kapp*.

"I have something to show you at the farm."

"Will I like it?"

"*Ja,* I think you will. But the more you pester me with questions, the longer it will take to get there."

Ellie laughed. "I think Partner could take us there himself, no matter how many questions I ask you."

Bram just grinned and slapped the reins on the horse's back.

Ellie hadn't been to Bram's farm since the shooting, but everything looked like a normal, quiet Amish farm as they drove up the short lane. She looked toward the house. Which stove had he ended up buying? And was the sitting room livable? It must be. Bram had been settled there for several weeks. She climbed down from the buggy and started toward the house.

"*Ne,* not that way. Come with me."

He took her hand and led her around the house and down a slope to a level spot near the creek.

"What do you think?"

Ellie looked around. The place was quiet and secluded, even though it was still close to the farmhouse. "It's nice, I guess. Why?"

He let go of her hand and paced along an imaginary line. "This is the front, and the door will be right here. The front porch will go around the corner—" he turned and paced along another line between her and the creek "—this way, so you can look out on the creek in the evening."

"You're building a house here? Why do you need another house?"

Bram acted as if she hadn't spoken. He turned another right angle and paced along a third side of the square.

"The back door will be here, with a walk going to the privy." He gestured toward the outhouse that sat at an equal distance between his imaginary house and the farmhouse up the slope. "And then on this side, there'll be space for a garden."

A garden? He was planning a house here, but that garden space looked too small for a family. "Bram, you already have a garden."

He walked back to her and took her hand again.

"*Ja,* I already have a garden, but Miriam likes to plant flowers, doesn't she?"

Ellie stopped, smiling at his sly grin. "Are you trying to tell me something?"

"I've already talked to Hezekiah and Miriam, and they're pleased about it."

"About what?"

"This." He swept his hand around them to take in the proposed house he had laid out for her. "This will be their *Dawdi Haus*. They're going to move in as soon as we can get it built."

Ellie's eyes blurred. He was doing this for a couple he wasn't related to? Why would he do that? But if they lived here, with Bram, she wouldn't have any more worries about them. They would be so close, only a couple miles away, and she'd be able to see them more often. Every day if she wanted to.

Bram's finger slipped under her chin and lifted it so she looked into his eyes. "Miriam can't wait to live next door to you and the children."

He moved his hand to the side of her face, and she felt him tuck the strand of hair behind her ear. Her breath caught as she realized what he had said. "What do you mean, next door?"

"Ellie," he said, his voice soft, intimate. He leaned closer to her. "I love you, and I want you to be my wife. Will you marry me?"

He smiled his crooked grin, but this time it was unsure, hopeful. She hadn't noticed the way his beard hid his dimple until now. He had stopped shaving again after the shooting, and his beard was getting so long he looked like a married man, but that dimple was still there. A secret they shared.

Just the first of all the secrets they would share. A wave swept over her, leaving her breathless. Bram wanted her to be his. How could she bear this joy?

"*Ja,* Bram, *ja.* I'll marry you."

He pulled her close to him, and she molded her body to his, pressing her ear against his chest to listen to his heartbeat.

Bram was kissing her forehead, her nose, nudging her face up with each kiss until he caught her lips with his. She lifted her hand to pull him closer as she let herself drown in his kiss. This was her Bram.

Epilogue

"Are you nervous?" Mandy's question after the family's morning prayers were over made Ellie laugh.

"Why should I be nervous? This is my second wedding day."

"Ellie won't have to be worried about anything," *Mam* said as she finished washing the dishes. "Everything is ready, thanks to all the willing helpers we've had."

Mam dried her hands and started the day's work with her usual brisk enthusiasm.

"Rebecca, remember, you and your friends are in charge of the little ones today. And, Mandy, will you please keep an eye out to give them a hand if they need it?"

"*Ja, Mam,* you can count on it."

Mam smiled at both girls. "I know I can. Now, let's bring up the jars of chow-chow from the cellar and start the chicken frying...."

Mam shooed the girls down the cellar steps in front of her, but turned to Ellie before following them.

"I have prayed for this day, daughter. *Gott*'s blessings will go with you."

"I know, *Memmi*. He is blessing our family already."

Ellie was alone in the kitchen—alone for the last time before her sisters and aunts started arriving to help with the wedding dinner. She looked around the spacious room. More than anywhere else in the world, this kitchen meant home and family. She had missed the significance of the kitchen before her first wedding. Perhaps she had taken it for granted, but she never would again. It was the center of the home.

She smoothed her hand along the grain of the old table and then rested it on the back of *Dat*'s chair. *Dat* had made this chair a place of humility, mercy and grace. She had learned about *Gott* as she listened to *Dat* read from the Bible as he sat here, and as he read their morning and evening prayers while they each knelt at their chairs.

Her whole life had been bracketed by *Dat*'s prayers at the beginning and end of every day. Even when she and Daniel had been married, he had included their names in his prayers just as he included Zac, Lovina, Sally and their families as they married one by one. Tomorrow he would start including Bram and their family in those same prayers.

Bram had taken her with him last night as they moved her things into their new house. The new table in the kitchen was as big as this one. His grin when she had protested that the table was much too large for the five of them still made her smile. They both hoped it wouldn't be too large for long.

Tears of thanksgiving came to Ellie's eyes as she thought of Bram's chair at the head of that long table.

He had built a shelf on the wall behind his chair and placed his Bible there, along with the copy of *Die Ernsthafte Christenpflicht*, the prayer book *Dat* had given him and the copy of the *Ausbund* hymnal that had been her gift to him. Bram was going to be a wonderful husband and father, leading his family as well as her *Dat* ever had.

Even as early as it was, the community would soon start arriving. First the women who would help prepare the huge amounts of food they would need to feed dinner and supper to two hundred people, and then the other families.

Then at nine o'clock the service would begin. She and Bram would miss the singing, as they would spend that time with Bishop Yoder, receiving the final counsel before taking their vows. Then the sermons would begin, the sermons that would lead the entire church in reflecting on the meaning of marriage and the solemnity and permanence of the vows she and Bram would soon take.

Ellie peeked in the doorway of the front room. All the walls had been pushed back to make room for the benches for the service, as if it were a Sunday meeting. She leaned her head on the door frame, her mind filling the benches with her family and loved ones of the community.

After the sermons, she and Bram would stand before the church with their witnesses—Matthew, Annie, Lovina and Noah—and then they would say their simple vows, promising to love and bear and be patient with each other until death.

Could she love Bram?

Ach, ja. She already loved him with all her heart.

Could she be patient with him?

Ja. Her love would provide the patience she would need.

Could she bear him? Bear his bad moods as well as his good? Bear his sorrows as well as his joys? Bear his failures as well as his successes?

Ja. She could bear anything at Bram's side.

The back door opened with a sharp squeak of the hinges, and Ellie turned to see Bram filling the doorway. His face broke into a grin when he saw her. "I hoped I'd find you here."

"Couldn't you wait until the wedding?"

"*Ne,* not today. I wanted to be alone with you for just a minute, before everyone else gets here. You know we won't have a chance until late tonight."

"A chance for what?"

Bram's crooked grin twitched, and he crossed the room to her. "A chance for one more kiss before you become my wife."

Ellie rose on tiptoe to peck him on the cheek. "There you go."

Bram growled as he pulled her into his arms. "You know I want more of a kiss than that."

And then he kissed her with a passion she had never felt before.

Ach, ja. She could bear even this.

* * * * *

WE HOPE YOU ENJOYED THESE
LOVE INSPIRED®
AND
LOVE INSPIRED® HISTORICAL BOOKS.

Whether you love heart-pounding suspense, historically rich stories or contemporary heartfelt romances, Love Inspired® Books has it all!

Look for new titles available every month from Love Inspired®, Love Inspired® Suspense and Love Inspired® Historical.

Love Inspired®

www.LoveInspired.com

Love Inspired ®

Save $1.00

on the purchase of any
Love Inspired®,
Love Inspired® Suspense or
Love Inspired® Historical book.

Available wherever books are sold, including
most bookstores, supermarkets, drugstores
and discount stores.

- ✂

Save $1.00

on the purchase of any Love Inspired®, Love Inspired® Suspense
or Love Inspired® Historical book.

Coupon valid until December 31, 2017. Redeemable at participating retail outlets in
the U.S. and Canada only. Limit one coupon per customer.

52615144

Canadian Retailers: Harlequin Enterprises Limited will pay the face value of
this coupon plus 10.25¢ if submitted by customer for this product only. Any
other use constitutes fraud. Coupon is nonassignable. Void if taxed, prohibited
or restricted by law. Consumer must pay any government taxes. Void if copied.
Inmar Promotional Services ("IPS") customers submit coupons and proof of sales
to Harlequin Enterprises Limited, PO Box 31000, Scarborough, ON M1R 0E7,
Canada. Non-IPS retailer—for reimbursement submit coupons and proof of
sales directly to Harlequin Enterprises Limited, Retail Marketing Department,
225 Duncan Mill Rd., Don Mills, ON M3B 3K9, Canada.

U.S. Retailers: Harlequin Enterprises
Limited will pay the face value of
this coupon plus 8¢ if submitted by
customer for this product only. Any
other use constitutes fraud. Coupon is
nonassignable. Void if taxed, prohibited
or restricted by law. Consumer must pay
any government taxes. Void if copied.
For reimbursement submit coupons
and proof of sales directly to Harlequin
Enterprises, Ltd 482, NCH Marketing
Services, P.O. Box 880001, El Paso,
TX 88588-0001, U.S.A. Cash value
1/100 cents.

5 65373 00076 2 (8100)0 12309

® and ™ are trademarks owned and used by the trademark owner and/or its licensee.

© 2017 Harlequin Enterprises Limited

LIINCICOUP0917

*When an accident strands pregnant widow Willa Chase
and her twins at the home of John Miller, she doesn't
know if she'll make it back to her Amish community for
Christmas. But the reclusive widower soon finds himself
hoping for a second chance at family.*

*Read on for a sneak peek of
AMISH CHRISTMAS TWINS by USA TODAY
bestselling author Patricia Davids,
the first in the three-book CHRISTMAS TWINS series.*

John waited beside Samuel's sleigh and tried
unsuccessfully to curb his excitement. He was almost as
giddy as Megan and Lucy. A sleigh ride with Willa at his
side was his idea of the perfect winter evening, especially
since he didn't have to drive. Lucy was the first one out of
the house. She quickly claimed her spot in the front seat
beside Samuel. Megan came out next and scrambled up
beside her sister. He'd never seen the twins so delighted.

Willa took John's hand as he helped her in. He gave
her gloved fingers a quick squeeze and saw her smile
before she looked down.

Samuel slapped the lines and the big horse took off
down the snow-covered lane. Sleigh bells jingled merrily
in time with the horse's footfalls, and Megan and Lucy
tried to catch snowflakes on their tongues between
giggles.

John leaned down to see Willa's face. "Are you warm

enough?" She nodded, but her cheeks looked rosy and cold. John took off his woolen scarf and wrapped it around her head to cover her mouth and nose.

"*Danki,*" she murmured.

"Don't mention it. In spite of the cold, it's a lovely evening to go caroling, isn't it?" The thick snow obscured the horizon and made it feel as if they were riding inside a glass snow globe. The fields lay hidden under a thick blanket of white. A hushed stillness filled the air, broken only by the jingle of the harness bells and the muffled thudding of the horse's feet.

Their first destination was only a mile from John's house. As Lucy and Megan scrambled down from the sleigh, John offered Willa his hand to help her out.

"Was this what you imagined Christmas would be like when you decided to return to your Amish family?"

She shook her head. "I never imagined anything like this. Do you do it every year?"

"We do."

"You aren't going to actually sing, are you, John?"

He threw back his head and laughed. "*Nee,* but I will hum along."

"Softly, dear, softly," she suggested.

He wondered if she realized that she had called him "dear." It was turning out to be an even more wonderful night than he had hoped for.

Don't miss
AMISH CHRISTMAS TWINS
by Patricia Davids, available October 2017 wherever
Love Inspired® books and ebooks are sold.

www.LoveInspired.com